DEVIL

in the

Detail

THE NORTHERN SINS SAGA

Book 3

NIK TERRY

Copyright Statement

Published on 30th June 2022 by Nik Terry.

The author can be reached by email on
nikterryauthor@gmail.com

Or Facebook https://www.facebook.com/NikTerryAuthor

Or Instagram https://www.instagram.com/nik_terry_author_/

If you enjoyed this book, please encourage your friends and family to download their own copy from Amazon and I would also love it if you could leave a review.

Chapters

A Note from Nik

Thank you for grabbing your copy of the third book in the Northern Sins Saga. This book is largely set in the north east of England, and as such, contains some local dialect. I have listed these below and hope you'll enjoy your introduction to some of our great Geordie-isms.

It is thought that Anglo-Saxon settlers influenced the Geordie dialect, and owing to a lessor Viking occupation than more southern parts of England, this wasn't as diluted over the years. The British Library points out that the existence of the River Tweed provided a significant northern barrier against Scottish influence.

Brief List of my favourite Geordie words and phrases

Canny – Good, nice, pleasant, OK.

Howay—This can mean different things depending on the tone. It can mean come on, hurry up, get off it, leave it alone. "Howay man" or howay over here (come on over here), "howay, man it's freezing" (hurry up, it's freezing).

Divvina (Pronounced div-in-ah) – Means "I don't know".

Fettle – Means in foul mood. "Are ye in a fettle, pet?" (Are you in a bad mood, pet). "He's in a right fettle" (He's in a right mood).

Gannin yem (Pronounced exactly how it looks!) – This means going home. "Gannin yem already?" (Going home already?) or "I'm gannin yem" (I'm going home).

Am Clamming – Means to be starving.

Da (Pronounced Dah) – Dad

Ma (Pronounced Mah – like a sheep but with an M) – Mum/Mother. But in the north east we often say mam.

Not all of these feature in this book, but you will see more and more in the upcoming series the Northern Kings MC.

How many can you find? Let me know – nikterryauthor@gmail.com

Chapter One

♋ Natalie ♋

"So, tell me again why you arrested my client?" My voice sounded strained in the small square room, ricocheting off the bare walls.

The boy beside me fidgeted, picking at his nails, his foot tapping the floor beneath him. The same rhythm for the last twenty minutes driving a pressure in my brain, and I watched a further minute of wasted time tick by on my watch.

"He matched the description of the suspect."

"And what description was that?"

"Tall, slim youth with a dark hooded jumper, dark trousers and trainers."

"So, you picked my client up because?"

"He matched the description," the young police officer repeated, narrowing his eyes at me.

"What colour was the jumper?"

"Well, dark."

"Is that black, navy?"

"The description was just dark," the young police officer looked flustered.

"What about the trainers? What make were they?"

"They weren't described."

"And the colour?"

"I don't know."

"Let's see if you can help me understand this. My client matched a very vague description. A description of nearly every youth that night. Why did you arrest *my* client?"

"Because he matched the description," the officer's face was growing ever more scarlet.

The boy beside me stopped picking at his nails, sitting up straighter on the hard plastic chair, a glimmer of hope shining in his eyes.

"And the victim. Did they say what sex they thought their attacker was?"

"No."

"Leon matched a vague description. One that couldn't identify whether the attacker was male or female. Given my client's short stature, his gender could not have been identified from his height and build alone."

The boy beside me shot me a look, one that I returned and hoped he had the sense to keep his mouth shut. The officer fell quiet again, exchanging glances with the man sitting beside him.

"He acted suspiciously when we approached him," the officer continued, and I noticed the hint of uncertainty that had crept into his voice.

"Describe how he acted suspiciously," I challenged.

"He just behaved like he was guilty," the young officer continued, sounding flustered, "he was shuffling and fiddling, and looking like he was going to bolt."

"Were you able to identify him at the scene of the arrest?"

"Yes."

"Then you would have been aware of his nervousness towards you. It was only last month he was arrested by your colleagues and left the station in an ambulance. The Independent Police Complaints Commission is still investigating my client's complaint."

The two police officers looked at each other, frustrated. The boy beside me smirked.

"Then I believe we are done here," I stated, "my client doesn't feel like answering any more questions and is exercising his right to leave."

The young officer opened his mouth to say something, but the older one beside him patted him on the shoulder and shook his head. The boy beside me beamed, his face smug with victory.

"Come on, Leon, time to go home."

I stood, the chair scraping back from the table, "now, if you'll escort us out."

The eyes of the officers burned into me as I beckoned for the youth to follow. I ignored the disgruntled mutterings of the officers seated in front of me, fixing them with an expectant stare as I stood waiting for them to let us out of the custody suite. We emerged into the waiting room at the front of the building, releasing the teenager to freedom and into the arms of his awaiting father, Jack Monroe, one of Newcastle's finest street criminals. Jack's eyes scanned over me, coming to rest momentarily on my chest before moving back to my face.

"Thanks for sorting me boy out, Nat," he said eventually, a cocky smile on his face.

"Just doing my job, Jack."

"Hmmm. I see Charlie's got herself right in there with the Irish mob. Always saw her potential when she used to run with my crew. Tell her I was asking after her."

Then he turned, nudging his son out of the door. I glanced around the room, eyeing up the miss-match of people sitting around waiting for something; two track suit clad youths with baseball caps pulled down low over their faces, slumped in chairs and playing on their phones, and an old man in torn jeans covered in stains. Next to him sat a man in a suit. Dark grey hair, peppered with white and a clean-shaven friendly face. He reminded me of my father, my thoughts trailing off to memories of long ago, or at least it felt like an age ago since I'd last set eyes on him. Two years ago, two very long years.

4

"Nat," a deep voice behind me almost made me jump, and I turned to the source of the noise.

"DI Burrows," I answered with strained professionalism as the tall, dark-haired man moved closer to me.

"Are we still going to do this?"

"I'm here to work, Steve, not for anything else."

"So I hear. My officers told me you're jumping up and down on my operations again."

"Then your officers should make sure they're not abusing their powers. Again."

I turned away from him. His hand wrapped around my arm, gently, but there was a meaning in his grip all the same. He stared at me for a moment, his eyes boring into mine, and I was sure I could see the twitch of his lips as he battled with whether to say more. I glanced at my watch meaningfully. His fingers relaxed, his hand dropping to his side again.

"Nice to see you, Nat. Don't make it a habit, ey?" his voice was low, laced with a soft threat.

*****

The sun was setting, casting an ornate orange glow over the river below it, making the dirty water seem almost golden. The triple glazed window didn't quite stop the rumble of noise below as the daytime businesses on Newcastle's quayside shut up for the evening, and the night-time economy roaring to life in

5

their place. I finished the last bit of dictation, winding the little machine back to check over the last line of the letter I had recorded, my voice sounding loud in the solace of my office. Satisfied, I slotted the machine back into its cradle and pressed the button.

The door pushed open slowly, a tentative knock of knuckles on the frame and a friendly face appeared in the gap that was created.

"Uncle Wes," I called, pleased to see the well-dressed man.

"Hey, Nat. How are you?"

"Yeah, I'm ok. Just getting finished up here before I have to make a run for the airport."

Wesley Weston smiled, and I knew that look; concern, pity, sympathy, understanding. Even now, two years on to the day, I'd felt the pain as raw as ever. Perhaps more.

"I miss him too, Nat," he said, his voice little more than a whisper, "we'll always miss your father; on this day especially."

I dropped my eyes to the desk, stuffing a pile of papers back into a folder, feeling the formidable burn of emotions at the back of my throat. I grabbed my suitcase from beside my desk and walked towards the silver-haired man. He was still tall and fit for his age, immaculately groomed, a neat silver goatee matching his hair, gentle brown eyes and barely a wrinkle for his 65 years. He was my father's best friend, not really my uncle, but we had called him that all our lives, and now, with my father and mother both dead, he was as close to family as I had.

He held out a big silver envelope as I walked towards him.

"For Charlie. I hope she has a fantastic day. I'll walk out with you."

Uncle Wes led the way to the lifts, and I pulled my case along behind me, the wheels rumbling rhythmically over the tiles of the floor in the corridor. There were still lights in the offices as we passed them and I nodded and waved to those still working, junior partners like me and those vying for the next round of promotions.

The receptionist stationed in the firm's lobby was tidying her desk up as we passed, stacking files and bits of paper, checking post-it notes for missed messages. She barely looked up as we got alongside the front desk. But then, as I reached the doors, I heard her light voice behind me.

"Miss De Winter!"

Turning, I noticed her step around the desk with a small, padded beige envelope in her outstretched hand.

"Sorry, this came for you a little while ago."

I looked at the small parcel almost suspiciously, feeling over the slight bulge of the padding behind the beige outer. It was handwritten with no postage stamps of any kind. The words floated in gentle swirls over the envelope, the graceful swish of the top of the letter 'N' to the loop at the start of the 'W'. My throat swelled as I took it carefully, as if it might disintegrate in my fingers.

"A courier," the receptionist added, probably reading the look on my face.

I turned the padded packet over, squeezing it gently, feeling again for any clue of what might be inside, the tiny lump of something only just evident under the cushioning of the little bubbles of air. I held it to my nose. It didn't smell of him, just the crispness of paper and the slight scent of the sticky gum securing it.

"I think you'll have to open it, Nat, to find out what he's sent you," Uncle Wes' voice was quiet next to me.

"You recognise the handwriting then?"

"I'll never forget your father's writing."

I swallowed and then eased open the top of the envelope and slipped my hand inside. There was nothing else in there except the cool metal object brushing against my fingertips. I pinched my fingers around it and pulled it out, holding it up to the light in the foyer. The thin brass key was elongated, longer than a normal house key, with a long stick of notches and nodules. The other side was smooth, save for six numbers engraved into the metal. I looked at the silver-haired man beside me quizzically, and he shrugged his shoulders in response.

"And there's nothing else in there?" He asked.

"Nothing at all. Just a random key."

A car horn beeped from the street outside. I dropped the key back into the packet.

"Gotta go, Uncle Wes, that's my taxi."

The man placed his hands onto my shoulders, looking into my eyes with an expression that read 'I miss him too' and then he kissed me lightly on the forehead.

"Have a good weekend, Nat."

I rolled my suitcase, manoeuvring carefully through the revolving glass door and out to the roadside. The taxi driver hoisted the suitcase into the boot of the black cab, huffing indignantly at its weight as I climbed into the back. As the car crawled through the rush hour traffic, I slid the key back out of the envelope, checking the packaging once again for anything else. Nothing.

Two years to the anniversary of my father's death, of his murder, he sends me a key. Nothing else, just a key. I felt a twinge of anxiety unravel deep in my stomach.

Chapter Two

❧ The Viking ❧

It was still chilly on an evening despite being the middle of spring. Or maybe the cool spring air was seeping into my bones from the last few nights spent stalking my target in the dark, watching him from alleyways in the cold of night and returning to a damp hotel room in the centre of Manchester. I was becoming sleep deprived from the noise of the other guests renting the place by the hour, groans and moans every night, reminding me of what I wasn't getting.

My target was like clockwork. Every night I'd followed him from the small flat in a tall block on the outskirts of the city, to the thrum of the city centre. He'd deal some gear along the way, pick up more from his supplier and then move the product somewhere else. Then he'd stop at a few bars, drink, deal some more and then pick up a girl or two and go home, like a regular gangster wannabe.

Unfortunately, he'd pissed off the Chinese along the way, and now he was in deep shit with no way out. The job was a big money one. Not the nice clean kill I preferred, but one where I'd been contracted to send a message at the same time. And that meant covering my tracks extra carefully. The Chinese didn't care that my rate for this one was sky high. He'd left a trail of gambling and whoring debts behind him, and his gang had also been encroaching on Chinese territory. And so, here I was, to collect their debt with his life, and dish out a warning to whoever might decide to fill his shoes.

His routine was the same tonight as it had been since I started watching him, and now I sat in a late-night café across the road from the bar he was living it up in. I could see his outline through the window, knocking back shots, waving his hands around to the music; he was becoming more and more drunk. A girl approached the side of him, and he pulled her into his lap, the silhouette of his hand coming up to his face as he took another swig of alcohol.

Someone approached my side, and slid a plate onto the table, the single greasy burger sitting on a white polystyrene dish, fat pooling in a dip. I barely took my eyes from the window as I lifted the soggy bun to my mouth, tasting almost nothing else but salt and grease. I was looking forward to my own kitchen, where I could get a decent meal and eat it while distracted by the TV instead of the constant attention that scoping out a target required.

Then, suddenly, the mark was up on his feet, moving towards the front of the bar, pulling the girl along behind him earlier than he was scheduled. Fuck. I pushed the bun back down on the table, the sorry half-eaten burger staring up at me as my stomach rumbled in anger.

I tailed the taxi they got into, staying well back even though I had no fear that he would even be aware I was following. I'd swapped the bike exhaust for a quiet one, and a fresh set of registration plates, just in case any nosey detectives tried their luck with their automatic number plate recognitions systems once the fucker was dead.

Winding in and out of the cars behind them, I kept a safe distance until they pulled up at the foot of concrete wonderland; numerous blocks of flats protruding into the sky. Tiny squares of yellow light glowed from windows, scattering around the sides, and illuminating the huge columns.

I waited in the shadows at the foot of the buildings, nestled between the industrial sized waste bins, trying to ignore the smell of filth, of rotting food and dirty nappies, of sour milk and mouldy bread. The target's window was only two floors up, so my climbing skills would not be put to the test tonight. I gave him an hour before I got bored standing in the dark and the stink at the base of the flats. One last hour to have one last fuck; I was a reasonable man, after all.

I wriggled my fingers into a thin pair of rubber gloves, pulling another set of black leather gloves over the top for extra protection, and the fact that shit was about to get messy. Then I smoothed the black hood over my head, carefully tucking in all my hair. With one last look around, I scrambled up on top of the bin, feeling for the inch wide ledge above my head and digging my fingers firmly into it as I heaved myself up the side of the building. The little balcony hung to the side just a few feet away and I inched forward until it was just in reach, curling my fingers around the rail and hauling myself up and over. It creaked threateningly under my weight, the noise ringing out into a charged silence, making me wince.

Dropping down into the shelter of the concrete wall, I wedged a screwdriver under the metal frame that held the glass window in place, popping it out easily. I jumped through the hole left behind, setting my feet carefully onto a cluttered kitchen bench, careful not to send the collection of dirty dishes crashing to the floor. Then I moved through the quiet flat towards the noise of grunts in a far room.

I eased the door open just a few inches so I could survey the room. The girl was on top of him, sliding up and down his dick as his hands roamed all over her. I pulled my gun out, taking the safety off, allowing the click to echo around the room. His hands paused over her tits, the sound familiar to him, but the girl continued, oblivious to the black spectre stood behind her. The man peeked around her, his eyes growing large as he made me out in the shadows, and hustled the girl to the side, before scrambling his naked body up the bed and cowering against the headboard.

The girl looked around, confusion turning to fear, and she opened her mouth.

"If you want to live, sweetheart, you'll swallow that scream," my voice drawled against the hood, a fake accent pulling from my throat.

She nodded, wide eyes glistening with frightened tears.

"Now. You're going to get dressed and go. And you're going to forget about tonight, unless you want me to come for you next."

She nodded, her face ready to crumple around her, but she got up off the bed and pulled her clothes on. I tossed some notes at her, more than enough for her taxi, and she stared at them.

"I'm not a...."

"For your taxi."

I waved the gun, and she snatched them up and rushed out.

"Look, mate. Whoever is paying you, I can pay you more," the man's voice wavered, his arms held in surrender above his naked body.

"I hear paying is your problem."

A look of realisation swept across his face.

"I, I, I can pay it all back."

"Then why haven't you?"

"I just need more time."

"Time's up," I said, slipping the safety back onto the gun and slotting into the back of my pants, moving round the bed towards him.

His eyes widened, his face confused with horror and uncertainty as he scrabbled against the crumpled sheets to get away from me. I could do without a game of cat and mouse; however quick the game would end. It was messy, and I was hungry. He leapt from the bed, catching his foot in a white sheet and stumbling forwards into the wall. I jumped onto the bed and then down beside him, my hand wrapping around his forehead and wrenching his head back. I reached for my knife, letting it hang in the air in front of him, the blade huge and sharp.

"Please," he whispered.

I pulled the blade across his throat, skin, tissue and tough sinewy tendons and ligaments giving way as blood spewed against the white wall in front of him. He gurgled for a couple of seconds, his head lolling back as if it would roll straight off his shoulders. Then I let his body sink to the floor. Stooping behind him, I eased the tip of the knife into his shoulder, carving the pound symbol into his dying flesh. Then I left the way I had come in.

Chapter Three

CB Natalie BD

I shivered in the chill of church, the mid-spring air cold in the confines of the old building, sending goose pimples chasing across my arms. The deep hum of the thick Irish accent of the Catholic Priest filled the air, the sound strangely amplified against the vaulted ceiling. I shifted uncomfortably, the hard wooden pew making my bottom numb. Carter rested his hand on my leg, the warmth of his palm radiating through the navy chiffon of the bridesmaid dress I wore. I moved my hand over his, my other clutching the small bouquet, Charlie's larger bouquet resting in my lap, as I watched the scene in front of me.

Charlie was beautiful. My baby sister. Adopted baby sister, but we were as close as any sisters would be. The cream dress sculpted over her chest, drawing in at a waist that showed no signs of being three months postpartum, and smoothing over her hips before fanning out like a mermaid's tail. It was simple, yet stunning. The pair of them stood at the altar, lost in each's other's gaze, totally consumed by the other, as the priest read out their vows and they repeated them like automatons.

I felt a prickle at the back of my eyes. My father would have been so happy to see her, and I was too, despite the fact that she was marrying the head of the Irish mafia. I glanced round the Church, noting the men in suits, their constantly alert looks and I wondered how many of them had a small arsenal stashed in their trousers as they sat under the eyes of God. It seemed hypocritical to me that these people had taken so many lives yet could sit in a church with no fear of dissolving into ash and flames. But then here I was too, an atheist, a non-believer; a lawyer who found loopholes to help criminals escape the law as many times as I had led a campaign of justice against them.

I fidgeted in my seat. Carter glanced at me and smiled, pulled my hand to his mouth, and kissed it gently. I forced a smile back.

"I now pronounce you husband and wife," the priest's voice echoed round the church, and a whoop from the audience of mafia foot soldiers sounded in response.

Charlie and Cian turned and walked towards us, hand in hand as they glided out of the church. Carter nudged me gently, and I stood, passing the enormous bouquet to the glowing bride as she moved towards me.

"Congratulations, Mrs O'Sullivan," I whispered in her ear, handing her the flowers and receiving the widest grin I had ever seen.

*****

I held the baby in my arms, staring into her eyes at the dark blue irises which were getting lighter each time I saw her. She cooed gently, smiling up at me as I made strange shapes with my lips and my heart swelled, warmth flooding through my chest.

"Are you ever going to put that baby down?" Carter grumbled beside me, chugging back another pint of lager, the foam clinging to his lips.

"Not if I can help it," I answered, my tone clipped.

"Don't know why anyone would bring a baby to a wedding. It's done nothing but take up all your attention since we got here."

"It's a she. Her name's Caragh. Remember?"

He took another mouthful of his drink, staring ahead silently and I turned my attention back to my niece as she smiled back with a big gummy grin. My heart melted all over again.

"Hey, Nat," Cian's low Irish rumble came from behind me, "can I steal my daughter for a moment?"

I stood up, half reluctantly, and held Caragh out towards him, watching the look in his eyes as he took her from me. The baby grinned widely, recognising him instantly. He kissed her tenderly on the forehead and tucked her against his chest, walking back towards the top table where Charlie sat. I watched as he took his seat beside her, propping the baby on his knee and grinning warmly as Charlie dipped her head to talk to her daughter. I couldn't help the pang of jealousy that ignited in my chest and radiated through my body, before fizzling out in a feeling of guilt.

The wedding party went on and on. I constantly stole glances at the happy couple, watching them genuinely swoon over each other and their baby, the feeling of envy burning low in my stomach. Charlie had what I'd always wanted, what I craved from being so young. I wanted a husband, a child, children, but so far, I'd not found anyone worthy of the challenge. No one willing to wait for me when I had to work late, or tolerate me leaping out of bed when I was called out to the Police Station to defend undeserving criminals in the dead of night. No one able to understand the massive ball of pain I dragged around with me these last two years.

"Please be upstanding for the new Mr and Mrs O'Sullivan," the DJ called over the microphone, as a cacophony of deep male voices whooped and cheered around me.

Charlie and Cian took to the floor, her dress sweeping gracefully around her as they whirled and danced, their eyes locked on each other, each other their only focus. My eyes blurred with captive tears, emotions threatening to overwhelm me, pride, a bittersweet happiness and a dark heavy sadness.

Defensively, my mind took me somewhere else, fluttering back to the key, and the sudden excitement at seeing the swirl of his handwriting on the beige envelope. But who had sent it? The last I'd checked; the dead didn't have a mail system. He had written it, his handwriting. There was no mistaking it. Uncle Wes had seen it too, and it displayed my father's typical crypticness. He was as mysterious in death as he was in life.

"Shall we dance?" Carter asked, taking to unsteady feet and holding his hand out to me when the music changed, and the dancefloor filled up.

I shook my head and reached for my wine glass.

"What the fuck is wrong with you, Nat?" He spat suddenly.

I looked up at him, confused.

"You wanted me to come here with you and then you've all but ignored me the entire time we've been here."

"I'm just not feeling it right now, Carter."

"You seemed pretty happy with that baby not so long ago."

"That baby is my niece, of course I adore her."

Carter sighed and sat back down beside me, "you're just such hard work. No one is good enough for you, are they?"

"What do you mean?" I asked, not turning to face him, already knowing what he was talking about.

"Me, the one before me and the one before that. No one is good enough for whatever fucking ridiculous standards you've got. I'd heard all the whispers long before we got together."

"So what? You fancied a challenge?" I shot back at him.

"I thought I could change your mind. Win you over."

"You mean by flashing all your cash in my face? Impressing me with your family's great wealth and prestige?"

Carter's face grew red, his lips pursing together.

"You know what, Nat? It doesn't matter. Us, this," he flapped an angry hand in the air, and I turned my face back to the view of the dancefloor, "fuck you, Nat. Enjoy the party. I'm out of here."

The chair scraped loudly against the floor, audible even over the heavy beat of the music. Then he disappeared.

I stared into the darkness sipping on the wine, the warm tingles washing over my body doing nothing to quell the battle taking place inside my chest; anger, disappointment, revelation. Emotions and memories consuming me from within, as I sat in my self-made loneliness.

I don't know how long I'd sat staring into the lights on the dance floor, lost in my own thoughts. I didn't see Charlie sit down beside me and I hadn't noticed the glass of wine she pushed towards me.

"Hey, sis. You ok?"

I took a deep breath, checking any stray tears were secured before turning to face her.

"Where's Caragh?" I asked, changing the subject from the mess that was me.

"The nanny took her home."

"I could have looked after her."

"You're supposed to be enjoying yourself, you *and* Carter. Where is he, anyway?"

"Gone."

"What do you mean, gone?"

"We argued. I told him it's over. He's gone," I lied, smoothly.

"What? Like left completely?"

"Uh-huh. Let's have a toast to the newest single lady in the room," I held my empty wine glass in the air.

Charlie shrugged.

"Hey, there's plenty more fish in the sea. Just look around."

"Yeah. I've looked."

"And?"

"Do they all have tattoos?"

Charlie snorted into the glass she was taking a drink from.

"Pretty much."

"I don't like tattoos," I grumbled, eyeing up the room that was overrun with men, mean and sultry looking.

"You know it doesn't define a guy, just cos he's got tattoos."

"Sure, it does. See him over there. He just looks like bad news."

I waved my glass over to the bar where the tall blond man stood, his long hair spilling down around his shoulders and the sleeves of his white shirt rolled up past his elbows. Even from this distance, I could see the dark ink all over his arms, from the back of his hands, disappearing up under his sleeves.

"That's the Viking," Charlie pointed out.

"Uh huh, and why is he called that?"

She rolled her eyes at me.

"If it's not because of the long hair, tattoos and beard, then it's probably because he's got a huge axe and not afraid to use it."

The laugh tumbled from my throat, and I felt my face pull with a smile; probably the first real smile all day.

Chapter Four

℘ The Viking ℘

The bar was quiet. How I liked it. How I needed it. It was an obscure pub, the sole building on the corner of a street long since gone, a redundant road leading to docks which had all but disappeared. I sat in the corner with a pint and a packet of pork scratchings, the place didn't even sell crisps. I glanced around, watching the old man flick through channels on the chunky old TV mounted on a wall at the side of the bar. If I didn't know what funded the place, then I would have been intrigued how it had remained open for so long. But I knew not to ask, and I knew not to stay for too long. Anyone in there not by themselves was conducting shady business deals, just like me.

The doors creaked noisily; swinging shut behind the bulk of the man who escaped the dull day into an even duller pub. I watched from the corner, catching his eye as he walked to the bar, grabbed a pint and brought it to the table. He sat across from me on the little bar stool that I was surprised didn't collapse under his weight.

"Hey, V," he wheezed into his drink, before slipping a meaty hand under his coat and sliding a thick envelope towards me.

I pulled it off the table and stuffed it straight inside my jacket, not stopping to count the notes inside. It would all be there. The Chinese were a lot of things, but they paid what they agreed on.

"What have you got for me, Bob?" I asked the broker.

"There's a few out today. Got you a handful to choose from."

He pulled out a fistful of folded brown envelopes, dropping them on the table in front of me, and I scooped them up, popping open the top and easing the photographs out.

They were the usual types: gang members, drug debtors and the odd rapist and abuser. I liked those the most, my soul partially cleansed for every dirty life I took. I was the angel of death; fallen, cast aside and ruthless. Today's offerings didn't disappoint: a drug dealer and rapist and a violent gang member that owed the wrong people money. They had good fees and were clean, simple kills. It was easy money.

"There's another one," Bob's voice lowered in the desolation of the bar, looking round uncomfortably. But I doubted the half-deaf old barman at the far side would even hear a bomb going off.

"It's a £100k job," he whispered.

I whistled and sat back. That was a colossal figure for one head. Someone must

25

have seriously pissed off the mob, or someone just as fucked up at that price.

"Lemme see."

I could have a year off with that sort of shit.

The man slid the envelope across the table, and I picked it up eagerly, popping the top off and dragging the pictures out.

The woman stared back at me. Mid-brown hair hung loose around her face and caramel-brown eyes which stared into me, as if she was sitting right there in front of me. As if I could reach and touch her plump lips with my fingers, smooth the skin over her high cheekbones. I swapped the photos round, pulling out the ones behind. In the second, she was dressed in a navy suit, bulging over reasonably sized tits, tapering in at the waist before blooming out over her hips. Her skirt finished just at the top of her knee, showing off shapely, well-defined legs down to an almost skin colour pair of stilettos. She carried a small briefcase and this time her hair was scooped up high onto her head.

"You want this one?" Bob broke through my thoughts.

She was a woman. I didn't kill women, period, but definitely not this one. There was something about her that caught my attention and drew me in, a familiarity perhaps? I pushed the pictures back into the envelope, my brain doing cartwheels inside my head.

"Not interested?"

"You know I don't do women."

"I know, but this job is huge. I thought you might change your mind at the price tag."

I gritted my teeth at the insinuation. It looked like it would be an easy, tidy kill. She was a businesswoman of some sort. She was dressed for power, for authority. Maybe a politician? I'd killed a few of those, and none of them were innocent. She had to be someone high profile, important. That would explain the price tag. Still. In the open with one smooth shot. Easy.

The broker went to secure the third envelope back inside his jacket.

"Wait. Let me have another look."

He handed the envelope back to me and I took the first picture out again. I studied her eyes, trying to concentrate on the uncomfortable feeling of déjà vu as I focused on her picture, on the flecks of gold and caramel that peppered the brown irises making them glow back at me. She wore red lipstick, enhancing the thickness and evenness of both lips, and for a moment I wondered how those lips would look around my cock, just like at Cian's wedding. Shit.

I stared at the other picture again and then back at the one just of her face. Fuck. Pushing the photos back inside the envelope, I slid them across the sticky bar table.

"Do you know who the client is for this one?"

"No. It's anonymous. They all are. You never ask that V?"

"I want to know the risk for this. There's a reason it's big money, and that has to do with the potential of exposure, or someone is very fucking desperate."

The broker shrugged but didn't answer further.

"No. Not this one," I shook my head.

The big man nodded and got up, leaving me with two of the three brown envelopes and another of cash. I stashed it all inside my jacket, not taking my eyes off him as he waddled out of the door, leaving me alone with the old barman. I fished out my mobile and scrolled through my contacts, my thumb pressing down on the one known only as 623, before holding the device to my ear. He answered in a few rings.

"Cian, you have a problem."

Chapter Five

ଓଷ Natalie ଅଠ

The sun was fading gently, casting a warm glow through the windows of my top floor office on the Newcastle Quayside. Even the murky depths of the River Tyne reflected the bright afternoon light, spring disguised as summer. The birds were happy with the weather, and I'd been regaled with the trumpeting songs of the kittiwakes and the purr of pigeons, interrupted occasionally by the baritone of the boats up and down the river. The day had felt fresh and positive, yet my mind had wandered relentlessly to the key safely tucked away in my purse.

I'd Googled pictures of keys. Keys to safety deposit boxes tucked away in banks, keys to lockers, I'd even reversed searched by uploading a picture of the small brass object, but nothing had got me any closer to finding out what it might unlock. If it wasn't for all the files of work I had stacked on my desk, then I would have allowed my distractions to take me home to rifle through my dad's belongings that I had stacked in my loft. That would have to wait.

I pulled a file from the top of the pile, sliding out the documents tucked just inside the folder and studied them. Witness statements and mobile phone transcripts. On the face of it incriminating, and I sighed at the challenge of trying to find some sort of defence in amongst the shit my client had given me. Why they couldn't have just entered a guilty plea in the first place and saved us all a whole load of hassle, I just didn't know. But that was my job, and their right, so I flicked through the list of calls and text messages, looking for something that would help blow the case out of the courtroom.

My phone buzzed beside me.

'Nat. Can we talk about the weekend? C'

'Is there something to talk about?' I text back, annoyance prickling at me.

'Please, Nat. Just give me a chance to talk to you.'

I put the phone down and pushed it out of the way, trying to concentrate on what I should be doing. But a few seconds later, I picked it back up.

'OK, Carter. El Puente. 8pm,' I relented, eventually.

'You know I don't like tapas, Nat.'

'You want to talk? El Puente.'

'Fine.'

By the time the evening came, I'd found the discrepancies in the mobile phone records. It was minimal, but enough to cast doubt, and I knew a jury could not overlook it. And it meant the case would probably be thrown out before we even set foot between the big doors of the courtroom. Another criminal left roaming the streets. I sighed, turning off my computer and tidying the files away into my drawers. Night crept in through the windows, broken up by the illumination of streetlights and bars, a rainbow of neon colours swamping my office, even from this height.

I moved across to the great panoramic windows, pulling the rope cord and watching the blinds sliding across, obscuring my view. Further down the river, nestled in a crop of buildings that contained Newcastle Law Courts and several bars and restaurants, my father's practice stood like a sentry, gazing out across the River Tyne and the millennium bridge. It had been renamed in the last year, my Uncle Wes bringing new partners on board. Porter Weston was now Weston Cooke LLP. It had hurt more than I could bear watching the sign come down, my father's name replaced on the huge building by someone I didn't know, who had merely bought in to the success and the work my father had put in.

Uncle Wes had offered me the chance to come on board with him. But I'd known he'd felt obligated, in honour of my father, and I was happy in my practice, with the people I had worked hard for. I pulled the toggle to the side of the window, turning the vertical blinds so they closed, blocking out the bright lights from the quayside.

The wind had picked up and rolled off the river as I walked along the well-lit streets towards the hustle of the city centre, yet the breeze was warm. My hair tangled as it blew around me, like the light caress of warm fingertips; reminding me summer was not far behind. A tiny sheen of hope in the darkness. I hated the winter and spring wasn't much better, but the promise of summer on the breeze made everything seem more civilized.

The little restaurant was tucked snugly in the arches of the old railway bridge, just at the top of the Quayside. Inside, the low hanging lamps glowed orange and waitresses milled about transporting tapas to tables. The bell on the door rang loudly as I stepped in. The restaurant was busy, and I was shown to one of the last tables, small and cosy but a little too close to the door. Yet it allowed a good view over the street and the people who walked past.

I ordered a glass of red wine while I waited, watching the clock on my phone change each minute. Carter was usually late, and tonight was no exception, but I was disappointed all the same. The bell on the door jangled, and I lifted my head up, half hoping to see the slim, well-dressed man walk in. But the man that walked in was clad head to toe in black leather, even down to the heavy-soled boots on his feet. My eyes travelled up him, catching the black tattoo that snaked over one side of his head where the hair was shaved away, the rest of his long blond hair tied neatly in a ponytail at the base of his neck.

He glanced at me, his eyes lingering over me far longer than they should have, and for a moment I wondered whether I knew him. He dropped his eyes after a further split second and made his way to the bar, sitting at the far edge as it trailed around a corner. For some reason I snatched another look at him as he spoke to the young barmaid, his face coming alive with a wide grin as he cocked his head to the side flirtatiously. He brought a tall pint of lager to his lips, his hands dark from the ink staining his skin, his eyes catching me looking and I turned away, back to the street outside, searching for any sign of the man I was here to meet.

My stomach rumbled loudly, and even in the electric buzz of the little restaurant; I was sure everyone could hear. I checked the display on my phone, annoyance infiltrating the blood in my veins. Or maybe that was just the large glass of red wine on a very empty stomach. I caught the waitress' eye and ordered, not waiting any longer for someone who may or may not show up.

My eyes flicked back to the end of the bar. The biker was still there, the pint in his hand hardly going down and his gaze wandered the restaurant, overly alert, suspicious. I grew wary, wondering what or who he was waiting for. A drugs deal maybe? A couple of little dishes were placed in front of him, the waitress smiling at him, loitering a little too close, tucking her hair behind her ear. Maybe he was just a boyfriend? An older boyfriend? That would be some age gap. He had to be mid-thirties and both the girl behind the bar and the one waiting the tables were barely older than late teens. Even from this distance, he seemed to radiate that life experience, worldly wise, confident.

I watched him scoop out the food on a plate in front of him, stabbing at it with a fork and shovelling it into his mouth, looking as hungry as I felt. My stomach grumbled again, and I reached for the basket of bread in front of me, thankful for any morsel of food. I'd skipped lunch again today.

My eyes wandered back to the biker. The food in front of him was almost gone, hoovered in moments. A tattooed hand wrapped round the pint, and he drank half of it quickly, never taking his eyes off the window as he stared out into the street, fixated on something. The tattooed side of his head was turned away from me, but even on this side he was everything I despised in a man. The long hair, the way it was shaved at the sides, the leather and roughness of the clothes he wore.

He turned and looked at me, capturing my gaze with an expressionless stare, judging me as I judged him. Then he tipped his head to the side and raised his pint glass in a light toast. I didn't smile or join in, but dropped my eyes back to the slice of bread I was picking apart, the crumbs spilling onto the red tablecloth in front of me.

The bell at the door tinkled again and my head shot sideways, expecting Carter to be charging through flustered and apologetic. The young couple eyed me quizzically when my eyes rested on them for too long, their expressions turning almost to pity when they noticed the empty seat opposite. I must have looked desperate. Pathetically waiting for a date who wasn't going to show. I swigged back the rest of my wine, angrily watching the couple be led to a vacant table towards the back of the restaurant.

I studied my watch. Carter was now over forty minutes late and I was starving and pissed off. The restaurant had slowed down, more people leaving than coming in. The young waitress approached; a tray full of small bowls that she pushed onto the table before sliding a large glass of red wine across to me. I looked up at her, puzzled.

"The bloke at the bar ordered it for you," she said flatly.

Glancing across at the blond man, he raised his pint glass to me once more, and this time flashed me a wide grin. I stared for a moment, not acknowledging his gesture whilst I decided if I would return the drink, before leaving it where it was and giving him a wry smile back.

I dropped my attention to the food in front of me. The powerful aroma of garlic, onion, and tomato made my mouth water, and I scooped a couple of spoonful's of each dish out onto the plate. A flicker of light danced across the table. I thought it was just a reflection of something outside at first, but when I looked again it wavered on the table napkin in front of me before creeping up onto my white shirt. The light seemed to form a tight red circle on the white fabric, slowly tracking up towards me and I swiped my hand over it, yet it seemed to come in from the outside. I flicked at the dot again as it climbed higher.

An angry screech rang out noisily to my right, followed by a thunder of hard boots and then the black shape came at me. I flew sideways, the air knocked from my lungs, the table upended, and the little bowls crashed to the floor. Something wet ran down my chest and across my stomach and I couldn't move. I couldn't even crane my neck for the hand that was wrapped in my hair, pushing my head into the leather of the long seat.

"Get the fuck off me!" I screamed.

Chapter Six

‰ The Viking ⚬

I'd caught the red dot of the sight of the rifle in the corner of my eye. It had flickered against the floor and crept across the table. I was already moving before the mark moved up the white fitted shirt she wore. She'd seen it too, batting at it like some annoying fly. I launched myself for her, pushing the table up on the side, ready to provide some cover from the onslaught of shots. I didn't know how many he would fire.

People screamed around me, plates crashed to the floor, and I felt something whizz past my head, far too close for comfort. I landed on top of her harder than I meant to, pushing her head down into the leather bench seat she had been perched on moments before. She wriggled under me, sharp elbows jabbing back at me angrily.

"Get the fuck off me!" her screams were muffled by the leather of the seat I had pushed her face into.

I relaxed my grip, not letting her up fully, as I searched into the street for the direction of the shot.

"Get off me!"

"We need to get out of here," I answered her angry shouts.

"I'm not going anywhere with you."

I let go of her hair, letting her sit up. Her head swept left and right as she surveyed the carnage before her, her hand dipping to her shirt as she rubbed the huge red wine stain that covered it. She opened her mouth and then closed it again. I tugged at her arm, pulling her to her feet.

"Come on. We need to get out of here."

"*We* need to do nothing," she snapped, her eyes narrowing at me, "what the fuck was that?"

She stood up from the seat, her whole body in view of the glass pane of the door.

"Get the fuck down," I hissed, pulling on her arm roughly and pushing her head below the upturned table.

She struggled against me, trying to pull her arm from my grip.

"Hey. Get off her," a male voice behind me started.

That's all I needed. I Ignored him.

"Natalie, I need you to listen to me."

She stopped struggling and looked at me.

"Someone has just tried to kill you. I need to get you out of here before they try again."

"What do you mean?" She whispered, fear now stealing her voice.

"You know. Like dead," I grumbled at her, knowing really this wasn't the time to be a smart arse.

She stared at me, searching my face, probably waiting for me to tell her it was some stupid practical joke filmed for shits and giggles for TV or something.

"Look at the glass in the door," I lowered my voice, pointing three quarters up across the right-hand side of the glass, "see that nice round circle right there? Uh-huh? That's a bullet hole. And that there is the bullet."

I pointed behind her at the bullet wedged in the wood panelling where her head had been a few moments before. She looked at the door and then the bullet, colour draining from her face.

"I need to get out of here," she whispered, terror creeping into her eyes.

"You do. Now follow me."

I ducked down, tugging her, pulling her along behind me as we ran through the back of the restaurant, eyes staring at us in confusion. I crashed through the fire exit doors and into a back lane littered with industrial sized waste bins and broken glass. The smell of rotting food hung in the air around us from the many restaurants that backed into the narrow lane. Pulling Natalie along behind me, I moved quickly over the pot-holed road surface, as she struggled on the black shiny heels she wore and the bags that she'd flung over her shoulder.

"Here, I'll get these," I said, stopping for a moment.

"Get off me."

I sighed. She was going to be fucking hard work.

"Who are you anyway?" She asked, stopping and looking at me.

I glanced around us before answering, checking how exposed we were, then seeing the recess of where a doorway tucked away in a wall, I pulled her across to where we would have some shelter.

"Cian sent me."

She looked at me, not sure which question to ask next.

"Why?" She asked, eventually.

"We got intelligence that someone had organised a hit on you."

"What do you mean?"

"Someone has taken out a contract on your life."

"Wh, what?"

Her face contorted, and she turned away from me, bending over, and I heard the splatter of vomit hitting the concrete at her feet.

"Babe, right now, I need you to do everything I say," I instructed to her back as she continued to wretch onto the ground.

She straightened, pulling the back of her hand across her mouth, her skin ashen, but the fear in her eyes a few seconds earlier replaced with a defensiveness. Then she shrugged her bags back on to her shoulder and walked away from me, heading towards the main street. Fuck. I didn't know where the shooter was or whether he had hung around, and letting her get her head blown off in the main street would really piss Cian off. I ran after her, flicking through the contacts on the phone and pressing it to my ear. I caught her in a few seconds, grabbing her arm.

"Nat, wait," I called out as she whirled around at me, shooting me a look so fierce I was sure a fist would follow. "Here," I said holding the phone out to her and letting out a sigh of relief when she took it from me.

"Charlie?" I heard her say, her voice wavering, showing the vulnerability that hid under the tough exterior, "ok...well I'm not happy about this, just so you know..."

"You gonna do as I say, then?" I asked, as she handed the phone back to me.

"You can ask for a start."

Her eyes held me in a steely stare and, although I'd just saved her life, I got the distinct feeling all she really wanted to do was kick me in the balls.

Chapter Seven

౧ Natalie ౧

"Charlie?" I was surprised by my sister's voice at the end of the strange man's phone.

"Nat. I need you to listen to me. You're in danger. Cian is on the way, but I need you to listen to the Viking. He'll keep you safe. But you need to do everything he says."

The Viking. I raced through my memories, familiarity niggling. The man at the wedding. I looked back at the biker, his eyes fixed on me, a cocky half smile on his lips. The long blond hair, the light beard covering his chin and jaw, and tattoos that I knew were hiding under the arms of his jacket.

"OK. Well, I'm not happy about this, just so you know," I said down the phone.

"I know, Nat. Stay safe."

I disconnected the call and handed it towards the biker, who seemed almost a little hesitant to come near me as if he thought I might bound away from him again.

"What now?" I asked, looking at the street in front of us, the dark bodies of people wandering past in the night.

"We need to get under cover. Your place?" the corners of his mouth twitched as he tried to suppress the smile, and I frowned back at him.

He moved forwards, grasping my hand and tugging me gently away from the main street and back into the shadows of the alleyway. I trusted my sister, but I couldn't help the unease forming in my stomach as I allowed myself to be led further into the isolation of the alleyway.

My heels seemed to echo noisily, bouncing off the walls, a mix of battered back gates, rusty metal shutters and some with empty doorways exposing the bars and restaurants beyond. Broken glass crunched under my feet, shards sticking annoyingly to the sole of my shoes, and I scuffed them free, wriggling my hand out of the biker's grip as I paused to pull one stubborn piece from the expensive shoes that were being covered in filth.

He turned and watched me, curiosity in his face.

"What?" I snapped.

"Someone's just tried to off you and you seem more worried about your shoes," he shrugged, as I teetered precariously on one foot.

"These are expensive."

"So will be my debt if I don't get you home in one piece," he grumbled, reaching for my hand again.

I moved it away from him, "I can walk without help."

He held his hands up in surrender before turning away from me.

*****

The taxi pulled up just outside the door, and at last I could escape the uncomfortable silence we sat in. I'd stolen glances at him for the last fifteen minutes, watching how he had been in a constant state of alertness, his eyes flicking around the taxi, his head pivoting from side to side and behind him as he glared out of every window in the vehicle. It had annoyed and frightened me all at once, and as the car rolled to a stop opposite my door, it took every ounce of self-control not to leap out and fly into the protective, thick walls of the Victorian mid-terrace house.

I walked ahead of him, my keys already out and aiming for the lock, wasting no time on the street as he looked around behind him. The lock clunked in the frame as it turned ever slowly, my heartbeat rising with the tension. Just a few more steps and I'd be safe. The door scraped across the floor, and I gave it a little nudge with my shoulder, making a mental note to get the sticking door fixed. For a split second I considered closing it quickly behind me, leaving the blond-haired man out on the doorstep, rather than allowing the complete stranger into my home. But I'd promised Charlie to behave, so I chased the thoughts from my mind. The door squeaked shut behind him.

The rattle of a chain made me turn, the metal scraping gently as it slid into place.

"Stay here."

"What?"

"Stay here. Don't move till I've checked the house."

"Could there be an intruder?" I asked, desperately trying to keep the fear from my voice, tension in my chest squeezing at my lungs, slowly pushing the air out of me.

"Dunno. Not taking a chance."

He stalked off and a couple of seconds later I could hear the chink of the curtains against the pole. Ignoring him, I followed him into the lounge, watching as he moved across to the other end and pulling the curtains closed on the other window.

"What are you doing?"

"If he can't see you, he can't shoot you."

"How do you know it's a man?"

"Female hitmen aren't really a thing."

"But they could be?"

"They just aren't. Trust me."

He wandered off, shutting the blinds in the kitchen and then bounding up the stairs to the second floor. I followed, kicking off my heels at the bottom step, my feet sinking into the thick carpet cushioning each step.

"Thought I told you to wait downstairs?"

"You did. I ignored you."

He shook his head, a strand of blonde hair falling from the ponytail. He moved out of each room, dropping the blinds and pulling curtains closed.

"You live here alone?"

"Yep."

Not the brightest answer to give a total stranger. He could still be a psycho for all I knew, and the fact he took orders from Cian O'Sullivan, the head of the Irish Mafia, meant he was a criminal at best. I trusted my sister, I reminded myself, trying to push the thoughts from my mind.

"Christ, this place is huge," he said after running up the next flight of stairs to the room at the top of the house, "why so big?"

"Because I can. And it means I don't have to move out again when, if, I have a family."

He didn't need to know any of this. Shock must have been getting to me. I was revealing far too much to a stranger, a mafia foot soldier. He stood looking at me for a second, as if pondering those last words, studying me, his head cocked to the side and for the first time I noticed the green-blue of his eyes, tranquil like the Mediterranean. The cropped beard that covered his chin, a slightly darker shade of blond than his hair, crept over his jaw as well and where that ended, the dark ink of tattoos started, rippling down his neck. Even with his leather bike jacket fastened to his neck, I could see the tattoo licking at the skin, closing round his throat and trailing off around the back of his neck. I didn't like tattoos.

"Now what?" I asked, pulling my eyes from his.

He shrugged, "you could make me a cuppa?"

I opened my mouth, an aggressive retort sitting on the tip of my tongue, but then I clamped my lips shut again. Supposedly, he had saved my life and I should show some signs of gratitude. Cup of tea it was. I tipped my head and led the way back down the stairs.

The kettle boiled furiously, the noise cutting through the house as if it had been amplified and then projected around the place. I took out a mug, clattering it loudly off the bench, my hands shaking suddenly, resolve eroded by shock and adrenaline. His hand was warm as it covered mine, taking the spoon from me.

"You're OK," he said softly, "we'll look after you. We'll keep you safe."

I nodded, silently, staring at the mug on the bench before turning to the fridge and emptying the last of a bottle of Pinot Grigio into an overly large wine glass. I brought it to my lips, gulping at it greedily, desperate for the warmth to trickle through my veins and numb the feeling of terror that had crept into me somewhere between the restaurant and my front door. How could this happen? Why would someone want to kill me? Surely this was a mistake; mistaken identity. I slugged another few mouthfuls of the liquid, hoping it would hit my empty stomach quickly.

I watched the biker finish making his own cup of tea, tattooed hands scooping two spoons of sugar into the mug and filling it with water, and then he peeled off his jacket and hung it on the back of a kitchen chair. He wore a grey t-shirt under his jacket, short sleeves gripping tightly over his biceps and the round neck of the t-shirt sagging almost to the middle of his chest. Across every bit of exposed skin all I could see were tattoos. They covered everywhere, a map of images drawn on his skin, bleeding into each other, a seamless blanket of pictures.

"Do you have a name?" I asked, the wine in my glass sinking quickly.

"People call me The Viking," he grinned.

"It's not really a name."

"I don't use it."

"Why?"

"In my career, you're best off not being identifiable."

"What career is that?"

"Nothing you need to know about."

He pushed the mug against his lips, blowing across the brown liquid before taking a mouthful.

"You can just call me V if you want. Most people do."

"Fair enough. When will Cian be here, V?"

"Probably not till the morning. You've got plenty space for me to crash here tonight, though."

"Here?" I looked at him and he nodded back, grinning at me.

I turned, rummaging in the fridge for an unopened bottle of wine, the fuzzy feeling of the glass I'd just gulped back infiltrating my body, the shake in my hands and the thoughts whirring round my head just slowing down. How the fuck had I got in this mess?

Chapter Eight

ಊ The Viking ಐ

I could hear Natalie moving about on the floor below and glanced at the digital clock beside the bed. 6.20am. I never got up this fucking early. I scrubbed a hand across my face and wrestled myself free from the sheets that had become wrapped around my legs after I'd kicked the heavy duvet off in the night. My head had sunk between countless pillows and cushions, the ones that had survived. The others lay scattered over the floor. There was no need for so many fucking cushions. I'd thrown most of them on the floor myself when I'd climbed up to the top floor in the early hours, and still the fuckers were trying to suffocate me.

The carpet was thick and soft on my bare feet as I swung my legs out of the bed. The room was bathed in daylight, the light-coloured curtains not keeping much out as it bounced around white and silver painted walls. Fucking daylight. Fucking 6.20 in the fucking morning. Fucking Cian. I kicked one of the shiny pink cushions across the floor as I got to my feet, the sound of a hairdryer whirring below me. I needed a cup of tea and a shower and then my bike, in that order.

As I got to the second floor I saw her, her reflection in the floor-length mirror, pinning her hair into a bun on the top of her head, a light blue shirt tucked into the navy skirt that stopped just above her knee, much like the pictures I had seen of her in that envelope. Her legs were lightly tanned, the slight bulge of her calf muscle probably a result of the ridiculous high heels she seemed to wear. Her tits bulged nicely in her top, definitely more than a handful. I tore my eyes away from her, my cock waking up quicker than me. I was pretty certain she wasn't a damsel in distress conquest and I would likely be castrated if she saw what Mini V was thinking right now.

I wandered down to the kitchen, pulling open cupboards and finding stacks of square plates and rectangular bowls, tiny serving dishes and wavy platters and thick butcher's blocks but no mugs. There was a cupboard showing off neatly stacked cans, grouped together by soup, or vegetables, tins of tuna and salmon, their labels all looking at me, tidy and ordered. But no mugs. I clicked the kettle on angrily, trying the final cupboard. Tucked neatly away behind the wine glasses were a handful of cups, ordered by their different patterns and sizes. I grabbed one, pulling it from the shelf and starting the next quest of finding where she kept the tea and wishing I'd paid more attention to her last night. I found the canisters above the tins, lined up neatly, labels facing the same direction, the same ordered way of everything in the cupboards.

The first mouthful of tea slid down my throat, heat warming my mouth and scratching against my tongue, but the smell, taste and anticipation of the caffeine hit was like the first lick of an orgasm. I closed my eyes, the faint smell of cotton candy and chocolate caramel filling my nose, sweet and strong. I looked up to see the woman standing in front of me, her eyes roaming my body, surprise and repulsion mixed with intrigue as she studied me. She pursed her lips together, red and full, the kitchen lights bouncing off the gloss of her lipstick. Her eyes were framed with a thin streak of eyeliner pulling off to a flick at the corners, making her eyes more oval shaped than I had noticed last night.

"Where are your clothes?" she said, her voice breathy, and I grinned back at her.

"Like what you see, babe?" I answered, my hand brushing over my bare torso as I stood before her in only a pair of boxer shorts.

She shook her head, "I don't like tattoos," her voice had cleared a little, her sharp tone of disapproval returning, "and you're just one big tattoo."

I took a bow, my loose hair falling over my face.

"My body is a work of art," I answered, "wanna see where isn't tattooed."

I took a step towards her, and she took a step backwards, teetering on a beige heel so high it threatened to bring tears to my eyes and might yet if I didn't behave myself.

"Don't be stupid," she spat.

I hadn't misread the intrigue on her face earlier, the subtle blush of her cheeks and the slight colour change at her neck. I hadn't missed the little lick of her red lips. And Mini V hadn't missed how her shirt pulled tight around a good rack, bulging out from her chest, the two undone buttons at the top of the shirt allowing a sneak peek down to the swell of two plump tits pushed together.

She turned away from me, striding down the hallway towards the door, her hips swaying from side to side like a catwalk model. I watched her pick up her laptop bag. Shit.

Shoving the cup down on the bench, I bounded after her, catching her arm and pulling her back towards me just as she reached the door, her fingers sliding off the door chain.

"What are you doing?" I hissed at her.

"I'm going to work."

"You're not."

"I am."

"Someone tried to kill you last night and very nearly succeeded. You're not going anywhere."

She looked at me furiously, her eyes smouldering with anger and hatred.

"Now go in there and sit down," my voice came out darker than I intended, harsh.

For a split second she recoiled, a flash of fear and uncertainty in the caramel brown of her eyes, and then she turned away and marched into the lounge, throwing her bag onto the settee as it dropped between another mound of cushions.

"So what am I supposed to do?" she asked.

"Call in sick or something. But you're not going out there."

"Fine. At least open the curtains."

"Nope."

I heard her swear under her breath as she dug the bag out from the cushions on the sofa. The sharp knock at the door startled the both of us. Natalie looked at me, alarm across her face as I moved to the bay window.

"Don't worry, babe. Hitmen don't normally knock," I chuckled, pulling the curtain back an inch.

Two suited men stood on the doorstep. The cavalry had arrived. Late as fucking usual.

I strode down the corridor and opened the door, ushering the two men quickly into the house. I led them through to the lounge as Natalie watched them intently, a flicker of relief in her eyes, her hostile stare warming slightly as Cian plucked a framed picture from the mantelpiece.

"That was the both of us with our father," she said, answering some sort of question only she seemed to hear.

Cian nodded, understanding in his eyes, and replaced the frame. He turned to me.

"What do we know?"

"Not much. She was on the list the broker gave me with a £100k offer."

Cian whistled but said no more.

"If the broker knows who wants the kill, he won't say."

"Why did you get a list?" Natalie asked suddenly. Her attention turned on me, those caramel-brown eyes pinning me with a look and a meaning that I suddenly didn't want to think about.

"The Viking is a hitman. The list of jobs he was offered had you on there. That's why we knew," Cian provided the answer that I was too much of a coward to give.

Natalie's eyes opened wide, shock pasted across her face, and this time there was no doubt in the way she recoiled from me.

"And you left me here with *him*?"

"He's one of the best there is. Sometimes it takes the devil to protect you from a demon."

Fucking great. Now she'd think I was psychotic too. Her eyes swarmed over me and although her face didn't exactly say it, I was sure that it took all her strength to stop her lips curling in disgust. I looked away.

"Nat. I need you to think really hard about who might want to kill you?" Cian asked, breaking her disgusted stare.

"N, no one. Why would someone want to do that to me? I'm just a solicitor, nothing special."

"Think, Nat," Cian probed, "who have you defended that you might have pissed off? Whose career have you fucked with?"

The anger flashed momentarily across her eyes, lighting up her face, her red lips almost sneering, and then she seemed to have the emotion under control again.

"Jaxon Blackwood, or his family. He was the kid who murdered my father. I put the case together against him, got him sent down. His family is notorious in Newcastle and across Gateshead. And then there is DI Burrows. He's an ex, but he also blames me for not getting his promotion."

"Anymore?" I asked, "whoever this is has deep pockets. This is way above average for one head."

She stared at me, a stare that told me to watch my step.

"I mean. This is out of the ordinary as far as hits go," I continued and breathed a sigh of relief that my nuts might live to see another day.

"I split up with Carter at Charlie's wedding. Carter Lawrence. His family has a shit load of money. He is a QC. But I don't think he would want to kill me. I mean, it would be a bit over the top, don't you think?"

"Let's start there," Cian instructed the other man, "me and Garrett will check these out. Natalie, until I say it's safe, you're on sick leave. V I want you here twenty-four-seven until this is resolved. Don't let her out of your sight and don't let her get killed. I'm only paying you if she stays alive."

I turned to look at Nat, who met my eye, the disdain and annoyance echoing my own feelings, emanating out of her and seeping into my skin. It looked like we were stuck with each other for a while.

*****

I groaned, turning over, trying to escape the searing heat of the twenty-five-tog duvet, sweat lying sticky on my skin. I didn't know what time it was. I'd spent all day babysitting, apart from a couple of hours whilst Cian was there where I went to fetch my motorbike from where I'd abandoned it in the centre of Newcastle yesterday. And then I was back to watching Natalie as she worked, listening to her as she spoke into the small machine she held in her hand, instructions for someone. I got bored quickly, regular checks through cracks in the curtains becoming mundane and so I was relieved when Natalie finally called it a night.

A scratch downstairs broke through my thoughts. I lay still and listened, concentrating on straining my ears to hear something other than my own breathing. Nothing. I rubbed my eyes, kicked the duvet clean off the bed, and turned over. The scratch came again, but this time there was the faint shuffle of something. Footsteps.

I launched myself out of bed, keeping my adrenaline under control as I padded quickly and silently out of the room and down the stairs. Below me, a dark shape slipped through

57

Natalie's bedroom door. I bolted down the last few steps, not caring now whether I startled the intruder. I heard her scream as I got to the doorway, loud and shrill and then suddenly muffled, a hideous gargle coming from her room. Running through the doorway, I saw the dark shape hunched on top of the bed, Nat's legs thrashing from under him. The scream from her throat now deathly quiet.

Chapter Nine

☙ Natalie ❧

The dip of the bed woke me, the sudden feeling of a presence in the room and the strong smell of a woody scent, and for a second I nearly called out, to tell the Viking to get the hell out. But then I felt the unforgettable feeling of someone straddling me. Their hands clamped down on my neck, a sudden vice like pressure round my throat, stealing the air and the scream that had escaped. I dug my fingernails into the hands, barely even brushing against the cold leather of gloves.

The pressure round my throat increased, my chest heaving from breaths it could not take, the blood draining from my brain, an unsettling peace trying its best to descend, contradicting the terrified fight of my body, of my legs trying to move the weight off me, my own fingers clawing at my throat. The grey light of the room faded, growing darker. The weight lifted suddenly, hitting the floor with a thud.

I inhaled, mercifully, air assaulting my lungs, blowing them up like a balloon, burning pressure throbbing behind my ribs. I turned onto my side, choking and coughing, my throat on fire. On the floor, a bundle of shadows thrashed around, grunts and thuds, the sound of a heavy boot crashing against the wardrobe. There was a hiss as air was sucked in through teeth and a then a dull thump. A shape staggered backwards, falling against the bed as the other shadow moved towards the door, growing smaller, each thump of feet on the carpet growing quieter.

I scrabbled for the bedside lamp, my lungs still screaming for air, coughing like an age-old smoker. The light lit the room in a soft glow, delicate, gentle. The blond-haired biker straightened up, his eyes fixing on my throat. Below us, a door banged.

"Are you ok?" He asked.

I nodded, the motion making my neck sore. Then he turned away and thundered after the intruder. The room fell into silence, the only sound the raspy intakes of air my chest was making. I staggered out of bed and slipped my arms through the silk dressing gown, pulling the tie tight round my waist. The stairs creaked lightly and for a moment my heart rate doubled, making my lungs feel like they were crushed against my chest.

I turned on the lights in the bedroom and then the hallway, a bright yellow glow chasing away the shadows, all shadows but the one moving back up the stairs, his body a tapestry of ink. I didn't know where to look first. At the ghoulish skull that covered his entire stomach, its mouth a gaping dark hole of crooked and missing teeth, or the faces painted onto his chest and the barbells through both his nipples. The tattoos continued down his thick legs all the way to his feet. There was literally no piece of visible skin un-inked.

"You ok?" He asked, ignoring that I was staring at him.

"My throat hurts."

"Lemme see," he said, moving closer.

Before I had time to answer or back away from him, his fingers had pushed my chin up gently, the action making me wince.

"It'll probably bruise. It's already going red."

"Who was that?" I whispered, my voice growing hoarse.

"A hitman. Could be the same one from the restaurant, could be another," he answered, shrugging as if it was no big deal I'd just been throttled moments before.

"There could be more?"

"Yeah, might be."

He dropped his hand from my face but didn't move away. I could almost feel the warmth of his flesh he was stood so close to me, and for the first time I noticed the way he smelled. New leather and soap, clean. I took a step backwards, creating some space. He was virtually naked, stood just in his tight boxer shorts and I had a thin pair of silk pyjamas under my dressing gown, hardly any clothes between us.

"I need to go secure the house," he said suddenly, turning away and wandering back down the stairs.

I watched him move away. The demon scratched into his back, looking at me as he went. Its soulless eyes stared at me as it sat on his back, a crown of shapes on its head and patterns emerging from between its eyes. I followed him, letting him get in front, hoping that if the intruder was still there, it would take him first, not me.

The Viking had the house lit up like a Christmas tree, each room flooded with the yellow artificial glow from the modern chandeliers I had hanging from every ceiling. I followed him, too scared to be left behind in my own house, too stubborn to admit it.

The biker opened and closed the back door, opened it again, studied the frame, and then shut it once more.

"Where's your tool kit?" He asked.

"What? Why?"

"A tool kit? To fix this door."

"I don't have a tool kit."

"Then what do you use to repair things?" He asked, crossing his arms over each other, the muscles of his darkened chest pushing together, biceps bulging under the tattoos on his arms.

Every time he moved, I noticed something new, every part of him different each time I looked at him. His lips curled into a grin. How long had I been staring at him for?

"I hire someone who fixes things," I answered eventually, trying to find somewhere else to look but at him, at the body that was perfectly sculpted under all those tattoos that I despised.

"Do you have a hammer?"

I shook my head.

"Ok, even just a screwdriver will do."

"Oh, I've got some of those. Hang on."

I turned, taking out a box from under the sink and rummaging through it, my hand clasping around the little plastic box about three inches long. I handed it to him. The Viking turned it over in his hands.

"Where the fuck did you get these? Out of a cracker?"

"Well, yes. But I thought they would come in handy."

"Fuck's sake," he lowered his voice so it was barely audible under his breath, "right. Get dressed."

"What?"

"Get dressed. I need you somewhere where I can actually protect you. And I can't do that here."

"I'm not leaving my house."

"You are. We're going to my place," he answered, moving towards me.

"I'm not going anywhere with you. I'm staying right here."

"You're not. Now be a good girl and go get some clothes on," his eyes held a twinkle, an amused smile across his face.

"I'm staying right. Fucking. Here," I said petulantly, anger simmering away.

The smile dropped from his lips, a darkness crossing his eyes and he took a step further forward, our bodies inches apart once more. I held his gaze, setting my jaw stubbornly, my head tilted upwards slightly to maintain my stare. His hand shot out so quickly he had wrapped it around my neck before I'd even seen him move, and I pulled in a sharp intake of air from the suddenness and pain from another person's hands. But this time I wasn't fighting for my life, this time I was fighting to keep control of my senses. Roughly, he yanked me closer, my breasts rubbing against his chest and his fingers pushed against the back of my skull. He trailed his thumb across my bottom lip, breath hot on my face.

"If you want to stay alive, babe, you'll do everything I say. And I mean *everything*," his voice was low, half-purr, half-growl, vibrating through me.

His thumb stilled, resting against the middle of my lower lip, just enough pressure that I could feel the blood pumping to where he touched me, heat rushing to the spot. I had a ridiculous urge to bite him, or suck on his thumb, or both. I shook my head free from his grip angrily, pushing away from him, that same heat now rising to my cheeks in embarrassment and frustration; a throb starting between my legs

64

that I would not be entertaining. In any way. What. So. Ever.

*****

I followed the motorbike through the tree-lined streets, the first light of day peeking through a cloudy sky. The roads were clear, commuters not yet on their way to work, curtains still pulled across the windows of the houses we passed as we left Low Fell and my home behind us. I'd stuffed a bag with clothes, and brought my laptop, although that had taken some negotiation. I'd found threatening to open all the curtains and expose us to eyes from the outside had been enough to persuade the biker that the computer was coming with me. Seemed he was easy to persuade when I could use my life as a bargaining chip, and the wrath of my now-brother-in-law as the final piece in the deal.

Traffic picked up on the motorway and the bike in front of me started to weave in and out of the cars ahead, my foot growing heavier and heavier on the accelerator as I tried to keep up. He'd given me no idea where his home was; no town, no place name, no direction. My only instructions were to follow him. And I was following a maniac on a motorbike. His speed crept faster and faster, breaking the speed limit. I fell behind.

An alarm sounded shrill and urgent from the dashboard and I jumped, my heart jolting against my chest. Lights flashed up in front of me, orange and red, as the car continued to play a chorus of warning sounds. It didn't make any sense. It was almost brand new. I edged my foot off the pedal, stealing looks at the dashboard whilst keeping some attention on the road, the black motorbike in front getting smaller and smaller.

I pulled off the dual carriage way, easing to a stop in a quiet road not yet woken up to the trucks that would pass shortly on their way to the factories and industrial premises that lined the banks of the River Tyne. A circular warning light flashed angrily back at me. Turning the engine off, I swung my legs out of the car and wandered around it. Both back tyres were as flat as pancakes. Shit.

A big black pickup truck drove up behind me, slowing as it passed and then reversing back.

"You alright?" The man inside asked.

"Flat tyres," I grumbled, opening the boot and looking into the space blankly.

"You want some help?"

"I, er, please," I said, eventually realising I had absolutely no clue what to do with the wheel in the boot that stared back at me.

He parked in front and came round to the back of the car, stooping over the top of me. The woody scent of his aftershave hung in the air, scratching at the back of my throat, and I coughed as it hit me, pain erupting, memories of a few hours ago rushing back to me. I turned, looking up at him. He was tall and wide, a nasty scar ran down a cheek, deep and jagged, and I'd seen plenty of those on crime scene photographs. A best guess was that he'd had a disagreement with the wrong gang. I sucked in a breath, tension creeping over me, the woody spicy scent hitting my lungs again. I tried to still the panic rising in my veins.

"You know. I'm just gonna ring my breakdown," I said, moving away from him, "you've probably got to get to work."

I turned to walk away, but he launched himself at me, wrapping his arms around my waist and pulling me back into him. I screamed, kicking out blindly, throwing my elbows back towards him, connecting with thin air. I pushed my fingernails into his hands, and he grunted, skin breaking under the pressure, but still he didn't let go. Bit by bit he pushed and pulled, edging me closer to the black pickup truck.

A rumble sounded in the distance, a prick of white light from a single headlight, bright in the spring morning. Then, like a missile, it headed straight for us, the exhaust roaring as it hurtled down the road. The man faltered, his grip on me loosening, and I kicked hard, my foot hitting his shin with a dull thump. He grunted again. I dropped, sinking out of his arms and down onto the ground, glancing over my shoulder to the leather clad man advancing, a huge knife glinting in the light.

The attacker turned towards the Viking, eyeing the hideous serrated blade warily, watching as he flicked it in the air in a series of arcs. He backed away towards his truck and I crawled around the side of the car, terror stealing my legs from me, my boneless limbs feeling heavy.

Chapter Ten

ഌ The Viking ൙

The red sports car slipped further and further back, and I checked my speed, slowing down a touch, hoping she'd put her fucking foot down and catch up. The longer we were out of cover, the more dangerous it was and the more likely she'd end up with a bullet between her eyes. I checked the mirrors again; the car slipping further behind, shrinking to a tiny speck in the glass. My eyes flitted to the front, moving out of the way of the car I had gained upon. When I checked the mirrors again, the red car had disappeared. Fuck!

I pulled the bike off the dual carriageway at the next exit, spinning round in the mouth of the road and travelling back down at speed. Natalie couldn't have gone far. She had just been behind me moments ago, albeit miles fucking behind. I slowed, glancing right, peering across the other lanes of traffic and down a road to my right that led off to an industrial estate tucked behind Gateshead's sports stadium, lining the banks of the River Tyne. Taillights glowed in the gloom, an April morning not yet warmed by the sun.

I whipped the bike to the right, leaning low over the road, the tarmac millimetres from skimming my bike leathers. The car was pulled up to the curb, the slim shape of Natalie at the back, a tall man beside her. A passer-by? A knight in dark clothing? He moved behind her; her shape disappearing from view completely and then appeared again, thrust to the left, arms and legs flailing. I revved the engine; the bike screaming as it burst down the tarmac, a guttural anger expelled from the exhaust. I slid to a stop sideways, burning rubber the only thing I could smell as the bike miraculously remained upright and I kicked out the stand, swinging my leg over the back and jumping off.

The man saw me and hesitated, readying himself for a fight as Natalie wriggled free from his grasp and slid around the side of the car. He moved his feet apart, planting long thick legs, his eyes focussed on me. Reaching round behind my back, I pulled the knife from under my jacket, sliding it from its leather sheath, the nasty serrated edge catching in the grey morning light. He didn't miss the size of the blade or the sharpness of the metal as I moved it through the air in a series of smooth moves, my wrist rotating seamlessly, gracefully, as the blade cut through the space in front of us. With a last glance at Natalie and then again at me, the money over her head slipping from his grasp. He turned and ran for the big pickup truck, moving across the road in big, long strides. The engine roared to life, and the tyres screamed, spinning and grabbing for the road surface before finally finding purchase and speeding off.

Slipping the knife carefully back into its sheath, I walked round the car. Natalie was propped up against the nearside front tyre, her arms wrapped around her knees, staring at the pitted pavement in front of her. I squatted down in front of her, watching her jump suddenly, eyes filled with fear, gazing up at me, glassy. Her hair had fallen free from her ponytail and a button missing from her cardigan allowed her tits to bulge out of it. I held out a hand.

She stared at it for a minute, her eyes wandering over the tattoos visible from where I'd removed my gloves. Her teeth raked over that plump bottom lip, today bare of her usual red lipstick.

"I'll not hurt you, babe," I assured her, "and these tattoos aren't infectious. You ain't gonna get one just by touching me."

Her shoulders slumped in relief or defeat. I wasn't sure which, but eventually I felt the cool touch of her fingers against my palm. I tugged, pulling her gently to her feet. Her lips trembled, and she hugged her arms around herself closer, and I noticed the slight shake in her body. I guided her back round to the driver's seat and pushed her gently inside.

"Wait here while I check the car out."

Wandering around the car, I dropped to my haunches at each tyre. The back two were flatter than pancakes, identical shaped holes in the tyre walls; screwdriver sized. The front tyres weren't much better and were losing air quickly. I opened the driver's door and peered in.

"All your tyres are fucked. This car is going nowhere."

Natalie ran her hand slowly through the loose strands of brown hair.

"So, what now?"

"We're gonna need some help fixing it. Follow me."

I straddled my bike, the engine roaring to life like a war cry, but this time I eased it down the road in front of Nat as she limped her car steadily behind me. My senses were on edge, every nerve ending tingling, watching, waiting for anything out of place, anyone or anything suspicious. The three-minute drive towards the river was excruciating, my head flicking side to side as I scanned my mirrors every few seconds.

We turned off the main road and down a steep bank, which always looked like it would take you right into the River Tyne itself until you reached the sharp bend. Natalie edged the car down carefully after me, gingerly letting it roll slowly down the bank. I imagined the relief on her face when, at the bottom, the road bent sharply to the left, following the river upstream, the road climbing once more.

At the top, the pub stood tall and proud, occupying a vantage point looking over the river, the carpark empty save for a familiar battered van. I pulled into the barren concrete square, the rumble from my bike exhaust carried on the still air, sleepy birds stirring in the thick bushes that surrounded the property. I looked up at the building, the wooden frames around the windows in need of painting, the slate of its roof mottled with moss. *The Dog on the Tyne.* Memories came flooding back, swarming around me like a load of angry bees, a buzzing in my brain as I tried not to focus on any of them, not even the good ones.

Natalie stepped out of the car, looking around quizzically.

"A pub?" She asked, her voice duetted against the scratch of wood against wood, tree branches creaking above us.

"What are you doing here, V?" The deep voice boomed from the gap he'd created in the old sash window.

"I need you, Indie," I answered.

The window clunked shut. Not a further word was uttered, and I stood in silence, waiting, hoping that after all these years he wouldn't turn me away. Beside me I heard the nervous shuffle of Nat's feet, scratching against the crumbling tarmac of the road.

The front door of the pub opened, and the man popped his head out, glancing around before tipping his head and beckoning us in. I waved my hand and Natalie led the way.

Inside, it didn't look much different to how I'd last seen it. A dark red carpet had replaced the previous green one, the bar top was still filled with dents, chunks missing from various brawls and stray knives, and the windows looked like they hadn't been replaced since the eighteen hundreds. Indie clicked on some lights, the golden glow exaggerating the defects in the carpet and the mis-matched bar stools.

Nat stood quietly beside me, gazing round the pub, her eyes stopping and studying, a look of distaste mixed with bewilderment.

Indie moved round the back of the bar, and I followed, propping myself against a tall bar stool, watching as he pulled one small glass from under the bar top and emptied some whisky into it. Natalie lingered some way behind me, unsure whether to approach or just stay where she was.

"What do you want, V?" the greying-haired man grunted after slugging back the entire glass of whisky.

I didn't blame him. Coming back here put all of us in some shit, but, right now, this was the least dangerous scenario.

"I need to fix that car and we need to get out of here."

"Why should I help you, V?"

I shrugged, "why not? But if you need reasons, then help me get out of here. Before anyone from the club turns up."

Indie's eyes bore into mine and he poured himself another drink.

"Too early for drinking that shit, cus. Look, I just need to get us out of here. Help me fix the car and then we're gone."

The man looked at me for a long time and I knew he would play out all the scenarios in his head, locking in to all the memories, just like I was as I sat there. He sighed, defeated.

"Your woman?" He asked, and I shot a glance over my shoulder.

I knew she had heard the conversation, despite our low tones. She was observant, clever, calculating. She wouldn't have missed anything of our exchange. Her eyes narrowed at me, but she kept her lips pushed firmly together and I turned back to my cousin.

"Nope. Just someone I'm looking after."

Indie nodded.

"Let's just get on with this before Ste comes back. Or both of us might not see tomorrow."

"Thanks, Indie."

I spun around on the stool.

"Stay here," I instructed Natalie as I followed Indie towards the back of the pub, hoping for once she'd follow some fucking orders.

Chapter Eleven

⊱ Natalie ⊰

I watched the two men working on my car from the pub window; a window that hadn't seen a good glass cleaner for a while. It was covered in fingerprints and marks; cigarette burns on the wooden frames. The building was old, and it felt it too. The air inside was damp and musty, and cold. Tiny droplets of moisture pooled on the single-paned windows, dripping into corners flecked with black mould. The carpet beneath my feet crackled, dried muck and congealed alcohol creating textures underneath me I didn't want to think too much about.

I'd stood for a while gazing out of the windows. The blond biker had pulled off his leather jacket, his tattooed arms escaping from the tight grey t-shirt as he bent over the car, the leather bike trousers tightening over his arse. The other man, Indie, was taller and broader. Once dark hair was invaded by grey, creating an almost two-tone look and the dark beard that covered his jaw was suffering the same fate. He wore a black hoodie with a picture emblazoned across the back as he stooped over the Viking.

Eventually, I relented and sat on the sticky seat of the cushioned bench that ran under the window. I must have sat there for hours, at least it felt like that, but when I glanced at my watch it was closer to forty minutes. I stared out through the streaked glass again, watching the two men doing nothing. Both stood with folded arms, inspecting the car and shaking their heads; gestures I didn't like. The blond man turned and caught me watching him from the window, smiling up at me, and I resisted the urge to duck down under the sill like an embarrassed teenager. He patted the bigger man on the arm and they both turned, walking back towards the building.

The doors at the back of the bar clattered noisily, and I rose to my feet.

"OK, babe…"

"Don't call me babe," my voice came out as a growl, the low heat of anger sparking in my stomach.

The Viking rolled his eyes and the man behind him grinned. I shot him a look as well.

"OK, OK. Your car is fucked. For now, anyway. It needs four new tyres."

"Can you not just patch them up?" I asked, anxiety prickling at my throat.

The Viking shook his head, "someone's gone to work on those babies. Indie's shit. He doesn't have the gear here to sort them."

I looked up at the tall man, whose eyebrows pulled together in irritation.

"Look," the blond man continued, "we have to get out of here and your car is not driveable. You're gonna have to jump on the back with me."

I shook my head violently. No. Fucking. Way.

"I'm not getting on that. No chance," I answered, my voice steely.

"Look, you'll be safe on the back with me. Indie's got a spare helmet."

I frowned, folding my arms across my chest, "Nope. Not happening," the blond biker went to open his mouth, probably to negotiate with me, but it would be fruitless. I saved him the energy, "I saw the way you drove. You're an absolute lunatic. There's no way I'm getting on the back of a motorbike with you."

"Well, what the fuck else do you want to do? Walk?" I could hear the frustration now in his voice.

*****

The van whizzed along the road, advancing on the cars in front until I was certain we were going to go straight into the back of them, and then swinging out into the other lane and around them just in time. The Viking's foot must have been as angry as his face. The van slowed suddenly, unable to move out from behind the car we'd just sped up on because of someone else in the other lane was driving at the actual speed limit. I hissed audibly as I was thrown forward, the seat belt yanking me roughly back into the seat, pain from my bruised neck shooting across my chest and shoulders. The bumper of the car in front seemed to just stare at me.

"Slow down! If you don't kill us, I think you'll make me sick."

"Puke in this van and you're paying to get it valeted," he grumbled, pumping the accelerator as he sat impatiently behind a car.

A set of eyes watched us nervously from the rectangular mirror of the vehicle in front, glancing at the road, then darting back.

"You're a dick. Do you know that?" I shot at him.

"Well, this dick is trying to keep you alive. And to keep you alive, this dick had to go running to the fucking Kings for help. If you weren't Cian's sister-in-law, you'd already be dead."

I swallowed, my throat feeling constricted, and any more angry words on the tip of my tongue now dried up from the combination of fear and pain, and the creeping nausea of travel sickness the Viking was inducing in me. We didn't speak again for the rest of the drive as we left Gateshead behind, heading east. Traffic filled the roads now, the black tarmac littered with vehicles. The Viking slowed but kept up his constant vigil, scouring the mirrors and continuously checking around him until we pulled into an industrial estate, the next town over.

The place was already busy with lorries and vans rumbling down the road, fully laden.

We took a left and then a right and then another right, twisting and turning down numerous roads until the busy morning quieted and the heavy vehicles became fewer. The Viking pulled the van alongside a row of garages. They were all the same; bare metal shutters, no signage, white-washed walls. The only distinguishing marks were the discreet numbers above each door. Without a word, he got out of the van and approached one of the metal shutters. Then, bending down and fiddling with the lock, he flung the metal door upwards, a clatter ringing out around us and making me jump nervously, before disappearing inside.

A low vibration from inside the chasm of the garage started, two angry looking headlights lighting up from the darkness before yet another van rolled out. It was as black as the Viking's motorbike, only two windows in the side of the cab, the rest of the vehicle, just one metal panel. The biker pulled it up in front of Indie's van and stepped out. Coming round to my side, he yanked the door open and for a moment I stared at him confused.

"Out," he instructed.

I hesitated and then eventually stepped out. Between the rows of garages, I stood almost nose to nose with him. He wasn't hugely taller than me, and he wasn't imposing, not with his tattoos covered, anyway. His eyes focussed on me, probably waiting for an angry retort, and I wasn't one to disappoint.

"You know people often comply quicker when someone says please?"

"I'm a dick, remember?" His voice was lighter than the scathing look in his eyes.

I stood still, crossing my arms over my chest and tilting my head to the side. He sighed and rolled his eyes.

"Can you *please* get your fucking arse in the other fucking van?"

I slid past him, yanked the back doors open and grabbed my belongings before depositing them in the back of the new set of wheels and slamming the doors shut. And then, after the Viking had safely tucked Indie's van into the garage, we were back on the road again travelling south.

"Exactly where are we going?" I asked, breaking the silence of the last twenty minutes as the vehicle crossed the Wearmouth Bridge, fighting its way past commuter traffic.

The Viking sat quietly, turning off and cutting down behind the centre of Sunderland and out towards the docks, eventually turning into yet another industrial estate. The roads were busy, heavy plant traffic and battered vans moving in and out of compounds, but he kept driving until right at the far end the van rolled to a stop.

Winding the window down, he leant out, punching a code into a keypad and waited. The big gates inched open, slowly, and as soon as they were wide enough to squeeze the van through, the vehicle crept forwards. Inside was a yard, stark and grey, leading to yet another garage unit, but this time over two storeys. The floor above had rows of rectangular windows, turned onto their long sides, divided up into individual oblong panes separated by white painted frames. The building had to have been from the seventies and looked nothing more than an abandoned industrial unit, although less dilapidated.

"Is this your place?" I asked, trying to keep my voice even, keeping hold of the judgement and the despair at the thought of what I was going to be staying in.

"Yeah. This is me," he answered, grasping the keys that hung from the vehicle's ignition.

The roller shutters covered the length of two garages, rolling up automatically as we approached and then shutting behind us. Strip lights lit up the inside, bike and car parts strewn around the place. Another black motorcycle stood, leaning sideways in the far corner. On the other side was a stack of cardboard boxes and then something large covered in dust sheets.

The roller shutters clattered noisily behind us as they hit the ground, stacking tightly together and cutting off the outside world. I glanced around again, wistfully, as I got out of the van. The air was thick with the smell of oil and grime and exhaust fumes. The Viking grabbed my bags from the back of the van and ushered me towards a door on the back wall. I tugged on it, having to give it a few good pulls before I wrenched the metal door open. A loud chime echoed round the cavernous space, bouncing off the walls and then coming back at us. I glanced at the Viking.

"Security system. That door makes a noise every time it's opened."

We followed a short corridor and then up a flight of stairs. Old vinyl tiles peeling on each step, the rubber of the black hand-rail uneven and scratched as I followed, letting the biker lead the way up the stairs, pulling my little jacket around me in the stairwell's coolness. I shivered, trying not to think about what sort of dirty hell hole I was entering. It was bound to be covered in empty beer cans and the smell of cigarettes or whatever substances he smoked, injected, or snorted.

This was a nightmare. I was in purgatory, being punished for some reason I didn't know, by someone I didn't know. And now my life was in the hands of a mad, knife-carrying biker. What had gone wrong?

At the top of the barren stairs, two doors stood opposite each other, bigger and heavier than the one downstairs, like something you would find in a bank, guarding cash and jewels. I followed the biker to the right-hand side, watching him push a thick key into a lock and turn it, a heavy clunking coming from inside the door. I followed him through, moving into the huge space, and for a moment I was stunned.

Inside was insane. The ceiling rose above us, metal beams criss-crossing, supporting the high ceiling. Rows of windows, stacked one on top of each other, let the light flood in. The windows were uncovered, the view of the North Sea in the distance unhindered. I gazed out through thickly glazed glass, my eyes catching the slight bob of tiny boats on unseen waves. The dark blue expanse of water ended as the light blue of a clear sky rose out of it. Tearing my eyes from the view of the windows, I glanced around the space, struggling to concentrate on any one area of the room long enough. It was almost entirely open plan. The kitchen was just inside the door, grey and black units contrasted against mat silver splash backs, massive industrial lights dangling over the top of a big island.

The room opened into a lounge area with two dark grey sofas sat at right angles to each other, then at the very far side, a mezzanine level rose over the top of what must have been the bathroom. It was stunning.

The Viking dropped my bags on the floor by the sofas.

"OK. Well, make yourself at home."

"Where are you going?" I asked, watching him walk towards the door.

"I'm going to find out who wants you dead."

"But what if they come here?" I asked, panic rising in my throat.

"This place is ridiculously secure. It's covered in alarms and cameras. Cameras I can monitor from my mobile phone. You'll be safe here. No one knows where you are, not even Cian."

"I thought you told him you were taking me to your place?"

"I did. Cian doesn't even know where I live. So you're safe. No one knows you are here."

Great. No one, no one at all knew where I was. This man could torture and murder and bury me. A man I only met a few days ago. A man that carried around a giant knife and lived in a fortress. I didn't feel safe. Not here. Not with him.

Chapter Twelve

❧ The Viking ☙

I locked the unit back up, leaving Natalie secured inside, and turned on all my alarms. The place was as secure as Alcatraz. No one was getting in, and no one was getting out. I checked the burner phone, the message on the screen giving me only an address of a pub out the other side of Sunderland. I pushed the motorbike through the busy streets, careful not to draw too much attention to the jet-black Kawasaki as it purred gently under me.

I wish I'd never opened that third envelope from the broker. I wouldn't have spent two days being slowly killed by pink and grey fluffy cushions. I wouldn't have had to go running to the Northern Kings Motorcycle Club to fix her car and leaving my beautiful Suzuki in Indie's hands, knowing I'm likely to get the oxygen squeezed out of me when I attempt to get the damn thing back. And I wouldn't have the hottest fucking woman locked in my home. The hottest woman with the highest price on her head who recoils every time she looks at the ink on my skin.

I found the bar further along the riverside, hidden behind the remnants of old heavy industry, of ship building, glass making and mining exports along the River Wear. The bar was quiet, tucked away at the back of a housing estate that had survived years of demolition, escaping only because there was nowhere else to move the displaced inhabitants to, and the Council coffers had dried up.

Sitting at a dark table at the back of the bar, I eyed each body that walked through the door, none of which were portly enough for the broker. He wasn't late. I was early. I pulled my phone out of my pocket and flicked onto the screen and checked the cameras. It didn't take long to find her, sitting on the sofa with a laptop on her knee. She wasn't looking at the screen, but across the room, distracted.

Movement caught my eye across the small bar, the bulk of a man poking his head through the door first. After a few seconds of scanning each table for me, he walked across and sat down, the wooden stool creaking in complaint as his arse spilt over the top of it.

"What's this all about V?" He asked, with none of the usual small talk, "you don't normally follow up on jobs."

"Tell me about the contract out on the woman. Who took it?"

"Why do you want to know?"

"Don't fuck about with me, Bob. Just tell me."

"You know how this works," he shook his head.

"Today it works differently. Either you tell me, or I find a new broker," he stared at me for a moment, not quite understanding the meaning behind my words, "I'm sure your wife and daughter will miss the income."

His eyes darkened, extra lines appearing on his expansive forehead, and he opened his mouth like a fish, wanting to retaliate, to tell me to 'fuck off' but he didn't have the balls to do it. Then he sighed and looked around him, checking he wasn't in ear shot of anybody.

"The first contractor failed. The mark is still alive. But I think you know that," he looked at me pointedly.

"Go on," I prompted.

"So it's been reissued. Unilaterally."

"Fuck," I breathed.

"And the price has increased to £200k."

Shit, that was an even bigger problem. Whoever wanted her dead was desperate. She'd been an expensive hit as it was and to double her price and offer it out to anyone who brought back proof had changed this from an assassination to a bounty hunt.

"Who is the hit for?"

"That I don't know."

I stood, the chair scraping back behind me suddenly, and grabbed the man by the collar of his jacket.

"You know I don't V," he said, his hands up in surrender.

Heads from the far side of the pub turned in our direction, eyeing us suspiciously, the landlord behind the bar watching intently for any further signs of violence. I peeled my fingers from the Broker's collar and lowered myself down on the seat. The man staggered up onto shaky legs, turning to leave, but then hesitating.

"I don't know why you are so interested," he said to me, "but this is big shit. You might want to stay well clear of it unless you're going to do the job yourself?"

I watched the Broker leave, a little bubble of anxiety starting in my stomach. This was all going south already. I scrolled through the code names on my phone and stopped on Cian's. The phone rang once, twice, three times, agitation nibbling away at my insides, but then there was a pause and a familiar gruff Irish voice.

"Hey, Kee, we have a problem," I started.

"Tell me she's not dead."

"No, she's not dead," I answered.

"Thank fuck."

"But we do have a bigger problem…"

I laid out the position, the Irishman listening intently on the other side of the phone.

"We need to know who's arranged the hit," Cian said eventually, "we need to know more. Get back and find out what you can from her."

I rolled my eyes but said no more. I had a couple of jobs to finish and then I'd get back to Natalie. She was safe in my place. No one knew where I lived, not Cian, not the Broker, not the Kings. Absolutely. Fucking. No one. Apart from her, and she could be my biggest risk yet. I dragged my phone back out of the pocket inside my bike jacket and turned the app back on to look at the cameras. She had moved from the sofa, her laptop on the coffee table and I scanned the movement. A cupboard door was open in the kitchen and she seemed to rake around, looking for something.

*****

It was a few hours before I returned. I'd finished one of my outstanding jobs after following him from the house of one of the girls he'd visit and then knock about when he wasn't happy with the services on offer. I didn't think she would miss him all that much. It hadn't taken much to inject a whole load of dirty heroin into him, and he had gone pretty quick, convulsing and puking everywhere. And then I'd gone to the supermarket like any normal fucker in society.

I parked the bike in its normal space at the back of the garage and moved through the door to my apartment above, the door chimes sounding noisily. Natalie was sitting on the sofa when I walked through the door, her legs pulled up underneath her, curled up cat-like, an empty glass and a bottle of vodka sat on the coffee table in front of her.

"Didn't have you down as a vodka drinker," I called from the kitchen island, pulling out the modest bit of shopping from my backpack and scattering it over the bench.

"I'm not. But that's all you had."

I grinned.

"Where've you been?" She asked, getting to her feet, wobbling slightly as she padded towards me.

Her feet were bare, her toenails covered in red polish, the same colour I'd seen on her lips. The oversized grey sweater hung down over one lightly tanned shoulder, the white strap of her bra on display. And she smelled fresh, freshly showered. Parts of her hair were still damp, collecting into gentle waves.

"I had some work to do. And I got us some tea," I gesticulated to the food on the bench.

"Hmmm," she said, "and what sort of work was that? Did you kill someone?"

"Just a bit of this and that," I replied, shaking off the way her words incited guilt. The guy was a violent druggie, beating and abusing women, pushing drugs to kids on the street. He deserved everything he got.

She moved closer, a sparkle of something almost devious in her eye and I could smell the floral and citrus scent of her perfume and the sickly, chemically smell of the alcohol on her breath. Her arm snaked around my back, her fingertips brushing the waistband of my pants. I could have pulled her to me then, felt the swell of her tits pushed against me and tasted her plump lips, but something slid against my back.

Natalie stepped away, waving the knife in front of me, the serrated edge and sharp tip much too close to my face, yet I didn't step away.

"What job requires this, then?" She asked, the caramel brown of her eyes narrowed, "because I'm not sure this is standard issue."

"Careful with that, Nat," I cautioned, more acutely noticing her unsteadiness.

"Tell me. Tell me exactly what you do. I need to know what I'm locked in this place with?"

"You don't want me to answer that question. You already know what I am. You don't need any more details."

"I do. I really fucking do."

She stepped towards me, pointing the tip of the knife up towards my throat, staggering ever so slightly.

"Does this make you feel macho?" She asked, a slight shake in the hand that held the knife much too close to my throat, "is this the sort of thing the women like when they see you? The bad boy. Mysterious. Dangerous. Is that what women like?"

I stepped back suddenly, knocking her arm to the side and grabbing her free one, spinning her round as I pulled her arm up into her back and forcing her face down onto the island in front of us. She released the knife in surprise, and it clattered along the stainless-steel surface and crashed onto the floor on the other side.

"Now what are you going to do?" She asked, her voice hoarse and ragged.

I let go, stepping away while she straightened herself up.

"So what? You don't even want to fuck me?" she spat, anger and arousal contradicting her facial features.

"You're drunk," I answered.

It was the safest answer to give. Of course, I wanted to fuck her. She was a good-looking woman after all, and I liked nothing better than getting my end away. But she was drunk, and I was supposed to be protecting her.

"Isn't that what people like you do? Save the damsel in distress, save her from the monsters and then she's oh so grateful and….."

"You've been watching too much James Bond, Nat."

"So what?" She answered.

She shrugged out of her jumper, dropping it to the floor. The white lacy bra pushing her plump tits together and then she reached round behind her and suddenly the bra joined the top on the floor. Her nipples were bared to me, pink and pebbled, just there for me to grip with my teeth or crush with my fingers. She cocked her head to the side, watching me watch her. And then she pushed her leggings down over her legs, revealing the matching white thong that sat high on her hips, making her slender legs look like they would never end.

"Nat," I warned as she moved closer to me.

"Is this not the sort of thing men like you want?"

"Men like me?" I asked, trying to keep the frustration and anger from my voice.

"Yeah, men like you and Cian. Men who are used to getting what they want, taking what they want."

Her words hurt. Words and insinuations I'd heard for years in my trade. And never had they made me feel like I'd been punched in the stomach until they came out of her mouth.

She stepped closer still, "is this what you want? How you expect to be paid for looking after me?" The rough need in her voice not going unnoticed.

None of her had gone unnoticed. Mini V had seen and felt everything. But this wasn't the time or the way or even a good idea. I hadn't brought her into my home to fuck her. I'd brought her here to keep her alive. Despite what she might believe.

She took another step forward, closing the space between us, tilting her chin up, her tits pushed against my chest, her lips just where I could dip down and taste them. Just one little taste. She brushed them against me lightly, gently dragging the smooth skin of her lips across mine, sending fire to my groin and a fuzziness to my brain. And so I dived against her. Driving my mouth against hers, pushing her back into the island, listening to the swish of breath that escaped her as I forced my tongue inside her mouth, as she parted her lips readily.

She groaned against me, the vibration running over my tongue and through my jaw and I caved, forcing my body against hers, giving her nowhere to escape me as I punished her mouth, plunging my tongue in and out, swirling it over her lips and driving it back in again.

Her fingers tugged into the top of my waistband. Fuck. This wasn't the assignment. I stepped away, my lips warm and tingly and my dick pushing uncomfortably against the tight material of the motorcycle leathers I wore.

"What did you stop for?" She asked breathlessly.

"You're drunk, Nat. Drunker than I realised."

"So?"

"You need something to eat."

I turned away from her and turned the oven on.

Chapter Thirteen

ᚲᛊ Natalie ᛒᚲ

Light flooded through the windows, the lack of curtains not shading any of the bright sunlight from my eyes. My head swirled and pulsed, my throat dry, almost stopping me from swallowing the bile that pooled at the very back. I rolled from my side onto my back, holding my arm over my eyes to block out the intrusive daylight. My other arm brushed the warm skin of someone to my left and I flinched, sitting up promptly, sending my head into a tailspin.

The covers dropped off me, my breasts bare, the slight coolness of spring air assaulting my nipples and they stood to attention immediately. The blond hair of the Viking spilled over his pillow, his eyes held tightly shut and an arm draped loosely over me, or at least where I had been. I picked the covers up and peeked down underneath, my skin exposed, not a stitch of clothing on me. Bracing myself, I lifted them off the man beside me, the dark ink of his tattoos creating chasms of shadows under the blankets, not a scrap of clothing to be seen between us. Shit.

My stomach lurched and the bile at the back of my throat rushed to the front, my mouth filling with water like I'd been drinking from a fountain. Throwing the covers back, I launched myself out of the bed, thundering down the wooden stairs from the mezzanine floor and hurling the bathroom door open. I hugged the toilet bowl for what seemed like an age. Every morsel of liquid and food expelled, the back of my throat burning from the effort as the pain pounded against the front of my skull.

The tiled floor was cool under the burning heat from my skin and I curled up on the ground, pulling my legs into my chest, waiting for the next bout of sickness to assault me. But he got to me first, pushing the bathroom door open, standing in the doorway, as naked as the day he was born, but much more inked. I snatched a towel from the radiator, covering myself as I stood up, my head spinning violently, and I staggered backwards.

Every centimetre of his skin was covered in art, every inch of his body apart from his face and the four, or maybe it was five inches, that hung between his legs.

I tried to look away, but I couldn't. My eyes held to the spot staring at him, the glint of something on the head of his penis catching the light. A piercing? His hand dropped to his dick, tugging at it, moving it in front of my eyes as if he was teasing me with it.

"Get some clothes on," I hissed, trying to move my eyes from his groin to his face.

"Why?" He asked, amusement shining in his eyes.

"Because…." I trailed off.

"Because what?"

"Please. Please, just get some clothes on."

I can't believe I was begging a man to put his clothes on. Not that I usually begged them to take them off. But something about seeing him naked, the artwork clinging to the muscle underneath, thick inked legs with tattoos designed to extenuate the curve of his muscles like some sort of masterpiece. The ripples of a washboard stomach almost made the eyeless skull on his stomach move, light and shadows clinging to all the right places on his body. And for some fucked up reason, I was damp; a warm, wet sensation starting between my legs. Maybe I was ovulating early? Maybe that was why I still hadn't taken my eyes off him.

He chuckled, a gentle low vibration which was almost like the purr of a lion, deep, guttural and sexy. Maybe I was still drunk? Then he turned and walked away, his tight round arse covered with pictures and symbols, almost like a map made from images and runes. I watched the tattoos fade, his body becoming only a patchwork quilt of shadows and skin.

Once I'd emptied the last bit of my stomach out into the toilet bowl, I wrapped the towel tight round me and wandered into the kitchen, each footstep, each tiny movement rattling my brain around my head. The kettle was bubbling furiously, and cups clanged off the bench, echoing around the vast space. I walked behind the naked man, desperately trying to keep my eyes off his body, and slowly opened the shiny grey cupboard doors, trying to make as little noise as possible.

Each cupboard let me down; food, crisps, chocolate, but no glasses. Until I got to the cupboard tucked away over the sink. It nestled into the corner; the door hinged so it covered the right-angled space. There was a crop of glasses in there, right at the back, my fingers just a fraction of a millimetre away from them. I could have jumped up to grab at them if I hadn't been clinging to the towel covering what might be left of my modesty and that the movement would have sent the hammer off in my skull again.

I groaned, loud enough for him to hear, and suddenly he was there behind me in all his nakedness.

"Will you please take…that away from me," I waved my hand in the air over his entire outline, careful to look him in his eyes, the blue-green of them creasing in the corners in amusement.

"That's not what you said to me last night," he grinned, turning in front of me slightly so that his naked torso brushed against the arm clutching the towel to me.

I drew in a breath, "did we…?" I asked, my voice coming out faint and pathetic.

He shook his head, and I was relieved, mostly.

"That's what you wanted. But see here," he took a step back slightly, my eyes being drawn down his body once again and I snapped them back up, "this is a gentleman."

"So why are we both naked?"

"I always sleep naked."

"You always sleep naked in bed next to a woman you're supposed to be protecting?"

"I always sleep naked. You were the one who got into bed with me. I told you to sleep on the couch, but you wouldn't. I couldn't have got you to keep your clothes on last night even if I tried harder," he grunted, reaching up above me and pulling down a pint glass.

He pressed the glass into my palm, the tall tumbler cool against the sickly heat of the hangover seeping through every pore of my skin. Scooting around him, I juggled with the grip on the towel and directing the glass under the cold tap, taking a few big gulps before setting it back on the bench.

"You weren't naked in my house," I said, turning to look at him, this time keeping my eyes fixed on his face.

He was handsome, in a rugged way. His blond hair fell to his shoulders, covering the tattoo on his head, and his eyes were a mix of green and blue, tranquil and gentle. He didn't have dimples, but the smile lines around his mouth, partially covered by a thin beard, were deep, making him look like he wore a perpetual grin, mischievous and enthralling. I'd never studied his face so closely, having spent too long distracted by his tattoos, but he was truly beautiful.

He grinned again, a wide, panty melting, if I had any on, sort of grin, his eyes alive with the hint of rowdiness. Dipping his head, his lips brushed my ear, the beard scratching the delicate skin there, sending tingles down my neck.

"I was being polite," he said in a half whisper, standing too close, my skin flushing with heat.

"So, you keep your boxers on when you are being polite, huh? And when you don't feel like being polite, you just…take everything off? Hardly offensive," I shrugged, my eyes fixed on his, my lips only centimetres away from where he had pulled back to look at me.

One side of his mouth curled, his hand sliding around the left of my neck as that thumb brushed over my lips again, tugging on the flesh of the bottom one, peeling it away from my teeth, parting my mouth as he stared down into it.

"Babe, if I was trying to be offensive, I'd be forcing you to your knees and putting my cock in your mouth."

His thumb pushed harder against my lip, the flesh forced across my bottom teeth. The cheekiness had gone from his eyes, replaced by tension, the blue darker, an ocean amidst a storm. And for a second, for some insane reason, maybe it was the fire that had been stoked between my thighs, the vodka I was sweating from my body, but I closed my top lip over his thumb, pulling back on it gently, watching the dark centre of his eyes dilate.

He grumbled gently, a low moan, that was almost too quiet to hear but my eyes dropped down his body, the naked flesh of his dick contrasted against the black of tattoos, its head pointed up towards me. My heart was beating far faster than it had any business to and I was too hot. I needed to take this towel off. But if I did, I was at real risk of impaling myself on something.

I backed away from him, just outside of his reach, refusing to let my eyes drop to where I knew there would be an erection staring up at me. He needed to be dressed. *I* needed to get dressed. He didn't stop smiling, smug and confident, as if he expected me to come running back to him with open arms, or legs. He was used to that. I could tell from his cool confidence, his calm arrogance. I would bet he barely had anyone turn him down. If it hadn't been for all his ink, then I may have struggled too. His face was captivating; angelic yet devious. The clear calm in his eyes pulling you under murky depths like some sort of male siren.

The smirk followed me, but his feet stayed put, mercifully. I padded away, escaping to the bedroom, although with the glass panels of the mezzanine floor it allowed little privacy. I scrabbled around in the bags of belongings beside the bed, noticing how he watched me through the clear barriers. Nearly the whole place was open plan, even the bedroom. I could sit at the kitchen island, drinking coffee and seeing straight up into the bedroom, to the bed and anyone in it. Maybe that was how he liked it. Some sort of voyeurism?

Eventually, after finding some solace in the bathroom, I had covered myself in clothes; jeans and a thin, long-sleeved top. Every area of skin all covered from him, from temptation. He was sitting on the sofa when I emerged, no longer naked himself, watching me as I came out of the bathroom. Did the man not watch TV? The thing covered the wall opposite, the biggest I had ever seen, more of a movie screen than anything else.

I sat on the opposite sofa, grogginess still clouded my brain and the dull ache of my throat from being throttled the day before reminded me why I was here. How had my life gone to shit? One day I was defending Newcastle's best criminals whilst helping take their mates from the streets to being holed up in some obscure bachelor pad in the middle of a half dilapidated industrial estate.

"What do we do now?" I asked.

He cocked his head to the side, his hair draping over one shoulder.

"I assume you mean our living arrangements?" He answered, his eyes bright and the usual boyish grin on his face.

I nodded.

"Nothing."

"What? Are just going to sit here? And wait? And what are we actually waiting for, anyway?"

"Cian will find who took the contract out. It'll just take some time. In the meantime, you get to stay here with me," he answered, running his hand through his long hair, muscle flexing against the arm of the t-shirt.

"So what, we don't go out? We just stay here?"

The Viking nodded.

"And do what? Just look at each other all day?"

He grinned widely, "I can suggest a whole load of things."

"I bet you can," I groaned, leaning back on the sofa, my head pounding again as I stared at the ceiling.

Metal girders stared back at me, high in the roof, running across from one side to the other like train tracks. I couldn't stay here, doing nothing, telling work I was sick. I just couldn't. I had a job, a career, a life. I had to do something.

"Has Cian found anything else yet?"

"I dunno," he shook his head, unconcerned.

"OK. OK. The leads I gave you. Did anything come up?"

He sighed, the smile peeling back off his face, his expression turning sombre.

"What is it?" I asked, my stomach tightening with the first hints of dread.

"The contract on you has gone unilateral, and the price has doubled."

"Wh, what does that mean?"

"It means someone is desperate. They'll pay whoever kills you. All the shitty criminals in the UK will want it. And they'll try. It also means the names you gave us are far too small-fry to afford this sort of money."

I felt sick again. My eyes prickled with heat and pressure, my throat tightened, and my mouth that was already dry felt more dehydrated than a mummy.

Chapter Fourteen

ಐ The Viking ಚಿ

There was no mistaking the look of horror on her face at my words. Her eyes widened, the caramel-brown tones darkening, the colour draining from her face. She'd sprung forwards, perched on the edge of the seat as if she was about to bolt but with no idea of where to. She looked at me, then at her hands and then out of the huge windows that led down to an old, abandoned forecourt, and for a moment I thought she might dash back to the bathroom.

I was pretty sure most normal women would have puked their guts up, or screamed and wailed when they learnt that the best and most greedy killers in the country were now looking for them. Yet, as I sat and watched her reaction, she pulled herself together. The shaking in her hands slowed down, the tremble of her bottom lip quieted, and the tears collecting in her eyes dissolved into nothing. Slowly, steadily, she reined it in.

"OK. So how do I fix this?" She asked, her head snapping back to me suddenly.

"I need to know every secret, every possible reason someone might want to kill you," I started, and she nodded, "I need to know if you've fucked someone you shouldn't, if you've done something you shouldn't. Everything. I need to know it all."

Her brow furrowed, as if searching for every despicable thing she might have done.

"Steve Burrows," she said, nodding to herself, "DI Steve Burrows. We had a thing…."

"A thing?" I asked, "I need you to be completely clear."

Natalie rolled her eyes.

"We were having casual sex. Not that it started out that way, but it ended that way. He was doing well in his career. We would attend the usual balls and charity nights together. It made him look good. It made me look good. We were both being seen together in the right crowds. Steve was looking good for a promotion; it was almost a dead cert. But then I was called in to represent a kid the police had picked up off the streets. The kid was connected to a string of gang offences, burglaries, low key stuff, but they'd picked him up for a stabbing. When I got there, he was in a state. Dishevelled, beaten. He was desperate to confess, but the details didn't add up. I got him out of there. I mean, he could have done it. It's not unusual for them to carry knives and things to go wrong, but I just had a hunch. There was just something else."

Natalie paused, her gaze going to the window, and I noticed how she pulled her nails across the back of her other hand, sub-consciously, not even realising that the skin underneath was glowing more red each time she scratched.

"A few nights later, we were at my place. We'd drunk a fair bit of wine and Steve had mentioned something about the stabbing. The alcohol was making his tongue loose, and he had talked openly that I'd caused a fair amount of shit for him by getting the kid off the charges. But when I pushed for more detail, he clammed up. I knew then that something wasn't right. I did some digging the night of the stabbing and managed to get the CCTV from across the street from where it had happened. That had been difficult as the normal CCTV footage had been wiped by a system failing, conveniently. But there was a house across the street, and they had caught some of it on the camera, not the actual stabbing but the group of kids who were there, including the Chief Super's stepson. None of the other kids had been arrested, just my client, like he was being scapegoated. I sent the footage to the Independent Police Complaints Commission anonymously. Steve never got his promotion. But I don't think he was the only one who was pissed off."

I listened intently, making notes carefully in my head, rifling through the information she had given me for anything useful. The man she was fucking was only a DI. There was no way that he had the type of money to pay a £200k bounty. But the Chief Superintendent might be connected enough that it was significant.

"The Chief Super, who is he?" I asked, feeling partly stupid that I probably should know who to keep my head down from, but I hadn't concerned myself with the police for years. To them, I simply didn't exist.

"Christian Johnson. Sixty something."

I rubbed my palm over my chin, thinking.

"Hmmm. And the stepson? Significant?"

"Only in terms of embarrassing the family. Johnson's married to a politician. His wife has been doing well, flying the flag for women in politics; some say she could be the next leader of the New Liberal party. I'm pretty sure they wouldn't have wanted the bad press from the son being in the extremely close vicinity to a fatal stabbing. But the police went after one kid, one kid who ran with a gang. My CCTV put Johnson's stepson with that group and therefore implicated in the assault. But from what I heard, no charges were ever brought against him."

"And the kid who got bust up?"

"Leon Monroe. He's still on the streets being a shit. I was sorting out whatever he'd got into again at the Police station the other week."

"When the other week?"

"Just over a week ago. Just a day before Charlie and Cian's wedding. It was the anniversary of ..." Natalie paused, staring at me as if I should know what was going on in her head. "Shit!" she continued, jumping up from the sofa and running to the stairs and up to the bedroom.

She ran around the side of the bed, snatching her handbag from the floor and taking something out of it. She fiddled around in what looked like a purse for a few seconds before bounding down the stairs again and back towards me, waving something between her fingers. For a moment, my eyes couldn't focus on what she held up. It was small and gold and a funny shape. She came closer, standing right in front of me where I could have grabbed her and pulled her towards me, pulling her onto my lap or close enough to feel those plump tits with my tongue. Instead, I grabbed her wrist and moved her gently closer.

It was a key of some sort. Not a house key by its shape and with circular indents along the blade. It was longer and not the irregular shape of points and divots. I looked up, confused.

"I was leaving my office on the Friday night when this turned up. It was in an envelope written in my father's handwriting."

"I thought your dad was dead?" I asked, immediately regretting my choice of words when I saw them resonating on her face.

"He is," she whispered, as if that was still difficult to say, "which is why this is odd. He somehow sent me a random key in an envelope, and it arrived exactly on the second-year anniversary of his death. Tell me that's not weird?"

That was weird. I nodded, running a hand through my hair, my brain firing inside my head.

"And then to top it off, someone wants to kill me the next week. It's got to be connected."

She was right. It was suspicious as fuck. I plucked the key from her fingers, weighing it in my hand. There was a tiny string of numbers engraved into the head. The blade was longer than a normal key, the tiny indented circles punched into the metal with a few small jagged cuts towards the tip. This was no house key.

"This is a safe deposit box key," I said, handing it back to her.

"I've never seen anything like this in all his stuff."

"Looks more like something you'd find in a bank or somewhere setup like that."

"Yeah. But I've searched pictures of keys, and nothing looks like this. I need to find out what it's for," she said, easing it from my hands as if she was scared she wouldn't get it back.

I got to my feet and cocked my head, beckoning for her to follow me. I led her out of my apartment and across the hallway, punching a series of numbers into the keypad next to the door opposite. The lights on the display flashed up red twice, and I placed my forefinger into the rectangular window that sat above it. The whole box shone green and a dull click came from the door.

I pushed it open, feeling for the light switch on the wall on the inside and the room lit up in a bright white glow, casting shadows against the rows of TV screens at the far end of the room. A computer stood to the right-hand side. Natalie followed behind me, silently, and I watched her eyes roam the space, stopping and looking at different areas and then resting on the steel cabinet at the very back.

I wandered to the computer, switching it on and entering my passcode. The large flat screen came alive quickly. I opened a search engine and poised over the keyboard.

"Pass the key," I instructed Nat, and she handed the little piece of brass metal to me.

I typed the code into the search box and it instantly brought up an address. But it wasn't a bank like I thought it would be. It was a storage unit in Gateshead, Northern fucking Kings' territory too.

"Why didn't I just do that?" Nat said from behind me, her warm breath against my neck, "can you take me there?"

I shook my head.

"OK. Can I borrow your van then?"

"No chance."

I felt her hand on my shoulder, pushing against me, spinning the desk chair round to look at her. Her face was tight with frustration, her eyes almost smouldering with anger as she glared at me. The muscles in her neck bulged as she fought it back, trying to keep calm. Something about the sight of her battling for her own self-control made heat rush to my groin, and I wondered how she would look when she was just about to come. When I brought her to the brink of ecstasy and not let her tip over the edge into oblivion. She swatted my shoulder, snapping my mind from my cock and where I wanted to put it.

"I need to know why he sent me a key, V," she said, her voice softer as if she was coaxing me, convincing me to yield to her will.

"That's fine. You stay here. I'll go and get it."

"No. I'm coming."

"You're not."

"Why not?" Her lips pouted a little, plump and inviting.

"Because you're too visible out there."

"Surely I'll be safer with you?"

I turned away and typed in a code into a keyboard next to the TV monitors. All six monitors flicked to the one screen showing the sofa in my apartment.

"I have cameras all over. I can watch you from anywhere."

I flicked to a different camera, bringing the bedroom up on the screen and then the kitchen, followed by the garage.

"Everything is alarmed too, and it all feeds straight to my mobile. Nobody other than Cian knows you're with me. And nobody at all knows where I live. There is nowhere safer than in this building."

Natalie folded her arms across her chest, her tits pushing against the thin fabric of her jumper. I remembered them from last night and I wanted nothing more to get my hands on them, knead the soft flesh and make her squirm. But for now, I had to find out what this key was, and what it might hide.

Chapter Fifteen

෮ Natalie ෨

The deep rumble of a motorbike faded away as the big steel gates at the entrance to the Viking's compound closed together, leaving me locked inside and alone. I took out my laptop and opened it up. I needed to do something, find something. My father had left me that key for a reason and in all the drama of the past week, the mystery of it had slipped my mind. Not now though. Now my brain fired on all engines, whirring and thinking, wondering what it could mean.

The internet connection failed again for the third time. I couldn't tether it to my phone, which was hardly surprising as there had been no signal here since I'd arrived, but I couldn't pick up the Wi-Fi that the Viking had used when we were in his odd office either. The computer in there must be hard wired in and I had no hope of getting in there. He'd typed in some code that was at least ten digits long. I'd counted them as he pushed them in, trying to memorise the sequence as his thick fingers flew across the keypad with a finesse he shouldn't have been graced with. And then he'd used a fingerprint scanner. Doubly secure. I'd need a few run throughs of the code at least to gain access and then I'd need his fingerprint.

I closed the laptop down again and wandered the apartment instead, opening each cupboard door in the kitchen, trying to get a feel for the man he was. Plates and bowls were tidy and ordered by shape and size, methodical. There was a small amount of food, mostly quick meals and tins, rice and pasta. The tins were in rows, neatly stocked on top of each other, almost like mine, but with the labels facing all over the place, haphazardly. I spun them round, making each label face towards me, and then restocked them all alphabetically. He was tidy and orderly, and that surprised me.

Growing bored with the kitchen and not finding much else of interest, I moved through the strange apartment. There was little in the way of storage. The coffee table between the sofas contained a few drawers, which were mostly bare apart from a couple of coasters and an old newspaper. I unfolded it, scouring the print for a date. Seven years old. I flicked the pages over, scanning the headlines, looking for some significance of why an aged newspaper would have been kept for so long. But there was nothing that jumped out. I folded it back into the creases I had found it in and slid it back into the drawer.

The flat was so minimally furnished. It was clean and uncluttered, but there were no pictures on the wall, no personal effects, hardly a thing that told me anything about him. I climbed the stairs to the mezzanine level and pulled open the wardrobe doors that stood against the wall. Inside was almost a room in itself. T-shirts hung neatly on hangers, carefully ironed, crisp and pristine. Jeans were folded and piled on top of each other, nearly all the same shade of blue stone-washed denim. I pulled a pair off the top of the pile, picking out the label. Levi. Figures. There were jumpers and hoodies, but nothing with any sort of detail. Everything was plain to the point of being boring. Yet the Viking was anything but boring.

I rifled further, the walk-in wardrobe going back so much farther than I had expected. There was a set of drawers pushed against the back with socks and boxer shorts, all black, no patterns or cheeky pictures. I pulled out the bottom drawer, expecting to find something boring, but instead there was a leather sleeveless jacket stuffed in the back. I eased it out feeling the need to take care of it. On the back it was embroidered. A huge skull was embroidered into the leather with a smaller skull on either side; their toothy grimaces menacing. Each skull, even the smaller two, wore a crown. The words embroidered around it were gold. Northern Kings Motorcycle Club. I held it to my face, inhaling a huge lung full of the Viking's scent. I'd heard him mention them like they were something to steer clear of. Was he one of them?

Carefully, I folded it back up, placing it in the drawer. As I pushed it back in, my hand brushed something hard and cool. I slid it out, careful not to catch it on the thick wood as I set it down in front of me. It was covered in a cloth, folded carefully, almost lovingly, and I peeled the fabric back. A woman's face stared up at me, her arms wrapped around a blond-haired boy, his blue-green eyes shining at the camera. I ran my finger over the image, concentrating on his face, an innocent joy and easiness emanating from him. The woman didn't share the same contentment. Her smile was forced, her eyes dull, her hands grasping the arms of the boy protectively. The corners of her eyes didn't follow the same curve of her lips and there was a darkness within them, even in the inanimate image. Suddenly, I felt like I was intruding on something hugely private. I wrapped the photo frame back inside its protective cloth and placed it carefully inside the drawer, closing everything back up to cover my tracks.

I glanced at my watch. He'd been away for a couple of hours. How long did it take someone to drive to the next town and retrieve whatever was in that safe deposit box? I pulled on my shoes and opened the apartment door, a loud chime sounding over the top of my head and making me jump. Pushing the little black button on the lock upwards to prevent the door locking me out, I wandered across the hall to the door to the Viking's office, or control room or whatever it was.

I stared for a while at the keypad, contemplating whether there was any way to override the biometric security system, before turning away and opening the other door that led down the stairs and into the huge garage underneath. The door screamed at me again as it opened, eliciting the same response. My heart skipping a beat even though I knew the door chime was coming.

The air was cool downstairs, and I fumbled across both walls, as my eyes adjusted in the dark and I eventually located a light switch. The bright white glow from three strip lights over head in the high ceiling washed over the garage. It was bigger than I remembered. It had a commercial feel. Boxes and crates were stacked all over the place and metal filing cabinets and cupboards were secured to a wall the furthest away from me. I pulled lids off, peering inside but seeing only metal parts for cars or bikes, or cans of oil and tools.

The place was dusty and stale, the smell of aged oil and grime filling the air kicked up as I moved across the floor, my eyes focussed on the thing covered in dirty dust sheets. I could see the bike's outline before I pulled the covers back, the off-white sheet dipping in the middle as it hung across the handlebars. I moved the covers, careful not to knock anything. The motorbike was impressive. It was covered in shiny chrome that looked like it had been recently polished. Not a speck of dust, grime or a fingerprint was visible on the mass of aluminium parts of the bike.

The seats were black leather, the tank in front was polished black, nothing adorning it save for the Harley Davidson sign. Underneath, the engine gleamed, splitting into two parts to form a heart in the middle of the bike. Two shiny exhausts led from the engine to the back wheel in perfect horizontal alignment. The leather seat could easily accommodate two people, and I ran my fingers across the material. It was gently worn, almost as if it had had little use, but the age of the bike from the number plate on the back of the seat suggested it wasn't new. The tyres were thick rubber, sparkling metal spokes in the middle, making them obsidian black and wider than the tyres of my car. I wasn't a fan of the noisy two-wheeled vehicles, but this was a good-looking bike. I pulled the covers carefully back over it.

The garage was secured by two long metal roller-shutters providing no means of exit, and even if they could be lifted manually, there was no way I would have the strength to prize them up. Yet in the opposite corner, a tiny slither of daylight poured through a crack, and I moved towards it. It was a door, the same metal type that was all the way through the house, or unit or factory, or whatever this was, and it was locked from the inside with a series of bolts and a Yale lock.

I slid the top and bottom bolts aside, having to stand on the tips of my toes to reach the very top one, and even then, it took a bit of convincing before it wiggled free. The door creaked inwards, scraping noisily on the floor, but this time I was prepared for the door chime shouting at me. The outside yard was bare, a huge, concreted expanse surrounded by a thick steel fence that was much newer in comparison with the rest of the building.

Walking around the perimeter, I peered through the gaps, seeing nothing but other gated units and a road that was riddled with potholes and plagued with a crumbling surface. The air was cool, filled with the smell of salt and seaweed, and seagulls screeched in the distance, their voices an angry squawk over the low rumble of traffic not so far away.

I pushed at the gates, the metal not budging a fraction in my hands. I was a captive, a mostly willing one, but captive all the same. I couldn't physically leave the compound if I truly wanted to and even if I could, would I even get far before someone rocked up to shoot me or strangle me? The thought sent bile rising in my throat, a frustrated sting at the back of my eyes. I had to solve this. I had to find out who wanted to kill me and why. Whoever it was had already taken my life from me. I couldn't go to work, I couldn't do…I sighed. I didn't do anything other than work, anyway. I tipped my face up to the sky, watching the wisp of clouds glide overhead.

Chapter Sixteen

℘ The Viking ℘

My phone vibrated in my pocket every few minutes, the alarms in my place having a hissy fit every time she opened or closed a door. I watched her move around, opening doors, sticking her head in cupboards, and at one point, she disappeared inside my wardrobe. There was fuck all I could about it. I could have used the intercom and warned her, but if I'd thought at any point since I'd met her that she might follow the most basic instructions, that idea had long since disappeared.

It hadn't taken long to get to the storage lock-up on an industrial estate barely a mile away from the Kings' club house. It was the second time this week I had breached our agreement and if anyone else other than Indie found me within three miles of them, I would be in deeper shit than I needed right now.

I kicked out the bike stand, letting it settle to the left-hand side, and swung my leg over the back. The storage unit was basic. Run out of a factory unit just like mine. There was a small reception area with just enough space for a few bodies to stand in, the only windows in the dirty brick building. I tapped on the sliding glass, peering in at a young, bored looking woman scrolling on her phone. Her head snapped up, her eyes searching my face, lingering on the tattoo over my head with a mix of interest and apprehension.

I smiled, watching the reaction in her eyes, gauging just how much negotiation I was going to have to do to get what I wanted.

"Hey, babe," I started, "I need to get to this. Reckon you can help me?"

I raised the key to the glass, and she stared back at me, her eyes focussing on the tattoos over my hand. The door beside me buzzed.

"You can go through," she said.

"It's my Da's key. He's ill and needs something out. Can you show me where it is?"

The girl nodded and slid the window open, and I passed the key in. Nudging a mouse on her desk, the computer monitor came alive, and she typed the code into the little box in front of her.

"Down the hall to the bottom and go through the last door on the right. It's locker 54."

The door buzzed again, and I pushed it open, following the hallway till it went no further, pushing through a heavy door at the end. Lockers filled the room. Row upon tidy row of numbered doors. I followed the numbers on the doors until I came to what I was looking for; locker 54. Slipping the key into the keyhole, I turned, listening to the muffled click of the lock sliding free. The little door pinged open, and I stared inside expecting folders or envelopes or papers or maybe even boxes and cash, but the only thing in there was a little black memory stick. I put it in the inside pocket of my jacket, zipping it up and shutting the locker door.

My phone vibrated against me again and I flicked my thumb over the screen, watching Natalie on the camera. She was in my garage, poking about in boxes and I watched as she made her way to the Harley, lifting the covers off it and standing back and taking a long look at it before covering it over again. Her shape moved in front of the camera, wandering across to the other side and opening the outside door.

"Fuck's sake," I grumbled, shoving the phone back into my pocket and leaving quickly.

I pulled out of the storage unit carpark, eyeing the traffic and wondering how quickly I could make it home again without drawing unnecessary police attention, and took the bend quickly, a sudden low guttural rumble of bikes coming towards me. Fuck. The Harleys slowed, the riders' heads turning to watch me as I passed them. I didn't need to see the faces under the helmets to know who it was, or the back patches in my mirrors to know just who I had ridden past. I caught the blond hair of the pony tail I'd forgotten to tuck into my helmet blowing in the wind as I eyed the men in my mirrors. Double fuck.

The bikes pulled to the side of the road, turning in a neat arc behind me. Exhausts roared loudly, the deep vibrations from the engines rumbling down the road behind me. I opened the throttle, tearing through the lights and out into the traffic, watching the bikes follow. Swerving in and out, squeezing the bike between cars and vans, shooting out in front of articulated lorries that blew their horns at me in rage. I raced the slower bikes behind me, and with each second, I gained more space between us. The guttural tones of the Harley's faded away, unable to keep up with the turn of speed of the black Kawasaki and the ease at which I could throw the nimble bike sideways. I headed out west, skirting around the edge of the town and onto the main motorway, making my way up to Durham before turning back towards Sunderland to shake anyone off my tail who might be still following me, Kings or otherwise. I rode a circuit around the outskirts of the town that straddled the River Wear before stopping to pick up supplies and heading back to the compound.

The door chimes sounded loudly after I climbed the stairs, my phone vibrating against my chest at the same moment.

"Where've you been?" Natalie's voice barked from the sofa.

I held up my hands, showing off the carrier bags in both of them.

"Did you find anything?" She asked impatiently, coming towards me gripping a small tumbler in her hand.

"I see you've started early," I said, eyeing the remains of the vodka that she'd started last night on the island.

"What else am I supposed to do? There's no internet. I can't go out."

"Watch TV like a normal person?"

"I don't normally watch television."

"Then what do you do for entertainment?"

"I don't know. I just work. Sometimes I'll go out for a meal," she answered, more quietly this time, self-conscious at her admission she was a serious workaholic.

I pulled the bottle of wine from the bag.

"Thought this might be more to your tastes," I said, pushing it towards her.

"Thank fuck. This stuff is hideous."

I couldn't help the chuckle that tumbled from my lips. I poured the wine into a tall, long glass and passed it towards her.

"I don't drink wine so don't have wine glasses," I said when she looked at it as if I'd handed her a glass of piss, "come on. Let's see what's on this."

I waved the memory stick under her nose, snatching it away from her when she grabbed at it.

"Was that what was in there? Is that all there was?" She asked, following behind me.

"Yup. Nothing but this."

I punched in the code on the other room and pressed my finger against the scanner, listening for the click of the door. The computer seemed to take an age to start up today and I could feel the impatient atmosphere in the room from both of us. I plugged the memory stick into the port, watching a bar loading on the screen before the password box flashed up.

I moved the curser inside and then vacated the seat, letting Natalie sit down. She stared at the screen for a while, and I wasn't sure whether she was searching for ideas on the password or whether she was worried about what would be on the memory stick. Her long, slim fingers danced across the keys, the password box filling with characters hidden by a long line of asterisks. A message flashed up on the screen.

'What's my favourite food?' it read.

Nat said nothing, but her fingers moved over the keyboard. Another message appeared.

'What is my favourite song?'

I watched her more closely now, the way her hands wavered slightly over the keys, hesitating for a fraction of a second before typing her answer. The computer came alive suddenly with a cross between soft rock and folk music, old and gentle, igniting a heavy pull from the base of my stomach, a feeling I'd hidden from for years as *Lindisfarne* sang out from the computer's speakers. Natalie paused, staring at the wall in front of her, fixed on the white-washed brick, and then with the tips of her fingers, she swiped at her eyes, concentrating on the folder icon sitting in front of her on the screen.

As the last words of *Lady Eleanor* died away, the room became silent again, a heavy atmosphere hanging in the air.

"That was my father's favourite song," she whispered, not really to me, "we played it at his funeral."

I heard the pain in her voice, the waver of her breath as she battled with the emotion welling in her throat and felt a burning sensation in the back of mine too.

"It was my parent's wedding song," I answered, not knowing why I offered her that information.

She turned her head and looked up at me, her rich eyes meeting mine, glossy from the tears I knew she had wiped away a few seconds earlier. For a moment, we held something between us. Something unspoken, a heartache and a comfort wrapped into one, a connection gone in a second. She sighed, turning back to the computer screen.

The folder opened and in it sat a single document. 'Make the connection', I glimpsed the title just before Natalie opened it and it sat there on the screen. The Word document was virtually blank, apart from a list of names and initials.

Archie Anderson

Jeremy Dodson

Lukyan Volkov

M. Lacroix

"You know who these are?" I asked, only recognising one on the list.

"Archie Anderson is a High Court judge, but I don't know about the rest."

"Lukyan Volkov is Russian mob. He's next in line to head up the family. The Russians are into all sorts of dodgy shit," I said from behind her.

"What sort of shit?"

"Drugs, prostitution, blackmail and protection rackets; the usual mafia stuff."

I watched her reaction, the flinch in her eyes, the way her jaw tightened. It was minimal, barely recognisable, unless you were trained to read situations and people. She glanced upwards at me and then back to the computer.

"Can I go on the internet?" She asked, which surprised me.

I nodded, watching her slide the mouse over the top corner of the document and minimise it before going to the search engine she'd seen me use this morning.

"Jeremy Dodson," she muttered, more to herself, "property mogul in the north east. He manages all sorts of property portfolios; student lettings, expensive short-term lets…"

Her eyes flicked back and forth over the screen as she jumped through pages on his website.

"I can't see what connects them all, though? Money laundering? Cases my dad worked on? I need to go home and get some of his stuff out of the loft."

"You're going nowhere," I mumbled.

Her head snapped towards me, frustration and anger ablaze in her eyes.

"You can't keep me here. I'm not your prisoner," she spat.

"You're not my prisoner. But you're still not leaving."

She pushed the computer chair backwards, getting to her feet and standing right in front of me, brown eyes meeting mine, searching, gaging.

"Why didn't you take the job, V?" She asked, the temper in her voice now under control.

"I don't kill women, Nat. And I only end those who deserve it, those who do bad things."

"So, you're more of a vigilante?"

I stepped closer so this time she had to tilt her chin up to keep the eye contact, my chest brushing hers.

"No Nat. I kill people. I take money from people to murder or assassinate someone. There's no romanticising it. It is what it is. I'm a killer."

Her eyes widened slightly despite the control she tried to maintain, her pupils dilating. Fear, and something else on her face. Did it excite her? Did she like that little sliver of danger or was it just because of the arm that I gripped suddenly in my hand, or the way I pulled her into me so that our bodies touched?

Chapter Seventeen

ೞ Natalie ೲ

The Viking pulled me into him, his fingers looped roughly round my arm as if he needed to demonstrate how dangerous he was. He should frighten me; with his long hair, his tattoos, his muscles and the ugly knife that he carried everywhere. There was no way I could match him, never mind defend myself against him. Yet, that realisation, that threat of danger, seemed to make me come alive. More alive than I'd ever been in the last two years.

The clean leather smell mixed with the light fragrance of his aftershave and a hint of mint as he breathed on me awakened all my senses and I felt that pull towards him, involuntary, intense. His head dipped towards me, his lips brushing the top of mine and then over to my ear, his light beard scratching my cheek, sending a shiver of sensation down my neck, resonating through my entire body.

"I won't ever hurt you, Nat," he whispered in my ear, "not unless you want me to. But that doesn't make me an angel. I'm the grim reaper. And I like it that way."

His voice was laced with promise, hoarse and deep, firing bolts of need and longing in me that were amplified by the situation we were in. The excitement and the terror, the boredom followed by the revelation, the loneliness followed by companionship. Controversial emotions plagued me, confused me, and heated me from the inside out.

He kept his face touching mine, teasing me with his presence and his touch, waiting for me to react, and neither one of us did. Neither one of us stepped away nor fuelled the flame that sparked between us, both of us too stubborn to succumb to the electric atmosphere in the odd little office. I nuzzled my face against his neck, his scent engulfing me, feeling the heat rising from his skin.

"I like beards as much as I like tattoos," I muttered, not able to keep the little exhalation of air from escaping my lips.

"There's a lot of fun to be had with a beard, Nat," he answered, nibbling my ear lobe as I desperately willed myself not to show a reaction, "I can make you scream from the feel of my beard alone, babe."

He pushed me backwards suddenly, his grip never loosening from around my arm, until my back hit the wall behind me. His body pressed into mine, heat raging between us, and he moved his lips against my cheek, kissing gently at the skin along my jawline. His beard scratched at me, the contradiction of sensations from the softness of his lips to the sharp scrape from the coarse hair of his face, sending pressurised tingles through my body. I closed my eyes to contain the moan that threatened to tumble out of my lips, refusing to let my mind think about the effect he was having on me.

"Get off me," the words came out as a whisper, not the command that I meant them to have.

The Viking stopped for a second, but then I felt his fingers drop to my wrists, yanking them up roughly above my head, his face in front of me, eyes never leaving mine.

"So it's get off me now? It wasn't that last night when you jumped on me in the kitchen. When you stripped off and pushed your tits into my hands," he growled, frustration hinting at his voice.

His eyes dropped to my chest.

"I was drunk last night."

His eyes moved back up to meet mine, blue-green orbs darkened with lust and need. He squeezed my wrists together, and I winced at the sharp pain as he crushed them in his hand, and then he let go and stepped back.

*****

I stared out into the evening, the last of the sunlight turning to a burnt orange as it crept from the sky and golden-bronze glowed through the mass of factory style windows.

"Does it not get cold in here in the winter?" I called from the sofa, the wine slipping down my throat way too quickly and the smell of meat cooking in the oven mixed with the potent scent of the onions the Viking was cutting. My stomach grumbled loudly.

He looked up, safe from me, safe from each other as he stood over the kitchen island.

"I mean, with all these windows and no curtains."

He shook his head.

"I have heating you know," he answered, his eyes dropping back to where he sliced the onion with an efficiency that probably would have seen me lose a digit.

"Yeah, but you don't have internet. You might as well live in the dark ages."

"I do. Just only on that machine."

"What's up with that?" I asked.

"I live under the radar. I actually don't even exist. The internet connection in that room runs through an onion router. It means no one can find me; not the law, not a rival and not a customer."

"Are you hiding from someone?" The more gulps of the wine I was taking the more it was loosening my inhibitions, it was dangerous, but I needed it, because it also numbed the pain inside of me, the constant ache and the relentless emptiness.

His head shot up, his gaze fixed on me, a hesitation that said more than it didn't. Even from a few metres away, I could see his eyebrows pull together in a scowl, his facial features going through a range of emotions.

"You'd be a shit poker player," I added, watching surprise cross his face this time.

"What?"

"You're rubbish. Who are you hiding from?" He stared at me, a challenge or an attempt to scare me off course, I wasn't sure which, but I was far enough away from him and under the influence of enough of the wine to ignore it. "The Northern Kings?"

He looked shocked now, as he ferreted around in his head to answer or deflect.

"Who are they, V?"

For a moment he said nothing, his face tense as he decided whether to answer me or ignore me. But in the end, he answered.

"They are an old motorcycle club I used to be a part of, but we fell out."

"Fell out how?" I asked, watching him turn around and throw something into a frying pan, an angry sizzle drowning out the tension.

He stood with his back to me, in front of the stove, moving something about in the pan and for a little while I thought the conversation was over. But as he turned around, he sighed.

"Let's just say I'm under orders to stay off their patch. If I don't respect those, they'll kill me."

"Why?" I breathed, more shocked than I had been expecting.

A beep sounded shrilly, making me jump, and the Viking turned his back on me once more, opening the oven, and the moment dissolved into the smell of food and the growl of my stomach.

I'd never really been a burger fan. They were messy, and I didn't like eating with my fingers, but I couldn't deny that this was delicious, and I was starving. And the wine I'd been consuming for the last hour really needed absorbing. Grease ran down my fingers and I licked at it, not wanting to put handprints all over the sofa. Blue-green eyes watched me intently from the sofa opposite.

"Starving?" He asked, the food on his own plate having disappeared in mere minutes.

I nodded, "you don't have much in your cupboards."

"My cupboards are well stocked," he complained.

"Yeah, with tins and chocolate. Not much fresh stuff. I need a salad, not all this grease," I mumbled, pushing the last of the burger into my mouth.

"Looks like you're doing ok with all the meat I gave you," the Viking said, raising an eyebrow, a boyish smile tugging at his lips.

I couldn't help but smile back at him. For a killer, he wasn't bad company, as long as he kept his clothes on and his hands off me.

We talked long into the night, tales of our childhoods, tales of adolescence, of youthful escapades gone wrong. We were the same age I found out, and he was intelligent, not the meat head, bully assassin I had first thought him to be.

He seemed to have values and morals, he just killed people; a contradiction I probably would never get used to. But I didn't suppose I needed to.

His blue-green eyes held a wealth of history, things he'd seen, things he'd experienced and if he had tried to conceal those from me, the tranquillity and honesty of his eyes had betrayed him. He'd become animated when he talked about the things he loved; his motorbikes, the feeling of freedom, of the wind in his hair as he rode through the countryside, and the exhilaration and adrenaline as he pushed the bike to its limit or took a bend a little too fast. He was everything I wasn't, a free-spirit, an impulsive risk taker, reactive and passionate. And I envied him.

I slugged back the last of my wine, feeling the fuzziness in my head and, more than certain, I was going to have a headache by the morning, but at least I hadn't tried to come on to a tattooed hitman tonight.

"What's the sleeping arrangements?" I asked, standing up.

The Viking looked up at me, a lopsided grin plastered on his face, "the bed's big enough for both of us."

"Uh uh. I'll just sleep on the sofa."

"That's great an all, but I don't have any spare blankets. Never have guests, remember?"

"Not any guests?"

"What are you asking me, Nat?" He stood up and moved towards me, and I pretended I hadn't heard the question, "if you want to know about girlfriends, I don't have any, and I don't bring women back here."

"So what? You just eat out?" The words fell from my lips before I had time to turn the filter on.

The Viking laughed, deep and strong, and despite the sudden embarrassment licking at my cheeks, I couldn't suppress the giggle that fell from my lips either.

"Babe, a man has needs. So yes, sometimes I eat out. I'm just not a regular anywhere. It's just too risky. So it's always just a onetime thing."

I don't know why that should have prickled me as it did, why his admission should have any effect on me. I liked my men in suits, clean shaven, free of tattoos and piercings and generally law-abiding citizens. This should have done nothing to me. Nothing. But it did.

"So you can sleep in my bed with me, or down here on the sofa without blankets. Up to you," The Viking said, pulling my concentration from the ridiculous feeling of jealousy building inside of me.

"Fine," I answered, "but wear some clothes."

He laughed, a low guttural, knowing chuckle.

*****

I woke up sweating. The room was so hot and so dark. A heavy arm wrapped around me, a

139

man snuggled against my back, his breath steady and relaxed. I was roasting. I'd changed into a jumper and leggings and positioned myself as far to the edge of the bed as I could. But now I was almost in the middle and wrapped in the arms of a hitman. I needed to take my top off, and right now I cursed my lack of preparation. I should have thought things through better when I'd packed in a hurry, the tattooed man goading me to go faster.

He moved, groaning slightly and pulling me back into him, my body melting against his, the feeling of something a little like contentment as I nestled in his arms, despite how hot I was. If I took my jumper off, I would feel his skin against mine, feel the gentle warmth from his body. But he wasn't my type, and I wasn't falling for some sort of warped version of Stockholm Syndrome. But I didn't move away from him either, instead I closed my eyes and concentrated on the feel of him around me, the scent from his skin and ignored the gentle tingle that was forming between my legs.

Chapter Eighteen

❧ The Viking ☙

I woke up to mouthfuls of hair splayed across my face and threatening to invade my throat every time I breathed in. The sun was only just coming up, pale gold light seeping in through my curtain-less windows, daylight chasing away the coolness of the spring morning. Natalie was still sound asleep, probably shattered after the amount of times she'd tossed and turned and threw the covers back, whimpering complaints of being too hot, yet too stubborn to take her clothes off.

The heat from her body sent her scent swirling between us, citrus mixed with vanilla and the gentle smell of her own skin, and strawberries from the hair that kept sweeping over my face. I stretched, careful not to wake her. I didn't want her to feel the bulge at her back from Mini V who was also wide awake. Who the fuck was I kidding? Of course I wanted her to feel it, just not at her back, in her. That's where I wanted her to feel it. I tucked myself back into her, winding my arm around her stomach and pulling her into me.

I thought I would have dropped back off, but I lay there enjoying the heat from her body, the little whimpers from the dream she was having, even the feel of her hair tickling my face. It was homely and normal, and for a little while it melted the loneliness in my heart. It couldn't last, no matter how much I might enjoy it in the moment, even if her company was prickly at best, it was company all the same, another human to talk to, another person to be with.

She stirred suddenly, turning over towards me, her eyes still closed, her face a few inches from mine. She was relaxed, her usual hostility replaced with a peacefulness that allowed me to see her properly. Her eyebrows were neatly shaped, like she'd taken hours to get them even. Not too thick, they tapered off gently at the ends. Her eyelashes were full and long, brushing the very top of her cheek as her lids stayed gently closed. Her nose was gentle and feminine, straight, possibly a little too small for the rest of her features, and her nostrils barely flared at the end, unless she was angry, which seemed frequent when she was awake. Her lips were lightly pushed together, plump and pink, pouting slightly at whatever was going on inside that dream. I bet they looked even better when she smiled, although I don't remember seeing much of that.

But I remembered the feel of them on mine, soft but persistent, moving against me, passionate, gentle, tentative. Even drunk, I could tell she was holding herself back, scared to let go, trying to remain in control. I'd wanted to take that control from her, show her how free she would feel if she let go. I sighed, my rampant thoughts doing myself no favours for the raging hard-on I was sporting. If I pulled her just a little closer, it would rub against her stomach. If I thought she might jump on and ride it instead of slapping me silly, then I might have just done that.

I looked at her lips again, now slightly parted, tempting and divine. I could just reach across and taste them again. But I didn't. Because as she lay there asleep, peaceful, no signs of anger, of pain and fear, she was truly beautiful. So I left her sleeping while I watched.

I lay there for what seemed like ages watching her sleep, until eventually, her eyelids fluttered open and the caramel-brown of her eyes stared at me. She recoiled almost immediately, pushing backwards like a magnet repelled, and the unfamiliar thud of heaviness in my stomach made me grind my teeth, even if just for a second.

"I, err, I'd forgotten where I was," she muttered almost apologetically, her voice husky with sleep.

Mini V reacted treacherously.

"Well, at least this time you kept your clothes on," I joked, but it came out more strained than I had intended.

"The other night," she began, her eyes studying my chest, "I don't normally do that sort of thing."

"The kissing me? The getting naked? Trying to force me to have sex with you?"

"I didn't force you."

"You took all your clothes off and rubbed your tits against me. I'd say that was force in my book."

"So, what's your excuse now?"

I felt her fingers wrap round my cock, gentle and careful, her gaze fixed with mine, watching for my reaction as she slowly slid her hand up and down my shaft in careful, shallow movements. Then she pulled her hand all the way up, her fingers closing over the head and then releasing suddenly, her eyes opening wide in alarm. I chuckled.

"What's wrong with it?" She asked.

I grabbed her hand and brought it back to me, wrapping my palm around hers and moving us both up and down the length in slow, long strokes.

"It's pierced, babe," I answered, curling my fingers over hers as she reached the head, pushing her hand against the metal in the end.

She tried to pull away, but I held her there.

"Why?" She whispered, her voice hesitated.

"Because it makes sex even better, for me and you."

"Does it hurt?"

"Find out," I answered, moving her hand up and down, pushing my hard-on into us.

Her tongue slid along her bottom lip nervously and then her eyes narrowed, her face hardening, and she yanked her hand free. Throwing the covers back, she darted out of bed, storming down the stairs and ramming her feet into some shoes. Shit.

I grabbed a pair of jeans, pulling them on quickly, watching as she marched to the kitchen drawers and helped herself to a set of keys. The door chain rattled, the scratch of metal inside the door as she turned the locks and I bounded down the stairs after her.

Door chimes rang angrily as she moved through my house, finding the right keys with ease as she let herself into the garage below. I caught up as she stepped through the door, grabbing her arm and tugging her back to me.

"Get off me!"

"Nat, wait, what are you doing?"

"I can't stay here."

"You have to."

"I don't."

"Nat, you'll not stay alive more than a day out there."

"I'll give it my best shot," she spat, trying to prise my fingers from around her arm.

"You won't, babe. They'll find you and slaughter you. That's how this works. I can't protect you out there. No one can."

Her face crumbled. Anger and frustration melting into despair as she bit down on her bottom lip, trying to keep control of her tears. But I could see them welling in her eyes, filling but being denied the opportunity to fall. She blinked wildly, determined not to lose the battle with her emotions, and then she drew in a breath.

"How do I make this stop?"

"There's only two ways. You die or we find the fucker who wants you dead."

"I think I prefer the latter."

"Me too, babe, me too," I pulled her towards me, wrapping my other arm around the back of her shoulders and for a few moments she let me hold her as we stood in silence in the garage, the smell of oil and fuel heavy in the surrounding air.

"I need to get my dad's stuff from home. I need to see what those names mean," she said, pushing herself away from me.

*****

Natalie's house was quiet. The back door had once again been bust open, my temporary repair to secure the place smashed to smithereens, but whoever had broken in had left everything else intact. I moved through the kitchen, having parked in the big paved yard at the back, and then headed up the stairs till I got right to the very top. Following Nat's instructions, I went straight to the top floor, pulling open the midget door in the side of the wall and crawling in through the gap.

Inside the loft were boxes all stacked neatly on top of each other. Everyone was labelled with some sort of description and arranged in numerical order of the numbers written on the front, methodical and orderly. I checked the box numbers she had instructed and started moving them through the gap until I had the four she'd asked for. At the bottom of the last set of stairs, I heard the scratch of a key in a lock. The front door opened, a dark-haired man in a suit stepping through.

"Who the fuck are you?" I demanded, moving the box to balance on my left arm as I reached behind me and under my leather jacket, my fingers closing around the handle of my knife.

"Me? I, this, I live here. Who the fuck are you and where's Nat?"

I moved towards him, watching his reactions. His suit was expensive, the material thick and the cut fit him so well, I was guessing it was tailored for him. He reeked of strong aftershave, heady, a mix of cardamom and Cinnamon, rich and woody. Expensive.

"You don't live here, mate. So tell me who the fuck you are before I break your face."

I took a step closer, and he took a step back.

"I'm Carter, Nat's boyfriend."

"Ex-boyfriend," I corrected.

"No. We're still together."

"That's not what I heard," I could hear the coldness in my voice.

"Where is she?"

147

"At her sister's."

"So, what are you doing here?"

"I'm doing some jobs for her while she's away."

The ex looked me up and down, analysing the clothes I wore, the tattoos on my skin, the length of my hair. I saw the disdain on his face. I saw it frequently when people looked at me, but from him, it made a knot of anger tighten in my stomach.

"Uh huh," he answered as if not believing me, "so if I ring her, she'll confirm that, right?" He asked, his accent thick with pomp.

We couldn't be so opposite to each other if we actually tried.

"No. Because her phone is switched off. But you know that already," I watched his expression, the extremely faint tension in his jaw as he clenched his teeth together and so I continued, "because she hasn't answered your calls and your pathetic texts for days. You broke up, remember, and then you stood her up in the restaurant."

His eyes widened and then immediately narrowed, undecided which emotion to allow to dominate in his attempt to remain stoic and indifferent to me.

"I didn't mean to not turn up. I just got busy with some, err, work stuff."

"Really? That was convenient."

I studied his face, watching the buttons I was pressing have effect. His already dark eyes had grown a shade darker, something untoward swirling in them, something that if I pushed just a bit harder might reveal a really interesting snippet of information.

"Who was she?"

"What?"

"The woman you stood Nat up for? Your secretary? The office junior?" the side of his face flinched with further tension. I was surprised his teeth hadn't broken with the pressure he was putting on them, "yep, it was the office junior, wasn't it? Young, impressionable, attracted more by that big wallet of yours than the tiny thing in your pants."

He was readable, like most men I tracked in the dark, but I hadn't quite seen the twitch of his fist and the quickness that it flew at me. The blow caught me hard above my eye, knocking me sideways, the box in my arms falling to the floor and the contents spewing out. Straightening up, I turned back to him. He shrank back towards the door, probably realising what a fuckwit he'd just been, watching me nervously, wondering whether I was about to return the favour. I should smack him straight in that posh boy face of his, send blood running all over that expensive suit. Normally I would, but today I restrained the anger pulsing through me.

I grabbed him by the collar of his jacket, pulling him towards me roughly, the heat from both our breaths mingling together almost as if that battled for dominance. He was a little taller than me, but it gave him no real edge. Pretty boys like this were no threat. He'd just got lucky with that punch.

"You give me Nat's key back and you walk away and never contact her again," my voice was low, threatening.

"Why? So you can shag her? See a pretty woman with a shit load of money and think you'd try your luck?" he spat back, petulantly, "good luck to you. She's a frigid bitch anyway. It's like fucking a dead body most of the time."

Rage flashed in front of my eyes, hot and irrational. His nose crunched, and he shrieked like a girl. Blood spilled over his expensive suit, pouring down from his squashed nose. I smiled, plucking the key from his fingers, and shoved him out the door. My forehead throbbed.

*****

"V! What happened?" Nat rushed to me as I ricocheted off the doorframe, blinded by the four boxes I'd staggered up the stairs with.

The cut in my eyebrow still oozed blood, although the frequency with which it had been spilling down my face had slowed down on the drive home. I'd mopped away at it continuously, scattered tissues all over the passenger seat of my van still, but it had been relentless.

"Your ex, or whatever he is, hasn't got a bad right hook for a posh fucker."

"Shit! You met Carter? I'm so sorry. He was a boxer in university, pretty good at it, by all accounts."

150

"Didn't realise that boxing was a thing that the toffs did? Anyway, why was he there?"

"He was in my house?"

I nodded, moving into the lounge and carefully lowering the boxes onto the coffee table. When I turned around, she was right in front of me. She had been showered and changed, her hair hanging slightly damp, gentle waves forming halfway down. The smell of strawberries hung in the air. She reached up and gently nipped my brow together.

"This is gonna need stitches," she said, her voice lower, the surprise dissolving.

"Apparently Carter had a key," I answered, as she tugged me towards the kitchen and pushed me against a bar stool at the island.

"Yes. I'd given him one. Never got the chance to get it back from him. Where's your first aid kit?"

I pointed to the cupboard over her head and watched her as she stood on her tip toes to reach a box at the back. She had a pair of slim fitting jeans on which hugged her arse, the cheeks round and pert. The lid clattered on the bench as she took it off and put it aside, turning back towards me with a bottle of antiseptic in one hand and a wad of cotton wool in the other. The liquid stung mercilessly, and I hissed at her as she dabbed a second lot on, suspecting she was enjoying my discomfort a little too much.

"What happened to your forehead? It's red too."

"I hit it off something."

151

Natalie took a step back, scrutinising me.

"You hit him back, didn't you?"

"Geordie kiss, actually," I grinned.

She pulled her lips into a half frown, not quite with meaning. She was stunning. Her tousled hair partially covered the bare shoulder that her over-sized jumper hung off, her tits bulged underneath, full of the promise of good times. Reaching out, I linked my fingers into the belt loop of her jeans and yanked her into me, grabbing the back of her head and tangling my fingers into her hair, leaving her no means of escape. I pressed my lips against hers, feeling the slight hesitation, but it was momentary. Nat didn't try to pull away or slap me and there were no stray knees to the groin. So when her lips parted slightly, exhaling a tiny breath of air, I pushed my tongue inside of her. Tasting her, my mouth grabbed at her hot, plump lips, devouring them, our breaths tangling as any resolve she may have had slipped away and she kissed me back, and we duelled, frenzied and passionate.

Chapter Nineteen

ℭ Natalie ℭ

His teeth nipped my lips, tugging on the flesh already made sensitive from the scratch of his beard. Heat erupted within me, radiating outwards like I could self-combust at any moment. Fiery tingles raced across my skin. His lips were soft, a contrast to the way he kissed me, hungry, desperate and forceful, pushing my lips apart for his tongue, the grip on my head almost painful. Yet, each little stab of discomfort from the hair wrapped in his fist ignited a deep prickle of heat, emotions and feelings welling in my stomach, pressure building inside of me, an ache forming between my legs.

I pressed into him harder, challenging him for control, my hands pushing into the hardened muscle of his stomach, a sprinkling of hair tickling my finger ends as I slid his t-shirt over his body. V took the hint, yanking the grey material off over his head, the marbled, inked torso naked under my touch, skin stretched over the ripple of muscle, smooth, hard granite under my hands. My fingers splayed outwards over the bulge of his pecs, feeling for the piercings in his nipples, foreign and contradictory against the heat of my skin, the coolness of the metal and the warmth of his flesh.

Pulling away from the assault of V's tongue, I slowed for a moment to gaze over the inked artwork on his skin. Brushing over the pictures, tracing the lines criss-crossing his tight flesh, the light wisps of the hair on his chest almost camouflaged by the tattoos. I pushed my lips over the stained skin, my tongue darting out, tasting a slight saltiness. Continuing I followed the contours of the muscles of his pecs until I reached his nipple, the sudden smooth texture of the metal barbell that was forced through it, stark against the softness of his skin.

The Viking groaned, deeply delicious, a low vibrating rumble and I flicked my tongue over the metal end, just to hear him gasp again. The ends of the barbell were smooth and cool against my tongue, the metal even as I glided across it. His hands squeezed into my stomach, edging me away from him, and for a tiny part of a second, I felt rejected. Then I felt the pull on my jumper, V's hands wrenching it roughly over my head, leaving me standing in just my bra and jeans.

"Let me look at you, babe," the Viking's voice was raspy, but there was no mistaking the command.

V's eyes drifted down over my chest and to my stomach before moving back up to fix on my face, a small smile creeping at the corners of his lips.

"You're beautiful," he breathed, pushing off the stool and closing the gap between us.

"It's not as if it's the first time you've seen me naked, V. No thanks to your vodka supplies."

"But it's the first time, I get to smooth my hands over your skin."

Fingers slid up my left hand-side, gentle and careful, pulling the strap of my bra over my shoulder. There was a little tug behind me as his other hand worked smoothly, flicking the strap at my back free and letting it slide down my arm and fall at my feet.

"And it's the first time I get to taste you, babe, all of you."

His face came down towards me, nudging my head sideways, his beard dragging across my neck, sending a shudder through my body, the space between my legs tensing.

"Your skin would look amazing tattooed," he whispered against my throat, sucking and kissing gently, moving over my collar bone and over the top of my chest.

"I don't like tattoos," I answered, my words disjointed with the distraction of the nip of teeth.

V's lips smoothed across, replacing the sharp little bites with kisses, the warmth tingling over the punished skin, before dipping into the small recess at my neck, and sucking against my throat. For a moment desire and lust filled the aching space inside my chest, making me forget about pain and the weariness of sadness, and the strain of fear. My nipples stood hard, desperate for his touch, yet he took his sweet fucking time to get anywhere near them, tasting every part of me but them. Then as he dipped lower, got just that little bit closer, I pushed my fingers into his hair, tangling them between the back of his head and the ponytail, pushing his head down to where I needed it.

His tongue darted out, flicking at the very end, and I exhaled loudly, pressing him closer, moving my chest into him until his mouth closed around the pert nipple, stroking it with soft lips, much too gentle. I needed more. I needed him rough and forceful like his kiss. I pulled him closer, biting my tongue so I didn't embarrass myself by begging him for what I needed. The tip of his tongue circled, lapping at the end of the peak, shivers surging through my spine with every tiny movement, my pussy pooling with wetness, hot and damp. I moaned loudly, unable to keep the noise from tumbling from my lips. The sound excited him, and he caught my nipple between his lips, sucking down hard, a delicious assault that took my breath away, and I pushed into him, desperately.

His teeth scratched over the sensitive peaks, sending a throb directly to my pussy, stoking the pressure between my legs until I was just a painful ache of want and need. I tugged at his jeans, my thumb flicking over the brass button and popping it free as he lapped and sucked, alternating between them, his fingers pinching and swirling the other. He was killing me. I yanked his trousers open, pushing them down his hips and over his pert arse cheeks until he took over and kicked them off.

The Viking's cock jutted out boldly between us, the veins protruding, and the head bulging. Four metal balls stuck out around the edge like a dial on a clock face. I swallowed, unsure suddenly. The metal ware in the end made the whole thing look brutal, weaponlike. The tip of his cock was smooth, like polished marble, and a sticky wet bead of pre-cum coated my fingertips as I brushed across the very top before feeling tentatively down the shaft, the hard bumps under my fingers jutting out at the sides.

"It won't bite," The Viking spoke into my neck, moving up from my nipple.

I closed my hand over the head, letting it slide over the piercings around the top and then glide down the shaft. It wasn't the biggest cock I'd ever had in my hand, but it was wide and girthy. My fingers barely closed all the way around it, and I imagined it inside of me, stretching me, forcing me open. I dropped to my knees, positioning my face in front of the Viking's groin, the tip of his cock just a few millimetres from my lips. Raising my eyes to look at him, I studied his expression, his jaw tight with tension, the blue-green of his eyes dark, shadows dancing in his pupils. Reaching out with my tongue I swiped it over the end, sliding my lips down the length of it, slowly, listening for the tiny gasps of air, feeling for the tiny pulses of reaction. Then I let my tongue glide back up, licking over his engorged cock to the bulge of the head and over the edge of the tip. Flicking at the ends of the barbells sticking out around the edge. V groaned again, sliding a

157

hand into my hair, grabbing a handful and holding my head steady above his cock.

He guided my head towards him, pushing me onto him and I let the satiny part glide past my lips. My mouth bumped over the barbells, one of them chinking against my teeth, and I winced, wondering whether I'd hurt him. But the look on his face didn't imply pain, only the agony of control. Gazing at him from my knees, I studied his reaction before sliding down on him again, taking a bit more of him, feeling the girth stretching my mouth open, the head of his cock knocking the back of my throat, and the tiniest hint of a gag forming before I pulled backwards.

V pushed his hips into me, his hand tightening into my hair, the taste of metal and the tiniest flavour of salt filling my mouth.

"Fuck, I knew there was a better job for your smart mouth," he growled, thrusting his hips into my face, making me gag and bringing tears to my eyes.

I quickened the pace, my fingers wrapping around the base of his cock, twisting and stroking in time with my mouth. His hands pulled my hair tighter, forcing even more of him into my mouth, the metal in the end bulging against my tongue. Then suddenly he tugged my head back, pulling me from him and to my feet.

"Don't think that's all I'm gonna get, babe," he growled, whirling me round and pushing my back up into the kitchen island behind me, "your mouth is a fine thing but I'm betting that sweet pussy of yours is even better."

158

V wrenched the button open on my jeans yanking them down my legs, pulling my knickers with him, and then his fingers covered me, gliding through my wetness. I moaned, flinging my head back and pushing myself towards his hand as his face dipped to my neck, biting and sucking.

Then the first finger pushed inside of me, and my pussy clenched around it like a vice, the brush of the heel of his hand over my clit flicking a switch deep in my stomach. Pushing myself against him I rocked my hips, rubbing against the roughness of his hands, a cry echoing around the apartment as he pushed another finger inside, his teeth nipping at my jaw. Shit, I was going to come already. The pressure built inside of me, heat swarming to my pussy, a static electric flooding through my body.

"More, babe?" He asked, his lips trailing back down towards my breasts.

"Yes," I breathed.

He pushed another finger in, slowly stretching me open for him, his thumb working my clit, swirling and pausing, in time with the fingers that circled inside of me. I pushed my hips towards him, riding his hand in lustful desperation, grinding my clit against his thumb as he pushed back against me, and then I felt the nip of teeth on my nipple, pinching it hard. My pussy clenched around him, my insides squeezing and screaming, my head lolling back as I pushed every part of me towards him.

"Oh. Fuck!" I shouted, bucking against his hand as the heat and pressure crashed together, an eruption within me, sending pulses of hot liquid electricity running through my body as I heaved and panted.

What the actual fuck was that? I stilled, feeling his fingers slide out and the rush of cooler air from where his hand had been clamped against me, from where I had ridden it like some needy whore.

The drawer next to me rumbled, and then his hands were fiddling between us, the swipe of knuckles gently grazing my over-energised skin. Glancing down, I watched the last of the condom roll onto his dick. It seemed wider than ever, and even with the condom covering the barbells, they still poked out like the top of a vintage tap. Nervousness settled in my stomach. But then he grasped the back of my head and kissed me, pushing his tongue into my mouth, his lips crushing into mine as he wrapped his arms round me, picking me up and pulling my legs round his waist. He carried me from the kitchen to the lounge, the top of his cock rubbing my pussy lips, igniting a fire in me again. Then bending down, he lowered me onto the sofa, climbing on top of me, his lips never breaking with mine, fucking my mouth roughly with his tongue.

His dick brushed against me, hovering just a fraction too far from where I wanted it and I arched my back, needing to feel him. He dipped, lowering himself against me, nudging my knees wider and lining the head of his cock up. I drew a breath, and he paused, his blue-green eyes staring down at me.

"Will it hurt?" I whispered.

"No one's complained before. I'll go slowly till you're used to me."

I nodded, biting my bottom lip, feeling the pressure as he pressed the head in, and the resistance as my pussy tensed around his girth.

"Relax, babe," he breathed into my ear, nipping at the bottom of my lobe and making me squeak.

Then I felt the stretch and the initial burn and friction, hot, rough friction as he slowly pushed his way inside me. I moaned loudly at the intrusion, at the stretching and how he filled me, his cock wrenching me open for him. He stopped a moment. His eyes wandered over my face, watching me and then pulled slowly backwards, the roughness from the wideness of his shaft and the metal on the end of it scraping my insides. His thrusts became quicker and deeper, and I could feel the barbells moving inside of me, the burn subsiding into heat and pressure.

The Viking's head dipped back towards me, kissing me as he moved, thrusting deeper. I ran my hands down his back, his lips moving to my neck, sucking at my skin, nipping along my collarbone. His hips got faster, his cock pulsing inside of me, battering my walls, pain turning to pleasure, the fire he was stoking in my pussy spreading through me. Fuck.

The air around filled with moans and grunts, our voices mingling with each other, and I dragged my nails down the Vikings back.

161

"Oh fuck," he growled, flinging his head back, ramming into me with a sudden deep thrust and I yelled out.

He pumped harder in response, a strangled growl coming from his throat, his cock pounding in and out.

V dropped a hand between us, his fingers finding my clit, rubbing and nipping, sending an explosion through my body, my back arching and my hips rising to meet him as he sank into me deeper and harder.

"Oh. God!" I shouted, feeling the build, the blood rushing in my ears, my heart hammering against my chest, "oh fuck."

Then my body shook, and my legs clenched around him, my mind and memories wiped clean as I sank in to ink black oblivion. He grunted from on top of me, but my head whirled, and ecstasy stole away any sense of where or who I was. V moved faster, his primal growls vibrating against me as he chased his own release and I lay momentarily delirious under him. Then he threw his head back and let out a strangled cry, squeezing his beautiful eyes shut, before sinking onto his forearms on top of me.

Caged underneath him, V's lips found mine, tasting me with shallow, careful kisses. My breaths slowed and my heart relaxed its frantic pace, our bodies still tangled together in a sweaty pile of limbs.

Pushing himself up onto his elbows, the Viking gazed down at me, smoothing strands of hair from my face. His own blond hair hung loose from his ponytail, sticking to the side of his cheek. Silently, with his eyes fixed on my face, he ran his thumb across my bottom lip and over my chin, splaying his fingers out and running them down my throat and my chest, tweaking my nipples gently, igniting a flame from the smouldering embers in my stomach.

The tranquil blue-green of his eyes had darkened, the colours bleeding into each other like a stormy ocean, and his cheeks flushed with colour. Gliding his hand back up my neck, his fingers curled round my jaw, pinning my face into the position he wanted it and then he dipped his head, grabbing my mouth with his and thrusting his tongue back inside of me. I breathed against him, my body responding immediately, tension and expectation flooding between my legs, where he was still buried deep inside of me.

"That was fucking incredible," he murmured against my lips.

He pressed his body to mine, bringing his weight down on top of me, pinning me against the sofa so that I couldn't move, captive underneath him. My pussy throbbed in response, demanding more.

163

Chapter Twenty

℘ The Viking ℘

Natalie's stomach rumbled loudly as she lay on top of me, her legs straddled either side and her forehead touching mine as her breaths came ragged and her orgasm ebbed away.

"I think we need to eat something other than each other," I laughed, tipping her onto her back and gently sliding out of her, seeing the wince on her face.

She had to be sore. We'd spent all afternoon fucking each other and now we were just a mess of hot, sweaty and starving bodies. I pulled her from the bed, leading her down the stairs as she staggered on shaky legs. Once the shower was warm enough, I backed her in under the flow of water, gently lathering her body with soap, smoothing it over her plump tits and over the swell of her hips and hour-glass figure. Her stomach was smooth but with a nice covering of flesh, womanly, beautiful.

I pulled her against me, and no matter how much attention I'd paid to her tits and her nipples while we had used nearly every surface in the apartment, just the feel of them under the soap, pressing against me, I was hard again. Ignoring the raging erection I was sporting, I dropped to my knees in front of her, nudging her thighs apart.

"What are you doing V?" She asked, her voice uncertain as I ran soapy hands up the insides of her legs.

"I'm taking care of you, babe. Legs wider," I instructed, giving her another nudge.

She hesitated a moment, staring down at me. I ran my fingers up the back of her legs and round the bottom of her arse cheeks, feeling the bulge of them in my hand, full and perfect, soft and fleshy. My hands dipped lightly over her arse, moving towards her pussy lips. She winced again.

"I'm sorry I hurt you," I said to her pussy that was centimetres from my face, begging me to taste it.

"It wasn't really intentional, was it? And I can't say I'm complaining. Just all that metal..." she sighed as my fingers brushed over the top of her, gently cleaning where I'd made her sore.

When I looked up again, she was biting her bottom lip between her teeth, the tiniest of moans only just audible and the caramel-brown of her eyes partially consumed by the dilation of her pupils. Rising to my feet, I pulled her face towards me, kissing her lips gently, backing her against the shower wall, taking my time with her plump pink lips and the softness of her tongue. It dipped in and out of my mouth tentatively, like she wanted more, but couldn't take another pounding. And I didn't blame her. She managed all my piercings much better than I had imagined she would, and every different position seemed to send her wilder still.

I pulled my tongue from her mouth, guiding her back into the shower stream and running my hands through her hair as the water cascaded down on top of her back, running off her shoulders, dripping off the end of her perfect tits. Her neck and collarbone were covered with marks I'd made. I brushed my fingers over her skin. They looked good on her.

"Right. You stay here," I instructed, pulling on a pair of jeans as she sat on the bed wearing just one of my t-shirts.

"Where you going?" She asked, rubbing her wet hair on a towel.

"I'm going to get us something to eat. Won't be long."

I hadn't been in the pizza shop two minutes and the alarms on my phone starting ringing like an orchestra. I untangled my mobile from inside the leather jacket and tapped into the security system, watching Natalie wander around the house again with a bundle of something in her arms. She eased open the door down to the garage and I watched her rake around until she found something in the corner. And then she opened the door outside. Fuck! What was wrong with her? Why couldn't she follow simple fucking instructions?

I eyeballed the fella in the takeaway shop, urging him to hurry the fuck up with my pizza, as I switched cameras to the one in the yard. I watched her poke her head through the door, looking left and right and then wandering across to the far side carrying a bin bag of rubbish. A pizza box slid across the counter towards me, the sudden hissing noise as it scraped the counter making me jump.

"What part of don't go outside do you not understand?" I asked a short time later, pulling the top off a beer and pushing a bottle of wine towards her.

"I, er, it was just the bin I was taking out. Besides, I thought you said no one knew where you lived. So I should be pretty safe," she shrugged annoyingly.

"You are babe. But I don't want to take any chances."

I dumped some slices of pizza on a plate and brought it to where she was sitting on the floor in the lounge with her legs crossed. Piles of paper were stacked methodically around her, multi-coloured cardboard folders in a pile to her left and a stack of thinner brown ones to her right. She flicked through the one on top of her legs, her eyes moving over the page and her brows furrowed.

"Found anything?" I asked between mouthfuls of pizza.

"Nothing yet, but these files are stuffed with old case notes that my dad kept. I don't know why he didn't just destroy them. Some of this is years old."

She frowned as she looked into the next folder.

"Like this," she continued, "a young girl that went missing back in 1993. And then a teenager who was reported missing in 1994. But I can't see the connection," she said, holding photos up so I could see them.

I sat quietly for a while, watching her thumb through the folders, sorting and re-sorting piles, picking up pictures, staring at them and putting them down again. Her pizza sat beside her, untouched.

"You need to eat something, babe," I commented eventually, "That pizza isn't gonna eat itself."

"I need to solve this, V. I need my life back. I can't stay locked in here with you forever."

The words cut me, stinging like a paper cut, shallow but effective. I didn't know why I should be as hurt by them as I was. The thought that she'd only fucked me to pass the time, because she was bored and there was nothing else for her to do. It shouldn't matter. It didn't matter. I'd had hundreds of women and that's all they were, just a shag, a convenience. But with Nat, it had felt different. I felt connected to someone, more than just physically. And I wanted to protect her. I wanted to look after her.

"I'll help you, Nat. I'll do whatever it takes to get your life back," I said, sitting on the floor beside her.

And I meant it.

She looked at me, the slightest glisten in her eyes, enhancing the sparkle that I could see every time I looked into them.

"Pizza," I instructed, pushing the plate closer to her and watching as her shoulders slumped in submission and she reached out for one of the now cold slices.

She continued raking through the boxes, taking a bite of pizza and then making her piles and I sat next to her watching, learning the sequence and the way she sorted it. I pulled a box towards me and started unpacking it, making my own piles of documents and folders around me. But in the same way she had been doing. At the bottom of the box, the beige folder bulged. As I pulled it towards me, an envelope dropped out, hitting the floor with a little thud, its contents spilling from the top.

I gathered up the photographs that had escaped, the face on the top catching my eye. She had warm-brown hair, slightly darker than Nat's. Her lips and eyebrows were thinner and a very faint cleft in her chin. But there was no mistaking the caramel-brown of her eyes. It was like there were two of them in the room with me.

"This has to be your mam?" I asked, tipping the photograph towards Natalie.

She smiled a shallow smile, full of sadness and loss, of memories flooding back, of fondness and love, and in that moment she was vulnerable, and truly beautiful.

"Yes. That was my mother. Where was that?"

"In this envelope inside that folder," I answered, pointing to the thin cardboard folder on the floor beside me.

"Let me have a look?" She asked, holding her hand out.

I passed her the beige envelope, watching as she took the pictures out, flicking through the photographs of the same woman. Photographs like I'd seen that day in the pub. She was dressed for work, smart, powerful. And then as she came to the last photo, the woman was sitting on a picnic bench, a child on either side of her. I recognised the brunette teenager. The same warm brown eyes were looking straight at the camera and on the other side sat a much younger child with ash blonde hair, dimples in each cheek as she smiled at something the woman seemed to have said. They were happy. The picture radiated love. Natalie swiped a thumb over it.

"Her name was Sophie," she said eventually, "Sophie de Winter. She was a barrister. That's how my parents met, in court, on opposite sides. She died when I was sixteen. Charlie was only four. This must have been taken days beforehand."

"What happened?" I asked.

"Hit and run. My dad took it really badly. It nearly ended his career, but my Uncle Wes got him through it. Without him, I don't know how we all would have managed. He looked after us when my dad hit the bottle, picked up the pieces at home when my dad couldn't cope."

"Why do you use your mam's name rather than your dad's?"

"He wanted me to. I always was a Porter but when I qualified, he wanted me to use my mother's maiden name in honour of her. And so I did."

I saw the tear trickle down her cheek this time, glistening on her skin as it rolled silently over her cheekbone. Reaching out, I covered her hand with mine, watching as the black, grey and white figures on my hand engulfed hers, her perfect, slender fingers peeking out underneath. She gave me a wry smile, her eyes lingering on my face for a moment. But then they darkened, her eyes narrowing, a faraway expression taking over her face. She bit her bottom lip, turning her head back to the piles in front of her, and I watched her eyes dart backwards and forwards.

"What is it?"

"I, I, dunno."

Natalie got to her feet, stepping into the middle of the piles and then bent down, opening the folders, pulling papers out, moving to the next and doing the same, mumbling something as she went. I leaned towards her, straining to hear what she was saying to herself.

"The children," I caught, her voice soft and airy, "the girls, the dates."

She looked back at me suddenly.

"V, get that box over there," she instructed.

I jumped to my feet and crossed the room to where I had left it and brought it to her, watching as she seemed to dance in the middle of the piles like she was performing some sort of pagan ritual. I put the box outside of the circle and watched as she rushed to it, grabbing a handful of files and throwing the covers back.

"The girls, the dates," she looked up at me as if I should understand, "these aren't my dad's cases V, they're my mother's!"

Chapter Twenty One

⊂∫ Natalie ∞

Excitement raced through my veins, and my heart pounded against my ribs. I pulled out the contents of the third box, making another set of piles on the floor. Towards the end of this box, the contents changed. I flicked through the newspaper cuttings of missing girls and women, recognising some of the names from the list on the single document, but this time, there were faces. I scanned the articles.

'*West-end kidnap case defendants found not guilty,*' one headline read, '*Newcastle sex-trafficking ring case thrown out,*' read another.

I rifled through the cuttings a bit more. There were hundreds of them, not all related to court cases. They talked about investments, local businessmen and then another caught my eye. It was dated in 2002, the same year my mother died.

'*Newcastle Business mogul cleared of rape charges,*' the headline blared. My eyes flew over the text, absorbing the words like I wasn't really reading them. Jeremy Dodson. He had been accused of imprisoning and raping a young Romanian girl.

"V look at these," I said, handing the newspaper cuttings to him.

His eyes flicked across them, his brow furrowing, and he dragged a hand across his face. I recognised the look, the worry in his eyes.

"What is it?" I asked, almost too worried to hear the answer.

"All of this," he mumbled, waving his hand over the piles on the floor, "the missing girls, these court cases, and this," he flapped the piece of paper in his hand, "it all reeks of sex trafficking."

Shit. A thick heavy feeling descended upon me, the deep tendrils of dread filtering into my blood, pushed around my system by the ominous thumping of my heart. I studied his face, an unusual frown on his otherwise perpetually amused features, his eyes darkening, a tick of tension in his jaw. There was more to this.

"What are you not telling me, V?"

He sighed, grabbed my half-drunk glass of wine, and took it to the kitchen.

"You're gonna need a drink for this," He muttered as he walked away, the sound of liquid glugging from a bottle the only evidence to what he was doing.

When he came back, he beckoned towards the couch, and I didn't need him to ask me twice. I sat beside him and waited.

"Sex trafficking has been going on for years, but recently it really stepped-up in the UK. There's a known cell operating out of Newcastle and the north-east and there's shit loads of money in it. I always knew, given the price on your head, it had to be someone with the means. And then I saw the list of names. Now all this. It has to be connected with the Northern Pipeline."

"Northern Pipeline?"

"It's the biggest sex trafficking operation in the UK. The Polish ran the operational side last year until Cian took out Kaszynski, the head of the Polish mafia. Now the Volkov's are in on it. Although Lukyan had been sniffing around it for ages, the vulture that he is."

"Are these all mafia?" I asked.

The Viking nodded, "yep. The Russians had been waiting for someone to weaken for years. Think they got excited when they thought the Polish might have taken out the O'Sullivan's last year, but either way, when Cian finished Kaszynski it left a gap and they filled it."

I felt sick and sipping wine on a full stomach of pizza wasn't helping. The dread that had infiltrated my body was knotting in my stomach, squeezing my insides and forcing bile to my throat.

"How bad is this, V?"

I didn't want to hear his answers. I wanted to bury my head under the cushions on the settee and pretend this wasn't happening. I wanted to turn back the time to just over a week ago and do something, anything, differently.

"It's pretty fucking bad," He sighed, clearly troubled by telling me the truth, "the Northern Pipeline has some of the country's most powerful people sitting right at the top of it. We've suspected for some time that it goes that deep that it was best to stay well clear of it in any of its forms. The O'Sullivan's and even the Chinese mafia have kept away from it, but the Polish were greedy and the Russians, well with old man Volkov on his last legs, Lukyan has been slowly building up his control. And he is a really greedy bastard."

"So have the Volkovs ordered the hit?" I asked.

The Viking shook his head.

"They have their own people who are quite capable of taking you out," he answered, wincing after he said it, "this has come from higher than them. The Pipeline is like a rose, each layer peeling away until you get to the real crux of power. I don't know who that is. The Polish and the Volkovs are just the workhorses of the operation. They get the women in and get them out again, like a logistics company. Above them, there are people who strategize and plan and above them are the people in control, the ones who will neutralise the other members if it keeps themselves from being exposed. And then there are the clients; the sick bastards who keep the demand for sex-trafficked women ticking over. I don't know who is worse. But whoever ordered the hit had to have been worried that you might expose them and so my bet is that, that list of names on that memory stick, you'll find something in here, in these boxes, that will connect them and expose them."

I glanced at the piles around my feet and the last unpacked box that sat on the floor next to the kitchen and sighed.

"When we find out who it is, how do we stop it?"

The Viking's face darkened again, and he turned away from me, looking out of the window, silence suspended in the air between us. When he turned back to look at me, there was a hardness on his face, a meanness.

"When we find out who it is, then I'll kill them," he said quietly.

It wasn't a threat, there was no anger present in those words, it was sincere, a consequence, a promise. The knot unravelled in my stomach, pushing out around my body, fear and dread and terror trickling into my cells. Something hot dropped down my cheek, splattering on the bare skin of my leg. The Viking tilted my head to look at him, his thumb brushing under my eyelid, swiping at the tears that fell without restraint.

"I'll protect you, Nat. From them, from this. I'll take whatever lives I need to, to make sure they don't take yours."

I stared at him long and deliberate, searching his eyes for comfort, for resolution, for anything that would make me feel better. The blue-green orbs were as beautiful as ever, but they were full of sadness and resolution mixed with an intensity I hadn't seen before. I pulled his head to me, brushing my lips over his, savouring the feel of the prickle on my mouth from his short beard, the sudden flicker of heat in my body, lighting the darkness swamping my heart. A small distraction amidst the chaos.

Pulling at his bottom lip, I nipped at it gently with my teeth as he exhaled into my mouth, and then I pushed my tongue against his, feeling the resistance immediately as his moved back against me. Our lips picked up a frantic waltz, our tongues duelling for power over each other. I spun round, throwing my leg over him so I straddled him, the roughness of the bulge in his jeans against my still swollen pussy making me stifle a wince. But even through the slight pain, the thrum of desire rang in my ears, something else coursing through my body and I concentrated on that feeling. Chasing it, hoping for distraction, hoping being with him would obliterate the all-consuming worry and fear, pleading with the biker to make me forget for just a few moments.

I pushed his t-shirt off over his head, diving onto the black and white patterns on his chest, my tongue tracing the lines as his fingers pushed into my hair. Then, pausing, I pulled off the over-sized t-shirt of his that I had been wearing all day, my nipples tightening further at the rush of cool air and the scrutiny of his eyes.

Reaching round the back of his neck I pulled the Viking's head down onto my chest, pushing him to where I needed him and he took a sensitive nipple into his mouth, sucking down on it so hard I yelped and groaned, rocking my hips against him, stroking my pussy on his denim covered erection.

"You're so fucking beautiful, Nat," he murmured, his mouth full of my delicate flesh and one hand cupping my arse cheek as he encouraged me to move against him.

He squeezed the other nipple between his fingers, pinching and swirling and pinching and swirling. An ache built between my legs, travelling upwards to my stomach, radiating outwards down every limb, making them heavy with lust. I moaned loudly, my hips rocking against him faster. The friction against my battered pussy was beautifully painful, a throb of an orgasm building.

"That's it babe, grind that beautiful cunt on me," the vibration of his voice against the nipple he was gripping with his teeth sent another wave of electric surging through my body.

"Oh, God," I called out.

"That's it babe," he said again, both hands finding my hips, pulling me down on the cock still covered in his jeans, the material rough as I rode the bulge in his lap even through the layers between us.

The blood in my veins felt like it was on fire, like it was boiling inside me; pressure

179

building like steam in a kettle, and I couldn't conceal the pathetic whimpers that were escaping my lips as I rubbed my clit against him. I rocked even faster, my pussy tightening. Closing my eyes, not caring he was watching me, not worrying about him not being inside me, just using his erection for my own benefit, until I lost absolute and complete control. Lights flashed inside my eyelids like the flicker of electric threatening to blow a fuse. And for a moment, the world disappeared around me and everything went black.

Chapter Twenty Two

❧ The Viking ☙

For the first time in years, I actually dreamed that night, even with the chaos that was erupting around us. It was the feeling of her in my arms, my skin against hers, the light sound of her breathing gently, lulled me into a sleep I really didn't want to wake from. I dreamt of strawberries and cream, of soap and freshly washed laundry, of fresh spring flowers and clean mountain air. The usual nightmares of dusty deserts and women screaming, of the roar of motorbike exhausts and blood on my hands retreated for the night, despite the fact I hadn't quelled them with alcohol.

And then I turned over, that side of the bed empty, cold underneath my hand and I shot upright. I scanned the mezzanine bedroom as daylight flooded through the mass of windows, the apartment alive in mid-morning sun. Swinging my legs out of bed, I looked at the floor below, seeing no sign of Natalie. I pushed my legs into my jeans with each step I took down the stairs, checking the bathroom before leaping out into the hallway. I hadn't heard any of my alerts going off, not one chime. I'd slept through my whole fucking security system.

I ran down the stairs into the garage, clicking light switches as I went. The doors were still locked from the inside and there was no one there. It only left one place to get into, and she couldn't get in without me. Had someone taken her while I slept? My heart hammered in my chest, heavy breaths sounding even louder in the silence of the garage. I darted back up the stairs, stubbing the toe on my right foot and falling onto my hands and knees, swearing loudly into the concrete. I limped onwards, the sudden pain dulling, the alarm of the door opening at the top ringing in my ears.

I looked to the left, at the computer room door, ever so slightly ajar where it hadn't clicked back into place properly. How? Pushing the door inwards, a sudden rush of relief hit me square in the chest as I saw Natalie sitting there, hands in her hair, staring at the screen of the computer.

"Couldn't figure out the password, huh?" I asked, watching her jump slightly at the suddenness of my voice in the room.

She scowled at me as if it was *my* fault she couldn't hack into *my* computer.

"How the fuck did you get in here, anyway?" I asked.

"I memorized your code," she answered, uninterested.

"And the biometrics system?"

"Took a print off your finger while you were sleeping. Seen it on Mission Impossible or some other shit. Seems the sticky tape thing actually works. Now can you please let me in to this thing?"

Half of me wanted to refuse, just to piss her off, particularly after the effort she'd gone to gain access. But I didn't.

"Shift over," I said, wheeling her away from the keyboard, "and turn around."

"Why? It's not like I'm going to post stupid statuses on your Facebook or Twitter account. Do you even have social media?"

"Just Tinder," I answered, amused and yet warmed by the scowl she shot me, "hitmen and assassins don't really post ads in the marketplace offering a buy one get one free."

Natalie harrumphed beside me but was quickly distracted by the computer coming to life in front of us.

"Are you really on Tinder?" She asked, a hint of worry in her voice.

"No babe, it doesn't really help the covert work I do," I answered, moving out the way and watching as she wheeled herself back to the computer. "What are you looking for, anyway?" I asked, watching her fingers dash across the keys with a speed that even Joey, my intelligence source, would be impressed with.

"There," she said, pointing to an old court listing.

I shook my head beside her, not seeing anything of relevance. She dropped the tab and put up another.

"And there," she said again, pointing towards the thick paragraphs of typed text.

"What am I supposed to be looking at?"

"These court cases, the ones about the missing girls, the sexual assault cases and the sex trafficking. The cases that were thrown out. The judge presiding over these was Mr Justice Archibald Anderson. Archie Anderson? He was on the list," she continued when I looked at her blankly. "He wasn't a high court judge then, just a county court judge, but it says here that he threw the case out, not the Crown Prosecution Service. The sex trafficking, the Northern Pipeline you called it. If this was what it was, then he has to be complicit in it."

I stood up, folding my arms over my chest, my eyes now picking out his name in the documents as Nat flicked through them.

"You know, I think you're right."

"I'm always right V."

I rolled my eyes, and she elbowed me in the side of my leg.

"We need to get over there and confront him. Bet he's got the money to k, k, to order the hit," she said, looking up at me now with caramel-brown doe eyes.

"I'll go and see him. You will be staying here, Nat."

"Please," her voice held a note of desperation, the slightest hint she might beg, and I really liked it, "please V, I need to do this."

"You don't," I answered, walking back through to the apartment as she followed me like a faithful sheep dog.

"V, I need this to end. I need my life back."

I walked up the steps to my bedroom and into my cupboard, rifling through my hangers for a t-shirt.

"You need to actually be alive to have your life back, Nat," I said, shaking my head and reaching for the black holdall at the top of the wardrobe, "it's a no from me."

"For fuck's sake, V."

My fingers felt for the hard plastic strips, and I pushed them in my pocket, turning to face her. Then, squatting slightly, I dug my shoulder under her tits, grabbed her and threw her over my back. She squeaked in surprise, the sound naïve and beautifully vulnerable for just a fraction of a second, before her arms and legs pumped in rage against me.

"What are you doing? Put me down!" she shouted angrily.

I walked her to the bed and dropped her onto her back, hearing the little whoosh of air pushed from her lungs, a mixture of surprise and the pressure from being deposited onto the mattress. Grabbing her right arm, I pulled it above her head and slipped the black plastic cable tie around it. I looped another through the plastic bracelet she now wore and secured it to the metal pole that ran along the entire headboard of the bed.

"What? V what are you doing?" She shouted as I got to my feet and made for the stairs.

"Just making sure you stay inside while I'm gone."

"No! You can't leave me like this!" she shouted after me, anger rising in her voice.

"Oh I fucking can, babe."

"V! Don't you dare!"

I left the apartment, the sound of her shouts and screams behind me sending a smile to my lips and the blood rushing to my groin. But first, I had a Judge to see about a contract.

*****

The little country road wrapped around sharp bends and hills; a biker's dream, but it ended far too quickly. I turned off the road, weaving the bike in and out of the potholes of the bumpy gravelled track, only wide enough for one car. It was flanked by a thick hawthorn bush on one side, threatening to tear holes in my jeans if I got too close, and a well-kept lawn on either side. Three huge chimneys poked above the trees as I approached the house, and, as I rounded the corner, the rest of the red brick property came into view. The house sprawled over the lawns that surrounded it, the driveway changing to pebbled stone. I slowed the motorbike down as it slid through the loose pebbles that led right up to three wide steps at the front.

The house seemed quiet, still. Even just approaching the front door, something felt off. I knocked and waited, listening for footsteps inside, watching for the twitch of curtains. Nothing. Two cars were parked in the drive, suggesting the inhabitants were home. I waited a bit longer before knocking again, the big brass knocker echoing around the grounds, but still no one came. I walked towards one of the bay windows that jutted out in its white painted frame and peered through the murky glass. The top of someone's head poked above the headrest of an armchair, a hand propped on the arm rest.

I went back to the front door, pulled my bike gloves back over my hands and turned the handle, feeling the little pop as the lock clicked out of place and the door sprung open. I didn't need to get much further in the house to know what lay ahead. The smell hit me first; a combination of rotten meat and rubbish, pungent yet sweet. Death. I pushed my hand against my nose, trying to concentrate on something else, not the putrid wisps of the scent that threatened to make me evacuate my stomach contents all over the floor.

Pushing the door open into the room I'd seen through the window, the smell hit me hard, like I'd stuck my head in a cupboard full of rotten food. I gagged, clamping my hand harder over my nose and mouth. A woman sat in an armchair opposite me, blank soulless eyes staring into nothingness and a neat hole in the middle of her forehead.

I looked across the room to the right, my eyes taking a bit more time to focus on the body that lay face-up on the floor. Blood that had soaked into the light cream carpet had now

187

dried, twisting clumps of the thick pile into twisted red peaks. The man stared at the fireplace in front of him, his eyes cloudy, his body empty of life, two bloody holes in his chest. They had shot the woman first, not giving her a chance to get out of her chair opposite the door. I suspected the man, Archie Anderson, had either run to her aid or for his life. Either way, a quick double tap and it had been lights out. And now this lead was quite literally a dead end. Fuck.

I left the house, carefully leaving everything as I had found it. I drove the bike off the pebbles, stopping on the pothole ridden drive and returning to kick the little stones over the tyre marks I made. Then I opened the throttle and got the fuck out of there.

I cut the engine of the bike off outside the gym on the south side of the Tyne Bridge, and, letting it settle onto the stand, I pushed the intercom button on the door entry system. Eventually, with a crackle, a body-less voice with a light Scottish accent greeted me.

"Someone need a Boneman?" I said into the intercom.

"Fuck," the voice on the other side rumbled.

The intercom clicked off, and a buzz followed, the light on the entry door turning from red to green. I pushed the door open and climbed the million fucking stairs into the gym, scowling at the red painted words of encouragement laced with sarcasm, plastered over the walls. *'There's no elevator to success'*, the red writing read as I heaved up each narrow step. Fucking Cameron and his wanky phrases. At the top of the stairs the atmosphere inside was buzzing, music pumping through the speakers, lycra clad women leaving a room in front of me.

"In here," the Scottish accent growled from the office to the side.

I walked in and shut the door securely behind me, pulling the horizontal blinds closed to cut-off any prying eyes.

"What's going on V?" Eli asked, sitting casually on a leather sofa against the side wall.

"I need you to get Cian on the line too. I'm gonna need a whole team approach to this one."

Eli exchanged glances with Cameron and then nodded and took out his mobile, his finger moving over the touch screen until a dial tone filled the room.

"What?" the Irish voice grunted over the speakers.

"Hey, Kee. We've got an even bigger fucking problem."

"She'd better be alive," he answered, and I felt the eyes of the others bearing into me, waiting for some sort of explanation for the unannounced visit.

"She's totally fine," I replied, "I've got Cian's sister-in-law at my place. There's a contract out on her head," I filled the other two in quickly.

"Do you know who ordered it yet?" Cian asked over the phone.

"No. I'm close, we're close. But it is connected to the Northern Pipeline."

"Fuck!"

Eli and Cameron looked at each other, a darkness creeping across their eyes.

"I need to get her somewhere safer. And I need you lot to figure this shit out, with all your sources. Because if we don't take the hit down soon, she'll die."

The words felt more sinister on my tongue than in my head, and a wave of coldness and dread crept through me.

"Alright, bud," Eli leant forward, "you need the cottage?"

I nodded. The cottage would be ideal. It was in the middle of nowhere and well stocked.

"But I also need to get her there safely."

Eli sighed.

"Bud, I'm sorry. I can man operations and intelligence from here. I can rough a few leads up for you. But I can't leave Ava. She's having some complications with the baby. It might have to come early."

"Shit, mate. I had no idea. Congrats," but I couldn't hide the disappointment in my tone.

"V, I'll get men up to you. You just need to sit tight a couple more days. We've some stuff to take care of here first," Cian offered.

My mobile buzzed, the alarm sounding in my pocket.

"Fuck!"

The room went silent, all eyes and ears on me. I checked the cameras, looking for the one that had been triggered, and Eli moved to stand over my shoulder. I stared at the screen, watching Natalie look directly at the camera in my bedroom, her hands between her legs, her fingertips moving under the fabric of her knickers, her eyes focused on me.

"Shit, mate," Eli grinned and stepped away.

"What is it?" Cian barked over the phone, "what's wrong?"

"V seems to have a woman tied to his bed," Eli chuckled.

"What?" Cian's voice rang through the office, "V you'd better not have fucked my sister-in-law. You're supposed to be keeping her alive, not fucking her brains out. And why the fuck have you tied her to the bed?"

I grinned and put the phone inside my jacket pocket.

Chapter Twenty Three

‍Natalie

I stopped screaming when I realised he wasn't coming back, when the motorbike in the garage below roared to life and the heavy metal shutter rumbled open. I wriggled, trying to pull the cable ties off over my hand, trying to slide it over my wrist, but no matter what shape I put my fingers into, the plastic wouldn't move. I tried pulling against it, even using my other hand to snap it, but all it did was cause the plastic to bite painfully into my flesh.

Kicking my legs in frustration, I shouted at no one, just into the silence of the apartment, and then gave up, lying on my back and staring at the ceiling. Even on the mezzanine level, the ceiling was still a good few metres high, its steel girders staring back at me. I'd bet it would cost a fortune to heat this place. There were no curtains over its millions of windows and I'd only seen a few radiators dotted about. The floor was all wood. The expensive real deal, and the only floor covering, was a rug in the lounge area. It was a bachelor pad, modern and simple.

I must have drifted off to sleep from sheer boredom as when I opened my eyes again, the sun was blazing through the windows, soft and warm on my skin. I turned onto my right hand-side, eyeing the red digits on the alarm clock beside the bed, my arm sliding all the way to the far end of the headboard, the ties moving easily over the singular metal pole that ran from one side to the other. The Viking had been gone two hours. And I was bored, really bored. And a really stupid idea had formed in my head.

I shuffled to the other side of the bed, methodically moving my arse, then my upper body and sliding my tied hand along the metal pole until I was on the other side of the bed where I'd seen him kick off a pair of boots the night before. They were still there, left where he just walked out of them. I reached a leg out, poking and pushing and pulling the boot towards me with my foot until it was close enough that my fingers just brushed the top. With another few moments of careful fumbling, I'd teased one of them into my hand, and then, with all my might, launched it over the glass barrier and down onto the floor below.

The alarm came blaring to life. Shrill and loud, and I clasped my free hand over an ear, pushing the other into the pillow below me, while my brain worked to get used to the noise. Then from above a camera whirred, the lens searching the room for the source of the disturbance, and I slid a hand down the front of my knickers. I focussed on the camera as it moved back towards the bed on its axis, and I let my fingers glide over my lips, moisture building

193

at my entrance, my body reacting to my touch. And suddenly it felt good, not just a gesture to goad the Viking. I liked it, the feel of my body reacting, my stomach tensing, the little throb developing with each pass of my fingertips, my pussy wanting more, needing more and I slipped my fingers inside myself, closing my eyes, enjoying the sensation.

The siren of the alarm shut off, a small series of beeps of the system resetting itself. I knew he had seen. And now I waited, watching the time flick by on the clock. My insides hot and heavy, tingling with promises of more, awakened and ready.

It took a good twenty minutes before I heard the roar of a motorbike. It was faint at first, a low rumble some way off, but soon the noise was definite and filled the silence around me. The garage doors rattled as the metal shutter was raised, and then the whole building seemed to purr with the noise of the bike underneath. I listened to the chorus of the various alarms, tracking him as he moved through the warehouse, tension and excitement building in me, the anticipation of seeing someone filling my chest, feelings I'd almost forgotten about over the last few years. I felt like a schoolgirl again, the flutter of new sensations and emotions stroking at my insides, desperation to see the face of your crush, to have their attention fixed on you.

The apartment door beeped shrilly, making me jump, even though I knew he was coming. Rolling onto my side, I peered through the glass barriers, his eyes meeting mine, a hardness on his face that made my heart stall with a sudden jolt of uncertainty. The Viking's footsteps were heavy against the wooden stairs, as if he was deliberately slowing himself down, teasing me with his presence. He moved round the edge of the bed, toeing off the boots he was wearing and stopping at the bottom, crossing his arms over his chest, the muscles of his tattooed biceps bulging against the short sleeves of his t-shirt.

"You're going to do it all again for me, babe," his voice rumbled through the apartment like the exhaust of his bike.

"What?" I whispered, feeling the heat of embarrassment licking at my cheeks.

"You wanted my attention? You got it now. So I am going to stay right here and watch you get yourself all wet and ready for me to fuck you."

"I, err…"

The bed dipped as he knelt onto it, stalking forwards like a predator hunting his prey. The blue-green of his eyes focussed on me and then he pushed my legs apart, positioning himself just between them. I scooted backwards, as far as the headboard and cable tie would allow, but he edged closer, until reaching up, he grabbed my free hand and pulled it down between my legs. Moving his hand over mine, both of us stroked over the fabric that covered me, blood rushing to the spot between my legs and my stomach clenched.

The Viking pulled our hands back up my stomach, before sliding them under my knickers, pushing my fingers over the smoothness of my skin, through the fire burning inside. Both our fingertips slid through the dampness that had begun the minute he had set that hungry stare on me. Then he pushed his fingers into mine, pushing mine inside of me, his hand stopping me from pulling away. Shamelessly I rocked my hips into both of us, feeling the pressure against me, in me. The two of us, fucking my pussy together with our fingers.

For a moment he took his hand away, and I felt the rough pads of his fingers on my hips, gliding my knickers down over my legs and I watched him watching me. His eyes had darkened, the dilation of his pupils stealing away the beautiful colour of his irises. The Viking's lips pushed together, tension in his jaw as I rubbed and moved in and out of myself, moving in tiny circles, my pelvis rocking to the rhythm of my fingers, grinding my clit against my own palm. My breathing picked up speed, a tingling starting deep inside of me, radiating upwards into my stomach. I moaned loudly, my head lolling back onto the top of the metal bar of the headboard.

Then he seized my hand, pulling it away suddenly, his fingers tight around my wrist as he wrenched it above my head, covering me with his body.

"You're not coming yet, babe," he growled into my ear, and I felt the cold of something slipping over my wrist.

I tried to pull my arm away, but it was now fastened as tightly as the other to the metal pole. His hands slid down my body, over the top of the t-shirt, and I felt him grip the bottom, pushing it up to my chin, exposing nearly every part of me to him. The slight chill in the spring air tickled at my skin, and my nipples contracted immediately. There was a look in his eye, a lick of his lips, but he didn't touch them.

Positioning himself between my legs once more, he grabbed at my thighs, digging into my flesh, wrenching me down the bed until the ties binding my wrists stopped me and I winced at the sudden bite of plastic against my skin. The Viking pushed my legs wider, his eyes dipping to where I lay helplessly exposed, his thumbs sliding up the inside of sensitive skin, making me flinch as the entire area came alive, stimulated. Then he pulled at the delicate skin, prizing me apart, a low grumble resonating from his throat, before dropping his head and I felt the first stroke of his tongue against me. I shivered.

V moved against me, lapping and then swirling around my clit, tasting and sucking, his fingers keeping me open to him, as his tongue dipped in and out. He growled with each thrust and lick of his tongue, wet vibrations coursing through me. My stomach somersaulted with each swipe, each time he sucked on my swollen clit, heat and pressure building and an overwhelming need to ride his face, to press myself against the scratch of his beard. But the ties stopped me moving the way I wanted to, and his fingers kept me in position, keeping me on the edge of orgasm, desperate for more.

I groaned, trying to move my hips into him.

"You ready to come, babe?" He spoke the words against me, sending another shiver through my core, massaging my insides, so, so close but not quite there.

"Yes," I answered, barely able to put the simplest of words together.

Then he stopped, moving away, and sitting up onto his knees.

"What are you doing? Don't stop. Please," I begged, shamelessly.

The Viking grinned mischievously, before pulling off his t-shirt and wriggling out of his jeans. The tapestry of black and white on his body seemed to tighten over his muscles, and the thickness of his erection was stark against the inked colour on his skin. And now I knew the piercings were there and the brutal ecstasy they offered, there was no way I could miss the metal protruding out the head of his cock. If he had still been touching me, I'm sure the very sight of him, hard and erect and the cheeky smile on his face, would have been enough to send me over the edge.

He crawled on top of me, teasing me with the tip, rubbing against me, forcing another flood of hot wetness to my pussy. Then he slid his tongue up my skin, trailing it from my belly button and up over my breast, swirling and nipping at the peaks that awaited him, moving to the other side and repeating as I pushed my hips towards him, desperate to feel him inside me, no matter how sore I already was.

I felt the fumble of his fingers, the sweep of his knuckles against me as he sheathed himself, rolling the condom on in painfully slow strokes, and I thought I was about to self-combust at the raw heat that was collecting between my legs. Then he leant forward, taking my mouth, thrusting his tongue and dick inside me all at once. No edging in. No time for me to adjust to the thickness of his cock or the bulge of the piercings in the end. Filling me full in one thrust, the barbells under the condom scraped and pulled, hurting and pleasuring, sending a flood of contradictions through me.

He moved on top of me, slowly at first, pulling all the way out and then forcing that thick shaft all the way back in, till he was buried in me, deliciously deep. Then slowly, gradually, he picked up speed, thrusting and moving and I clasped my legs around his waist, drawing him closer, taking every bit of him. The Vikings lips moved over my body, sucking my neck, my collar bone, pinching my nipples, whilst my hands were bound, unable to touch or feel him through my fingers, unable to slide over his skin or round his back to pull him against me. And I was at his mercy.

His hand dropped in between us, his thumb swirling round my sensitive swollen bud, forcing electric through my body and I gasped as a heaviness built in my pussy. His pierced cock still punished my insides, relentless, his fingers teasing my clit in furious time with his thrusts.

"Oh fuck," I cried out, biting down on my lip, trying to keep my screams at bay as the

199

piercings pulled and pushed against the delicate skin inside me.

"Not yet, babe. You're not coming just yet. Don't think you can finger fuck yourself on camera to get my attention and not get punished for it," the Viking muttered, his lips hot on my neck and he moved his hand away, slowing down and pulling out of me.

"No," I whimpered, "please, I need this. I need you V."

"Oh, you're gonna get me," he growled, just under my earlobe, sending vibrations washing over my skin, his hands moving to my hips.

Then, with one fluid moment, he tipped me over onto my face, my arms twisting painfully above my head, crossing on the headboard, the plastic ties biting into my wrists, pain and a peculiar pleasure hitting me in the stomach. I felt the bulge of his cock against me, sliding through my juices, teasing over my entrance as one hand grabbed my hip, forcing me down on him. My pussy clamped and strained against the tightness as he made his way inside of me, against the bumps of the barbells, setting a fire off in my stomach. I cried out suddenly, my voice echoing around the apartment, coming back at me as if was someone else's and he grunted behind me in response.

Chapter Twenty Four

❧ The Viking ☙

I flipped her body round, her arms twisting under the ties that held her to the headboard. I let my hands run down her body for a moment, feeling the weight of her tits as they hung from under her and the roundness of her hips as they bulged out from her waist. Her arse was round and fleshy, and her pussy was hot and tight.

Then I rammed my dick inside of her, listening to the gasp as the barbells at the end pulled against her flesh and tugged against my cock. I groaned, low and animalistic as she settled back around me, stoking the burn in my groin, my hands slipping over her beautiful, naked body. Digging my fingers into the flesh of her arse, I parted her cheeks, watching my dick sliding in and out, pleasuring and punishing with the metal I was forcing inside of her.

Pumping my hips, slowly at first, enjoying the feel of her tight pussy clamping around me, pulling against me with every tiny movement. She squeezed and tormented me, grabbing hungrily at my cock, tightness clutching the barbells in the end, forcing a fresh set of electrified pulses along my shaft. Her insides clenched and dragged at the piercings with each stroke, the tiny movements of the metal on the end throbbing up my length like static electricity, tingling and biting, goading me to go faster, to pound into her until I erupted. But I didn't. I waited, and I savoured her; my eyes roaming all over the back of her body, on her unblemished skin, not a piercing nor a tattoo in sight. Her skin was pure, untouched, like her soul, like her heart.

Leaning forward over the top of her I wrapped a hand round her neck, sliding another underneath her, my fingers skimming up the smooth flesh of her stomach, over the bulge of her tits, her nipples mere hardened buds, ripe to be squeezed, and twisted. My hips pistoned steadily, rhythmically into her and she sat back into me with each thrust, meeting each movement, a strangled cry each time I bottomed out. I trailed my lips over her back, dancing across her shoulders, nipping the taut muscle of her traps that were pulled tight by the tension against her arms where she was tied to the headboard.

She couldn't get away from me. I had her impaled on my cock from behind and restrained. She was a fucking beautiful sight. And everywhere I kissed her, everywhere my hands wandered over, was mine, mine to do with as I wished, mine to bite and lick, mine to suck and pleasure. My hips picked up speed, my hand squeezing tight round her neck, the other kneading at the flesh of her tit, teasing the sensitive nipple, sending her body squirming against me, unsure whether she wanted to get away or whether she was desperate for more.

Natalie's breathing became ragged, her moans loud, her hips bucking against mine as she whispered 'please' over and over again. And I would give her what she wanted. I would fuck her sweet cunt until she cried and begged for me to stop. Heat and pressure and static electricity gathered between my legs, my heart racing, my body thrusting into her wildly, my grunts filling the apartment. Fuck, she was amazing. My body tensed, my balls shuddered and contracted and I threw my head back as I buried my cock into her as far as I could. She whimpered underneath me, like an animal caught in a trap, her strangled voice all kinds of delicious, knocking me right over the edge.

"You're fucking mine, Nat," I roared, pumping hard into her, my hands moving to her hips to pull her against me with each urgent thrust, the barbells in her pussy clawing against her, my head thrown back in glory as her cries filled the apartment and I hammered into her relentlessly. Fuck.

Collapsing on top of her, I pushed her flat against the bed, the pair of us panting together, her arms still twisted above her head, straining against the cable ties that held her in place. I could leave her there all day, naked and tied up. I could lie here next to her and let my hands roam all over beautiful body, let my fingers investigate every curve, every angle, see if there was anything less than perfect on her amazing body, on her smooth skin and soft flesh.

"V," she whispered, her voice hoarse, "my wrists hurt."

I prized myself off her, turning her over and then feeling around the floor for my knife. Carefully, I slid the tip of the blade under the black plastic, tugging gently and then feeling the pop as the ties broke in two. Natalie sighed, pulling her wrists into herself and rubbing around her bare skin. I lay back down next to her, propping myself up onto an elbow, and pulled one of her arms towards me. The skin around her wrist was red and angry from where I'd tied her, a mark that she would wear for the next few days. I turned her hand over and kissed her wrist gently, as if I could taste the damaged skin underneath, taste my claim on her body.

When I let go of her hand, she shuffled closer, the heat of our bodies mingling, our scents joining together, a light mix of sweat, the modest tangle of her perfume and my aftershave and the heavy muskiness of sex. Natalie reached forward, pushing back some hair that hung round my face. Her fingers were gentle, lingering on the side of my head and tracing my tattoo, her keen eyes mesmerised by the shapes and swirls. She dropped her hand to my neck, swiping over the images inked there, feeling over every little detail like it was some sort of braille, her fingertips reading the pattern on my skin.

"Do these mean anything, V?" She asked.

I thought of all the things I could tell her, that I just like a certain artwork, or that the hundreds of individual pictures etched into my

204

skin meant nothing more than my love of tattoos. I sighed, searching her eyes, finding the courage to put it into words. I wouldn't lie to her. I could avoid the truth over and over, but I couldn't lie.

"There is a picture on my skin for each life I've taken. So that I never forget that I've killed someone, that I've ended someone's life. That it was never my right to do that."

"I thought you only killed bad people?"

"I do. Now."

"What do you mean?" She asked, her voice a little fainter.

"When I was in the army, that wasn't always the case. Sometimes we'd get bad intelligence and the people we killed were innocent. Sometimes civilians, women and children, got caught in the crossfire."

I felt the dark chasm of sadness peeling open inside my chest, precariously heavy, a great Pandora's box that I was scared of opening.

"For each of those lives, I tattooed a reminder on my skin. So that I will never forget them."

Natalie snatched her hand away, as if she'd touched something putrid, something diseased, and I recognised the look in her eyes; disgust, disappointment, judgement. I'd seen it for years when people looked at me, but seeing it on her face, even though I was expecting it, felt like she'd kicked me in the balls. My stomach flinched, the deep, sickening feeling of nausea sinking into the pit of my gut.

"So many lives," she whispered.

I nodded, silently, watching as her eyes roamed my skin, darting from one tattoo to the next, fear and loathing making the caramel-brown darken, widen. Yet she didn't shuffle away from me as I expected her to, but stayed close, letting her fingers wander back over my skin as if she was following a map, her face contorting into a mask of thoughts and expressions I couldn't decipher.

"Why? Why do you kill people?" She asked.

"The army trained us. We were elite soldiers Eli, Cameron, Cian and I and some others in our unit. Talented, strong, ever so slightly psychopathic. You have to be to continually take lives. To ignore the guilt that you have taken that away from someone, taken away someone's dad, son, brother, sister, mother. They took us and they trained us harder. Made us lethal. In the end, I was sick of the collateral damage, the shit intelligence and the innocent lives. My skin was stained with their blood, the tattoos filling in the space quickly. So I left. I went AWOL, and I have been that way since.

"And now I don't exist. I'm not even a ghost. It's hard to get work. So I started doing odd jobs for some of the more dubious people I knew. I would scrape together some cash, drink it away in a bar and piss it back up a wall. It was the only way I could stop seeing their faces. I took on bigger and more dangerous jobs. The adrenaline rush stilled the screams in my head for a little while, chased the guilt into a dark corner for a few hours.

"Then one day a guy walked into a bar. He was well dressed, looked like he earned a bob or two, but his eyes were wild, his face contorted in anger and pain. He asked around the bar about a few gang members. Wasn't too discreet about it. Turns out the bastards had raped his daughter. I offered him my services for a fee, and that's where it started. Every kill after that diluted their voices in my head, dulled their faces when I closed my eyes."

"Do you like it? Your job?" Natalie asked, her voice weak, a slight tremble to her lips.

I nodded, "Yes. Every time I pull that trigger, every time I thrust my knife, it's one less scumbag on the street. One less dealer peddling drugs to kids, one less rapist, one less wife beater. I'll never take an innocent life again. There will never ever be innocent collateral damage ever again."

Natalie watched me intently, the warm brown of her irises back, the earlier revulsion replaced by something else; understanding.

"I think you are the only man who has never lied to me, V. The only one who answers me honestly, even if I don't like the answers you give."

And then she pushed her fingers into my hair, pulling my face towards her and brushing her lips across mine, gently tugging hers against them. A delicate, meaningful kiss. It wasn't lust and desire, or control and gratification. It was raw, and tender, and passionate. And I kissed her back the same way, not letting my thoughts sink to my groin but staying with her in the moment, feeling the soft flesh of her lips, the gentle tentative swish of her tongue against mine. I ran my hand up over her beautiful hips, over her silky skin, and rested it between her shoulder blades. I didn't force her into me, but I held her there, holding on to the gentleness of the moment, holding onto the feeling of being emotionally close to someone for the first time in years, the cage of loneliness around my heart cracking ever-so-slightly.

Chapter Twenty Five

☙ Natalie ❧

The Viking's arm lay heavy around me, a great tree branch stretching over my stomach, holding me possessively. My eyes moved over the symbols and pictures scratched into his skin, a tapestry of black and grey, devoid of colour, ominous and sorrowful. Pictures of lives taken too soon. The thought still frightened me, filling me with a sense of dread and foreboding, of disgust if I let it. And I should let it. I should let it fill me with fear and hatred to think the man I lay with had killed so many people. And enjoyed it. But it didn't. There was a stark honesty in his soul, black though it was.

My life had changed so much in so little time. I didn't even know what day it was, what work was thinking about my sudden sabbatical, what Charlie was doing. Had Uncle Wes tried to contact me? Had anyone told him what was happening? Or were they keeping him in the dark just as much? How had my life become so fucked up? Not that long ago, I was a mere solicitor, doing my job, living my life. I had a partner, a career, freedom.

But had I really been living? My heart felt heavy, swelling with emotion, feelings I normally kept buried. For the last two years I'd focussed on moving forwards. Finding someone to settle down with, having my own family, filling the huge hole my father left after he was taken from me so brutally. Yet all I'd left behind was a plague of broken relationships. DI Steve Burrows, Carter, they were the same as the men that had come before. Not one of them feeling right.

Yet here I was, wrapped in the arms of a hitman, the pair of us so far opposite each other we'd need a map to somehow find some common ground. He was all I hated in a man; tattooed, heavily muscled, hair as long as my own, a criminal, a killer. Yet I felt the most comfortable lying naked next to him, after he'd ravished my body with the metal in his dick with the best sex I'd ever had, and been more honest with me than any man in my life, including my father.

My own father.

Something in my head clicked. A sudden need to get back to the files. Some information coming to life, buried in my memories long ago. A piece of a jigsaw puzzle snapping into place. I wriggled out from under the Viking's arm, pulling on some clothes to ward off the cold night air that had crept into the apartment.

Lights twinkled in the distance, an orange glow from the streetlamps of the industrial estate outside the perimeter of the hitman's compound. I pulled the boxes out from behind the settee, thumbing through the reorganised papers. I'd seen an envelope, thick with information and cuttings, yet I'd filed it, thinking it was the same as most of the articles in the boxes. I pulled the manilla envelope from the back of the box, peeling the flap loose, years' old gum cracking under the assault.

Family photos. I pulled the first out. Sixteen-year-old me sat with my mother, both of us smiling. Not a care in the world, no idea of the hell that was waiting for us around the corner. I smiled, sadness rising inside me. The next photo was the three of us; my mother, father and I. I was younger; eleven, maybe twelve. Then another photo. This time, there were two women. My mother and a blonde girl. The blonde girl was young herself, maybe eighteen, possibly older. The girl sat with my mother in the next picture, a baby held in her arms, with dimples in each cheek. But as I looked closer, holding the picture up to my face, I could see the faint dint of dimples in the girl's cheeks too and the same baby blue eyes. I recognised the baby from the pictures my father had all over his house. The ones I'd packed carefully away after he had died. Me and Charlie, and my mother, all of us. But I had never seen the blonde girl before, with her ash blonde hair and dimples in either cheek.

I swivelled, wrenching the lid off the other box, pulling out the pile of newspaper clippings, the girl in the photo with my mother, familiar. I pulled out the article I had seen, two articles stapled together. The first article detailed that millionaire businessmen Jeremy Dodson had been helping the police with enquiries following a complaint of rape at a party held at his Newcastle mansion. The next article was eighteen months later. It told of a missing girl, twenty-year-old Valentina. She was beautiful, her face radiating from the picture on the paper. The same face of the girl sat with my mother and the baby. The baby with Charlie's dimples. Shit.

I sat staring at the pictures, looking from one to the other and then at the newspaper cuttings, horror seeping into every part of me. An idea formed in my head, a horrific, sickening feeling that there was something far sinister to all of this, to the boxes in front of me, the price on my head and the nauseating feeling of dread that my parents' deaths were all connected.

Something shrill pierced the air. A scream. A siren. A banshee. For a moment I sat confused, pressing my hands to my ears to block out the hideous shrieking. Feet thundered down the stairs above me, heavy boots on the bare wood. A voice getting louder.

"Nat! Nat!"

A bang roared through the building from below us, shaking the floor like a mini earthquake. I looked around wildly, my brain desperately searching for some sort of sense amongst the chaos. A hand grabbed my arm roughly, fingers biting painfully into the muscle, yanking me to my feet.

"Nat!" the Viking's voice was right on top of me, pulling me back towards him.

He pulled me across the room, moving fast, my feet missing a stride and stumbling. But his arms were under me in a second, holding me up, hauling me back up the stairs to the mezzanine bedroom, to higher ground. The door to the apartment burst inwards, the sound of an explosion ripping through the air.

Grunting beside me, muscles bulging in his arms and across his chest, he moved the bed onto its side, propping it against the glass barrier. He tugged my arm, pulling me down behind the cover of the mattress and the wooden base.

"Stay here. Don't move," he said, then he darted away, the air filling with loud pops.

I watched him jump into the wardrobe, fumbling around in the back, the swish of doors sliding back as he grabbed black objects and tucked them into the waistband of his jeans, his chest bare. Below us, heavy feet pounded the wooden floor. I strained my ears listening. The air had gone silent, taken over by the slight clump of footsteps moving towards us. I couldn't make out how many pairs of feet moved in the apartment, but there was definitely more than one. The Viking slid back in next to me. The sound of hollow metals moving across each other caught my attention, a sound I'd only heard in films, and I glanced across at him. The black object was snug in his hand, dark in the dawn of early morning that lit up the apartment in filtered light and shades of grey. I swallowed, trying to keep control of the fear that swelled in my throat, unable to tear my eyes away from the gun in his hand, of the reality of the situation

213

and the controlled ease with which he hunkered down beside me, checking and preparing his weapons like we were in the middle of a battle.

And this was a battle. A battle for our lives as the booted feet moved closer. The Viking stood up, pushing his head slightly above the upended bed, then ducking back down as something flew past us, the glass of the windows smashing behind me. He jumped up again, the gun in his hand going off loudly beside me. I flinched, my hands cradling my ears, my heart thumping in my chest, my insides heavy with terror. Boots thundered up the stairs, moving closer. I wanted to bury myself at the base of the bed, hide from reality and pretend that none of this was happening.

V moved out from beside me, his gun sounding again, and there was a dull thump on the stairs and a shout from below.

"Stay here and keep your head down," he growled at me, his eyes hard and focussed and for the first time I saw him for the killer he was.

He scuttled across the room, into the doorway of the walk-in wardrobe, then just as a man reached the top of the stairs I saw the Viking's arm move, the glint of metal gliding through the air lodging in the forehead of the man advancing. V's massive knife was wedged right between his eyes. The man looked up, a fleeting moment before his eyes rolled back and his body collapsed to the floor.

V ran forward, yanking his knife free, blood exploding down the dead man's face like a cork had just been removed and pooling out onto the floor below him. I watched the biker charge down the stairs, a gun in hand, shots firing madly. I peeked around the bed frame. Two heads bobbed from behind the kitchen counter where they had taken cover from the Viking's sudden onslaught, and one man stood exposed in the lounge. Not for long. Two pops tore through the air and the exposed man slumped to the ground, a dull thud below me.

But as that man became merely a body, one of the men from the kitchen charged forwards towards V, knocking the gun from his hand and the room below me erupted into grunts. The assailant threw punches, fast and hard. The Viking blocked and whirled, snapping the man's head back with a blow to his face, parrying and darting out of reach as the man came back at him. V was toying with him, batting his punches away like a bear swatting flies. The tattoos all over his torso seemed to have come alive, moving on their own over his skin as his muscles flexed and his arms moved. And then he seemed to get suddenly bored. Spinning the man round in front of him, he grasped his attacker's head with both of his arms and then pulled it sideways. The attacker looked shocked for a split second, but then V stepped away, the limp body falling to the floor.

The man who remained behind the kitchen counter stood up, grabbing something from behind him, holding it out in front of him as he stalked forwards towards the Viking menacingly. He was huge, almost as broad as he was tall, dwarfing the biker. V pulled out the blade tucked in the back of his jeans and flicked

215

it through the air, the serrated edge moving in a series of arcs, slicing through the tension. And then he dropped lower, beckoning for the gigantic man to come at him and the dance began again as they circled each other.

I hadn't realised I'd crept to the top of the stairs, staring through the glass barrier, pulled into the action like I was entranced. And I was. I hadn't been able to keep my eyes off the Viking. I'd never seen anyone move so gracefully when they were killing someone. Although I'd never seen anyone killed. But now he was retreating. Jumping back as the long kitchen blade wielded by the big man swiped at him. He blocked a tree-branch like arm flailing towards him, but it knocked him backwards under the force alone. He ducked another swipe, dropping to his knees and spinning out sideways, yet the big man still came at him, moving him backwards all the time.

The Viking's legs hit the sofa suddenly, falling backwards and the huge man ran at him. My heart felt like it was going to explode in my chest, the manic beat now morphing in to one long heavy drone of pressure. The big man's arm flew towards V, the kitchen blade grasped in a fist, crashing down on top of him. V rolled sideways and off the sofa, landing on the floor and scrambling back up to his feet. He slashed his serrated blade round, dragging it down the man's back and he howled like a tortured dog, arms flailing, catching the Viking round the side of his head, knocking him to the floor. V's knife clanged on the floorboards and bounced away out of his hand.

The Viking crawled towards it, reaching for the weapon just as the big man regained composure and turned, darting at the blond man, kicking the blade further from his reach before digging his toe hard into V's side. I thought I heard the whoosh of air that was forced out of the Viking's lungs. The heavy booted foot collided in his side again, and he grunted, rolling onto his back. The big man was quick, much quicker than he should be for all that bulk he carried.

The Viking pushed to his feet, not quite straightening, and I could see he was injured. He limped sideways, glancing at the knife that lay across the floor, too far away for him to reach, then his eyes were back on the big man, watching the arm that swung the kitchen knife. The huge man lurched forwards at the biker again, and V darted out the way of the blade, ducking right and then diving to the left, but his movements weren't as nimble and I saw him wince, grabbing at his left arm, red soaking through his fingers.

The big man was going to kill him. My heart felt like it shuddered to a stop, the heaviness in my stomach radiating outwards, all my limbs feeling like lead, despair stoking a darkness in my brain. The Viking needed a distraction. If the big man killed him, there was no way I would survive. And in that moment, I didn't want to survive without him. I couldn't have another person who I care for taken away from me.

Chapter Twenty Six

ఴ The Viking ಞ

My arm stung, blood pulsing from a heavy cut in my bicep that my own bastard kitchen knife had made. My work knife was strewn across the floor, out of reach, and the big man advanced on me. I wasn't small, but he dwarfed me, like some sort of giant hybrid. His arms were heavy and under all the flesh, I could tell he packed some muscle. My ribs felt like they were on fire from the kicking he'd just given me. My gun was out of reach and the big geezer had cut off my route to my weapons store at the back of my wardrobe.

Moving quickly, I ducked away from another swipe of the knife, retreating towards the kitchen, towards a dead end that promised a shit load of weapons if I could steer clear of the massive kitchen knife he wielded. I moved backwards, leading him to where I wanted him. He moved in on me, stepping just in firing range as I wrenched open a cupboard door, bouncing it off the middle of his forehead. He shook his head, a smile tugging at his lips.

"Now, now, doll," he rumbled, "maybe I'll fuck up that pretty face of yours before I slit your throat."

"Ooh, Daddy," I ribbed back, "sounds like my sort of shit."

I backed away a step, watching his face darken a little.

"You like fucking boys, do you big guy?" I continued, watching his jaw tighten, "are you a top or a bottom? Or maybe you don't care as long as you get that dick that you love?"

He launched himself towards me, the knife swinging wildly. I ducked underneath it, sliding past him on my knees, grabbing for the cupboard door behind him that sat just under the counter. My fingers clasped the pan handle, pulling it from the pile of metal pots with a clang. I wrenched it upwards, the massive man turning just a smidgen too slow as I swung the heavy, copper-bottomed pan across the side of his head. Bone crunched under the blow and the big man didn't utter a word as he fell forwards, the knife tumbling from his hand.

I straddled him, reaching forwards and grabbing the knife, yanking his forehead backwards, exposing the soft flesh of his throat. The knife slid across easily, the thin, sharp blade gliding through the fat of his neck, hitting a bit of resistance as it moved across his oesophagus and out the other side. Blood gushed out from the hole and his eyes widened in horror, big brown irises staring up at me. He tried to breathe through the blood slipping down his throat and into his lungs, but the only sound coming from him was a low gurgling noise. And then his eyes went blank, and the bulk of his body went limp under my grip.

I breathed deeply, taking in the soft, fresh metallic smell, tasting the adrenaline coursing through my body and dashing across my tongue. My heart pounded in my chest, adrenaline hitting my brain like an orgasm. The sweet feeling of another life taken rushing through me.

"V?" Her voice was faint behind me.

I turned. Her hands grasped the gun, shaking, but pointing it in my direction all the same. I slid the bloodied kitchen knife onto the bench and turned fully towards her, watching her eyes drop to the corpse at my feet and back at me. The melted caramel had solidified to a darker brown, horror and fear replacing the stubbornness I was used to seeing in her eyes. I moved towards her, and she stepped back, afraid. Then I looked down at myself.

Thick blood ran down from my left arm, soaking my skin in thick gooey claret. My chest was soaked, blood splattered across my tattoos in various different patterns, and my hands were coated red from the jugular of the man I'd just sliced through.

The gun wavered, her arms sinking under the weight, her body convulsing, shock and adrenaline colliding against each other. I held out my hand, beckoning for the weapon, and she pushed it towards me.

"I, I thought you might need that," she whispered, her voice on the very edge of cracking.

"Thanks, babe."

I took the gun from her hand, sliding it on to the bench, watching as her eyes darted over me, to the body behind me, her head turning to eye the scatter of bodies in the apartment. Her lips trembled and her skin washed over, pale and grey. Then she turned and ran towards the bathroom. I followed her, the adrenaline in my body dying down, pain replacing it, heat surging from my ribs and a sharp sting to my bicep. I stood outside the bathroom door, listening to her vomiting.

"Hey, Nat," I called softly, when it sounded like she had finished, pulling a clean t-shirt over my blood-stained body.

No answer.

I pushed the door open tentatively. Natalie was sitting on the floor by the toilet, her arms wrapped round the knees she hugged to her chest. She stared ahead silently, her eyes not even flickering as I walked into the bathroom. I dropped to my knees stiffly, positioning in front of her, blocking her view of the nothingness she stared into.

"Natalie. I know you've just seen some really crazy shit, but I need you to forget about it for a moment."

She didn't move, didn't look at me, just continued to stare straight ahead as if she could see straight through me.

221

"I don't know how they found us," I continued, "but if they have, others will be here soon. We cannot stay here. We've got to get out of here."

She looked at me then, tears collecting in her eyes, shock and terror etched across her face and all I wanted to do was hold her, to tell her it was over and she would be alright. But it wasn't over. And right now, if we didn't move, it wasn't going to be alright. I took her hand gently and pulled, guiding her to her feet, feeling her whole body shake through her slim fingers. I tugged her back up the stairs, stepping over the body slumped at the top and towards the wardrobe. Pulling the bed back into position and then pointing at it.

"Get some stuff together. Make a pile on the bed. Essentials only," I instructed, before turning and walking into the wardrobe, rifling through the back.

I lifted a set of leather motorbike panniers from the shelf, stuffed some clothes in and packed some weapons in amongst them, covering them carefully. Then I collected the clothes Natalie had piled onto the bed and shoved them in the other side.

"What are we going to do with those?" She asked, her voice faint, staring at the corpse going stiff on my stairs.

"I'll come back and sort them later."

"Where are we going?" She asked.

"Somewhere… else."

I rubbed a hand through my hair. This might not be my best idea yet. But I had no other choice. I grabbed the panniers and Natalie's hand, pulling her past the body and out through the apartment. The door to the landing was bust open, the locks dangling from the frame and the wooden surround splintered in all directions. The door down to the garage was the same. I led her to my black Kawasaki and was just about to throw the panniers over it when I noticed the tyres. They were pancaked, huge slashes tearing the rubber. The van beside it had suffered a similar fate. Not one of them was driveable. Fuck.

"What are we going to do?" Nat asked, looking about, bewildered.

I slid my hand down my face, glancing across to the far corner of the garage at the undisturbed dust sheets, eyeing the shape of the bike concealed underneath. We needed to get out of here. This wasn't the time for a flood of painful memories, but I couldn't move towards it, because the minute I cocked my leg over it, it meant something.

"V?" She asked again, panic rising in her voice.

I squeezed my eyes shut and took a deep breath, then stepped towards the bike, whipping the covers off it. The garage lights bounced off the shiny metal of the dual exhausts underneath, the black of the petrol tank gleaming, not a fingerprint or fleck of dust on it. I flung the panniers on the back, securing them and then rummaged in a corner for a petrol canister, emptying the liquid into the tank, the sweet smell of fumes mingling with the sweat from my skin and the metallic smell of the blood still running down under the arm of my leather bike jacket.

A screech tore across the garage floor as I opened the metal cupboard behind the bike, the door catching on a lump of concrete. My fingers ran over the black and white motorcycle jacket, the leather soft underneath the callouses of my hands, sadness echoing around my head. Pulling the zip down, I peeled it off the hanger and grabbed the helmet that sat on the shelf underneath, handing them both to Natalie. My mother was relatively the same size, so the jacket would fit. Natalie shrugged into it without a word, zipping it up snuggly over her larger tits, the leather clinging to the curves of her figure and had we not been running for our lives, I probably would have taken the time to admire her in it. Instead, I inserted the key into the ignition of the bike and turned, the sudden roar from the Harley making the whole garage feel like it was vibrating and then it settled into the guttural purr, low and workmanlike. Natalie pulled the helmet over her face, the black tinted visor obscuring her eyes and stood there sedentary beside the big bike.

"What's wrong? Hop on."

"I've never been on a motorbike before," she answered, her voice heavy with fear once more.

"There's nothing to it, babe. Just keep your feet on the rests and don't put your foot down when we stop. Simple as that."

She nodded silently and tentatively swung her leg over the back, shuffling in behind me. Then, when I felt her arms grip me tightly, I let out the throttle. The roar from the engine filling the garage and pulled away, relieved that the big metal roller shutters still worked, even if the garage door to the side was damaged. But there was no time to properly secure the building. I just had to hope no one would come sniffing about, or they'd get a hell of a shock at what lay waiting for them inside.

The Harley felt alien against me, the vibrations from the engine rattling my bones, sending pulses through my fingers, and the sensation of dread writhing through me. Natalie clung to me tightly, pushing herself into me as if she could sink inside of me and dawn broke around us in its entirety. The bike was loud, turning heads from the occupants of every vehicle we passed. If we were being watched and followed, there was no way I could stay covert on this thing. The steering was heavier, the acceleration slower, and it just felt cumbersome and archaic.

I'd long since given up any respect for the Harley that had all died with my father. But on his bike I felt like a kid again. And part of that felt good, not having anyone rely on me, no real fears, no real responsibilities and no one that I had to keep alive. Yet, over the last week, my duty to keep Cian's sister-in-law breathing had transcended to a raw desire to protect her, and that now made everything fucking complicated.

We passed through Sunderland, weaving ungraciously through the early morning traffic, heads turning to inspect us as the bike rumbled loudly onwards. I checked my mirrors continuously, noting cars and then losing them again a few moments later. No one appeared to be following us. We headed across the Western Bypass, cutting through Birtley, skirting around Gateshead until there was little choice left but to take the road into Northern Kings' territory.

The roads around the back of the riverside industrial estates were almost deserted, factory and industry workers not quite woken up yet. The bike glided over the mottled roads as I steered in and out of potholes until the factories fell away and the trees grew denser.

There were no lights on at the Dog on the Tyne and I pulled into the old car park, the rumble of the heavy engine echoing in the thick mist rolling in off the banks of the Tyne. Indie's van sheltered the row of motorbikes parked up behind it and I counted the number of them, knowing that shit was about to go south when I knocked on that door.

I kicked out the stand, carefully allowing the heavy chrome bike to lean to the side and killing the engine. Holding out my hand I helped Nat off, watching her unfold her legs stiffly as she stood up, the tight jeans and even tighter leather jacket making her a biker goddess as she pulled the black helmet off, her warm brown hair falling loose and catching in the light morning breeze. She smiled at me nervously, reacting to my tension and studying my face, trying to read me like I was her opponent in a courtroom.

Gently, I pulled her along behind me to the paint stripped doors of the pub. My knock filled the air around us, loading the atmosphere with tension and trepidation. The door creaked open, a face I'd not seen for years standing in front of me, sleepy at first but becoming wide awake with realisation. The punch hit me square in the face, my nose splattering under the assault, hot liquid spilling over my lips as I staggered backwards, gentle hands behind me just keeping me on my feet.

"Got a fucking death wish, V?" The voice on the other end growled.

"See you've been working on that right jab, cus," I grumbled, wiping at the blood streaming from the end of my nose.

Chapter Twenty Seven

ඥ Natalie ඞ

The balled fist came from nowhere. The door hadn't even fully opened before the arm shot through the gap, landing square on V's nose. The crack sounded louder in the thick air, the fog not letting the sound dissipate but instead lingering between us. He staggered backwards, cradling his face, and I held my hands out, modestly trying to hold him on his feet.

"What the actual fuck? Why the fuck are you here?" The voice behind the door was filled with anger.

"I'm here to see Indie," the Viking replied, mopping at his nose, his own blood staining his hands red.

"He's not here."

"Indie's always here."

"Not for you, he isn't."

"Just go and fucking get him," the Viking's voice lowered, almost growl like, but the warning in his tone was clear.

The man at the door stepped forward. He was taller than the Viking, but slimmer. His thick, dark hair was cropped short, longer and fuller on the top of his head, where it spiked up on one side and lay flattened on the other as if he had been lying on it. His eyes were dark, dark-brown eyebrows drawn together, making his features even more formidable and a long thin nose that ended in a sharp point.

"You know you've signed your own fucking death sentence coming here, traitor?"

V shrugged his shoulders but said nothing. The man stepped forward again, sizing himself up against the Viking, staring down at him with a cruel, angry glare.

"You've grown, Demon," V answered eventually, looking the angry man up and down, the threat of the man standing mere centimetres from him having little effect, "what are you now, twenty-one?"

"Twenty-eight, fuckwit," the man spat back.

"If you wanna see your next birthday from this position, then you'd better go get Indie."

"You're threatening me?"

The man's hands balled into fists, tension and veins bulging over tightened skin.

"Consider it a polite request to get Indie before I break your legs."

The dark-haired man stepped forward, his body almost touching V's, faces millimetres apart, holding each other's glare like two raging cats.

"Fuck's sake," I muttered from beside V.

I moved around them, leaving them staring angrily into each other's eyes, pushing the pub door open and stepping into the building.

Inside, the expanse of the barroom was dark, a dull orange light from outside casting shadows, thick bundles of black, darker black and grey all over. The sickly stale smell of alcohol on breath hung in the air, collecting with a haze of cigarette smoke. I moved to the bar, scanning the room, catching the tiny tendrils of light that had escaped through the thick curtains reflecting off the liquid spilt over the countertop. Shuffling in the darkness, my eyes struggling to adjust, my toe caught, sending me stumbling forward.

My feet and legs tangled in something on the floor, and I fell sideways, landing heavily on top of a lumpy object. The trip hazard groaned underneath me, as my arms flailed, and I scrambled to my hands and knees. Clinging to the bar counter, I pulled myself upright, my fingers dipping into liquid that lay in puddles, sticky and wet. Then suddenly the pub was bathed in light, every lightbulb in the heavily artexed ceiling ablaze.

A tall figure stood in the doorway behind the bar, his frame filling it, naked apart from a pair of tight boxer shorts.

"What the fuck is going on?" His voice rumbled across the room.

Straightening myself up, I glanced round the pub. A body on the floor propped up onto elbows, thick dark blond hair pushed back over his head, completely naked, and I suddenly realised I was staring at him. I flicked my eyes back to the man in the doorway.

"Hey, darlin'. This cock is free if you wanna hop back on it," the sleepy voice from the floor floated up towards me and I glanced away, trying not to let my eyes linger on any other naked men.

"For fuck's sake, Tiny Tim, get some fucking clothes on," the Viking's voice rumbled from behind me and suddenly the atmosphere in the pub stilled, as if everyone was holding their breath in anticipation of a bomb going off.

The naked man jumped up off the floor where he had been lying, moving to a stretch of padded seats behind him and sliding his legs into a pair of jeans. The tall man that had been standing staring out V walked up behind us, and the grey-haired man in the doorway tipped his head in unenthusiastic greeting before moving to an optic and pushing a shot of dark bronze liquid into a small glass tumbler.

The atmosphere was thick with tension. Half-naked men surrounding us, looking at each other with silent stares and looks of hatred, predators waiting to pounce the minute the grey-haired commander in the boxer shorts gave the nod. What the fuck had we walked into?

"What you doing back here, V?" the grey-haired man asked, then necked the liquid in his glass.

He was nearly as covered in tattoos as the Viking. A colourful trail of ink coated both arms. Pinks, blues, greens and reds. A myriad of colours all over his skin. His grey hair was mussed up, thick tufts straying in every direction, and he looked like he had barely slept. And looking at the mass of glasses that littered the tables, unemptied ash trays and a bar top covered in a cocktail of spilt alcohol, I was thinking that the occupants of the pub hadn't long closed their eyes before we had gate-crashed whatever this was.

"We've been compromised," the Viking replied from beside me, his hand gently looping around my waist and for once I was pleased with the comfort it gave me, even if there was a quiet message at the heart of it.

"Still don't know why you are here, V."

"I need your help, Indie."

"This fucker gets no help from us," the angry tall man spat from behind me.

"Whoever is coming after Nat found us. I've got bodies piling up at my place, Indie. I can't keep her safe anymore."

"And what about your Mafia mates?" The grey-haired man asked calmly, shoving the glass tumbler back under the optic.

"They're at least nine hours away. We didn't have nine hours."

Indie glanced at V and then around the bar and I followed the movement of his head. The angry young man now came and stood beside me, leaning an arm on the bar, his eyes glancing up and down, inspecting me. The man on the floor was now fully clothed, his hair messy, but just behind him was another one. Exactly the same. A carbon copy, wearing the exact same clothes and for a moment I wondered whether I had hit my head. But he nudged his doppelgänger in the arm as he approached, and the two exchanged a glance.

"I don't know how you fucking dare…." the tall angry man stopped when Indie shot him a look.

"What do you want me to do about it?" Indie asked V, sipping at his drink more slowly this time.

V sighed from beside me, shrugging out of his leather biker jacket, wincing as he tugged his left arm free and the grey-haired man's eyes stared at the wound. One of the twins whistled, high-pitched, just a little way off.

"I need this stitching and I need her protecting, even just enough to get this closed up, and the bodies cleaned up at my place. It'll buy us some time. Just a couple of hours."

"You're not really gonna help this twat?" the tall man piped up beside me.

"Shut up, Demon," Indie answered gruffly.

"But our Da…"

"He's not here, is he? Besides, he'll be buried deep in his pit till gone lunchtime. He'll never know V was here. Will he, lads?"

The question was answered in silence and Indie addressed the room again.

"Because if Ste even gets a whiff we didn't break his face the moment we opened the door this morning, we're in as much shit as this twat."

Indie looked around the room pointedly, his eyes lingering on each person until there was a nod of agreement from each twin and eventually the tall man everyone called Demon. The nod was half hearted, a mere dip of his chin, but it came, and I let out a little sigh, my legs suddenly going weak.

"You look like you need a drink, lass," Indie spoke to me, "what's ya poison?"

"Wine, normally. But I'll take a vodka, please. With some coke."

The man nodded, turning back to the optics and pressing a glass up against the dispenser, the clear liquid tinkling into the glass. He slid the tumbler across the damp bar top after adding the coke and I grasped it, gulping down the liquid, the taste hitting the back of my throat and making me pull a face.

"So how bad's that arm?" He turned to the Viking.

V turned sideways, pointing his arm towards Indie and rolling up the sleeve slowly, his eyebrows nipping together in pain. Indie's eyes swept across the split bicep before he pushed his lips together and turned towards the twins.

"Your lass. She's a nurse?" He grunted in their direction.

One of them shrugged.

"Aye, well, she works at the hospital," the other one answered, rubbing at his eyes.

"Get her up."

Twin two turned away and walked to the back of the pub and I could hear the muttering of voices, a drone of tiredness, and then two people moved towards us. The girl was young. Probably Charlie's age, twenty-three, maybe twenty-four at a push. Her highlighted blonde hair stuck out at all angles, and she smoothed it down over her head as she approached, her eyes heavy, still half asleep, or half-cut, or both.

"Can you stitch that?" Indie asked as she approached the bar and stared at the Viking's arm.

She squinted and rubbed her eyes again, stepping closer and screwing her face up.

"I'm just an auxiliary," she said, squeezing the gash in V's arm together, peering at it with one eye, "I just clean people up, and help them eat and that sort of shit."

"So, you can't stitch this?" V grumbled as she prodded around it.

"I mean, I'm studying to become a nurse, but I've never really done any nursey stuff yet."

I rolled my eyes and took another swig of my drink.

"We could glue it, though?" She asked, looking around at the blank faces, a mix of inebriation and confusion, "got any superglue?"

"What? V, I think we should get the hospital to look at that," I waded in, eyeing up

235

the young blonde who was still prodding at the slash in his arm.

The Viking shook his head, "I don't exist, remember? That means no hospitals. Indie, glue?"

The grey-haired man nodded and left the bar, returning a short time later with a tiny tube and some gauze and bandages, and the young girl got to work. Indie slid a bottle of vodka across the bar towards her and I watched the Viking wince as she wiped a vodka-soaked piece of gauze over the wound and then squeezed the glue onto it, nipping it together. Then she pulled the bandage around it, pulling it tight, forcing the injured flesh together and giving the glue time to do its job.

"There," she said eventually, "that should hold. But you're gonna need to rest it."

"Cheers," V answered and then turned back to Indie, staring at him pointedly.

"Thanks lass. All right, Dumb and Dumber, I need you to get your lass out of here. Club business to discuss. Bring Fury back with you."

The twins nodded and ushered the blonde girl out of the bar, Indie and the Viking watching the three of them leave.

"Fucking rest," the Viking muttered, grabbing the bottle of vodka left on the bar and bringing it to his lips, "I've got a fucking house full of bodies. It looks more like a morgue than an apartment."

Indie looked at the tall man who continued to stand beside us, scowling.

"When Fury gets back, I'll get him to drive you over."

The Viking shook his head and went to speak, but the older man cut him off.

"You're compromised anyway, V. We won't come after you. The rest of the Kings don't need to know you are here. They can't know you're here, or we're all in the shit."

The Viking nodded silently, and I glanced sideways at the man they called Demon, whose eyes seemed even darker as he stood quietly, listening and festering.

Chapter Twenty Eight

℘ The Viking ℘

Natalie sat at the bar on a stool at the corner, silently watching, lifting her second glass of vodka and coke to her lips with a slight shake. The place had descended into a strained silence, eyes stealing glances at me and then back again. Apart from Demon, who had spent the last hour as we waited for Fury trying to insert his own eyes into the side of my head by thought alone. And Fury was fucking late, as usual. I needed to get out of here, get the bodies stashed away somewhere, secure my home, and hope that I'd be able to come back to it.

I stared into the little tumbler of neat vodka sitting in front of me. This had all gone tits up. I never once thought protecting Cian's sister-in-law would bring me home to face my demons, and *the* Demon. I was a sitting duck here in Northern King's territory and I was only here by the grace of Indie. I had been warned on no uncertain terms to never return all those years ago, yet here I was. I was as good as dead if Uncle Ste walked in, but so was Nat if I didn't do something. And I could no longer protect her by myself.

Whoever these guys were that had attacked us, with their eclectic jumble of accents and their mismatch of a team, they were good enough to find me. For years I'd cruised around the north east undetected, using different names, different identities and not even my friends knew where I lived. Now that had been blown out of the water by a team of mercenaries. I'd bet the price on Natalie's head had risen. It had to for so many to come after her, which meant that someone, somewhere, was getting desperate.

Whatever information they thought she had, had to be big. It had to blow the entire operation out of the water or else implicate some very important people. My money was on the identities of some of the bigwigs running the pipeline, and that meant, even if I could find the person responsible for the hit, I didn't think I could ever keep her truly safe. And that little nugget of information was manifesting its way inside of me, eating me from the inside out.

Natalie wasn't just any old assignment from Cian. She wasn't just Cian's sister-in-law. And I don't know when everything had suddenly changed. My memories fluttered back to the day in the dingy bar in Sunderland. My mind filled with the recollection of sliding her face out of that thin beige envelope. Her keen stare, her rich brown hair hanging either side of her face, and those red lips. They mesmerised me before that day, just a pair of red lips at Cian's wedding. It was the way she held them tightly together, condescending, arrogant almost, and then when I had pulled that photo out of the packet I'd remembered them. I remembered what I wanted to do to them, where I wanted them to be.

And now I looked across at her. The slight shake to her hand every time she brought the glass to those lips, naked and natural. The tiny way they pushed against the glass, nipping it between the soft flesh, tension clear in the long slow sip she had taken. Her eyes stared at the wall of optics, glassy and distant. I didn't know what she was thinking about, but now and then her brow furrowed and the rise and fall of her chest would speed up before slowing down a short time later as she willed herself to stay in control, of her emotions at least.

I sighed and slid off the bar stool, walking towards her stiffly as my battered muscles ached and my jolted joints creaked. My arm throbbed from the wound the twins' plaything had put back together, flesh swelling under the tight bandage, the vodka doing nothing to numb the pain.

"Hey, babe," I said softly as I got closer, sliding up towards her and leaning over the bar, "how are you holding up?"

Nat took another long sip.

"Why are they coming after me?" She whispered, her eyes still trained on the wall in front of her. "Why me?"

"Somehow, somewhere, even if you don't know it, you hold some valuable information. They know that. And they won't stop till you're dead."

Her head turned towards me slowly, fear and panic in her eyes, the caramel-brown orbs dancing with terror. Yet the rest of her was composed, stoic.

"Then if they'll not stop, what is the point of all this?" She asked, looking around the pub, the interior growing lighter as morning was taking hold.

"Because I'll find a way to stop them. I'll find the person who can make it all stop. I'm not going to let anyone hurt you, babe. No one."

Natalie's lip trembled. Just for a moment and then her top teeth raked across it, biting into it, holding it still.

But right now, even though I'd uttered those words, I didn't know how I was going to protect her. I was an outlaw, running from the military I'd turned my back on, exiled by my own family and I killed people to feed myself. I couldn't raise an army and I couldn't go to the police. This should have been a simple job. Keep Natalie safe, give Cian time to work out who was trying to kill her and instead I had fallen in love with the prize. I'd fallen for the mark. I was an assassin. I was paid to kill, not to keep people alive, at least not anymore. Yet Natalie had become so much more than just a job. More than just a threat from Cian about consequences I didn't want to dwell on. And I'd known it the minute her face had slid out of that envelope.

I needed a plan, and fast. Turning away from her, I pulled the burner phone from my pocket and wandered outside into the morning air, spring sunshine fresh and warm on my cheek, the rumble of traffic on the roads a little way in the distance. Birds tweeted a chorus from the bushes that surrounded the pub and the gentle swish of the water against the banks of the Tyne stilled my whirling brain.

I pressed the phone to my ear, listening to the gentle purrs of the ringtone and eventually there was a click and a second of silence.

"V?" The voice was groggy on the other end of the line, "you know I don't fucking open my eyes at this time of the day. It's practically still night-time."

"Maybe not your eyes, but you're definitely opening that big mouth of yours, complaining like a little bitch."

"What do you need?" He grumbled down the phone.

"I'm going to give you some names and I want everything on them. Everything."

"Got it."

I rattled off the names that were on Nat's dad's list and then added my own.

"Sophie de Winter, Anthony Porter and Natalie de Winter. I want everything from medical records and qualifications to any scrapes with the law."

"Got it. When do you need it by?"

"Yesterday."

I ended the call. A Harley Davidson rumbled in the distance, and I hoped it was the lesser of two evils, because if it was my uncle, I was dead already.

Fury came crashing into the Dog on the Tyne a few moments later, the rage in his eyes making him live up to his nickname.

"Where the fuck is that Barbie doll little cunt?" He roared.

Natalie whipped around, alarm clear on her face, glancing at me, then back at the man standing in the doorway, pulling his helmet from his head. Long, dark hair spilled around his shoulders, a similar length to mine.

"Nice to see you too," I answered, squaring myself up and preparing myself for the wrath I knew was coming.

Fury strode across the space, his steps never faltering, picking up speed as though he was going to ram straight into me. Yet suddenly, from nowhere, a body intervened, intercepting his path, standing and facing him, keeping him from me.

"Enough," she growled, "I've never seen such a bunch of testosterone ridden idiots in one place, and I've worked in youth courts."

"Who are you?" Fury asked, his advance faltering.

"I'm the reason he is here. So, take a breath and stop being, whatever it was that was supposed to be."

Indie chuckled from behind the bar, and I let out a breath, relaxing a little now that I thought it was less likely that Fury was about to rearrange my face. Fury shot her a look, like a petulant child, but moved to the other side of the bar.

"That was pretty brave, or stupid, jumping in front of a raging bull," I said to her quietly, eyeing up the man looking angrier than even Demon was at that moment.

Natalie shrugged.

She swigged back the last of her drink and settled herself on the stool. I stood looking at her, mesmerised. She was intoxicating and interesting, endearing and sexy all at the same time.

"What?" She asked suddenly, "don't you have bodies to bury or something?"

*****

The ride back to Sunderland was anything but comfortable. Fury kept his eyes on the road, never even glancing at me as I directed him through the traffic, and he silently followed my instructions. His jaw clenched tightly together, his eyes narrowed, rage and hatred bubbling just under the control. If I stepped a foot out of place, he would explode.

Fury was formidable. Ex-forces like myself and older, yet where I had gone AWOL, he had been discharged. His temper was too hot to even channel into the job. Even amidst a gunfight, he was just too unstable. Like nitro-glycerine. If you shook him, he would explode. And so I sat in silence.

Eventually, the grey steel fence of my compound loomed up before us. The gates remained locked, the yard clear, looking like the factory unit it was supposed to be. To outsiders Indie's van turning up looked perfectly legitimate, even if we were about to pile up bodies and clearing out any evidence.

I jumped out of the van as it purred beside me, trotting around in front of it to the keypad and stealing a subtle glance at Fury in the driver's seat to make sure he wasn't going to crush me against the fence. The gates unlocked, slowly gliding open to let the van through.

"You live here?" Fury grunted, stepping out of the vehicle as the big roller shuttered door secured us from the outside world.

"Yeah," I answered, a heavy feeling in the pit of my stomach.

I had kept this place secret for years and in a brief space of time, every criminal fucker and his mate now knew where I lived. The door to the side of the garage was bent, the locks blown clean out. The main gates were completely unscathed, and the only conclusion I could make was that they'd scaled the fence. And I hadn't even heard the alarms going off till too late. I'd slept through it. The first time in years.

I tipped my head, beckoning for Fury to follow me. The door at the top of the stairs was bust open, the locks bent and wrenched off. The apartment door had also suffered the same fate, although I'd closed it over when we had left, to hide the bodies a little. I pushed it open and stepped inside.

Fury whistled. The sound stark in the silence of the enormous room. It looked like a massacre had taken place. There was blood splatter up the walls, pools of red soaking the floor and bodies lying where I had dropped them like some sort of war scene.

"Shit, man!" Fury breathed, "someone really hates you."

"It's not me they were after. It was Nat."

"Your lass?"

"She's not mine. Not like that. I just have the job of keeping her alive."

"And satisfied."

I whirled around, taking a step towards him, much too close and getting in his face. He was taller than I was, by a good few inches. And for the first time, he smiled.

"Aye. Right. Come on Barbie, let's get this lot cleared out," he responded before stepping around me and kicking at the first body with the toe of his boot.

Chapter Twenty Nine

⊗ Natalie ⊗

I moved from the bar and sat in the corner by the window. I was tired, and I was terrified. A knot of dread and horror tightening deep in my stomach, radiating outwards from within me, making my limbs feel like lead and my head feel like it was floating. Adrenaline had been good company the last few hours, but now, as it dissipated, the enormity of the situation was closing in.

The threat had worsened. Someone had sent a small army after me and if it hadn't been for one man, I would be dead. But then I would have been dead weeks ago. It was only because of V I was still alive.

"Are you ok?" A gruff voice asked, making me jump.

For a moment I reeled around wildly, ready to dart sideways, or up, or away; a rabbit ready to run from a predator.

"I'm sorry. I didn't mean to frighten you," his voice sounded again, lower, more of a rumble.

"It's ok. I'm just a bit on edge."

"On edge? Think I'd be more than on edge if someone was trying to kill me."

The seat beside me dipped as he perched on the edge that wound around the corner of the wall. I tried to smile, the movement of my lips becoming more of a grimace than anything else.

"Do you have any idea who is behind all this?" Indie asked.

I shook my head.

"Not really. Someone with a lot of money and a lot of clout."

The doors to the pub swung open, the movement catching my eye, and I looked across eagerly, the bodies swamped in the bright back light of the sun outside. But it was two identical men who walked into the bar, not the Viking. They laughed and joked, looking fresher than when I'd first met them, or stood on one of them as he lay sleeping off a skin full on the floor of the bar.

"He'll be back soon, Natalie," Indie rumbled from beside me, "you're safe here with us till then."

"And what after? Am I not safe when he returns?"

"Of course you are."

"And what about V? Is he safe here?"

Indie didn't answer. He sat watching me, deciding what to tell me. His brow furrowed as he contemplated his response.

"The Viking is no longer welcome here," he said eventually.

"Why?"

"We all fell out with him a long time ago. It was not long after his Da died. Death does funny things to you."

"Yeah. It does."

"You sound like you know a thing or two about it?" He asked, his voice lighter, relief at the subject moving from him.

"Both my parents are dead. And somehow my father is sending me messages from beyond the grave. And it's all to do with this mess."

"Connected?"

"I have a horrible feeling it is, somehow. It's like I'm holding all the jigsaw pieces in my hands but can't work out how they go together yet."

"You eaten today?" Indie asked, suddenly.

I shook my head, "didn't have time to grab breakfast. There was a cereal killer on the loose!"

I snorted loudly. The attack of the giggles catching me by surprise, taking hold until my body was shaking, and I was wiping tears from my eyes. Indie grinned back at me, his brown eyes wrinkling at the sides in amusement. Shit. I was cracking up under the pressure. But stupidly, it felt good. I don't think I'd really laughed like that since my dad had died. I'd barely smiled. Yet here I was sat in a pub full of bikers after I'd narrowly survived a group of blood thirsty bounty hunters. I giggled again.

Soon the place was filled with the smell of breakfast wafting in from the kitchen at the back. Demon and the twins were huddled at the bar, talking amongst themselves and occasionally glancing over at me. But I was too tired to feel uncomfortable and too hungry to even care. As long as no one was trying to kill me, I was quite content to sit on the creaky padded seat of the bench that lined the wall.

The big room was bathed in warmth, heat from the sun gently warming my back, lulling me into a false sense of security and making me sleepy. I could just dose off. Just for a few minutes, safe for now amongst these strangers. These men that the Viking seemed to trust despite their disdain for him.

The smell of bacon drew closer, my stomach growling in response. A floorboard close by creaked, my brain firing inside my head and my eyes snapped open, fear sparking in my chest for a split second until I remembered where I was.

The plate dinked on the table in front of me and I rubbed my eyes, my focus sharpening as Indie slid two cups across the table.

"Didn't know whether you were a coffee girl or a tea girl," he said, smiling warmly.

"Actually, I'm more a wine type of girl," I answered, my stomach growling impatiently, "but tea is good, thanks."

"I can get you a wine too?"

I shook my head, swallowing down a mouthful of sandwich.

"No. This is great, thanks."

"Howay, man," one twin called from the bar, "where's ours, like?"

"You lazy fuckers can get your own. You know where the pots are. Don't mind them," Indie continued, looking back towards me.

I smiled, gratefully taking another large mouthful of the bacon sandwich, suppressing the pangs of hunger in my stomach. I almost felt normal. Just for a split second. A belly filling with bacon and relative safety, and someone else to talk to.

"So how do you know, V? Other than being in the same bike club, of course."

Indie's face flinched. His jaw ticked ever so slightly, but the movement stilled as quick as it came.

"I'm V's cousin, and the moody twat over there at the bar is my brother," I followed his gaze to Demon, who was watching me intently, "we have different mothers, thank fuck. At least I'm not completely related to that grumpy shit."

I smiled again. This was becoming a habit.

"The rest are members of the bike club. There's more of us. These are just the reprobates that hang around here like a bad smell; drinking my booze and eating my food."

"Thanks for the food," I gestured towards my plate, the bacon sandwich almost gone, "it was really good."

"I'd say anytime, but really, we don't want the Viking back here."

Indie smiled, but this time the intent behind it wasn't quite there. Instead, his face was contradicted, sad almost.

"That's right," a gruff voice suddenly added from just above us.

I hadn't felt his presence, hadn't heard him creep closer, but he had appeared, quietly in front of us. The grey-haired man glared up at him. Some sort of silent command I couldn't decipher, but the look on Demon's face only darkened.

"We should have slit his throat for returning," the angry man spat, hatred rolling off the end of his tongue.

I glanced from Indie to Demon.

"Why I do I get the feeling that threat is serious?" I asked, unease unravelling in my stomach.

"It's just a disagreement," Indie replied.

But I looked up at the angry young man, darkness emanating from his eyes. He moved quickly, the thump of his fist on the table making me scramble away from him, fight-or-flight senses igniting.

"You like him, don't you?" Demon asked, his tone icy.

I swallowed; my throat suddenly dry.

"The Viking is lucky my Da let him live. I wouldn't. I would have killed him for what he did," the man growled, leaning in towards me.

"Demon," Indie cautioned him, but the words didn't seem to register.

And I shouldn't have let my words slip from my throat, but they did.

"Why?"

"Because he killed my uncle," Demon paused, staring at me, waiting for me to understand. But I didn't understand. Or really, I didn't want to hear it.

"He murdered his own father."

The words hit me hard, slicing through me, my heart staggering in my chest. Shock, disgust, fear and disappointment expanding in my chest like someone was blowing up a balloon inside of me. Yet the worst feeling was betrayal. We'd talked about his parents. I had no idea. None.

A door creaked to my left and two figures moved into the shadows from the bright spring sunshine outside. Masculine voices, chattering and jovial. My head followed the sound of his voice and I watched as he walked towards me. Confident, suave, beautiful. His lips pulled into a smile. How could I have been so stupid? How could I have been so blind to what he really was? I knew what he was. An assassin. A killer. A murderer.

Chapter Thirty

ഌ The Viking ൙

"I need to make a detour," I told Fury as we made our way back towards the Gateshead clubhouse.

"Where?" Fury grumbled.

"The gym."

"You want to go to the fucking gym when we've got a van laden with fucking corpses? Are you for real?"

I shook my head, suppressing a smile.

"I'll be in and out."

The man beside me scowled, but he pulled off the main road, taking the back streets through the industrial estate to the gym, a stone's throw from the Tyne Bridge. Fury tucked the van around the side, cutting the engine and trying to look inconspicuous.

I ran up the stairs and punched the code Eli had given me into the pad at the door, listening for the click of the floor-to-ceiling turn-style as it unlocked to let me in. Inside, the gym was bustling. Men and women lingered around lockers chatting, and above me I could hear the rhythmical pulsing of machines contrasted against the sporadic thump of weights being released onto the floor.

The office door was pushed to but unlocked and I nudged it open. Eli's head snapped upwards, alert and ready to fight, as always.

"Hey V," he greeted me, "what's up?"

His keen eyes studied my face, slowing over the cuts and the fresh bruises.

"I need your cottage keys, Eli. I've been compromised."

"Shit, course V," he answered, rifling in his drawer and then tossing a keyring of chinking metal towards me.

"I'm gonna go off grid until Joey and Cian can work this out."

Eli nodded.

"It's well stocked. Look under the rug."

"Thanks mate."

*****

The pub on the banks of the Tyne was immersed in sunlight when we returned, the fog that had rolled in along the river now chased away by the sun. It was picturesque and peaceful, if you could ignore the dull roar of the traffic on the Old Durham Road not all that far away.

It brought memories back. Of a childhood riding small scrambler bikes around the carpark and up and down the little hillocks at the back of the pub, now rammed tight with trees and weeds. Then later, as a teenager and young adult, of spending my nights getting roaring drunk with the rest of the club, singing and shouting, and vomiting into the River Tyne below. That was when I had friends. Family. Before I joined the army and before I'd killed people. The blackness of those thoughts swarmed around me, constricting my throat and pushing against my chest.

I shook my head and pushed the doors open, the sudden darkness of the pub swallowing me. I blinked, chasing the shadows from my eyes, my pupils struggling to adjust from stepping out of the bright sun outside and into the cosy gloominess of the Dog on the Tyne.

Natalie was sitting at a table, Indie sitting to one side of her and Demon stooping over the top. His shoulders were bunched up, his head low, his gaze locked on to her as he said something to her. Her jaw clenched, and she tipped her chin up at him in a half challenge, but her hands worked against each other, her fingers scratching over her skin. Subtle, barely noticeable, but I'd seen it before. Anger swelled in my stomach and I bounded forward, crossing the bar in a few strides, my fist ready to break Demon's face at the slightest suggestion he was any threat to her.

Her head turned, her brown eyes pinning me, stopping me still with a chilling stare. A silent warning like a royally pissed off lioness. I stopped, looking between them, catching a glint in Demon's eye and the smug smile on his face as he straightened up. I looked back at Nat, searching her face. Her eyes were filled with horror, and fear, and disgust. I could see it right there, burning into me, boring into the shards that were left of my soul.

I looked back at my cousin, the smirk on his face, pulling into a wide smile as anger simmered away deep in my chest. I knew what the bastard had done. I knew why Natalie now looked at me with contempt in her eyes. Demon winked, ripping the last shred of control from me. I launched myself towards him, my fist already formed, catching a glimpse of Indie jumping to his feet much too slowly.

My first punch landed right against his jaw, sending his head snapping sideways. Demon staggered backwards, blood splattering across my face, and I swung again, connecting with his nose, feeling the crunch of bone as he swayed backwards. My heart hammered against my ribs like a drill, rage soaring through my veins, the dull pinch of skin of the wound in my left bicep barely registering. I took another step, watching the tall man wobble as he stepped backwards.

Fingers closed around my arms, yanking me backwards, my fists still flailing, punching the air in front of me as Demon scrambled free of my blows.

"Enough!" Indie shouted from beside me, pulling me away from the young man, now covered in his own blood, "you don't fucking waltz back in here and start pummelling your fists into our members."

"You know what he told her, Indie. I saw it in her eyes."

"Then you should have told her the fucking truth. It should have come from you."

I stilled, a forced calmness coming over me, the anger I had felt towards my dumb-ass cousin now turning inwards. Indie was right. I should have told her what had happened. She had asked, and I'd fed Natalie a load of shit. Glancing across to the table she was sitting at, I caught her gaze, wide- eyed, shocked, disappointed. And I felt it all too. Flooding my veins, forced round by my pumping heart, resonating within me and feeding off the anger already reaching boiling point. I was losing my mind around her. Losing my identity. I needed to get this job finished.

Fury ushered Demon away, but he eyed me angrily, and I wouldn't put it past him to fling a few punches back the next chance he got.

"You need to sort this out, V," Indie hissed next to me.

"I am. We're going off grid. I can't protect her here. I need to get her away."

"And how are you going to do that? There could be people watching this place right now."

"I have nothing else, Indie. It's all I got."

Indie looked back at the table, his eyes focussed only on Nat for a moment as he let out a sigh.

"Me and some of the boys will ride with you. We'll give you cover," he said eventually.

For a moment, relief washed over me. It was momentary, but it felt good and it broke a hole in the despair I'd been wearing the last few hours.

"Thanks, Indie. I really appreciate it."

"I'm not doing it for you. I'm doing it for her," he answered, his gaze returning to Natalie.

*****

Fury and I had barely slept, having spent the cover of darkness depositing bodies at random locations, searching graveyards for recently buried family members and adding an extra after a quick excavation. Joey had jammed cameras, providing us with a veil to get around Gateshead and neighbouring Newcastle unnoticed, or at least unnoticed enough not to be implicated if any of these dead fuckers later showed up. And now, as morning was breaking, I packed essentials into panniers and loaded them onto bikes.

Natalie watched us roaming around the place, lost in her own thoughts, her eyes flicking to me and away again. And I hadn't approached her. I couldn't stand that look in her eyes. Even when she had first met me and she recoiled at the tattoos, she had never looked at me like that. Repulsed, disgusted. And it burnt into me, searing into my skin. I was used to being shunned. By my father, by my club, and then my tattoos did the rest. But for days I'd felt like I belonged with someone, no matter how very different we were. And now she shunned me, too.

She had every right to. Every justification. I'd had plenty of time, locked together in my apartment, plenty of time to tell her the truth about my family. She had asked, and I still hadn't told her, never really lying, but never telling the full truth. My chest was heavy, the pain of loss pressing against my ribs as if it was forcing them apart.

"We're all packed," Indie's voice from behind me made my heart jolt.

I got to my feet, getting up from the side of the bike I was tinkering with, checking the oil. I wiped my hand over the leather seat. I nodded at him and then tossed the keys at one of the twins. I couldn't tell which and moved to his bike.

"Dunno why I had to be the one to swap fucking bikes," he grumbled to Indie.

"Because you're the one with the girl," Indie answered him, looking over at the young woman dressed exactly as Natalie had been, in tight jeans and the black and white leather bike jacket.

"Fuck's sake," he mumbled as he walked passed me, dropping his keys into my open palm, "if you scratch her, you're buying me a new one, Viking."

I forced a grin, silently agreeing. We were splitting up, Indie, Demon and Fury riding with us to the cottage whilst the twins and their girl were riding decoy, hoping that if anyone was following me, they'd go after them. It was risky. Really risky, to the twins and the girl more so. But I was blinded, and keeping Natalie safe was all I cared about. And they were fast riders. Throwing tails off would be a breeze.

My father's bike started up under Cade, his girl hopping deftly onto the back and with his brother flanking them, the Harley's roared out of the carpark.

I looked towards the door of the pub where Natalie was standing watching. The full leather bike suit clung to her. Shapely breasts bulged under the material, which pulled tight over her waist and hips and elongated already long legs. She fiddled with the black helmet in her hands, turning it over and over, nervously.

"Time to go," I walked over to her, gently touching her elbow to guide her towards the Harley Davidson, that wasn't too much unlike my dad's.

"I'm not getting on there with you," she said angrily, shrugging my hand free of her and moving away.

"Nat, please. We don't have time for this. It won't take someone long to realise they've followed the wrong bikes. We need to go now."

"Get off me, V."

"It's ok. You can ride with me, Nat," Indie offered, and I watched her shoulders slump a little, a small amount of the anger and tension dropping from them.

She nodded at him, pulling the black helmet over her head and obscuring her face

261

from me. She kicked a leg over the back of the bike, sliding into place behind my cousin, turning her head to watch me.

I didn't need to see her face to know the look that she was giving me under the dark visor, to feel the hatred and distrust radiating from her. I pulled on my helmet, swinging my leg over the bike and firing it up; the deep, guttural purr of the Harley joining the others like a group of bass vocalists, the ground vibrating beneath them. And then with a deep roar, the bikes peeled off, and I watched Natalie's arms cling to Indie snuggly.

Chapter Thirty One

⚹ Natalie ⚹

The motorbikes moved in convoy in the early morning light, gliding easily through the traffic, commuters just taking to the roads. Indie's bike roared beneath me, the frame vibrating violently, sending a shaking all the way through me almost to my bones. For the first few minutes I clung to him anxiously, unable to focus on the scenery that whizzed by, the bikers taking advantage of the light traffic on the motorway which skirted the city centre, taking us further and further north; away from Gateshead, away from Newcastle.

V stayed close, flanking us, and when I relaxed enough to lift my head from where I had buried it between Indie's shoulder blades, I stole snippets of glances, watching how the Viking constantly checked mirrors, his head darting from side to side. He snatched a few glances back at me, but I couldn't, wouldn't, let him hold my gaze.

Demon's words soared around my brain, stoking up a thick fog of confusion and hurt, filling me with dread and anger and disappointment at V and at myself for my own weakness. For getting caught up in the adrenaline rush of the situation and succumbing to the charms of the tattooed biker. But the internal retribution continued, and my mind flittered back to all the other disastrous relationships over the years. Every one of them had ended. No one was good enough for me, no one stuck around long enough, and no one had made me feel like he did.

Fuck. Anger and irritation formed a dangerous cocktail inside of me, fuelled by the silence and isolation inside my helmet. Despite the man I wrapped my arms around and the men surrounding me to keep me safe. To keep me alive.

The time ticked by. Suburbs changed to green fields, lush colours of differing shades of green. The verges were spattered with spring flowers; the purples, pinks and whites of crocuses and the multitudes of different yellows as the daffodils challenged the grass for dominance. The colours entwined, bleeding together as we sped past like a melting rainbow. We climbed on through Northumberland, rolling agricultural land broken up by copses of dense trees and woodland, the road leading us higher and higher until we were swamped either side by the purple hue of heather and the bright green of moorland fern.

The spring morning was fresh, the sun not quite chasing away the chill of a cloudless night, and I shivered. But it was colder on the bike, the cool air streaming past, working under the gaps between the leather and my helmet, infiltrating through the seams. My finger-ends became numb with the cold and my toes had given up, the feeling in them becoming more and more fuzzy. Cold swarmed under the visor of my helmet, whipping away the tears that squeezed out the side of my eyes from the assault of air that attacked me, and even when I tucked myself behind the big man in front, the wind still battered me. I was cold, and I was uncomfortable.

I glanced left and right occasionally, glimpsing road signs, noting where we were as we drove deeper and deeper into Northumberland until we hit the border of Scotland. And still we continued, breaking speed only to counter the pockets of traffic we would meet. Jagged hills reared up on our left, growing in height and ferocity with each minute that ticked by. I had no idea where we were going. Only north. North into Scotland, where the air grew colder with each mile that passed. My stomach rumbled loudly, a deep basal sound that was answered by the pulsing of my bladder and the early morning coffee that was winding its way through me. The cold wasn't helping, nor the creeping uncomfortable feeling of sitting on a vibrating Harley Davidson for much too long.

I tried to distract myself by thinking about something else, anything else, but every time my thoughts would revert to the revelation in my father's boxes and then the army of men that had been sent to kill me. Neither was comforting, only making my stomach flip faster in turmoil and dread, adding nausea to the list of complaints.

The bikes roared on. Never stopping, continuing their relentless pace, the boom of the vibrations of the exhaust constantly running through me till all I could hear, all I could feel was the unforgiving reverberation of the heavy engines. But nearly four hours in, my bottom was numb from the cold and the constant pulsing of the engine, and I was sure the ends of my fingers had dropped off somewhere just over the Scottish border. My bladder tensed, full of liquid, the cold of the Scottish air and the constant shuddering of the bike beneath me exasperating the problem, and desperately, I tapped Indie on the shoulder. He glanced behind him, and I did my best attempt at a made-up sign language, trying to communicate the predicament and eventually he nodded.

The bike roared louder, a surge of speed as he opened the throttle and pulled past the outliers in front, overtaking them and wafting his arm at the leather clad bikers. A collective of nods was passed between them and at the next exit the group of bikes peeled off the busy road, driving down a meagre track, gravel scattering as the thick wheels kicked up the loose road chippings behind us. A few minutes later, the bikes rolled to a stop, pulling into a layby next to a thick line of pine trees, crowded and dark, that skirted the road.

The men shoved visors up, their faces revealed by the small slit in their helmets, looking at Indie for further instruction.

"Piss stop," he grunted, letting the bike lurch suddenly to the left on to the metal stand,

and I gripped him harder for fear I'd be ejected out the side.

Stiffly, I climbed off the motorbike, looking around, seeing no toilets or amenities of any kind.

"Where's the toilets?" I asked.

Indie smiled and pointed into the woods.

"Take your pick."

"You've got to be kidding," I hissed, watching the smiles erupt on the faces of the bikers.

Indie shook his head, "wild wees only."

"Fuck's sake," I cursed, half under my breath, traipsing off to get lost amongst the trees.

The forest floor was spongy beneath my feet, the odd twig cracking and making me jump, my head snapping side to side as anxiety reigned down upon me. And then, when I had gone far enough that I was consumed by tree trunks and shadows, I wrestled from the tight leather suit and relieved myself. Not my finest moment squatting amongst the pine trees, the fresh air tickling at my naked flesh. What I would give for loo roll and a coffee. My stomach complained, the sound bouncing off the trees around me, reminding me it had been hours since anything had passed my lips.

Back at the road, the men were standing around, a thin tail of smoke coming from Demon's cigarette as Fury leant against his bike with his arms crossed over his chest. Indie and V seemed deep in conversation, talking in hushed

267

tones, the discussion stopping as I emerged from the treeline. Indie nodded at Demon and Fury and the men remounted. The older man sat on his bike, waiting for me to get back on.

"How much further?" I complained, eyeing up the hard leather seat and already feeling the ache seeping into my seat bones.

"Few more hours."

"Few? I need food and coffee."

"You can eat when we get there."

"And I can't sit on this moving pneumatic drill any longer."

Indie pushed his visor up, fixing me with a stern stare, his dark eyes boring into me.

"You've got two choices: my bike or his," he tipped his head towards the Viking, and I sighed, acknowledging defeat and kicking my leg over his bike.

"That's what I thought," he said again, tapping my leg and turning the ignition.

The rest of the motorbikes started up in response, the engines deafening in the silence, sending a murder of crows shrieking indignantly from the trees.

The journey continued, stiffness claiming my joints as we sped past mountains, dropping into the belly of valleys and skirting lochs of various sizes until my head lolled sideways, tiredness making my eyelids feel like heavy lead shutters. I leant forward, my weight dropping against Indie's back, my limbs turning limp as the vibrations lulled me to sleep.

Fingers gripped my leg, then an urgent pat, the tone of the motorbike underneath me changing, the pace slowing. I snapped my head up, opening my eyes, jolting upright from where I had slumped over the man in front.

The bike pulled over to the side of the road and the Viking glided to a stop behind us.

"Shit, Nat. You were asleep," Indie half shouted over the deep rumble of the idling bike, "V, we need to stop for a few minutes."

The Viking shook his head.

"We're almost there. It's safer to keep going."

"And if she falls off the side and someone runs over her head?"

"Nat'll be fine. Just keep pinching her leg or summit."

I glared at him, and for a moment, the lips that pulled into a lopsided grin tugged at my heart. But it was short-lived as the memories of Demon's words came flooding back. He was a wolf in sheep's clothing, the devil in disguise.

"I'll be fine," I said eventually, drawing in a lungful of cool mountain air and pushing my visor up so it circulated around my helmet, crisp and refreshing.

The Viking was not wrong. We only went a further twenty minutes before turning off the main road and onto an unmarked track of loose road clippings with enough room for a single car to fit down. In places, the road bulged into the grass verge, enough space to pull into, to allow another vehicle to pass. It was narrow, with sharp bends, slowing the bikes down. The road wound around the foot of the mountains, cutting through a tiny village of around five buildings before the Viking, who was now leading the procession of bikes, took a series of turns, taking us deeper into the foothills and further away from civilisation.

Then, as the tiny road rose before us, a climb that seemed to have gone on for miles, we turned off onto an even rougher track, riddled with potholes. My bones and joints jolted as Indie did his best to avoid the uneven ground, catching small pockets and bumping over mounds and cracks and the sides of holes in the road. But eventually, right at the very end, the white-washed cottage stood nestled against the rocky crags of a foothill that reared up behind it.

The lane was flanked by thick fern and clumps of dark-grey rock and a dry-stone wall, separating the unfenced farmland from the grounds of the little building. As we got closer, a cluster of outhouses stood behind it, a myriad of doors leading off into various small stone buildings. The bikes drove around the back, collecting in the tiny courtyard at the rear. Indie helped me off his Harley, my legs now half numb from the hideous vibrations of the engine for nearly eight hours and the lack of circulation from sitting still for so long.

We all piled into the cottage behind the Viking, Demon and Fury running for the toilet that seemed to be just off the kitchen and Indie pulling off his helmet and propping it on the table. V walked around, still on high alert, examining the windows and testing whether they locked shut, grimacing every few steps as his eyes stilled over the various features of the cottage. I watched for a little while until my stomach growled like an angry bear, the sound echoing off the thick walls of the property.

Rummaging through the cupboards, I finally found a kettle. It was old fashioned and designed to go onto the hob, on a stove that I couldn't fire up. Reluctantly, I followed the men through the house to where the Viking had dropped to his haunches and was fumbling around on the floor. He pushed the rug to the side and tugged on something, till part of the floor came away in his hand, tilting up to the ceiling.

"Fuck!" Fury said suddenly, and Demon let out a long whistle beside him.

I moved closer, trying to get a glimpse of what they were all looking at. There was a hole in the floor into some sort of chasm or tiny basement, but inside was a small armoury. Guns, knives, even cross bows. They were arranged neatly, every weapon having its own place. I didn't know whether it was relief washing over my body or a sense of foreboding.

Chapter Thirty Two

✑ The Viking ✒

"Jesus! Look at this shit," Fury babbled excitedly beside me before dropping himself into the hole and gazing around it like a kid in a sweetshop.

"Whose place is this?" Indie asked.

"I told ya. Just an old army bud."

Fury picked up a handgun, turned it over in his hands and then ejected the magazine and inspected it before sliding it back in.

"This is a canny collection," he said, replacing the handgun and picking up a knife, spinning it round in his hand and then slicing it through the air, the thick blade making swooshing noises as it carved up nothing.

"What does he need all this for?" Natalie asked from over my shoulder.

"Just hunting rabbits," I replied, flashing her a smile and immediately regretting it when the sternness on her face never faltered.

Natalie sighed and turned away, leaving Indie, Demon and Fury to play with their toys while I cruised the little cottage, inspecting each window, each way in and out.

I pulled the curtains across each space, plunging the lounge into darkness, barely a stitch of daylight creeping through the thick drapes over the windows. I moved upstairs, the leather panniers slung over one shoulder, to the single bedroom over the lounge. Depositing the panniers on the bed, I continued surveying the property, pulling the wooden shutters across the windows which protruded out of the slanted roof. Nat had already rummaged around, peeling the leather suit off and sliding her legs into a pair of jeans.

"There's only one bedroom?" She asked from behind me.

"Yes, babe."

"Don't call me babe."

"Why not?" I asked. But I knew why.

"I'm not your babe."

Natalie turned to walk away, and I caught her wrist, whirling her round to face me.

"Nat, wait."

"Don't touch me."

Her voice was a growl, low and dangerous. A warning that I should heed. A warning that she was way out of my league. But my heart beat faster and my stomach filled with despair, as if touching her skin, feeling her soft flesh in my hands was enough to remind me what I was about to lose. Even if I kept her safe, even if I kept her alive, the light in her eyes now dulled when she looked at me. Pure and simple disgust. I got it. I really did. I understood why the revelation had rocked her so much.

The murder of her own father was still raw, and she couldn't perceive how anyone could do that to the person who had brought them life. She didn't need to say that to me. I could see it in her face, deep in her eyes. Family was everything to her, current ones and the ones she had lost, and the ones she saw in her future. I understood that. But my father had brought me only misery.

I dropped her arm, and she took a step away from me. For a second, I was prepared to let her go. To bury the thoughts of her, of how my heart swelled every time I looked into those caramel-brown eyes, at the heart-shaped face and defined cheekbones.

"Nat," I called gently, taking another step.

She looked at me, half warning, half pleading. Her bottom lip trembled. Just for a split second, the tiny loss of control almost unnoticeable. But I noticed it. I noticed everything about her.

I took another step, and she retreated half a step, as if we were in a waltz. And maybe we were. A tangle of hearts, a mix of emotions, crashing together and whirling away.

"Nat."

"Don't. Just no."

She held her finger up at me, like the stern wave of her index finger would keep me back. I stepped towards her again and she took another step backwards.

"Nat. What Demon told you…"

"I don't want to hear any more of your lies."

I shook my head vehemently.

"I've never lied to you," I said, more quietly.

"Really?" She spat the words, a challenge.

"Really. You never asked how my father died. At whose hand he died. And I never told you."

She shook her head side to side, as if trying to keep my words from entering her brain.

"No. You don't get to do this."

"Do what, Nat?"

"This. Make up excuses. Pretend to be someone that you're not."

"I've never pretended to be anyone else. I've never hidden who I was from you."

I moved in on her again and she moved backwards, Eli's tall chest of drawers rattling as she stepped back into them, cornering herself, the open door stopping her from escaping me.

"You're a killer. A criminal."

"I am. And you've always known that Nat."

"I can't do this."

Tears welled in her eyes, her words hitching in her throat, a woman on the outskirts of control.

"Do what?"

"Us. This," she waved her hand in the air, "being hunted. People trying to kill me. All of it. I just want to go back to normal. I had a normal life, a boring life, but it was normal, quiet. I want to go back to mourning my dead parents, to second guessing whether I could have prevented their deaths, done more for Charlie. I want to go back to wondering whether I'll ever get a chance to have a baby. Ever get the chance to settle down into a normal relationship?"

"I'm not stopping you, babe. I want you to have all that. Whatever you want."

I pushed the words out, burning my throat like poison. But they were out there.

"I'm going to keep you alive. Cian and my man, Joey, they'll sort this out," I continued, watching her shake her head at me, "I just need you to be patient just a bit longer. Then I'll get you back to your normal life. And you don't need to see us, me, ever again."

I bit the inside of my cheek, a burning sensation taking over my throat and my chest. A tear rolled down her face, her eyes even more beautiful from the sparkle of those tears that had yet to fall. She bit down on her bottom lip; her face glowing more and more red, and then she pushed off the drawers. I took a step back, letting her move past me and out of the room, listening to the creak of the stairs beneath her feet.

Slumping onto the end of the bed, I focused on the wall in front of me. It was painted white like the rest of the house, clean and sterile. Nothing hung on the wall, but on the chest of drawers one picture stood. Eli and Ava, together, happy. And here I sat, surrounded by my club brothers, ex-club brothers, feeling as alone as I ever had.

"V!" Fury shouted up the stairs, "V!"

"What, man?" I yelled back, angry that he'd disturbed the self-loathing I was wallowing in.

"Is your lass supposed to be wandering down the road by herself?"

Fuck! I bolted down the stairs, missing the bottom two steps and slipping down them, skinning the back of my leg and wrenching my shoulder from hanging on to the handrail, the pain of bruised ribs biting my side. The cottage door clattered noisily off the wall where I wrenched it open, launching myself out into the late afternoon sun.

My feet hammered on the road, hurried footsteps ringing out into the quiet countryside, as Nat glanced over her shoulder before breaking into a run, her long legs covering the ground much quicker than I had expected. I pumped my arms, picking up the pace and closing the distance between us.

"Nat! Stop!" I called after her, but she didn't break her stride, veering off suddenly to the right and heading for the thick trees of the woods in front of us.

I was gaining quickly, a metre or so behind her but not yet near enough to grab hold of her, and she disappeared into the darkness of the trees, the shadows consuming her. I barrelled in; my eyesight ripped from me from the thick canopy of leaves over our heads. In the seconds that blackness filled my pupils, I listened, picking out the rushed sound of feet, soft thumps on the cushioned floor of dead pine needles and rotting leaves.

The trees got thicker, the undergrowth dense, and I heard a rustle in front of me and the slight exhalation of air followed by a whimper. Natalie picked herself back up, but she'd lost the advantage and she had nowhere else to go. She wheeled around, the thin wisps of light that filtered through the leafy canopy overhead catching her tear-streaked face, dirt clinging to one side.

Defeated, she bent over, her breaths raspy and fast, and then she sank against the trunk of a big pine, sliding down onto the ground and pulling her knees to her chest and burying her face in her hands. Her sobs broke the silence around us, filling the woods with her despair.

"Nat," I said softly, dropping down in front of her.

"I can't..." her breathing was erratic, "I can't. I, I, I just can't."

"You can't do what?"

"I'm so scared. I don't want to die. I'm not ready to die. I thought I had more time."

I wrapped my arms around her, pulling her into my chest, kneeling on the dirt in front of her. Her body vibrated, her sobs vicious and uncontrolled.

"It's ok," I whispered, stroking her hair, "it's ok."

For a while I just held her, till her sobs died down to inconsistent hiccups and the convulsions of her body stilled. Till she had nothing left to let go of and the only thing that disturbed the peace in the trees was the rhythmical beat of our hearts, beating together in harmony.

"Everything has changed, V," she said eventually, her voice muffled against my chest, "and I don't think I can cope with that. I'm scared of everything. But I wasn't scared of you. Not until I saw you kill those men in your apartment. When I saw for the first time how dangerous you were. And then, when Demon told me about your father…."

Natalie pushed away from me, her eyes fixing on mine, the caramel-brown orbs boring into my head, like she was excavating my soul.

"What sort of person kills their own father, V?" Natalie whispered.

Chapter Thirty Three

‿ Natalie ‿

The Viking put his hands either side of my face, tipping it up slightly, his gaze burning into mine.

"My father was a drunk. He'd been that way for as long as I could remember," the Viking sighed, a wash of sadness filling his eyes, there in a moment before the shadows took it away again.

His thumb traced the line of my cheekbone, swiping at the tears that lay on my face.

"I didn't realise what I was hearing when I was younger. They had a lot of arguments. I'd hear the odd noise that would wake me, but I didn't know what it was. Later, though, it changed. The first time I really understood what was happening, I was seven or eight. I heard my Da shouting in the night and bangs from downstairs. I got up to see what was happening. The kitchen door was open a fraction, just a small crack, and I peeked through, watching. Watching him bounce my mam off every surface, hitting her, letting her fall to the floor, picking her up and punching her again. She never whimpered, never cried out, never begged him to stop. She just took it. And I just stood there watching. Doing nothing.

"The next morning when he had gone to work, I noticed how she moved stiffly, the tiny winces of pain. Yet every time she saw me, she straightened up and smiled like there was nothing the matter."

The Viking paused, pushing out a tense breath.

"Then I heard it more and more at night. The muffled bangs, the grunts of my father. And I was too scared to do anything. I was twelve, maybe, the next time I got up in the night. Something stirring in me. By that time, I was larger and stronger. I heard them earlier than usual, my Da staggering in from a club night, pissed and angry. I'd heard the door slam, knew what mood he was in. And then the thumps from the kitchen started as he knocked my mother about. This time I went downstairs. I ran at him, shouting for him to get off her, to leave her alone. I'll never forget the look on his face when he turned to see me. I'd always feared him, but this time it was as if it wasn't him at all. And he came at me. I wasn't big enough to defend myself, not strong enough to take his punches. My mam begged him to stop, but he didn't, not till I was bruised and bloody. It was as if he couldn't stop, that blood lust had kicked in and it took him over.

"She kept me off school for days, till the bruises faded. And for a while, I didn't intervene again. But I got bigger, and I got stronger, and I always knew one day that I'd be able to take him. That day came when I was eighteen. We'd both been drinking, in the club house, in Indie's pub. By then I'd grown a reputation as a brawler in the bike club and amongst anyone who pissed me off. It had been a way of channelling all of this, almost a transfer of anger to anyone else but my Da. I came home after him and found him beating my mam again. And this time, whilst he was still stronger than me, I had the benefit of raging hormones. We fought, my mam screamed at us to stop, we broke things, broke each other, but for the first time I got the upper hand. And I was ruthless.

"After that, I found the confidence to stand up to him. And for a while, it kept him in check. But my anger was getting the better of me and with my growing strength, the hours in the gym, testosterone, and I was becoming more and more like him. I was half cut when I walked through Newcastle one afternoon, alcohol stoking the usual rage in me, and a girlfriend had just dumped me. The army office was right there, fancy posters and a film showing on the TV inside. When I came out, I had signed up."

The Viking paused, his face distorting, fighting with a memory of years ago.

"Instead of staying to keep him in check, to protect my mother, I ran away to the army. And I loved it. I didn't have to walk on eggshells, to be ready to fight him, to keep him off her when he was angry or drunk. And for a long while I didn't come home. I think I was too scared to see what had been going on while I was away. Or maybe it was the guilt that I'd left my mam, that all I had thought about was myself?

"We'd had a particularly bad few months. We'd had an extraction mission, a rescue of our own soldiers, and we lost one. It tore us all apart and our team started to break away, go on to other things. The family and the brothers I had were moving on. I took leave, eventually. I needed a break. A break from the mindless killing, the civilian casualties. The people blowing themselves up in the name of their cause. And I came home.

"Yet the minute I got back, I could see he had been up to his old tricks. I bundled in through the door, and the first thing she did when she saw me was to recoil in fear. She was so thin, and she looked so old. Like she aged at double the speed from me leaving. She'd been beautiful. Slim, blonde, blue-green eyes. Now her hair was greying and her eyes dull, lifeless. Her nose was crooked, broken many times from the beatings he'd given her. A bruise was fading away under the wrinkles below her eye. He'd broken her. Physically and mentally.

"I went after him. Found him at the bike club with another woman. I didn't care about the other woman, she could have had him. We raged at each other. He threw a load of punches, but I was faster, stronger, and I was a trained fighter. A killer. I told him he could come get his bags. That I'd have them packed ready for him. He never came for them. At first, I thought he'd just cut and run. I was stupid.

"Instead, he'd been on a three-day bender, drinking, smoking, probably all sorts of other shit. He came home in the middle of the day. I was out. When I got back, I found mam in a puddle of her own blood. He'd absolutely pummelled her. She was a pulp, a piece of meat chewed up and spat out. He must have spent hours torturing her."

V shifted, unfolding his legs and then dropping on to his bottom on the forest floor. A breeze moved through the trees, gentle and cool, picking up the bits of blonde hair that had worked loose from his ponytail and blowing them across his face. He took a deep breath and looked to the side, staring somewhere into the distance, unable to maintain eye contact.

"I was angry. Angrier than I'd ever been in my life. I wasn't thinking straight. It didn't take me long to find him and I'm sure he was expecting me. He was with my Uncle Ste, and a few others, older bike club members. I remember the smirk on his face when I walked in. He knew what he'd done. But I didn't stop. The others tried to get hold of me, but I was pumped, red-hot with rage. They went down quickly. I still remember the feel of that first fist I forced into his face, the pop of his lips and the way his head snapped backwards. It shocked him. But I didn't stop. I couldn't stop. That same blood lust pumped through my veins and no one could stop me. Or maybe they were too scared to. I didn't stop. I didn't stop even when I knew he was dead. When the limpness under my feet and fists took its last breath."

The Viking looked back at me, holding my gaze this time, a ferocity in his eyes, burning into me. There didn't seem to be any remorse, no sign of guilt, just crystal-clear acceptance. He grabbed my hand, my brain telling me to pull it away, but I resisted.

"I would do it again," he said, searching my eyes. "I would do it again to protect my mother. I would do it again to protect you. If that makes me a monster, then I'm sorry."

I opened my mouth, but my brain had nothing. Nothing to give him. Not a word of comfort, not a word of condemnation.

"Your mother?" I whispered, even that sounding loud in the eerie calm between the trees.

"She's alive. I took her home to Sweden, back to her family. She'll never be the same, physically or mentally, but she's alive."

"And what about the tattoos? Do you have one for him, too?"

The Viking stood up, shrugging out of the leather bike jacket and pulling his hoodie and t-shirt over his head, the dark patterns on his skin looking even more ominous in the shadows of the woods. He turned away from me, standing still, the demon staring at me. I understood then.

"My Da will always be the demon on my back. I should never have left my mam. I should have made her leave him. We should have run away. And even in death, he haunts me, punishes me. He changed me. I don't exist because of him. I'll never be the boy, or the

285

man, that I was then. And no matter the reason for his death, the reason for my actions, I'll always carry around the guilt of what I did. I ruined my life. *He* ruined my life."

I nodded, understanding, but still a great confusing sadness descended.

"I really don't know you, V, do I?"

"I haven't hidden anything from you. If you've asked, I've answered."

And he was right. I hadn't asked. I'd never wanted to know the answers. It had been easier that way. I stood up, moving towards him, linking my fingers against his, his naked chest in front of my face.

"I don't even know your name," I looked at him.

"I'm Scott. Scott Lundgren."

And for a moment I stood watching him looking at me, my hand linked in his, the beautiful tapestry of tattoos on his body almost animated in the small streams of light that penetrated the great green canopy above our heads. The forest was still, save for the occasional tweet of a bird, of the rustle of nearby leaves in the breeze.

"Nice to meet you, Scott."

I raised up on my toes, kissing him gently on the lips, his stubble prickling over the skin above my cupid's bow. The tension dissolved slightly from his body, relief flooding through mine and an acquiescence of who he was, seeped into my veins.

He would never ever have fit the description of my ideal man, but he was right he had never lied to me. He'd protected me even if it meant his life was on the line. Going to the Kings for help, against their banishment of him, had been dangerous. The quiet safety of his home had been compromised because of me.

I pushed my lips harder against his, my hand snaking up to grasp the back of his head to pull him closer, my tongue teasing over the gap in his lips, until I heard the small exhalation and his guard slipped. I pushed into him harder, the tip of my tongue flicking into his mouth to meet his. And then he groaned, his arms wrapping round me, a hand raking through my hair, clamping round the back of my head, as he kissed me back, deep and penetrating.

Our tongues tangled, desperation and ferocity smouldering between us, a spot of heat igniting in the pit of my stomach, radiating further with each swipe of his tongue against mine, each grab of his lips and the graze of his teeth against the soft flesh of my bottom lip. I clung to him, pulling him closer, feeling the hardness of his muscled torso against me. A flush of warmth dashed across my skin and then we were walking backwards. Step by tiny step until the rough trunk of the pine tree behind stopped us from moving any further.

The Viking pressed against me, his hands moving under my jumper, rough fingertips brushing my skin, igniting a feverish heat everywhere they touched as he dragged a small amount of friction across my body. I kissed him deeper, as if I couldn't get enough of him, like I was starving. And I was. I was starving for him, for his body, for his hands, for his tongue and his expert fingers, for feeling him inside me, any of him, all of him, connecting with each other.

He yanked at the bottom of my top, pushing it up my body and over my head, the Scottish air surrounding my naked skin in an instant, cool and brisk, in direct contrast from the surging heat of his hands and then his lips. They moved to my neck, tugging and sucking on my flesh. The bark on the tree trunk at my back prickled and scratched, but his lips were soft, caressing my skin with urgency. He traced around my collarbone, to the soft dip of my neck, before running his tongue down my chest and dipping between my breasts.

The Viking's breath was hot, the tip of his tongue gliding over the top of my cleavage, teasing over the flesh that was not hidden by my bra. My nipples hardened, pushing against the fabric, the slightest movement making them prickle with sensitivity. His hand slid round my back, squeezing the clasp in one quick snapping action, freeing me for him as he swiped the straps off my shoulders and let the bra fall to the floor.

The forest air rushed at me cold and assaulting, sending a shiver running over my skin, but then his mouth and hands covered me, his tongue flicking over the tight peaks, sucking my nipple into his mouth as his hand cupped the other. I ran my hand into his hair, grabbing a handful and pulling him to me, thrusting myself into his mouth, gasping and writhing under his touch. Pressure built between my legs, feverish, pulsing, and I squeezed my thighs together to feel the friction, to keep control.

V took his hand away from my other breast, sliding down my naked stomach, popping the button open on my jeans, and pushed them down over my hips. My stomach clenched and my insides flooded with desperation, the tingling sensation within me turning to electricity and all I could think about was how I wanted him inside of me, how I needed him inside me. His fingers brushed over the top of my knickers, sending another pulse of fiery need racing through my veins.

I took my hands from his head, my own fingers searching for him, running over the ripples of the muscles of his stomach, fumbling over the button of his jeans.

"Fuck!" I breathed into the crook of his neck, "fuck, V. I need this. I need you."

And as if my words broke the last of any resolve, he grabbed my trousers, yanking them the rest of the way down my legs. Then reaching round behind him, he pulled at the knife tucked in the waistband at the back of his pants and slid it free. The blade caught in the light that filtered in through the leaves, sparkling menacingly as he brought it towards me, the steel cold against my skin as he dipped it under the material of my knickers, slicing through the lace without even a tug and the white thong fell away, leaving me bared to him and the forest surrounding us.

Chapter Thirty Four

ॐ The Viking ॐ

I let the knife fall onto the soft bed of pine needles and leaves at our feet, as I lowered myself to my knees. My tongue roamed all over the soft flesh of her stomach, listening to the inconsistency of her breaths, the tiny inhalations of air as I sucked harder under her belly button, the stubble on my chin scratching the delicate area on her lower abdomen.

I could smell her from this angle, the light oil of her skin, the fading scent of soap and the musky femininity of her beautiful cunt, the heat from between her legs making it stronger. I nipped at the smooth skin in line with her hips, nudging her legs apart for me, tracing my tongue along the join between her groin and her hip, feeling the shudder of her body with anticipation.

Then I pushed my face into her, inhaling her, tasting the juices already wetting her slit with one long swipe of my tongue, and she whimpered into the air above me. Her cunt was the flavour of woman, musky and earthy, but with something inherently unique that reminded me of her and no one else. I took a long slow inhale of air, and I willed myself to slow down and not devour her like some wild animal that hadn't eaten in weeks. I slid the point of my tongue over her clit, the nub swelling under the pressure of my lips as I nibbled and sucked, then moving down, following the line of warmth to the moisture that pooled at the juncture of her legs.

Her fingers raked over the top of my head, fiddling with the strands of hair, but nothing could distract me from her, from her awaiting pussy and what I needed to do to it. I pulled my tongue back over her slit, dipping in teasingly and listening for the gasp I knew would come from her soft lips. And then I settled over her clit, sucking it into my mouth, swirling my tongue over the top of it as she let out a strangled shout, a bunch of birds erupting out of the trees above. Her hips pushed into my face, smothering me as her hands tightened in my hair.

My tongue swirled like crazy as I alternated between licking and sucking and nibbling, hearing the heightened gasps of her voice in the stillness of the woods. And then I sunk lower again, tasting the delicious wetness of her pussy, feasting on her like I was starving, driving my tongue inside. She rode my face, pulling my hair, her fingernails scratching my scalp, her hips writhing against me.

"V," her voice was hoarse, strangled as her thighs clasped around my head, holding me in place, her orgasm teetering on the edge, ready to explode all over me.

Knowing she was almost there I grazed my teeth over her clit, biting the little fleshy nub, and I pushed two fingers inside, feeling the tremor of her legs against my cheeks. She cried out, her voice shrill and loud. Curling the ends I drew circles inside of her, stroking and massaging. Nat's fingers scratched my scalp, the muscles in her thighs tightening, pushing up on to her tip toes, trying to escape the heat and tension I was forcing into her. But my tongue and lips kept her in place, and she ground her sweet wet cunt against my face; searing whimpers changing to strangled cries. And then she came, her body taking over, her pussy clenching greedily on my fingers and her hips bucking wildly into my face.

As the movement of her body died down, I removed my face from where I had buried it between her legs, pushing to my feet as I ran my hands over her naked flesh, goosebumps covering her skin and her nipples standing hard in the cool forest air.

I wrapped my hand round her neck and pulled her mouth to mine, letting her taste her own juices that had smeared my face. She moaned into me, sending vibrations running rampant through my flesh, stoking the fire already burning in my groin. Fingers slid down my body, pushing at the fabric that covered my legs.

"I can't," I breathed into her mouth, "I don't have a condom."

"I don't care."

"Nat…"

"I'm on the pill. I'll not make you a father, don't worry."

Her hands continued to push my jeans down my thighs, my cock springing free from the cage of denim. Her fingers wound round the shaft, the pad of her thumb running across the tip, shivers cascading down my dick to my balls as she gently flicked the barbells around the head.

"I need you, V," she whispered against my neck, "I need you in me, filling me. Please."

I pulled the jeans down my legs with the toe of my foot, guiding them off and kicking them to the side. Grabbing Natalie's thigh, I pulled it around my waist, edging towards her till I was a fraction away from her, almost feeling the desire of her soft, delicate flesh on the end of my cock. Her lips moved cross my neck, nipping and pulling at my skin as she traced a path from my earlobe.

"Are you sure, babe?"

"Yes," she mumbled, as her lips tugged at the skin of my throat.

Holding her leg still around my waist, I guided my cock towards her, pushing into her wet folds, swiping the head through her juices, lubricating the end before slowly pushing into her. Her mouth fell open in a soundless 'o', her eyes widening at the same time as her cunt, as I moved slowly into her. The soft flesh inside pulled at my shaft, gripping against the piercings, fitting around me tight and hot.

Then slowly I pulled almost all the way out, my fingers gripping at the soft flesh of her arse cheeks that I held in my hand and I closed my eyes, distracting myself from the friction of her tight pussy as it fought against me. For a few moments I went slowly, letting her adjust to me, relaxing the soft tissues inside of her. And then, after pulling tortuously slowly out of her once more, I rammed back in, forcing through the tightness of her cunt. A delicious scream ripped through her lips, like a siren in the quiet of the woods. My hips pumped, hard and fast, self-control leaving my body, her back forced against the rough bark of the tree that held us both up. The piercings in the end of my cock grabbed and punished the sensitive flesh, as my grunts and her screams joined the cries of the birds escaping the hell we were releasing on each other.

I pummelled into her, losing all control, fucking her hard and ferocious, like I'd never fucked anyone before, like it was our last night alive. Her tight cunt would never want for another cock again after I'd finished with her, would never yield for anyone but me. And suddenly this was so much more than sex. I was marking my territory, making her mine, imprinting my very being inside of her. My hips thumped against her, Natalie's nails clawing down my back, her cries filling the air around us.

"Fuck, V."

"You coming for me, babe?" I asked, barely able to form the words.

"Uh-huh."

I angled my hips up into her, forcing myself against the flesh covering her pubic bone, bottoming out as I ground into her with shallow thrusts until I felt her legs shake around me and the scream about to tear from her throat. I clamped my lips against hers, kissing her deeply, thrusting my tongue inside her mouth, my lips grabbing at her urgently as I took the cry of orgasm from her, my own body tensing in anticipation. Then as her yell died down, my balls clenched, a bolt of lightning travelling down my shaft, tensing and pulsing, as I emptied myself inside her, burst after burst of hot cum filling her pussy, making her mine.

My lungs were heaving, my thighs raging from exertion, and my heart pumped furiously in my chest. I let her leg drop to the ground, easing gently out of her, the tiniest of winces slipping between her lips.

"I'm sorry," I muttered. "I didn't mean to hurt you."

"I liked it V. I like the way it feels, even when it hurts and scratches."

I rested my forehead against hers, the pair of us standing naked in the woods, the cool air kissing at our skin, cold caresses dancing over us. I pushed my lips against her, kissing her slowly, tugging at the soft flesh of her mouth, feeling the heat of her tongue against mine. She was delicious in every way. Her hands traced over the bottom of my back, skimming over my arse and cupping my cheeks, exploring and stroking, sending soft tingles racing through me.

Or maybe that was a shiver from the nip of Scottish air.

Overhead, the shadows were becoming denser, daylight fading, and the breeze growing stronger as leaves rustled around us.

"We need to get back," I mumbled with reluctance, enjoying the quiet calmness of our skin pressed against each other.

Natalie nodded, her body shaking now against the cold in the air. She bent down, scrambling around on the forest floor for her scattered clothes. Snatching the white scrap off a tree stump, she held it up, letting the material hang from between her fingers, a grin tugging at the sides of her face.

"I would have taken them off if you'd just asked," she chastised, a giggle just about suppressed in her throat.

I shrugged, sliding the knife back into its sheath.

"Admit it, babe. You loved how quickly I got them off you."

I offered a wide smile, watching the light catching in her warm brown eyes, rich and beautiful even in the concealment of the shadows.

The wind was stronger when we emerged from the cover of the trees, a storm cascading down the mountains at the back of Eli's cottage, bringing with it a sense of foreboding and trepidation. I glanced around discreetly, checking for unusual movement and shadows, but not seeing anything out of place. Just a storm.

The cottage had warmed through once we had got back. A fire burned in the stove and the low rumble of voices murmured behind the door to the lounge. I pushed the door open, a roar of cheers erupting around us, and I felt Natalie's hand tense in mine.

"All friends now?" Fury grunted, smirking into the bottle of beer he held between his fingers.

I ignored them, watching as they flashed knowing looks at each other. The curtains I had drawn closed were open, light from the lounge flooding onto the green hillock the cottage stood on.

"For fuck's sake," I grumbled, striding across the room and yanking them closed again, "the curtains on every window stay shut."

"You don't expect them to really find us here?" Fury retaliated, taking a long pull on the beer bottle and fixing his stare on me.

"Not taking any chances. And while we are here, I want all phones turned off."

"Paranoid much?" Demon muttered from beside the fire, poking at the wood in the grate, a small flame growing larger.

"You haven't lived, kid," I answered, feeling the heat of irritation bubbling inside of me, "the people who are coming after Nat are professionals. They have access to the best communications, the best technology. We might be out here in the sticks, but while we are, you do as I tell you."

Demon rolled his eyes and the rest of the room turned silent, chastised. Natalie shrugged her hand from mine, cradling the back of it with her palm, her fingers scratching at the skin, incessant and determined. The earlier peace in her face now replaced with tension and fear.

Chapter Thirty Five

C3 Natalie 80

My arms were cold, the skin on them tight and goose bumps prickled at the surface. Shivering, I tucked myself against the Viking, the warmth from his naked body enveloping me, but not quite chasing away the crispness of the Scottish morning. The fire in the only bedroom had burnt away to ash, not even a slither of warmth coming from it, and a tiny crack of light fought through the gap in the shutters.

The Viking moved his arm, swinging it over the top of me and pulling me closer, his even steady breaths comforting, driving some of the anxiety away. For a moment I could lie here and pretend everything was ok. That we were merely holidaying at the foot of a Scottish mountain, that there wasn't a room full of men below us and then a small armoury below them.

My heart beat faster, pummelling my chest, tension creeping to every part of me, the threat of losing control, of my mind and my resolve. I shuffled backwards, feeling his skin against mine and his decorated member stirring between us. How had I got here? Where had it all gone wrong? Yet here, in the Viking's arms, it felt so right. More right than I had felt with anyone else. I closed my eyes, inhaling the scent that surrounded me; the remnants of yesterday's aftershave lingering on his neck, the natural oil on his skin, and something else that wasn't as much him as it was us.

Eventually, my stomach grumbled. The meagre meal we'd eaten last night, a mix of sandwiches, crisps and alcohol, no longer providing my body with any sort of sustenance. And my bladder was uncomfortably full. I wriggled out from under V's heavy arm, poking my legs out of the covers to be immediately assaulted by the brisk air of the countryside. I raked in the leather panniers that now stood in the corner of the room, teasing out a pair of jeans and a clean jumper.

The floorboards creaked behind me, and I straightened, turning into the tattooed torso stood in front of me, naked, chiselled and beautiful.

"I'm starving, V," I complained, my stomach grumbling again as if it felt the need to add authenticity to my statement.

The Viking nodded, pulling a pair of jeans up his legs, tucking his thick cock behind the denim as my eyes lingered on the spot for far too long. The stairs creaked under our feet, obscenely loud in the silence, and we padded over the stone flags of the kitchen. I filled the kettle, firing up the stove and depositing the copper-bottomed pot on the ring.

"Is there no heating in this place?" I grumbled, opening each cupboard door until I found an eclectic mix of mugs and cups; some with stripes, some with spots, some with chips in the lip.

I pushed them together, lining them up by colour or pattern and then plucking a couple from the reorganised cupboard and rinsed them out.

"Eli likes this place rustic," the Viking answered, "plus I don't think he and Ava use anything other than their bodies for heating."

V smirked. I rolled my eyes, a hungry irritability firing at my synapses. The Viking wandered off, pushing open the lounge door, unleashing the percussion of numerous snores from the bodies littering the room. I watched as he walked in, kicking the lumps on the floor with the toe of his boot, groans and grumbles coming from the dark shapes in response.

Turning back to the kitchen, I scanned the jumble of groceries dumped on a tiny table that would barely sit two, and the almost empty pannier on the floor. It should encourage me that there were only a few days' worth of supplies and not more. But the haphazard groceries and tins, merely accompaniments to a meal, chased away any sort of relief. What were we going to eat while we were here? Leaves? Soup? I didn't think the supplies would last us long, particularly with four big men to feed.

The facilities in the cottage were sparse. The kitchen had a row of cupboards on either side of the window. The cupboards under the benches didn't possess doors, only a row of flimsy curtains on thin poles hid the interior, like something I'd only seen in pictures or in a museum. Even with a thick pair of socks on, the tiled floor under my feet pulled the chill up my legs. Daylight filtered in through the crack in the curtains and I pulled the thin fabric back slightly, checking over my shoulder that V wasn't watching, and peeked out.

The little road wound down the hill that the cottage stood on, the dark thick band of trees part way down, lining the road and engulfing the view of the countryside in pine and shadows. Tiny droplets of condensation hung on the windowpane, catching the light and looking more like lots of tiny crystals. Muffled voices in the lounge grew louder, and I dropped the curtain, tucking it back into place.

"Morning, Nat," Indie said, walking through the kitchen and straight out the back door, cool air rushing in. His boots crunched on the pebbles outside and a door in the distance banged against its frame.

I followed V into the lounge, swamped in darkness.

"Come on, princess," I heard him say, nudging the lump on the floor with his toe, eliciting a grumble of curses from under the heavy blankets.

"Fuck off, V."

The blankets moved. The lights clicked on overhead and boots echoed on the wooden floor of the lounge.

"Rise and shine, ladies," Indie called out from behind me.

Voices on the floor groaned again and covers were thrown backwards, bodies pushing up onto elbows.

"Fury, are you naked?" V asked, a laugh catching in his throat.

"Aye, he fucking is," Demon complained from beside him, rolling out from under the blankets fully clothed, "the bastard's spooned me all night."

The lounge erupted in deep chuckles, the atmosphere feeling less strained, even for a moment. Fury stood up, the blankets falling off him and I gasped and turned around, heat grabbing at my cheeks.

"Howay, man," V complained, "I don't want her to put off men for ever, put it away."

"Nah, mate. You're more worried she'll realise she's been *short* changed."

I rolled my eyes and left them to it, walking back to the tiny kitchen while half listening to the jabs and jibes flung around the lounge. At least it was words that were being thrown and not punches. The kettle on the stove bubbled, a faint whistle becoming suddenly angry as the little room was consumed by the loud shrieking noise. I turned off the gas, pouring the bubbling liquid into cups. An arm pushed one across the bench towards me and I took it from him without looking up and filled it.

"Will the others want something?" I asked, turning to see Indie clutching armfuls of wood.

303

He shook his head grinning, "not unless it's got alcohol in it. Bacon sandwich?"

"No thanks. I've never eaten so much protein since V started...." I paused, suddenly self-conscious and confused. Too many emotions and questions struggling for control.

"Since V started looking after you? Been filling you full of protein, has he?" Indie turned, a low chuckle emanating from him as he threw some rashers into the pan, the meat hissing furiously from the heat of the metal.

"Since he started keeping me alive."

A smile pulled at my mouth, spreading to my cheeks, a stab of happiness assaulting me, taking me by surprise, and I waited for the fleeting moment to pass.

And although everyone seemed to want to kill me, and it felt like they were getting closer to succeeding, I had never felt so alive. Terror had awoken something in me, something long buried. The ability to feel again. I'd locked those feelings away, guarding them, never getting too close to anyone for fear that I would experience pain like it again. I'd started withdrawing and internalising the moment my mother had died. Yet, feeling again didn't scare me like it ought to, like I thought it would. Inside something had thawed, a warmth gradually radiating through my body, melting my snow queen demeanour, dislodging the shards of loss and grief in my heart.

I shook my head, melancholy trying to get the better of me, but I couldn't help glancing into the lounge at the man with the long blond hair, the man whose almost entire body was covered in inked images, the man who wore barbells in his flesh like expensive jewellery. He was the polar opposite of me. He couldn't be further from me in personality and the side of the law that he existed upon. And here I was watching him, feeling the swell of something in my chest, knowing he had entered my body in every way possible and I would never be the same again.

Eventually, after hungry bellies were filled and the meagre supplies had taken a hit, we'd congregated in the lounge. A fire blazed in the hearth, the earthy smell of burning kindling filling the room, a cosy warmth making me feel uncharacteristically relaxed.

"So what's the plan, V?" Fury asked.

"Don't really have one. Just wait."

"Wait for what?" The dark-haired man pushed, "for these fuckwits just to rock up here and take her out?"

All eyes turned to me, and I chewed on the inside of my mouth.

V broke the silence, deflecting the uncomfortable stares. "My intelligence guy is working through some leads, and Nat's brother-in-law is working others."

Fury looked at me again, his head tilted to the side, his eyes roaming over me as if I was a piece of data he was analysing.

"And this brother-in-law, is he well connected?" He asked again, turning away from me.

"Mate, he's Cian O'Sullivan."

"Shit."

Fury turned back to me, a look of genuine interest on his face.

"And what did you say you did for a living?" the dark-haired man asked.

"I didn't."

Fury rolled his eyes, "thought I'd heard you mention youth court."

He was observant.

"Yes. I'm a solicitor."

"And here I thought you were just a posh bit? Guess you're O'Sullivan's get-out-of-jail-free-card, huh?"

I felt the flush of annoyance hit my face, the retaliation stinging the tip of my tongue. But I swallowed it. These men didn't have to accompany us to the north-west of Scotland, and they didn't need my rudeness.

"I've got Cian out of a few scrapes. I'm sure he'll return the favour."

Fury nodded in understanding.

"So, do we just lie low while someone works this shit out?"

"Guess so," V replied.

"Fuck," Fury complained, running a hand through his hair.

"I need everyone's phones, too. No contact with the outside," V said again, holding out his hand and waiting.

"You for real?" Demon retaliated.

The Viking nodded.

"Fuck," Fury swore again, "I got a tight little ass in Newcastle going on. Was hoping to get some entertainment while we were holed up in the back of beyond."

But he handed his mobile to the Viking, anyway. Indie and Demon followed, piling their phones on top of his outstretched hand, and then he turned to me.

"And you, babe."

"What? I'm not going to use it."

He smiled, shaking his head.

"Sorry, babe. But I've told you not to do a shitload of things, yet you've done them all. Phone."

I harrumphed. There was probably no signal here, anyway. I pulled the mobile out of my back pocket and handed it to him.

"Hope Eli has some board games or something," I sighed, glancing around at the thinly furnished lounge, its lack of TV, its lack of anything to play music on.

"I know a good game of cards," Fury commented, the side of his mouth curling into a smile.

I rolled my eyes.

"I'm going for a walk."

I turned to leave, feeling the immediate curl of fingers round my arm, my body pulled back to face the Viking.

"I'm sorry, babe. No one goes out. No curtains are opened. I'm not taking any chances."

"Fuck's sake," I muttered, "guess I'm going back to bed then."

I shrugged V's hand free from my arm and left the room.

Chapter Thirty Six

ഋ The Viking ര

Natalie's feet stomped across the wooden floor, her plump arse cheeks and her hips swaying as she all but flounced out of the room. Then I heard the angry creak of the stairs under her feet, and I followed the sound, the floorboards above my head shifting slightly under her modest weight. I sighed.

"You can't keep her locked up, V," Indie said, suddenly beside me.

"Fucking can."

"She'll go stir crazy, mate, we all will. We'll be safe here."

He rested a hand on my shoulder, an attempt at reassurance that I wasn't prepared to accept.

"This is huge, Indie. No one has found me for years, not the Kings and not the Military Police, no one. I thought I could keep her safe at my place, with all my equipment and my surveillance, but I couldn't. Someone found me, found her. That shouldn't have been able to happen."

"You sure you're not just feeling guilty that they got close to her? That you were distracted by her?"

"I wasn't. I just didn't hear the alarms," I protested, the deep knot of something sinking into the pit of my stomach.

"Yeah, cus, keep telling yourself that. We can all see how you look at her," Indie continued, looking around the room as if he needed backup.

Fury smiled at me, but Demon just folded his arms and rolled his eyes.

"They're not gonna find her," Indie continued, "you've got all our phones. No one followed us. There's no way anyone would know where we are. So relax. And let her do something."

I chewed the side of my cheek.

The shrill sound of a mobile broke the silence, high pitched and annoying, and for a moment I stared at each of the men in irritation.

"It's coming from your pocket, mate." Fury crossed his arms over his chest, frowning at me.

I pulled the burner phone from the back of my jeans and pressed the button on the display and held it to my ear, ignoring the annoyed faces of the men stood in front of me.

"V," Cian's Irish accent rumbled down the phone, "where's Nat?"

"Gone for a lie down," I answered.

"Haven't you all just got up? OK, OK, I don't wanna know," Cian continued before I even attempted any answer, "we've been tailing that ex of hers."

"The posh bastard? How's his eye?"

"The copper? Didn't look like anything was wrong with his eye."

"Nah, he wasn't a copper. Some posh twat in a suit."

"That was Carter Lawrence. I'm talking about another one, Steve Burrows. DI Steve Burrows."

I swallowed the hot lump of lead that had risen to the centre of my throat.

"She's upstairs," I answered, "I'll go get her."

The stairs complained as I leapt up them. They were steep and narrow and bare and my feet echoed around me loudly. When I pushed through the bedroom door, Nat was already on her feet, her chin set, defensive. I pushed the handset towards her, her fingers brushing mine as she took the small phone from me.

"Cian," I grunted, stepping back and propping myself up against the set of drawers at my back.

Natalie's eyes flicked back and forth, not focussing on anything particular in front of her, and I could hear the low grumble of Cian's voice on the other end. She frowned, her brows pushing together.

"We dated for a few months. I liked him," her eyes flicked to me and away again, "he seemed a nice guy. I could see how he would fit into my life, how we could have been a family, had kids."

She paused, listening to whatever Cian was saying to her on the other end of the phone.

"He always seemed like a good guy. I became more and more involved with defence cases. It was a rite of passage in my firm, but I was good at it too, just like...." she stopped herself, slightly shaking her head as if she was chasing a memory away, "these kids were getting roughed up in the cells, yet every time I started to question police brutality, the CCTV was missing or damaged. It happened too many times. I complained to Steve, warned him to sort it or I'd take things further. He didn't. I suspected there was someone above him pulling those strings, someone who would help him get a promotion. But it kept happening."

Natalie dropped down on the edge of the bed, listening.

"I put in a complaint to Professional Standards," she paused, looking at me, "This was the first of two. The other was similar, about the use of evidence and police brutality in another case which involved the Chief Super's stepson. Steve never got the promotion. In fact, he got demoted. So yeah, he's canny pissed at me."

Natalie nodded and then stood, holding the phone back to me.

"What you thinking?" I asked Cian, turning on the loudspeaker.

"Your dead judge and his wife? They frequently had dinner with the Chief Super. Until the day they didn't. There were dinner reservations, but they didn't show. Strangely enough, it was a DCI and the Superintendent who were first on scene."

"Are you sure?" Natalie asked, shuffling closer towards me, "even at a murder scene it's usually uniform who respond."

"Exactly," Cian continued, "so why were two high-ranking officers the first ones on the scene?"

"Cian?" Natalie asked from beside me, "I need you to find out who were the Police Officers involved in the Dodson case. It was a high-profile case back in the nineties and Judge Anderson threw it out on a technicality. I'm almost certain those officers at the top of the food chain will have been involved. I knew that someone was influencing Steve back when we were dating. I just didn't know who."

"OK, Nat, on it."

The line went dead, leaving us standing in silence in the bedroom staring at each other. I slid the phone onto the dresser and crossed the room till there was barely any space between us. I pushed my hands into her hair, tipping her head back, spreading my fingers through the rich brown strands. Nat's eyes closed, her lips pushing together, thoughts and emotions tangling together.

"We're a step closer, Nat," my voice was a half whisper, the richness of her caramel-brown eyes catching me off guard as she opened them, beautiful. Desire, need, fear, all melded into one. She was delicious when she was vulnerable.

I pushed my lips against her forehead, lingering there for a moment, enjoying the warmth of her skin, the slight shake from her body, the way her tits pushed into my chest. She drove me crazy with just her mere presence. Nat tilted her face, her eyes burning into mine, the fear and anxiety stripping back to a perfect innocence and purity of soul, the intensity of her ripping my heart open and my demons spilling out. And then the fear of losing her hit me again in the chest, hard and irrational, driving a dread into me, a knowing feeling of doom crushing me, stealing my breath. I slid my hands from her hair and pulled her into me, feeling her melting into my arms and sinking against me, letting her guard down.

And suddenly, I never wanted to let go of her. But how could I keep her when we were so far apart from each other, both in lifestyle and personality? Nat needed her life back, wanted her life back. Yet I had no life to live. My chest ached, like someone had ripped my heart out, stomped on it and pushed it back into the cavity, misshapen and swollen.

Reluctantly, I let her go, grabbing my phone as I turned out of the room. Back in the lounge, three faces looked at me quizzically.

"What the fuck was that?" Demon asked.

"Cian. Checking in with info."

"No, I mean the phone. You get us all to hand our phones in and yet there you are with that thing."

I glanced at the smart mobile device in my hand and shrugged.

"It's fine. It has PGP."

"What the fuck is PGP?" Demon asked.

"Yeah. I'd like to know that too?" Natalie's voice called out from right behind me, "why do you get a phone and we don't."

I sighed.

"PGP. Pretty Good Protection," I answered.

"Fuck off!" Fury piped up from beside Demon.

"No really," I pushed, "it's an encryption programme on the phone. It's unhackable, untraceable and I can wipe the kit if it gets too hot. Anyway, I'm the only one who gets a phone. At least till this is resolved."

"Or I'm dead," Nat said flatly from the doorway.

"There'll be no dead, babe."

"If no one shoots me, then I'll die of boredom, or starvation judging by how much these guys eat."

Demon grinned, his hand rummaging around in the huge multipack of crisps in front of him.

I took a deep breath.

"OK, OK. You can go outside, as long as it's with either me, Fury or Indie."

"Why not me?" Demon asked indignantly through a mouthful of crisps.

"Because you don't have any military training, pup," Indie added, "we need the right sort of eyes on this."

"So why the fuck did I have to come?" Demon retorted.

"Because we needed the extra body. And if merry hell does break loose, at least we can rely on you to get fucking crazy quick."

Demon grinned, like a dog that had just been patted on the head, and went back to shovelling crisps in his mouth.

"Nat's right, though. We are going to need more supplies."

Indie nodded, grabbing his leather bike jacket off the back of a chair and sliding his arms inside, shrugging it onto his shoulders.

*****

I watched Natalie from the window, watching as she stood in front of Eli's cottage, her arms wrapped around herself, looking out over the Scottish countryside. The outside air was still cold, despite May creeping ever closer, and she shivered. My eyes scanned beyond her, looking for any sort of movement, any sort of indication that there was someone else with us at the foot of the mountain, the peak obscured by a sinking cloud.

Reaching out, I wrapped the leather bike jacket around her, watching as she slid her slim arms inside and pulling it around herself.

"Indie will be a while before he's back with anything to make a meal out of. And the sun is about to set. Fancy a walk?"

She looked at me, a faint smile stretching her lips, but it didn't tease the sadness from her eyes. I slipped my hand into hers, our fingers entwining, holding on to each other, and for a few seconds I stood enjoying the feeling of her palm against mine, of holding each other like we meant something. Gently, I tugged her along beside me, guiding her to the tiny pathway the sheep had created, winding up the side of the foothill behind the cottage, higher and higher, until the climb steepened further, and our calves burned from the effort.

Natalie's breath came in heavy gasps behind me, and my own heart beating heavily in my chest, each step up the steep incline pushing blood faster around my body until eventually the stony path widened and we stepped through crops of scattered heather and sharp rocks. For a moment, the climb finished, and I stopped on a flat ledge.

The land fell away in front of us, the single-tracked road to the cottage winding into a thin grey line and the forest of thick, dark green trees no longer rearing up before us. In the distance, we could see where the trees ended; the tiny patch of blue taking over the landscape as a loch stretched out from behind them, the lines of blue and grey of the tributaries flowing into it from the mountains either side of us.

And then, even further away, the sky looked like it was simmering; a shade of oranges bleeding across the horizon as the sun dropped lower and lower in the sky. Natalie squeezed my hand.

"This is so beautiful," she said quietly beside me.

"You know, in the winter, you can see the Northern Lights from here?"

"I've always wanted to see the Northern Lights," she said sadly.

"You know you can see the Northern Lights even better from Sweden. Maybe I could take you there?"

"Maybe," she whispered, a hint of uncertainty in her voice, but I chose to ignore it, to ignore that feeling within me that what we had right now was only temporary.

Chapter Thirty Seven

ೞ Natalie ೲ

The Viking tugged at me, nudging me backwards until we could go no further because of the rock that pushed up against the back of his legs. His arms wrapped round my waist pulling me towards him till I was sat between his thighs, my back nestled into his stomach, and we stared out across the rugged Scottish countryside. And for a long moment we just sat quietly, watching the sky grow more orange, the light breeze periodically blowing V's loose hair across my face.

"What's Cian going to do when he finds out who's behind this?" I asked, already knowing what the answer would be.

"He'll kill them," the Viking responded, "but not before he dismembers a few limbs. It's kinda his thing."

"What do you mean?"

"He likes to send a message. That normally involves someone missing a few fingers first. Occasionally he'll hack off something more."

"That's disgusting."

"So is putting a contract out on someone's head for no good reason."

"Maybe they think they have a good reason."

"I'm sure they do," V continued, "but it's still shitty."

"It's what people in power do," I sighed, "corruption just seems to be everywhere. And they think I've got the means to blow something up. I just wish I knew exactly what it was."

"Your Da, must have known," V answered, turning sideways slightly and swiping the strands of hair that the breeze had blown across my face.

The movement was so light, barely a whisper of flesh brushing across my cheek, but it made my skin erupt in tiny goose bumps of electricity. I closed my eyes, feeling the cool air on my skin, everywhere but the side of my face that was the closest to his, heat radiating between us, an unseen connection.

"I'm certain of it. I just don't know exactly what, though. Charlie is something to do with it all," I added.

"What do you mean?"

"In the boxes, I found newspaper cuttings and photographs. We both knew my dad had destroyed all her birth information. I never understood why. I always felt it had been something to do with my mother, some sort of weird grieving process. But then I found a picture in the box. It was Charlie as a baby, sitting on this young girl's knee next to me and my mother. Their smiles were the same. The same dimples, the blonde hair. The photos were all together with newspaper clippings of Jeremy Dodson. He was *helping* the police with his enquiries after a rape allegation at one of his parties. I remember my parents going to his parties occasionally. They were big posh affairs, put on for the social elite; judges, lawyers, businessmen. And then, in the same bundle of photos and clippings, was another article of the same girl in the pictures with my mother. Valentina. She had gone missing. Charlie would have been six months, maybe nine months. Not long after that photograph of us all was taken.

"I don't know whether to tell her. She'd always wondered about her parentage when we were growing up, but my father would never tell her, said it didn't matter."

"And does it matter now?" V asked.

"I don't know. I think I'd want to know."

"But not everyone does. Does Charlie really need to know she's the by-product of some sex trafficking depravity, that her birth mother was likely exploited and raped by a bunch of elitists who think they can get away with selling and abusing women? What do you think that would do to her? She's angry enough already. Do you think she would just sit there and dwell on it, or do you think she'd take it upon herself to reap some sort of revenge?"

I glanced sideways, tilting my body so I could see him better.

"Are we talking about Charlie here, V, or someone else?"

The muscle in his jaw flickered and for a short time he stared straight ahead, quiet tension stiffening his body against mine.

"Demon is my half-brother, only he doesn't know it. No one does. My Da was fucking about. Always did, and as I got older, he'd gloat about it to me. Whether my mam knew or not I was never sure, but I didn't tell her either. My Da loved to wind me up, elicit any sort of response in me. The day I signed up, he'd told me he'd been fucking my Uncle Ste's lass, Indie's stepmother. He told me about Demon. He was beaming about how much better a son he was than me. And he looks like my Da; the same sharp nose, the dark eyes, the temper. I should never have let it get to me. But I did. So I went on a bender, got dumped by my girlfriend and signed up for the army. And became a shit son for my mam, too."

I closed my hand over the Viking's, squeezing gently, the tattooed skin cool under the heat from my palm. He turned his wrist, his fingers entangling in mine.

"Demon hates me for killing his uncle. If he found out it was actually his father I killed, he would come for me. And I would be left with a choice of whether to defend myself or let him kill me," the blond man paused, and I watched as he glanced at me sadly, "and I don't know which one I would choose. So yeah. If it was me. I wouldn't tell Charlie what you found. She doesn't need to know."

For a while we stared out silently over the hills. A thick mist collected in the lower parts, clinging to the sides of the valley, rolling forward as the cool spring air dropped into the troughs between the mountains.

I sighed, letting out the big breath of tension that had been building, the Viking sitting beside me in quiet contemplation, but there with me, his hand squeezing my thigh.

"After my father died, I became obsessed with finding his murderer. It didn't seem long to find a trail. Steve... DI Burrows... he helped. He put all his resources on it. No stone was unturned, no shadow left alone. Or at least that was what he told me. Now, though, now I suspect he was in on it, or at least covering for someone. It was too easy. The court case, the evidence. It just went together so well."

A single tear rolled down my cheek, hot and obscure, the cool mountain air wicking away the heat immediately, the trail turning icy on my skin. I stopped talking, fixing my eyes on the mountain peaks in front of me, a silhouette forming behind them, darkness tracking the orange glow of sunset.

"You know I've always had shit taste in men," I continued, and I felt V straighten slightly behind me. "I've always had an idea what I wanted from the men in my life: integrity, honesty, safety. And I've never found that. Until I met you."

I slipped off the rock we sat on and turned around so that I faced him, pushing myself back in between his legs, between his thick thighs, my

323

hands sliding over the contours of hardened muscle under his jeans. V's eyes never faltered, never moved from mine, clear, resolute, mesmerising. He was the most beautiful man I had ever laid eyes on. From the golden blond of his hair, the light beard that hid the strong jaw underneath and the blue-green eyes, tranquil and calming like the Mediterranean Sea lapping against a secluded cove.

V stretched out his arm, sliding the tattooed hand against my neck, his thumb rubbing over my lips, and I sucked the rough pad just inside my mouth, kissing against it gently. He was a contradiction, a disparity. He searched my eyes, his brows pulling together in a frown, the angelic features of his face becoming suddenly dark and dangerous, and I pulled back slightly, watching his jaw tick in tension.

"I like you, Nat," his voice was hoarse.

I grinned, feeling the weight lifting from my shoulders, even just for a fleeting second.

"What are we, V? Thirteen?"

He grumbled, a low rich thrum, a spark in his eyes. Linking his fingers in the loop at the waistband of my jeans, he wrenched me closer, popping the button open and sinking his hand down the front.

"Don't think we were doing this at thirteen," he breathed into my ear, his fingers pushing into my knickers, slowly, teasingly.

My stomach clenched, his fingertips skimming over the skin of my groin, and I flinched, my pussy tightening, my stomach stuttering, waiting and feeling. His free hand wound round my neck, pulling me closer, his breath tickling my face, his lips millimetres from mine, tension and anticipation suspended in the air between us.

"I don't know how we would work, V?" I breathed the words, "we're so different. We want different things."

"What do you want, Nat?"

"I want a family, V. I want kids. Kids are all I've ever wanted."

"I never wanted kids. Why would you want to bring them into this fucked up world?" The Viking asked, a hint of disappointment in his voice.

"I dunno. I just want someone to love me back the way I would love them. Like my mother and my father did. There's just this immense hole in here." I touched my chest, watching V's eyes follow the movement of my hand.

"You don't have to have kids for that. You just haven't found the right person. Let me be that right person, Nat."

"And how could that be? You're a killer, a hitman. And I'm a solicitor, the person who upholds the laws you break."

"Justice comes in all different forms, babe. And your shitty, half-arsed prison sentences aren't always it. Sometimes the only price is blood. The only retribution is a life for a life."

I cocked my head upwards, studying his face again. The reaper disguised as an angel.

Then he pulled my head into his, his lips attacking mine, his tongue pushing into me and the fingers tucked tight against my pussy, suddenly impaling me as my gasps were swallowed by his mouth on mine. Heat flooded my body, my stomach flipping and tightening as his fingers punished me, moving in and out, the tightness of my clothes creating an irritable friction as the heel of V's hand rubbed and nudged my clit. Distracting me. Reminding me of the physical attraction. Reminding me he was the only man who had satisfied the primal urges within me, and had shown me that passion could really prevail in the place of love. We were so different, worlds apart, but when he touched me, those worlds collided, and there was not a thing I could do to stop myself from enjoying every bit of it.

I pushed my hips back against him, riding the fingers that were tucked down the front of my jeans, nipping at his lips with my teeth, our tongues battling as the sun set around us at the foot of a mountain.

Chapter Thirty Eight

ஒ The Viking ஐ

By the time Natalie climbed off me, the evening had turned to night. She shivered, her hands shaking over the button of her jeans as she pulled the waistband round her. Behind her, the blackness crept in, the tiny dark red embers of the sunset smouldered away to almost nothing as it dropped below the horizon.

I grabbed her hand, slim and cold against mine, and her body shook harder. But I didn't let go of her right then. I tugged her into me, spinning her so her back pressed into my stomach and I pointed up to the sky. Thousands and thousands of stars twinkled down at us, swamping the sky with tiny pricks of light as if someone had splattered white specks of paint over a black background.

"I've never seen so many stars," Nat whispered in awe, her teeth almost clattering together.

"You can see so much more without all the light pollution," I answered, my face pushed upwards, "it's almost as if we are among them not beneath them."

I wrapped my arms more tightly round her body, tucking my chin against her shoulder, staring out into the abyss of stars and space, as if in that moment, we didn't have a care in the world.

Below us, a small spot of light moved, gradually growing bigger, brighter, as it bounced along the road. I flicked on the torchlight of my mobile phone and laced my fingers into Nat's, leading her carefully down the narrow, winding sheep path as we descended to where the little cottage stood, its white walls almost a beacon in the growing darkness.

At the back of the cottage, a bike rumbled, low and guttural, echoing off the walls of the little house and the outhouses that stood behind it. And then suddenly the noise stopped, the only sounds the crunching of our feet moving against the smooth grey stones. The bike was caught in the glow from the cottage, a shadow swelling up the wall of the storage buildings, moving slightly as it settled onto the kick stand.

Indie raked around in the panniers, standing suddenly as we came round the corner.

"Fuck's sake," he cursed at us, "I was ready to kick your heads in."

"Hitmen don't normally make as much noise as that, Indie," I teased, watching him shake his head at me in a light-hearted warning.

"At least make yourself useful and carry all this shit."

Indie handed us a couple of carrier bags each and we followed him into the kitchen in the little house. Heat hit us the minute the door was open, the air filled with the rustic smell of burning kindling, and my stomach groaned.

"Hope you got something tasty in there, Indie," Fury called from the lounge.

"Can you cook, Nat?" He asked suddenly, rummaging through the old cupboards under the benches.

"Depends what it is," she answered.

Indie pointed to the white carrier bag I'd deposited on the tiny table. The bag rustled as Natalie rifled through it, pulling out trays of red meat and pulling a face as she handed it to Indie. He chuckled, taking it from her.

"If I stuffed some metal in one end of it, maybe you wouldn't look at it in such disgust?"

"Hey! Mini V doesn't look as mangled as that," I protested.

Natalie turned and fixed her stare on me.

"You've called your dick 'Mini V'?"

"Yeah. Why not? It's just a mini version of me," I shrugged.

"So you're saying that you're thick and veiny and a real stand-up guy?"

"Mainly."

"Mini V isn't tattooed," she shrugged, grabbing a bottle of beer from the bench and prising the cap off with the opener, "don't think I'm giving it a name, or addressing it by that," she grumbled waving her hand in front of my crotch, dismissively.

"There's time yet," I protested.

"Well, you're all sorts of firsts, that's for sure," Natalie answered, taking her beer and leaving me with Indie, who's shoulders were shaking from laughing as he peeled potatoes onto the bench top.

"Yeah, cus, she's got the measure of you," Indie said between fits of laughter, "I like her."

So did I. I liked her too much, and that bothered me. I watched her move through to the lounge and plop down onto the sofa, dropping her head back against the worn cushions and letting her eyes slip closed. And I wondered what she was thinking.

*****

The rain hammered the windows, bringing with it a coldness that seemed to have crept into the cottage through every tiny gap and crevice. The wind whistled through those same gaps around the windows upstairs, the wooden shutters banging against the frame, a soft persistent knocking adding to the noise of the weather threatening the Scottish countryside.

Natalie stirred beside me, the rhythm of her breathing changing slightly, and I pulled her against me, wrapping my arms around her. The skin of her stomach where my hand fell was smooth under the tips of my fingers, her flesh soft and warm. Her hair was splayed out on the pillow, wayward strands brushing against my lips and cheeks, surrounding me with the fruity scent from the shower she had taken before she'd come to bed last night.

A blast of wind hit the front side of the cottage. No shelter from the storm that creeped ever closer, rolling down from the mountain ranges that surrounded the property. The gust seemed to shake the little building then, the windows and shutters rattling.

Natalie jumped, startled, pushing onto an elbow to sit up. I pulled her into me tighter, my arm locking around her waist, the swell of her arse cheeks tucking in against my groin.

"It's ok, babe," I called out gently, "it's just the wind."

I ran my hand up her stomach, feeling the ripple of her skin reacting against my touch, dragging my fingernails across her delicate flesh and listening for the little gasp that tumbled from her lips. Mini V had already woken up the minute the wind had interrupted my sleep and now I couldn't think of anything else but where I needed to bury myself.

I stroked up her body, my fingers dancing lightly over her tits, skimming the skin but not yet stroking over her sensitive nipples. I nuzzled at her neck, my tongue darting out to taste the tiniest hint of salt and the scent of her dying perfume firing a rage in my groin, the addictive swell of heat diffusing outwards. I pulled my lips over her shoulders, gently sucking, teasing, feeling for the firmness of light muscle before nipping her sharply. Nat gasped, loudly this time, pushing her arse into me, the gentle flesh against my cock, begging to be fucked.

Running my hand lightly over her nipple, I felt for the hard bud beneath the pads of my fingers, listening for the little moan out of Nat's beautiful lips. The wind buffeted the windows again, and she jumped against me, her body forcing more pressure on the engorged part of me that was begging to be inside of her. I bit my lip, forcing restraint into the body that raged with a primal lust, a fever of heat even in the cold Scottish spring air around us. My palm grabbed at her tit, the heavy swell of flesh not quite fitting in my hand, spilling around it as my finger and thumb rested over the tight nub. I twisted my fingers sharply and Nat gasped, her hand rising to her mouth to stifle the cry at the sudden pain response.

My lips trailed across her shoulder again, as I dragged them up her neck, feeling for the tiny flicker of her pulse. It drummed under her skin, beating frantically against me. I grazed the spot with my teeth, listening to the rasps of her breath, following with my tongue and lips. Releasing her nipple, my hand snaked down her stomach, dipping between her thighs, meeting the warmth of her bare pussy and she exhaled loudly. My fingertips skimmed across her, sliding through the slick juices coating her, wet and ready for me.

Gripping her thigh, I moved it forwards, pushing it away from the other and I dipped my body closer to her, my hand now having better access as I glided my fingers into her from behind. Nat gasped as I filled her, dragging them in and out, making sure she was ready to take me in this position because I couldn't wait any longer to bury myself in her beautiful cunt. I pulled away, grabbing my length, guiding it towards her, the pre-cum coating the tip of my cock, lubricating the resistance of the barbells dotted around the head.

But it didn't matter how wet she was. The minute I entered, she gripped me tightly, pulling against the metal running through the head of my cock and I couldn't hide the heavy grunt that escaped against her back. Her pussy was warm and wet, and greedy. It groped and pulled at me, straining against me, sending furious surges up my dick and into my groin, filtering up into my stomach, leaching away any control and restraint that I had. I plunged the rest of the way into her, forcing her pussy open under the thrust, as she cried out loudly at the pull and scratch of the metal forcing its way through delicate flesh.

I didn't give her the chance to adjust to me. I couldn't. The sensation burned in me, primal and basic, the need for pleasure, a total lack of control over the animalistic instinct inside of me. I pulled out and pushed back in, grunting loudly, my other arm wrapping underneath her to hold her into me as I fucked her with long, hard thrusts. I closed my eyes, trying to keep control, trying not to think of just my cock and nothing else, but each time I rammed into her, the sensation intensified.

She was just perfect. My fingers grazed over her tits, listening to the noises leaving her mouth, my hand moving over the smooth flesh of her chest until I reached her throat, soft and vulnerable. I shouldn't have wrapped my fingers around her. I should have slowed down and savoured the tight pussy that milked my cock, but I couldn't. My fingers tensed around her, grabbing at her neck as I moved faster, my grunts growing louder, mixing with the soft whimpers tumbling from her lips.

I felt around her with my other hand, sliding between her legs, the swollen nub of her clit at the end of my fingers. She bucked her hips, not knowing whether to push into the fingers that swirled against her or back into the cock that punished her from behind. I pulled her pelvis into me, not letting her move away, keeping her in place as I fucked her, drumming into her, hearing the whimpers grow to cries. Between her legs, my fingers whirled, nipping and rubbing, swirling and teasing. Her heavy breaths pushed against my forearm, her pulse thrumming against the fingers that I wrapped around her delicate throat, squeezing as I held her still, fucking her harder and harder.

"Shit, V!" she cried out, her voice ringing around the bedroom.

The bed bounced on the floorboards, moving under our combined weights. Bumping and groaning, but the noises from Nat's gorgeous mouth and the growls ripping through my throat drowned out the pounding of the bed on the floor.

My fingers picked up the punishment on her clit until she was thrashing underneath me, her body trembling from where I had her pinned against the bed, unable to get free, unable to move her body against me like she wanted. Her pleasure was completely at my mercy. I dipped my mouth to her neck, sucking on her skin and nipping along her shoulder with my teeth. Heat swelled in my stomach and I bit down harder. Nat threw her head back, her hair falling in my face, her stomach flinching and her hands scrabbling against the covers. Her pussy tensed around me, and her hips desperately tried to move but my hand and cock held her in place and as I sucked against the skin I'd just bitten, she cried out, a string of expletives until her body went limp against me.

I rolled her onto her front, adrenaline racing through my veins. Propping my arms either side of her head, I pounded into her, urgent, desperate. The headboard of the bed thundered against the wall as I grunted like a wild animal, the wind and storm not quite able to drown out my own carnal sounds. My stomach tightened, my breathing hitched, and I closed my eyes, feeling the pressure pull against my shaft, my balls tensing and wet, sticky heat flooding out of me.

"Fuuuck," I growled into the back of her head, my body flattening her to the bed, powerless underneath me as I took what I needed from her tight pussy. She was fucking incredible.

Chapter Thirty Nine

❧ Natalie ❧

The wind rushed around the cottage, driving the rain against the windows. Yet the sounds of the storm had become barely audible as we distracted ourselves with each other's bodies. It was only as I lay in the Viking's arms that I heard the anger in the storm. The roof creaked loudly overhead as another blast of wind hit the house and I glanced around the room, half expecting to see it ripped clean off.

"Relax, babe," V purred from beside me, his eyes half-closed, a tattooed arm lying across his inked, naked chest, "the cottage has stood here for years. No Scottish storm is gonna knock this place down. We're as safe as houses."

Then he laughed to himself, boyish and light, nipping the bridge of his nose as he tried to contain his amusement. I sighed, snuggling back under the covers and wriggling into his side, lying my head on his chest, ignoring the prod of the nipple piercing sticking into the side of my cheek.

"It sounds crazy out there," I said softly.

"It is. Scottish mountain weather is pretty fierce. But not as fierce as mini V."

I felt him smile, as I lay on his chest, staring towards the dying light that had done its best to penetrate the windows all day.

"You're gonna have to get better craic than that, if we're gonna keep doing this," I answered.

The Viking turned onto his side, his face now in front of me, blue-green eyes searching mine. A look of seriousness crossed over them, a frown pulling momentarily at his mouth, the mouth that had been driving me insane only a few minutes ago.

"And are we going to keep doing this?" He asked.

"There's not much else to do here."

"I don't mean just over the next few days."

V's face was stern, tense, almost.

"I, I don't know how this is going to end, V. I can't even see further than a few days at a time."

"I've made a promise to you, babe. I'm not going to break it." His hand brushed over my cheek, the dark tendrils of his tattoos catching in my peripheral vision before his fingers disappeared, brushed up into my hair.

"You should never make promises you can't keep," I answered, staring into the tranquil blue-green orbs that stared at me.

"I will keep my promise, Nat. I can't.... I won't lose you." His hand tightened to a fist in my hair, little pricks of pain exploding in my scalp, followed by the rush of heat through my body.

The Viking pushed his forehead to mine, his scent encapsulating the space we lay in, the wind whistling in the background as the rain slowed its steady beat against the windows.

"You're everything I didn't realise I needed, Nat. I won't lose you."

My teeth raked against my bottom lip, partly to stop it trembling, partly to focus on reality.

"Let's just assume that I'll live to see next month," I started, "how would any of this even work? You're a criminal. You don't even exist and if you did, the world and its wife would be coming after you. How do you see this working?"

The Viking drew a breath, his lips parting to say something and then stopping himself. His hand relaxed in my hair, sending surges of tingles running over my skin.

"I've had the most amazing sex in the time you've been protecting me. I really have. But I don't see how a relationship can work," I continued, watching my words destroy him just a bit more.

But we didn't make sense. How could we? We walked two different sides of the law. Our lives were too different. It couldn't continue. It would never work. We were too different, too opposite, no matter how I felt about him.

V's hand trailed back down the side of my face, as he shuffled away from me slightly, far enough that I was sucked into the blue-green abyss of his eyes until I felt like I was looking deep into his soul, and I was sure I could see the pain festering there. Or maybe that was my pain reflected at me, because saying those words to him, no matter how true, how sensible they were; it hurt, low, dull pain opening out in my chest.

"I know I'm not your usual type, Nat. I'm not a wealthy lawyer, I don't make an honest living. But I'd look after you."

"I don't need looking after, V. I'm good at doing that myself, present situation excepted."

He pushed his lips together, his eyes narrowing with defeat, letting out a long breath, the shunned sigh that he was trying to control.

"I'm hungry, V. I need to get something to eat," I said suddenly, unable to break the tension between us.

Throwing the covers back, I darted across the room, the air assaulting my naked skin as I pushed my legs into underwear and then my jeans, yanking a thick jumper over the top half of my body. I didn't look behind me as I padded down the stairs, unable to see the look on the face of the man I'd just rejected. The only man who made me feel alive, even in the face of death.

I shook my head angrily at myself, the stairs creaking under my feet, rushing to get away from him. Low voices and laughter came from the lounge, the door standing open and a faint heat drifting into the cold kitchen from the fire burning fiercely at the far side of the other room.

The stove seemed to take an age to heat the water in the kettle as I peeked out of the curtains into the failing light. The rain had stopped, but the wind stubbornly attacked the little cottage. In the distance, the trees waved furiously, and I could almost hear the angry swishes of branches knocked against each other as the trees in the forest collided. The sky was grey, consumed by clouds full of rain yet to fall as the storm refused to compromise.

The kettle shrieked suddenly, making me jump, just at the same time as the Viking appeared behind me. He loitered for a moment, as if he intended to say something and then thought better of it and wandered into the lounge. I poured the bubbling liquid into a mug and sloshed in milk on top before cuddling it between my hands, ignoring the burn on my palms.

I could see the men from where I leant against the bench, sat on the floor in a circle, a roar coming from Fury as he threw something into the middle, and after a little while I wandered in to join them, avoiding V's gaze.

"Hey, Nat," Indie greeted from where he sat crossed legged on the floor, a hand of cards in his grasp.

"Hi," I returned, watching the card game in front of me, "what you playing?"

"The noisiest game we could think of," Fury answered, "anything to drown out the sound of the bed hammering against the floor and the walls and fuck knows everywhere else all day."

"Ignore Fury," Indie commented, "he's just pissed off he doesn't get the chance to get his end away all day like V."

Heat rushed to my cheeks, and I glanced at the Viking, who was leaning against the dresser that stood alongside the wall between the lounge and the kitchen, a slight smirk tugging at his lips.

"Lucky we didn't let him play strip poker, like he wanted," Demon added, "he might have tried to join in with you guys."

"Hey! Do I look like one of those twins? I don't share. My women are mine and no one else's," he retorted, "but if you get bored with Barbie here, I'll happily provide you a new ride."

He grinned widely as Demon and Indie chuckled. I chanced a glance at the Viking, who smiled, the corners of his lips pulling upwards, but his eyes told another story. I moved back towards the kitchen, away from him, from the hurt on his face that he was trying so hard to hide.

The sound came suddenly, the chink of breaking glass and a whizzing noise, almost at the same time. And for a moment, it felt like time stopped. I turned towards the noise, catching the Viking moving towards me. In the distance Indie, Fury and Demon rose to their feet. The whistle of the wind grew louder, and the air seemed to move around me, yet I felt I was stuck in some sort of bubble, watching everything and everyone in slow motion.

He came at me in a flash of blond hair, the patterns etched over his arms coming alive, moving on their own. His arms wrapped around me, grabbing me roughly before his weight hit me, tipping me over, the hard floor rushing up towards me. My head clattered the floorboards; my brain feeling like it ricocheted against every internal surface of my skull.

More glass exploded; a high-pitched whistle as tiny missiles drove through the air. The Viking was heavy on top of me, forcing the air out of my lungs, my head dazed and confused.

"Fuuuuck!" a man yelled from the other side of the room.

"Get down, you fuckwits!" the Viking yelled from on top of me.

V wriggled off, taking the weight from my body and I panted, my lungs desperately trying to inflate. A man's voice continued to groan loudly from the side of me. A hand clasped mine, fingers wrapping around my palm, pulling at me.

"Keep your head down and crawl," V instructed, dragging me to the centre of the room.

I followed him, crawling across the floor, letting him pull me across the floorboards, my heartbeat filling my ears, panic swelling in my throat. In front of us, Fury lay on his back, clutching his thigh, blood soaking into the floorboards and creating a pool of red underneath him. The Viking stopped for a moment, taking hold of Fury's hands and pushing them against his leg. V's mouth moved as he uttered something to him, but the humming in my head drowned out any sound. Then fingers wrapped round my hand again, pulling me across the floor.

I glanced up, watching Demon moving on his stomach in front of me and then drop away out of sight. We kept crawling, moving quickly, dragging our bodies with our elbows. The wind rattled around the lounge, the curtains billowing where they covered the windows, the whistles and whoosh of the storm drowning out any other sound.

Ahead, the trap door in the floorboards stood upright, and the Viking slid me towards the hole, towards the outstretched hands of Demon who tugged me in, catching me before I dropped onto the ground below.

"Indie, get Fury in here and then I need a distraction," I heard V from above me.

"Got it," Indie's deep voice rumbled overhead.

The Viking jumped down into the hole, and for a moment I felt relief to have him next to me. He grabbed a gun from Eli's stash, pushing a black cartridge up into the bottom of it and then throwing it up towards Indie. I looked around, bewilderment stealing any words my brain could form. And then I looked back at him, a strand of long blond hair fallen, draping down his face, his eyes narrowed, concentrating on the weapon he held in his hands as he loaded ammunition and checked the sights.

Dread filled my stomach, like a balloon slowly filling with air, watching helplessly as he slung the huge gun over his shoulder and hoisted himself out of the hole in the floor.

"If I'm not back in an hour," I heard his voice rumble over the top of the hole as he spoke to Demon, "get her out of here and don't stop riding. Get her to Cian in Cork."

The Viking turned.

"No. Wait!" I shouted after him, my hands scrabbling against the shelves of guns to get purchase as I tried to pull myself out of the strange cellar under the lounge floor. But the Viking didn't stop. He didn't even turn around. The dread filling my stomach doubled, nausea clawing at my throat.

Chapter Forty

ೞ The Viking ೦೩

I hadn't heard the first shot. It had sailed through the glass cleanly, the bullet from the rifle lodging in the far wall with a quiet thud. Nat had turned, flouncing to the kitchen just at that moment. I would never have reached her in time otherwise, and the thought had knocked me sick. But the bullets didn't stop as we scattered across the room.

I dragged her across the floor, pulling her as she crawled, keeping her as low as possible. The windows popped around us as bullets filled the air. He was shooting blind now, no particular focus on any of us. He had lost his mark. I pushed her through the hole in the floor, Indie pulling her in towards him as I leapt into the underfloor hatch beside her.

Eli had an impressive selection of weaponry, but nothing like the sniper rifle that had just been shooting at us. I pulled a mean-looking hunting rifle from where it was secured on a shelf, locating the right ammunition for it and packing a bag of extras. My knife was upstairs, beside the bed, but I had no time to fetch it. I'd make do with what Eli could offer me, and there were plenty of smaller knives in here.

I shot a look at Indie, who nodded, acknowledging the orders I gave him, and then jumped out of the hole.

Nat's voice rang out behind me, shrill and terrified. But I had no time to look back, no time to worry whether any of us would survive this next hour. With the mountain at the back of the cottage, we couldn't be surrounded, but we also stuck out. I didn't know how many shooters there were. There could be one. There could be more. And I had no idea how they'd fucking found us but found us they had.

A dull moan sounded behind me as I crouched and jogged through the lounge, hoping the shooter wouldn't catch me with a lucky shot. Safe in the thick doorway between the lounge and the kitchen, I watched Indie and Demon drag Fury into the hole, a long line of red trailing behind him. And then Indie was up and out of the cellar, crawling across the floor, scurrying towards me.

"What's the plan, cus?" he asked, leaning against the deep threshold.

"Draw his fire. He'll be in the trees, I'm sure, but I need a clue."

"Then what?"

"Keep low and get ready to ride. If he starts shooting again, I failed. If I'm not back in an hour, I failed."

Indie nodded, resolution creeping across his eyes, his lips pushed together in a mixture of concentration and tension.

We burst out of the door from the cottage, guns drawn, half expecting to be dropped the minute we stepped foot outside. But the shots didn't come. Indie shuffled round the corner, sinking to his stomach and crawling around the front of the cottage. The tiny grassy hillock at the front of the house provided some cover, enough to tuck in behind. And then he fired, the shots ringing out behind me as I bolted for the foothills at the bottom of the mountain that reared up behind us.

The wind was even stronger without the protection of the thick Scottish masonry, and I scrambled up the first incline, my feet slipping on the scree of the sheep track as I kept low, hoping the shooter's attention was on Indie. The noise from Indie's gun was quickly muffled, the wind swallowing the sounds and disguising any sense of where the sniper was positioned. But there was no doubt that it was the forest with its natural cover of thick pines.

The ground under my feet squelched, soaked from the rain that had pounded the countryside, unrelenting for the past few hours. The narrow sheep track wound higher and higher, till the drop on one side would break a leg if I slipped. Another thud vibrated in the distance, the whine of a bullet in answer as the wind picked up the sound, driving it towards me. I ducked instinctively, my foot sliding in the mud and I tipped forwards onto my hands,

347

sludge and saturated peat sliding between my outstretched fingers.

Pushing back up, taking care as I edged around a steep, rocky mound, the earth dropping away almost from under me as the narrow track made by the sheep became almost non-existent. I breathed heavily, pushing on as quickly as possible, without falling to my death, or paralysing myself in a fall down the steep valley sides, rocks rearing out the ground with razor sharp peaks.

I'd now skirted around to the side of the forest, creeping closer to the tree line. The foothill had risen suddenly, and the only way down was to half scramble, half slide down the sharp rocks and shale, making as little noise as possible. Even from this distance, a good sniper would pick up movement, or at the very least my movement might startle nearby wildlife. Slowly, carefully, foot by foot, I moved down the steep decline, the hunting rifle slung over one shoulder and the small holdall across the other.

The ground was slippy, the earth under my feet moving a millimetre with every cautious footstep. But, bit by bit, I descended. It was slower than I would have liked, slower than I planned. I checked the digital watch I'd taken from Eli's weapon's room, noting the slow progress I had made and the hour's deadline I'd given Demon and Indie. I wanted to quicken my pace, run over the soggy heather and fern grabbing at my feet, but there was no margin for error. Natalie's life depended on it. So I trotted carefully, sinking low, ducking behind mossy boulders and vast patches of reed, my feet sploshing through bogs, freezing water soaking up my legs.

The air seemed to grow darker as I got closer to the treeline, the sentries of huge pines standing ominous against the storm collecting overhead. The wind blew the branches, the swishing movement from the trees masking my approach. And then I slipped into the forest, the floor beneath my boots dryer, as my soaked socks squelched uncomfortably inside the leather.

Keeping close to the line between the woods and the bare moorland, I moved back towards the cottage, treading carefully to avoid the dead branches that littered the forest floor. The shadows enveloped me, allowing me to creep forwards, a predator tracking his prey. Every few metres I stopped, scanning up into the trees, looking for a shape that didn't belong, a disjointed movement too big for a bird or a squirrel. Indie's shots had stopped and so had the response from the trees and so I crept into nothingness, with only my sense of intuition and the experience of a killer to guide me.

I skulked deeper, skirting around where I thought he'd be positioned, where I would position myself if it was me looking for the kill. My footsteps were soft, almost soundless, creeping ever closer, glancing occasionally at the watch and seeing the minutes flashing by, precious time ticking away.

A bird flapped above me, suddenly, overly loud in the oppressed silence of the trees. For a few short moments, it set off a catalyst of noise, triggering every bird that had settled into branches to escape the storm as they shot off wildly, running from an unknown predator. I sank to the ground, crouching in the shadows, keeping as still as possible, even my breathing sounding amplified in the strained silence.

Minutes ticked by as the forest settled and the birds came back to roost. The ruffling of feathers and the flapping of wings dying down, and I crept forward, one cautious foot at a time.

The shooter had to be far enough into the tree line to give himself some cover, but not too far back that he couldn't clearly see his targets, even with the sights of his weapon. I moved forward, silently stalking the prey I couldn't yet see, scanning the trees for the lump of shadows. And then, five metres from where the trees cleared, and the heather littered lowland started, I saw it. The dark shape bulged out of the tree branch, huddled against the thick trunk of an aged pine.

He barely moved, but every now and then, he shifted slightly, as if his legs were plagued by painful tingles from being in one static position too long. I knew. I recognised the ache that would be thrumming through his limbs, the tiredness behind his eyes from constant surveillance, the fuzziness in his brain from watching the movement of the leaves in the wind and the headache from the constant tension of concentration.

But this wasn't Iraq or Afghanistan, and this wasn't a police stakeout. I was willing to bet he had no idea who or what I was. Nor would he be expecting me. I stayed back and dragged the gun off my back, positioning it in the crook of my shoulder and checking the aim. I had two seconds to make the shot and then a further thirty to get to him before he could fire back. The second I cocked the rifle, he would hear it. And I didn't want him dead just yet.

I checked my aim again and for a split second, a tiny tendril of doubt raced through my veins. If I had made a mistake, that the dark shape in the tree was not the shooter, we were all as good as dead. I positioned myself against a rough tree trunk, took a breath, and slid the bolt of the gun back. I saw him move as I pressed the trigger, the dull sound of the gun quickly swallowed by the noise of the wind. The shooter didn't shout. If he grunted, the wind took that too. Slinging the gun across my back I bounded forward.

He was on his feet the minute I got to him, reaching a hand behind him, the other lying limp at his side. His arm swung back to the front, my foot connecting with the object in his fist, knocking it to the ground with a dull thump. He teetered sideways, a wince pulling across his face.

"Who the fuck sent you?" I growled, my eyes sweeping over his body, ready for any other weapon he might pull out of his clothing.

White fluff hung out of the black padded jacket he wore, hiding the real damage, and I suspected the exit wound just under his collar bone was messy from the hunting rifle's bullet. And even in the shadows, I could see the clamminess of his face. The skin was grey, a trickle of light through the canopy of leaves providing enough to see, and tiny beads of sweat prickled on his forehead. He was probably slowly bleeding out from beneath his jacket.

He smiled at me, his lips forming more of a grimace from the pain of the wound.

"You know I wouldn't tell you if I knew," he answered.

He stepped to his left, his movement stiff and clumsy, circling me.

"Who gave you the job?" I asked again.

"Everyone in the field knows about this job. Whoever ordered this hit is desperate. The bitch must have some shit on them."

I threw my fist before I'd even thought about knocking his teeth out, but even injured, he was quick, slipping to his right, feigning and then driving into me with a left hook. I staggered backwards, my head reeling, his left fist jabbing and punching as I struggled to get my hands up in front of me. Then he ducked, swinging his leg and kicking my feet out from under me, sending me crashing down onto my back. He reached down to his ankle, lifting the leg of his trousers and slipping out the black handled object and flicking open the thick silver blade. Light caught off the sharp edge that whizzed towards my face. I rolled sideways, the mulch of the forest floor muffling the travel of the knife, spearing itself in the soil just where my neck had been.

The man above me faltered, confusion washing over his eyes, and then they rolled back into his head. The first drop of blood spattered onto my face, then turning into a sudden gush as I dislodged the heavy serrated blade from his temple.

Chapter Forty One

ೞ Natalie ಬಿ

I glanced at my watch again, the faint ticking sounding like it was pounding in the strained silence. I'd barely taken my eyes off the little crystals embedded in the face, watching the hands move, counting down the time from when the Viking left. My memories flitted back to the look on his face, to the quiet resolution, to the setting of his shoulders and the stoic calmness. To the kill or be killed demeanour in which he flung the terrifying rifle over his shoulder and bolted out of the cottage.

It was in that moment, as I watched him leave me behind and charge out into the storm and the danger beyond, that I realised I was in love with a hitman. An assassin.

And there it was, the admission that somewhere, somehow, I'd fallen for this guy. A guy who wore jewellery in his cock and all over his body, the same body I couldn't see for tattoos. A man who doesn't talk to me about which new legal precedent has been set or how he is expected to make QC in a few years and a peerage next, who doesn't play golf and drink fine wine.

We're opposites. Entirely. We couldn't be further from each other if we each stood at separate poles. We're fire and water, night and day. And that there was the realisation that all I had ever wanted, a respectable job, a husband, a child; the Viking wasn't any of that. He wasn't stability; he wasn't the family man, the father, the breadwinner, the man who would sit by the fire on a night reading the newspaper and talking politics with me over cheese and wine. He was everything I didn't want. But he was everything I needed.

He was all I could think about. He'd wiped those desires from me, stripped me bare and for the first time, I realised what love truly was; the irrationality and the fear, the unrelenting attraction to that other person, to the kindness in their soul no matter the exterior.

It wasn't what I was looking for, and it wasn't how I'd envisioned it. The Viking had changed me, enlightened me. And I understood then that's why no one else had ever worked for me. And now I felt the fear; the fear of losing someone, the fear of wanting and needing someone so badly, mentally, physically, that everything and everyone else is forgotten about.

Almost.

I hadn't forgotten V's instructions. The hour was up and more. I glanced around nervously from where I sat on the floor, my back propped against the upturned leather sofa, providing some sort of barricade to the bullets.

Fury sat not far away, a belt secured around his thigh. The blood from the wound congealed and drying. Indie and Demon worked on all fours, stuffing weapons and supplies into panniers, talking amongst themselves in low urgent voices.

"You gonna be able to ride?" I heard Indie's voice as he shuffled over, crouching in front of Fury.

"Dunno. This fucker hurts like hell."

"Demon," Indie called across the room, "Fury will need to ride with you. I'll take Nat."

I shook my head, pushing onto my feet.

"No. No," I started, watching three heads turn in my direction, "we can't go yet."

"Nat. V said…"

"I don't care what he said."

Indie shook his head, his eyes full of pity.

"Nat. It's been an hour."

I tossed my head from side to side.

"I'm not going."

Indie straightened up slightly, stepping over Fury and moving towards me in a half crouch, keeping his head low. Reaching out, he rested his hand on my shoulder, squeezing it slightly.

"Nat. V knew what he was doing the minute he stepped out that door. He calculated the odds, and he went out there, anyway. His instructions were clear. He's not come back. It's been over an hour. We need to move."

I shrugged his hand free, "I'm not leaving without him."

"Nat," Indie warned.

I shook my head again, my throat swelling and my eyes burning. I swallowed.

"No. I can't...." my voice came out as a whisper catching in my throat.

After all of this. After everything. I couldn't lose him. I couldn't lose another person I loved. The tear trickled down my cheek, warm, tickling my flesh. Indie pulled me into him, wrapping his arms around me. For a few minutes, I didn't fight the comfort of the strong arms holding me. I rested my forehead against his chest, biting my lip as I took long, deep breaths, fighting back for control.

"What's this?" The voice sounded from the doorway, light and cheeky and beautiful, "stealing my girl already, cus?"

I whipped my head round, relief jolting against my chest like an electric shock and I pushed out of Indie's arms, my legs carrying me across the wooden floor, not caring whether my head would get blown off at any minute. I bounded the last few strides, jumping at the Viking and throwing my arms around his neck. His lips were hot against mine, and if he was taken aback by the sudden public display of attention, it didn't show. His tongue moved against mine in a desperate waltz and for a moment everyone faded away into inexistence, and it was just us in the cottage in the mountains.

"When you two have stopped eating each other's faces, we've got a getaway ride to make," Indie interrupted.

V propped me back onto my feet and I hadn't realised that I'd wrapped my legs around him, hanging on him like some horny teenager.

"We've got another storm coming over," his voice rumbled, "and the shooter is dead. We leave at first light."

Indie nodded, turning back to Fury.

"Ok. Gives us time to get Princess here sorted out," he motioned towards the man still sitting on the floor.

"Fuck off, Indie. If someone shot you in the leg, you'd be fucking rolling around crying."

"How bad is it?" V asked, a look of concern crossing his face.

"The bullet glanced the side. Took out a nice chunk of flesh, but not much else. Fucking drama queen."

The Viking's face lightened, his lips pulling into an amused smirk, and I noticed for the first time the blood drying on his face. There was a cut to the right of his eyebrow and a bubble of partially clotted blood sticking out from the wound. His cheek bone was shadowed with the start of a bruise. I turned back towards him, cupping his cheek, my thumb smoothing lightly over the marked skin. But all I could think about was how I was touching him again.

His fingers closed against my hand, pulling it away from his face, touching his lips against my palm with an angelic softness that was as contradictory as a monster with morals, and I closed my eyes, savouring the feel of him.

*****

As the grey light of morning trickled through the bullet holes in the curtains, the wind having scaled back to a light breeze, I pushed myself closer into V's body. It was cold in the cottage, more so because of the draught coming in through the holes in the windows. My back and hips ached from lying on the hard wooden floor and my head pounded from lack of sleep. We'd stayed on the ground floor, sheltered behind the old leather sofa, fully clothed and ready to make a midnight escape if it had come to it. The men had taken turns to watch the cottage, between them wandering the perimeter or perched at the upstairs windows, watching for any flicker of unusual movement in the dark.

The Viking shook me gently.

"Time to get up, babe."

I nodded, urging my stiff body from the floor, my eyelids heavy from lack of decent sleep. The men hustled about, packing the last bits of clothing into the panniers.

"I'm not leaving my bike here," I heard Fury complain.

"Well, I'm not leaving mine," Demon answered.

"Yours is shit. It'll probably not even make it back in one piece," Fury continued, hobbling around.

"Got here, didn't it?"

"Ladies!" Indie interrupted, "just get on a bike. I don't give a fuck who's. We'll come back for whoever's bike we leave."

"I'm taking mine," Demon finished petulantly.

"Fine. You're a shit rider, anyway. Wouldn't want you fucking mine up."

"You're just bothered you're gonna have to be my bitch all the way home," Demon retorted, grinning jubilantly.

"Aye. Enjoy it. It'll never happen again," Fury growled, his eyes growing darker the more the younger man taunted him, "V, it's all your fucking fault."

The Viking chuckled, a low rumble, his eyes sparkling with mischief. Fury hobbled towards me, the irritation across his face fading away.

"So, who did you piss off then?" Fury asked me, limping past, carrying the leather panniers over his shoulder, "some drug dealer you put away?"

I shook my head.

"We don't know. Someone with a lot of money connected with the Northern Pipeline," I answered.

Fury raised his eyebrows and Demon stilled, resting against the upturned sofa with his arms crossed against his chest.

"Northern Pipeline? What a gas company?"

I snorted, trying to stifle the giggle, a tiny element of lightness awakening within me and then extinguishing just as fast.

"Sex trafficking, mate," the Viking explained.

"Fuck."

Demon whistled, "jeez, you've got yourself in some shit, lass."

"Wasn't me," I protested, "somehow my parents got involved with it a long time ago. It's killed them both."

"Then why are they after you?"

I shrugged, "my father must have some incriminating evidence somewhere. Someone knows that. On the anniversary of his death, someone delivered me a key. It led us to a list of names. Jeremy Dodson, Luckyan Volkov, Archie Anderson, and M. Lacroix, whoever that is."

Demon scoffed, "M. Lacroix? He sounds like he's got a right face on him."

Four heads turned towards him quizzically.

"M. Lacroix. Maurice Lacroix. It's the make of a watch," he answered, shrugging.

"Shit," I blurted, "my father's watch."

Attention turned back to me, the Viking searching my face.

"My Dad always had a favourite watch. My mother had bought it for him as a present one year. It was a Lacroix. After my mother died, it stopped working. Then, a couple of years before he was murdered, he started wearing it again. It didn't work, but I just assumed that he felt closer to her."

I turned to the Viking.

"That watch. I need to get back home, V. The key to this is sitting in that watch. In the loft."

Chapter Forty Two

❧ The Viking ☙

We rode all day, stopping once, only to piss in a bush on a country road. As we made our way through Northumberland, I could feel Nat shivering against me. We'd met wet weather again just before Edinburgh and, despite the protection from the thick motorcycle leathers we wore, the rain had been relentless and was seeping through the saturated material.

A few more hours and we were nearly home. I pulled off the motorway just before Gateshead, taking off down a small road that wound its way back on itself and dipped under the main road. Sheltered from the traffic, the weather and prying eyes, I cut off the engine and kicked out the stand. The heavy bike settled to the left, and I slid my leg over, helping Nat off, watching her straighten up stiffly.

"What's up?" Indie asked, pushing his visor up.

"We need to get back to Nat's place. But I need to pick the van back up and drop off Tweedle Dum's bike before he cries. How clear will the clubhouse be? Don't fancy running into

Uncle Ste. I've fought to the death enough for one twenty-four-hour period."

Indie studied my face, a sudden look of sadness crossing his, and then it was gone as quickly as it came.

"Get Nat home. I'll get your Da's bike and meet you at her place. We'll swap back then."

I nodded, telling him the address and then ushered Natalie back to the Harley. She climbed back on behind me stiffly, wrapping her arms around my waist. Then we peeled away, leaving the escort of Northern Kings behind.

Natalie's street of family houses radiated homeliness and familiarity, and I could feel the exhale of air, her body relaxing as we drove down the street. I cruised slowly, looking for anything out of place in a street of family cars and terraced homes. It was early evening, the light was fading and already lights blazed in windows as the grey sky leached the natural light away, making it darker than normal for the spring evening.

I made two passes, checking everything, front and back, before driving to the back of the mid-terrace house. Parking up at the back gates, I kept the bike ticking over, the throaty rumble of the engine echoing down the back lane of wooden gates and garage doors. The gates leading to Nat's concreted backyard swung open haphazardly, and I checked the back of the house carefully before riding the bike in and closing the gates up behind us.

I'd seen the back door when I scanned the yard, noticing the shards of glass on the step below it and the dark hole just alongside the door handle. Pulling my helmet off, I cut off the bike, beckoning for Nat to shelter behind me. The door was unlocked, the door handle broken and the door itself ajar.

"Shit," I heard Nat mutter behind me.

"Stay close," I instructed, pulling out the knife tucked in the back of my bike trousers, "like fucking glue."

She nestled in behind my back, and I felt her duck down, shielding herself behind me. Slowly, quietly, we crept through the house, sweeping each room for intruders. The place was a mess. The contents of drawers were pulled out, strewn over the floor, ornaments smashed and picture frames knocked over.

"Someone was clearly looking for something," I muttered when we were back downstairs again.

Nat looked around, her eyes ablaze with the contradiction of relief at being home again and distress that her place had been ransacked.

"Fuck, they've made a mess," I grumbled, righting a picture of Natalie, Charlie, and their father.

"Looking for the same thing we are," she muttered, standing in the middle of her once tidy lounge, her eyes sweeping across, surveying the damage, "only they won't really know what they are looking for."

"And you do?"

"It has to do with that watch. He's left me clues."

I sighed. The thoughts troubling me on my way home expanded now that we were back in the belly of danger. I fiddled with the cuff of my bike jacket, the chill of being wet through starting to get to me now.

"What?" Nat asked suddenly.

"What do you mean, what?"

"You look uncomfortable," she cocked her head sideways a little, keen eyes boring into me, "there' something on your mind."

I sighed again, chewing the inside of my cheek, my mind jumping over all the answers I should give.

"I don't get it," I said eventually, "if knowing about the pipeline and who was involved was so dangerous for your Ma and Da, then why did they bring you into it? Why not keep you out of it?"

Natalie looked at me, her eyes capturing mine, the rich caramel-brown burning into me, and for a moment I thought she was angry.

"I can only assume he wanted me to figure it all out, take them all down," she said after a long, pondering pause.

"It's a fucking big thing to bring down, babe. The people involved are much bigger than you and me, bigger than Cian."

She sighed. Her eyes filling, the beautiful brown orbs sparkling with tears.

"I don't know, V. But he wouldn't have steered me towards this unless he wanted me to do something with it. I need that watch."

I nodded, resigned that she wouldn't rest until she found it.

"Where is it?"

"A box in the loft."

I grabbed her slim hand, tugging her with me up the first set of stairs. The first floor of bedrooms was as messy, clothes and papers strewn about and the little room she used as an office completely turned upside down. They'd left nowhere untouched. As we got to the top floor, the picture was the same, drawers pulled out and items disturbed. The little door to the back of the attic was wide open, boxes of clothes thrown over the landing.

Nat's face tensed, her jaw tight, a look of immense concentration, and I suspected she was fighting the tears that I could see welling in her eyes. A man's clothes lay over the floor, dragged out of boxes and pulled about. She dropped to her knees, moving the items of clothing out of the way and crawling forwards into the little space nestled into the rafters.

"Hey, babe, you need a hand in there?" I asked when she hadn't emerged straight away.

I stuck my head in the hole, my eyes adjusting in the glow from a tiny, dull orange light hung overhead from a rafter. Objects scraped against cardboard, Natalie's attention in a particular box, right at the back of the loft. Dropping to my hands and knees, I crawled forwards, inching through the tiny door, filling every bit of it as I moved across the wood ply flooring that stopped us falling through the ceiling of the rooms below.

Peering over Nat's shoulder, I could see what she sat staring at. Photos. Pictures of her childhood, of two live parents, of ignorance and naivety. Charlie wasn't in them. She wasn't even born, even Nat was so young. And the smiles on their faces. Everyone was so happy. She stuffed them back in the box suddenly, inhaling sharply as if pushing those memories aside. Then she pulled out the watch and turned it over in her hands.

Back downstairs, she sat at the kitchen table. The watch was old. A mid-brown leather strap and a hugely detailed face stared back it me. There were three little black dials within the face of the watch itself, intricately detailed, and a little rectangular box showing the day of the week. The hands and case were gold, and I suspected they were a decent carat.

"My mum bought him that watch when he set up his own practice. It was such a huge point in his career. Him and my Uncle Wes. And it went from strength to strength, attracting huge clients," Natalie reminisced, studying the piece in her hands.

She turned it over again, so it was face down in her palm, running her fingers over the back of it, inspecting it. She tilted it sideways, holding it in front of her face, directly in her eye line. Then she closed one eye and moved a millimetre sideways.

I waited, watching her turn it over and over, looking for something.

"V," she said suddenly, "the drawer over there," I followed where she pointed, "the little kit of screwdrivers. Get them for me, please."

I moved to the kitchen drawer and rifled through it, my fingers moving over the little rectangular box.

"These?" I asked, pulling out the box not even the size of my mobile phone.

Nat nodded.

"Really? Your Christmas cracker screwdrivers?" I mused.

"They're perfect," she answered.

And she was right. Nat took out one of the tiny screwdrivers and eased it into a space at the back of the watch, bouncing the little metal screwdriver until the back popped clean out. Something dropped out from inside, landing on the table with the tiniest of noises. I picked the little bit of blue plastic up from where it lay.

"It's an SD card," I said, "got something to put it in?" I asked.

Natalie shook her head.

"I do." I answered.

A rumble sounded at the back of the house, formidable and unmistakable. Natalie looked at me.

"Bike exchange," I explained, and she nodded in understanding.

Indie rode the bike into the yard, dropping it onto the stand and swinging his leg over the back of it as he got off. He patted it, as if remembering the owner, or maybe it was just memories of a time long ago.

"Thanks mate," I greeted him, throwing the keys for the other bike towards him.

"It's been good to see you, V."

"Good seeing you too, cus," I answered, holding out my hand in a strained goodbye.

Indie clasped my hand, and then, pulling me into him, hugged me before letting me go. He smiled faintly, but in his eyes was a deep sadness. And I felt it too. Then he climbed on the borrowed Harley, backed it out of the yard and rode off, the roar fading away into the distance.

Natalie stood beside me, sliding her hand into mine, her beautiful rich-brown eyes looking up at me with understanding.

*****

Darkness was rolling across the north east as we rode home, stopping only to pick up a takeaway, the first food we'd eaten in nearly twenty-four hours. The industrial estate just on the dockside in Sunderland was quiet, shut down for the night and the only people we saw walking the gated roads were the usual ne'er-do-wells, looking for no good or waiting to meet for drive-by drugs deals. I drove down the streets cautiously, taking in every movement and every shadow, paranoia spiking my every synapse. But there was nothing out of the ordinary.

The gates to the compound stuttered, creating a moment of panic in my chest, but then mercifully whirred to life, slowly peeling open. I didn't wait for them to open fully, squeezing the bike through the moment there was enough space.

Fury and I had secured the place pretty well after we'd dealt with the bodies and rid the place of DNA evidence, or most of it. The alarms showed no sign of any further attempts at entry, and I felt myself exhale, a small amount of relief trickling into my body.

Nat stood in the garage impatiently, pulling out the tiny SD card and twiddling it between her fingers.

"Food first," I warned, seeing the stubborn look appear in her eyes, "then we'll look at that."

Whatever was on that tiny memory card was not good news, and I really needed some food before the shit hit the fan.

We ate like starving animals, and I wasn't sure whether it was because we genuinely were famished, or whether both of us needed to get the eating part out of the way and satisfy our curiosity. I took out the little card and pushed it into the side of the USB stick and then into the computer portal. A bar appeared on the screen, a pulsing blue line for a few seconds before the file opened, filled with several coded documents. I stepped back, letting Nat jump into the driving seat, watching from over her shoulder.

She opened the first JPEG file, a photograph appearing on the screen of two men in suits shaking hands. For a moment she stayed still, staring at the screen, her breath shallow. Then she closed it down and opened another, the same two men. And then another, but this time one of the men was different. And I recognised him, my last memory of his cold, dead corpse in his lounge on his estate on the outskirts of Durham. Archie Anderson, sitting in a restaurant with the man in the suit that had appeared in all three photographs.

"Your Da seems to have a fascination with this bloke in the suit," I muttered from over the top of her, seeing the same man appear time and time again, "he must be significant somehow."

"You could say that," Nat answered, her voice wavering, "it's my Uncle Wes. My father's best friend."

Well, fuck.

Chapter Forty Three

෬ Natalie ෨

He was there in every photo. My father's best friend. The best man at my parents' wedding. The man who supported me through university, who would let me talk boy troubles with him, who helped raise me when my mother died. I dug around in the other folders, looking for something that wasn't Uncle Wes. I found a bank account statement. Uncle Wes' bank account. My eyes scanned over the entries, the frequent deposits of large sums of money. And yet more photos. I recognised most of the men he was with: the high court judge Archie Anderson, the millionaire businessman Jeremy Dodson, my ex, Steve Burrows and his senior at the time. But there was another man in the photos, one I had never seen before.

"Do you recognise him?" I asked V, my voice cracking as I desperately tried to maintain control.

"Yeah. Lukyan Volkov. Russian Mafia."

I leant back in the chair, staring at the screen. I was numb, shocked. A trickle of bile rose in the back of my throat, burning my chest.

Or maybe that was the tears and hysteria that I so desperately tried to contain. Uncle Wes. He connected them all.

"M, m, maybe there is some other explanation?" I asked aloud, unsure whether I was asking the Viking or trying to quell the chaos of thoughts and emotions pushing against my chest.

V looked at me, pity in his eyes, waiting for me to accept what was in front of my face. He shook his head, his eyes holding mine.

"I'm sorry, babe," he said, resting a hand tentatively on my shoulder, like I was an unexploded bomb.

A tear rolled down my cheek, warm and wet.

"Do you think, h, he had anything to do with the d, deaths of m, m my parents?"

The Viking pulled the chair away from the desk, dropping to his haunches in front of me, grasping my head in his hands. There was a storm in his eyes, the murky bleeding of blue into green, any tranquillity disturbed by an undercurrent.

"Yes."

That's all he said. One word. One final word. I crumpled. My face feeling like melting wax, a strangled sob ringing out in the air between us. And then I was in his arms, my body shaking with sobs, my chest aching from the pressure of the pain. It was like they had been taken from me all over again.

The shrill ring from the Vikings phone made me jump so high I nearly fell off the computer seat. He pushed the phone to his ear, nodding his head before lowering it, and a thick Irish rumble filled the room.

"Your boy Joey's come up trumps with his search for dirt on Nat and Charlie's parents," he started, and I held my breath. "Anthony Porter was a member of an old boy's club. You know the type of thing: cigars, golf, shady business deals. I'm willing to bet they also had a wanky secret handshake. Sorry Nat."

"It's ok. Go on."

"His membership with them stopped sometime in 1997."

"The year Charlie was born," I muttered.

"What was that, Nat?" Cian asked.

"Nothing, Cian. Continue, please."

"The other members were Jeremy Dodson, Archie Anderson, Wesley Weston. I know you know all those names, Nat," he paused, "V you asked me to see who investigated the cases that Anderson threw out? Christian Johnson."

"The Chief Super," I breathed.

"Uh, huh. And I'll bet that's why he's where he is today."

"So my dad was connected to the Northern Pipeline all along?" I asked.

"Sorry, Nat. Looks that way."

Oh God.

*****

There was a scratching noise, a rustling from beside me. I turned, sliding my arm across the bed and feeling nothing but wrinkled sheets. My eyes were heavy, still swollen from a night of crying, but slowly I opened them and tried to focus. Sunlight flooded the mezzanine floor, a deceptive warmth as it poured through the bare windows. The Viking was in his walk-in wardrobe, pulling thick legs into a fresh pair of jeans, hiding the tapestry of pictures that covered his skin.

"What are you doing?" I whispered, a second attempt, the first not yielding any words.

"I'm going to do my job," he answered, not meeting my eyes.

I snapped upright, kicking my legs out of bed and moving towards him.

"No, you can't," I breathed, panic almost silencing me.

"I have to, Nat. It's the only way to stop them coming after you."

"But what if it's not what it seems?"

"How can it not be? You've seen all the evidence. Your Da has been sending you messages. Leading you to what really happened."

"You can't just go in there and kill him. We have evidence. I can send him to prison."

"Do you really think you'll get a conviction? Look who he's involved with. This goes way up. He'll get off with it or those higher up will take him out. Just like they took Anderson and his wife out."

"We don't know that's what happened to them," I protested.

The Viking moved towards me, the tattoos on his chest moving like they were alive. He reached out, his hands covering my biceps, gently squeezing.

"It can't be anything else. That's how these people work. You've seen how deep this goes: the Police, the lawyers, the judges. I'll bet there's some politicians connected to all this. The Chief Super's wife, probably. Corruption is like the plague, winding its way through society, leaving nothing untouched."

"But it's broad daylight. The office will be packed. You'll not make it out of there."

"I'm not wasting another hour on that fucking scumbag. I'm not giving them another hour to come after you, babe. This ends, now."

He turned away from me, grabbing the white t-shirt and pulling it over his torso, the demon on his back staring at me.

"I'm sorry," he said, tucking the ugly knife into the back of his jeans and reaching for his leather jacket.

I stood watching him go, my head whirling, unable to sieve through all the resonating thoughts. I was like a deer staring down the barrel of a gun. A rabbit staring into the bright white headlights of death moving towards it. I was confused and scared and contradicted.

An exhaust rumbled suddenly below me, metal clanking loudly as the big garage shutters rolled up over head. I grabbed for my jeans. Forcing my legs into the material, throwing a jumper over the t-shirt of V's I'd worn to bed and scooping my hair on to the top of my head in a messy bun.

Downstairs, the shutter had returned to its lowered position. I scanned the garage. There was nothing to drive and I couldn't ride a bike. I had no idea how. Thundering back up the stairs, I raked through the meagre belongings I had brought with me. V still had my mobile, but my purse was snuggly tugged into my laptop bag. I wrenched it free and ran back down the stairs to the garage. There was a keypad on one of the pillars that supported the floor above, with a number of buttons. I pressed a couple, listening and waiting until something, anything, happened and then moved on until I found the one that opened the shutters. I punched the button, listening to the metal rattling as it wound upwards.

The metal gates of the compound were slowly closing. The gap getting smaller by the second. I raced across the yard, my lungs on fire from the effort of throwing myself sideways as the heavy gates brushed against me. I wriggled through, just before the metal crushed my chest. And then I took off down the street, my feet hitting the pavement in a steady beat, as my heart pounded and my lungs opened.

I jogged down the pitted street, machinery and vehicles passing me steadily, the industrial estate traffic in full swing. At the main road, I dropped to a walk, a burning pressure in my lungs from the small exhilaration and a sharp stitch developing in my side and the mounting panic building in my veins. A taxi drove past, and I waved frantically, but the car didn't slow down. I kept going, breaking into a jog before my lungs burned and I had to slow again. I watched every approaching vehicle, hailing anything that looked like a taxi.

I was almost in the city centre before I stopped one. The green arch of the Wearmouth Bridge reared into view as the traffic streamed across it. The white saloon car pulled into the side of the road and I jumped in, offering a tumble of garbled instructions as my chest squeezed against me, anxiety gripping tightly to me.

The journey into Newcastle was painstakingly slow, traffic building at every light, a constant start-stop, and with each second that ticked by, tension built within me. Eventually, the taxi pulled up alongside the quayside offices; three floors of enormous glass windows and the massive glass atrium that looked like a glorified goldfish bowl. My father's old practice. People poured out onto the street, agitated, scared, and confused. I scanned the pavement, catching sight of the black Harley Davidson that stood almost abandoned in the middle of the forecourt.

"Looks like there's a problem," the taxi driver muttered as we came to a stop.

"Yeah, looks like it," I answered, thrusting the money under his nose and clambering out of the vehicle.

Outside, there was a clamour of voices: exaggerated, worried, bewildered. I skirted round the people spewing out through the main doors, a hand catching my arm as I slipped inside.

"You shouldn't go in there," the man's voice said, "the police are on their way. There's a madman on one of the floors. Disgruntled client or something."

I shrugged the hand free.

"Yeah, something like that," I answered, pushing my way past.

A woman hung around the reception desk, chewing her bottom lip with worry. I recognised her. She'd aged, wrinkles setting in deeper round her eyes and flecks of grey through once dark hair. My father's old PA. She looked at me curiously for a moment and then a faint smile came to her lips, something dark crossing her eyes.

"What are you doing here, Natalie?" She asked.

"Got to speak to Uncle Wes."

"Someone else came to do that too," her eyes fixed on me, searching my face.

"Yeah. I know."

I darted away, bowling into the lift when it pinged and the doors slid back, a couple of worried looking people in suits rushing out, eyeing me quizzically as I brushed passed them, punching in the button for the top floor.

It was quiet on this level, save for the ping of the elevator and hiss of the doors swishing open. Uncle Wes' office was along the far side. It occupied most of one side of the building, with its sofa, desk and a small boardroom style table. I edged closer, hearing the dull tone of male voices as I crept along the corridor.

"Did they send you?" Uncle Wes's voice drifted towards me, strained.

The Viking said something, the low rumble of his voice the only thing I heard.

I picked up my pace, breaking into a run, my footsteps pounding down the corridor. The door to his office was ajar and the blinds wide open, allowing me to see straight into the huge glass room. Uncle Wes was still seated, calm and resolute, staring up at the long-haired hit man in front of him. I grabbed for the handle, pushing the door open fully as it squealed in protest and I bundled into the office.

"Nat?" my uncle asked, puzzled, "what are you doing? You need to get out of here. This man is dangerous."

I slowed, closing in on the desk, approaching the two men. I slid my arm around the Viking's back, reaching up on my toes and drifting my lips across his cheek.

"Please, let me speak to him," I whispered in V's ear.

The Viking nodded, dropping his hand and the ugly knife he held onto the desk. My uncle's eyes watched my every move, suspicion morphing into realisation. I watched him take a breath, a forced smile pulling at his lips, tight with tension.

Chapter Forty Four

౫ The Viking ౚ

"You've got a lot to tell me, uncle," Nat started, her voice cool.

The silver-haired man stayed sitting, his brown eyes fixed on Natalie, the jaw hidden by the silver-grey goatee growing more tense, and I could see the muscles pulsing just at the sides.

"What are you talking about, Nat?" He asked, his voice surprisingly steady for the apprehension that filled his eyes.

"I'm sure you know. But you can start with the Northern Pipeline."

"I have no idea what you mean," he answered flatly.

He was stalling. Wasting time till the police got here. We didn't have time for this. Nat knew it, too.

She sighed.

"Look. We can skirt round the subject as much as you like. But neither of us are going anywhere until you tell me the truth," the grey-haired man looked from Nat, to me, and then back again. "And don't think I don't know that you pressed the alarm under your desk. He can, and will, make you talk, and since I've spent the last few weeks avoiding the contract *you* put on my head, I'm not in any mood to stop him torturing you for the information I need. An eye for an eye? Ey?"

There was a flicker across his eyes, his jaw slackened slightly and then shut again. Slowly, he drew his arms against his chest, staring silently at Nat.

"OK then," she continued, "let me tell you what I know. I know what the Northern Pipeline is, the sex trafficking ring run by the elite and powerful in society, using young girls as sex slaves, tempted from eastern European countries with the lure of work and a better life. I know Charlie's mother, Valentina, was one of them."

Nat paused, watching his reaction. His brown eyes softened, but his lips clamped more tightly together.

"My mother worked it all out, didn't she? She tried to take it down, but it went too deep, didn't it? Judge Anderson, Jeremy Dodson, the police. They are all involved. Did you kill my mother? Or did you just fund it?"

He said nothing, but Nat didn't falter.

"At some point dad realised you were the link. So, you got rid of him too, didn't you? Did you pay someone? Or did you do it yourself?"

He continued to sit there staring at her, saying nothing, and I watched as she subtly sucked in a lung full of air, bracing herself, keeping tight hold of the frustration that must have been simmering inside of her. Because it was reaching boiling point inside of me.

"Really, Uncle Wes, I don't need you to admit any of it. I have all the evidence. Photographs of you with Anderson, Dodson, the Police bigwigs. Photographs of you with the Russian mafia. And I've got your bank statements with the deposits, regular big deposits, not the sort of money you get from a case, no matter how high profile. And there's more."

"Then why are you asking me?" His voice was low, controlled.

"I'm giving you the opportunity to tell me. Did you kill my parents?"

"Yes."

"And you hired the hit on me?"

"Yes."

Nat held his gaze, and I could see the anger flash across her face, mixing with pain and disbelief.

Wesley Weston sighed suddenly.

"Why?" She asked, her voice barely more than a whisper.

"You know."

"There had to be another way out? A plea bargain, at least?"

He shook his head.

"There never was. It started with a few jobs. Hide some evidence, tamper with witnesses. Once I'd done it the once there was no going back. Only forwards. I can never get out," he said, almost with a sadness. "It was hard killing your mother. She was a wonderful person. I'd known her for so long. It destroyed your dad. And I knew he would never stop looking for her killer. It took him longer than I thought for him to find me. But when he did, there was nothing else I could do. It was easy enough to plant the evidence on the Blackwood boy and you did exactly what I thought you'd do. And then I thought that was it. But then that key arrived. And I knew that, somehow, you were about to be pulled into it all."

He stopped, taking a breath, wetting his lips, eyeing me.

"So I got in contact with some people and put a contract out. I couldn't do this one myself. You meant too much to me."

"Not enough to not kill me, though?" Nat's voice was harsh, the words strained as she kept her emotions in careful control.

"Once you knew, once you started digging, *they* would find out. You were dead anyway, one way or another."

"Who's they, Uncle Wes?" Nat asked, her voice strained, cracks in her composure starting to show.

"You're right. This goes far deeper. You can never stop it. Never," then he turned to me, "and you, you can never protect her. They will find her. They will kill her. They'll kill you both. I put the first contract on you. But it failed. I put more money into it, but that failed too. Then someone started digging around Anderson. It alerted *them*. Anderson would have been an easy kill. Probably long overdue; he'd acquired a conscience in his old age. But then *they* came after you, too. You've done well to survive so long. It's good to have connections to the criminal underworld, isn't it?"

I'd heard enough. I stepped forward, my fist slamming into his mouth, his head snapping backwards. Natalie turned towards me, and I shrugged.

The grey-haired man looked up at me grinning, blood spilling down his expensive suit from the cut in his lip.

"Ah, the hunter fell in love with his prey," he laughed, a manic hideous noise, leaning back in his chair.

Natalie flinched but held strong.

"So tell me who is at the top of the chain, Uncle? If we're all going to die anyway, what difference does it make me knowing?" Nat continued.

"I don't know. But you're right about the people you mentioned. The Chief Super has been involved for years. They have their hooks in the government and the judicial systems. They control who can take action against them with bribery and threats and those they can't control, they kill. It's been like this for decades. The rich always find a way. Nothing you can do will change that," Wesley Weston mopped at his mouth with the handkerchief he pulled from the breast pocket of his suit.

"And my dad? The Club? He was involved in this too, wasn't he?" Nat asked, struggling under her attempt at indifference.

"We'd been involved on the outskirts for a while. Business meetings, lunches, the usual things as we won clients. It drove the firm forwards. Being members opened up a vast realm of opportunities. Your Dad could turn a blind eye to most of it while it was making us money, but then he started to notice the other things. The things I'd become more involved in. Discrepancies. Hints of secrets. Of young eastern European women on club grounds; there one minute, gone the next. I'd noticed them too, but I wasn't about to bite the hand that fed me. And for a while, I convinced your father to keep his head down too.

"Soon, though, I was sinking deeper and deeper into it all. Business was booming, we had clients paying us retainers. The firm was going from strength to strength until the Club had the annual ball that year. Wives and significant others had been invited. It was the usual loud affair, drink, drugs, business deals. I don't know how she had found out, gone wandering round Dodson's mansion, I guessed. But she found the Valentina girl distressed and undressed in one of the rooms. Your parents left the party early. And the girl was gone too.

"Sophie, your mother, she tried to bring Dodson to account. Guess she thought she could finally pin something on him after all these years. It wasn't the first sexual assault case she'd brought against him. But for Dodson, it helped to be well connected with people who can help these problems go away."

"What happened to Valentina?" Nat asked.

The older man shrugged, "I can only guess. But I suspect *they* got rid of that problem. I convinced your parents to falsify the adoption paperwork for Charlie. It wasn't difficult, given the connections I now had. It was the cleanest way for all of us. But your mother never stopped going after them and soon she was coming after me, too."

He looked at me again, then back at Nat, his face relaxing, the serenity nauseating.

"They'll come for you both," he continued, "and they will get you. No amount of mafia connections will keep you safe. *They* have access to the entire intelligence system: cameras, satellites, purchase records, mobile phones, IP addresses the lot. There is nowhere to hide."

Then he sat back in his chair, gazing over the top of us and out of the window. I caught the movement, the little red spot moving over the desk, tracking up over his chest. Fuck.

Chapter Forty Five

❦ Natalie ❧

My head whirred, anger and rage pressurising my brain. This couldn't have been the man I knew all my life. The kind, caring, honorary uncle who had treated us like his own. I thought I knew him. I thought he had loved us. But instead, he had taken everything from us. Everything.

His words rattled against me. *They would never stop.* I was as good as dead. There was never a future for me.

The Viking crashed into me, sending me hurtling to the ground, knocking the air from my lungs. There was a smash of glass and a sudden draught. V scrambled to his feet, pulling me with him, tugging me around the desk. Straining, he pushed at the heavy wooden structure, tipping it onto its side and sending the contents sliding to the floor, crashing and banging. Then I was pulled behind, my head pushed down.

"Uncle Wes!" I shouted.

"Nat, I'm sorry. That was a shot. He's dead."

"No," I whispered.

No. This wasn't what I wanted. This wasn't supposed to happen.

"No," I said again.

"I'm sorry."

We crouched behind the desk, but no other shots were fired. The air stilled around us, and everywhere was silent for a moment, as if the entire Newcastle Quayside was holding its breath. I glanced up from where we were hunkered down. Uncle Wes' legs sat still beside us, and for a while I strained, concentrating in the silence, but the only breaths I could hear were our own. Down on street level, I heard the whine of sirens; a tiny shrill wail at first, growing louder and angrier. I tried to count them, but the screeches became too loud, the individual sirens merging into one monstrous noise.

"What do we do?" I asked the Viking.

He closed his eyes, pinching the bridge of his nose, thinking.

"I need you to get to Cian. Use public transport. Stay in crowded areas. Cut your hair or something, but change your appearance."

The Viking pulled out his mobile, swiping over the screen several times, and then handed it to me.

"Ring Cian. I've taken the biometrics off. There are no names on the phone, only numbers. His is 623. It's part of his service number," he added when I looked at him quizzically, "now I need you to get up and walk slowly out of here."

I nodded. The Viking's hand clasped mine, and I gripped it tightly, like he would be ripped away from me at any second. He nudged me forwards on to my knees, pushing me out from behind the table. I could hear voices now, breaking in the silence. Lots of deep male voices. The Viking skirted around the side of me, blocking my view of Uncle Wes in the chair.

"Please, Nat," he whispered, tugging me away from the seat, "don't look. You don't need to see that."

But he was wrong. I did. I did need to see. Tilting my head slightly upwards, I looked into his eyes, unable to say the words and instead willing him to understand. And he did. Raising his hands to my shoulders, he squeezed the top of my arms, giving me one long last look as he stood barring the way. I nodded, and he stepped aside.

Uncle Wes looked like he was staring out of the window. Except his arms hung limp at the sides and his body was slumped back in the chair. There was a perfect circle between his eyes, dark and red, gooey looking, but no trickle of blood fell from it. Yet behind him, on the floor behind the desk, a dark pool of blood gathered, and tiny pinkish-red spots sprayed on the white wall behind him.

I should be sad. I should be weeping and wailing, another family member dead. Yet I wasn't. I was just numb. Inside, the emotions congregated, a storm gathering but not yet unleashed. Anger, pain, sorrow, dread, fear. All of it balled up in my stomach, threatening to overwhelm me at any minute. But I couldn't let that happen. I clenched my jaw and allowed the single tear to fall, just enough to release the pressure, and then I wiped at my eyes, taking in a deep breath, the metallic scent of spilled blood filling my nostrils.

"What are we going to do, V?" I asked.

"Get to Cian," he whispered, pulling me into him suddenly, touching his lips to my forehead, the kiss so gentle yet full of meaning. And then my stomach dropped, and dread won out over all my emotions.

The Viking pushed himself away from me, just as the sound of feet crept steadily along the corridor. He met them at the door, his arms in the air. Guns pointed at him as the first police officer stepped forward, pulling his arms behind his back and securing them. There was a mumble. Rights being read, and my head whirled, and I staggered back against the desk.

The rest of the unit poured into the office, filling the room like a swarm of flies. I lifted my arms into the air, nervously.

"Name?" The officer holding the gun towards me asked.

"Natalie de Winter. Wesley Weston is a family friend. I came here to warn him…."

"Right. The receptionist said you'd bolted up the stairs to his office. Said he was your uncle."

"Yes. Not officially, but I called him that, yes," my voice wavered, the other emotions that had not yet been freed fighting for dominance.

The police officer lowered his gun.

"I'm sorry for your loss, ma'am."

I nodded in thanks, unable to form anymore words and allowed him to usher me out of the office. I followed the procession of officers, the Viking's blond locks occasionally catching my eye in the gap as he was led away, and my stomach felt heavier still. Down in the reception, Uncle Wes' personal assistant loitered, looking anxious and as I came more fully in to view, she stared at me meaningfully.

"Please excuse me," I said to the officer escorting me from the building, "I need to check on the staff. They've had a shock," moving away from him and towards the older lady almost hopping from foot to foot.

I ushered her towards a couple of armchairs in a corner of the foyer, my eyes flitting between her and the plain clothed police officers who entered the building. I suspected our time here was limited, and I needed to get hold of Cian.

"Do you remember me?" The personal assistant said suddenly, snapping my attention back towards her.

"Yes, I do."

She smiled weakly.

"Is, is he dead?" She asked, looking up at the ceiling, but I knew who she meant.

"Yes."

"Good."

I turned and looked at her. She was angry, not shocked. There wasn't a fleck of fear in her eyes. She licked her lips.

"Then I can assume you found whatever that key was for?" She continued, her keen eyes burning into me.

I nodded, "how did you know…"

"I sent it to you. Your father had given it to me. Told me that if something happened to him, to send it to you but to wait a year or so. I waited two. I guessed it was as dangerous as it was important. He'd spent the last few years of his life skulking around the office late at night, scurrying over bits of information. I always knew that it wasn't just that he was working on cases. He was all but destroyed after your mother died; but in the last few years of his life, it was as if he had come alive again.

"So I forged his handwriting on the envelope….," she paused, offering me a small smile, "I was his secretary for many years, Natalie. I knew his handwriting as well as you."

She was right. She'd worked for my father for years and he'd spoken about her fondly. I didn't doubt she couldn't have imitated his handwriting.

"Was it Wesley?" she asked, her voice suddenly little more than a whisper.

"Yes. It was."

The woman sat back, her eyes filling with tears as she struggled for control.

"I always thought that," she nodded, more to herself than me, "he always wanted all of the business. Didn't like to share."

I stood, resting my hand on her shoulder, "yes. Something like that."

Then I walked away, pulling V's phone out of my pocket and locating the number 623. I tapped the screen and pushed the handset into my ear. The dialling tone clicked off, followed by a moment of silence before I heard Cian's Irish rumble.

*****

The police station was bustling with officers, the atmosphere full of static energy. I'd raced home, showered, changed and called in a favour from the Northern Kings. And now my heels clacked across the shiny tiled floor with the stomp of authority. It seemed like an age since I'd been in a suit and heels. I clutched the handles of my leather bag tightly, tension filling me with anxiety like never before.

The young police officer on the desk looked at me with familiarity, the excited expression in his eyes deflating when he recognised me.

"Ms de Winter," he acknowledged, "how can I help?"

"I'm here to speak to DI Burrows."

"He's busy at the moment."

396

"He's not too busy to see me," I corrected. I glanced at the bustling seating area. "I'll wait over there. He'll want to see me as soon as possible. Tell him it's about the Pipeline."

The young officer stifled a look of annoyance and nodded his head, reaching for the phone beside him. Turning, I scanned the room. On the far side was an older man and woman, sitting patiently beside each other and staring off at the wall ahead of them. There was a gaggle of track-suit clad youths taking up the middle chairs, mobiles in hands and talking and laughing amongst themselves. Then closer to me was a couple of men in their thirties, dressed in the same Adidas tracksuits of the youths. They sat silently, reading whatever was on the devices in their hands, and the man closest to me had his other hand tucked down the front of his trousers. Nice. I sat next to them. And waited.

Eventually, I caught movement on the other side of the room, a shape sliding out behind a door and stalking across towards me. I rose to my feet, steeling myself for the conversation I'd practiced in my head on the way over here. Steve Burrows looked annoyed. He barely slowed as he approached, reaching out and grabbing my elbow suddenly. I shrugged my arm free and glared at him, watching his expression change from irritation to exasperation.

"What are you doing?" He hissed, moving much too close to me.

"Thought that might get your attention," I shrugged, defiantly holding his gaze.

"And every fucker else in here."

"There's something, or rather, someone, I need."

DI Burrows looked at me, cocking his conventionally handsome face to the side slightly.

"You talking about the biker we just brought in?"

"I am. I need him out."

The dark-haired man looked at me as if I was crazy.

"We both know you have some serious procedural misdemeanours going on and now I have evidence to involve you in the Northern Pipeline. Photographs. Seems you also like a drink with the next head of the Russian mafia. Not sure how you would explain that to the Independent Police Complaints Commission? I'm sure you can release him on bail."

He took a half-step backwards, studying my face as he tried to decide if I was bluffing. Then he grabbed my arm again and tugged me away from the seats filled with people in the waiting room. Tucking us into a corner, he glanced around the room and I followed his gaze. There was no one watching us. The young officer on the reception was reading something, probably his phone, not so covertly under his desk.

"Are you for real?" He said again, the hiss turning into a growl, "you can't come in here and start flinging that shit around, Nat."

"Can't I? Because you're worried someone up on high will find out you're compromised and you'll be the next body? Or that you'll be incriminated in a sex-trafficking ring? Which is it?"

Steve Burrows shook his head.

"I've got a ton of pictures that put you with those involved. Anderson, Dodson, The Volkovs and Wesley Weston. And of course, the Chief Super. That's right, Steve. I know all about his involvement in the Northern Pipeline. It's all in the 'Cloud', Steve, ready to be disseminated to the papers in the next 48 hours. Only I can press that button and stop it. There's only so much covering up you lot can do."

"What do you want, Nat? I'm assuming that you haven't just come in here to brag about how clever you are to uncover all of this?"

I rummaged in my bag, pulling out the A4 envelope and handed it to him. His stare fixed on me, barely moving as he slid the photographs out of the packet. Then he glanced down, his brow furrowing and his eyes darkening. As he looked back up towards me, I smiled, passing him a basic looking mobile phone. He inspected it for a moment before looking up at me, a silent question on his face.

"There is one number programmed into that phone, Steve. You're going to take it to the Chief Super and you're going to ring that number. My representative will deal with all the formalities."

"And who is that?"

"I'm sure he'll introduce himself when the Chief calls him."

DI Burrow's face looked thunderous, tension creeping into the corners of his eyes as he furrowed his eyebrows, trying to control the scowl that I knew he wanted to give me.

"Oh, and that biker in there," I gestured, pointing my thumb over my shoulder, "he is part of this deal. So if you don't want this whole thing blowing up, I suggest you get him the fuck out of there."

"You know he's wanted by the Military Police for being AWOL, don't you?"

I nodded.

"He's been AWOL for the last eight years, Steve. Let's say we keep it that way?"

The detective inspector glared at me, his lips firmly clamped together as he tried to contain his anger.

"And how do you want me to fabricate releasing him? He's charged with murder."

"Thought you were good at that? But as you asked. Wesley Weston was killed by a sniper. The bullet entered the office window. Apart from the fact that the biker wasn't in possession of a gun, the trajectory and blood spatter on the wall behind him won't conclude that a handgun was the murder weapon. At best, you have him for possessing an offensive weapon. I reckon you can charge him with that and bail him."

"And is he likely to return to go before a Court?"

I smiled. DI Steve Burrows knew he wouldn't see either of us again.

The inspector shook his head and walked away.

Chapter Forty Six

℘ The Viking ℃

I wandered through the halls of the police station, officers eyeing me with disdain, as the tall, dark-haired detective inspector ushered me out.

"Don't suppose I can have my knife back?" I asked lightly, watching the scowl creep across his face.

"Just get out of here," he said, his voice low, as he opened the door from the custody suite to the free world.

I chuckled, walking away.

She was standing just outside the entrance, spring sunshine catching the rich brown of her hair. Dressed in a navy skirt suit and neck-breaking high heels, she leant against the red convertible sports car with her arms folded across her chest, oblivious or unconcerned, I wasn't sure. What I was sure of was that she was beautiful, and I'd missed seeing the bright red on her luscious lips.

"You got your car back?" I smiled at her.

"Yeah. Indie dropped it off. Rescued your bike too. It's nice to have my wheels back. Think we'd better make a run for it before the MPs get here," she said, a look of jubilation lifting her features even more.

"So you broke me out of the cop shop, huh?"

Nat nodded, "if *they* weren't absolutely sure I knew about the Pipeline, they do now."

"Fuck."

Nat shrugged, "when do we leave?"

*****

We'd spent the last few days lying as low as possible as I packed up the warehouse. I was exposed, and it was time to move on. The panniers for the black Kawasaki Ninja were already secured onto the bike, filled with as much as I could put in them, a one-man tent and sleeping bags strapped on the top of them, ready to go at a moment's notice. The alarm for the front gates rang out shrilly and Nat jumped, searching for the source on the cameras. I laid a hand on her shoulder, squeezing it in reassurance and then pressed the button, allowing the car through the gates.

The metal shutter rolled up slowly, letting the big, black 4x4 roll into a space in the huge garage. Cian stepped out, shutting the door behind him and giving the place a measured scan.

"Interesting place," he murmured, thrusting a brown envelope in my direction.

Teasing the little books out of the envelope, I flicked open the pages and thumbed through them.

"They're the best I could get at short notice," Cian added when he saw me inspecting the passports. "I suggest you get new ones wherever it is you're going."

"They took the deal, then?" Nat asked, and Cian nodded in response.

"What deal?"

"Nat shared the pictures her dad had taken and copies of the newspaper cuttings. I completed the deal with the Chief Super. It gets them off your backs for now. Until I can work out the rest. Joey sorted out the passports and a program. Here's the phone you need."

Cian passed the handset to Nat.

"Has it got Pretty Good Protection?" She asked, flashing me a smile.

"It does. You need to log in to the program every day. If you haven't logged in for more than seven days, then it'll fire the details to all the biggest media outlets in the country."

"It won't work forever," Nat said, turning to me, "but it'll keep them off our backs until we set up somewhere else, or Cian can take the whole thing down."

"And if whatever this program is doesn't work?" I asked.

"Then I'm dead. And if I'm dead, there is no one to log in and delay that email from being sent to the media. If they kill me, the secret's out."

She shrugged, pleased with herself. Then she turned back to Cian.

"You'll take it all down one way or another?"

"Nat," Cian warned, "the Pipeline is much bigger than me, much bigger than the O'Sullivans. It goes much deeper than we even know."

"I know. But those girls."

"I can't keep those girls safe. But I can keep you safe, Nat, in some part. And I can keep *my* girls safe. And that's what I'll do."

Cian smiled sadly.

"Charlie says take care," he placed his hands on her shoulders, "we'll get this sorted Nat, somehow. I promise. And when it's done, you can both come home."

She nodded, biting her lip and inhaling sharply.

"Give Caragh a kiss for me. Don't let her forget me."

"I won't, Nat. I promise."

As he turned back in my direction, I threw a set of keys at him.

"What's these?" Cian asked, dangling them from his fingertips.

"See that bike over there?" I tipped my chin to my dad's Harley Davidson, "I need you to drop it off at the Dog on the Tyne in Gateshead. Tell Indie it's for Demon. A peace offering. I'll have no more need for it." It seemed only right that he have our dad's bike, even if he didn't know its significance.

Cian nodded.

"Come on then, babe," I gestured at Nat, who moved towards me uncertainly.

I swung my leg over the black bike, kicking up the stand as I balanced it between my thighs and felt for the little dip as Nat climbed on behind me. Then with a roar it came to life. Another angry boom echoed around the garage as I wrenched the throttle and tossed another set of keys at Cian.

"Keep this place locked," I shouted over the sound of the exhaust, "I may come back for it one day."

And then I rolled forwards, leaving my home and memories behind, leaving behind the docks on the edge of the city of Sunderland that had kept me hidden for nearly a decade.

We rode all night and the best part of the next day, stopping only to go to the toilet or refuel. I chose the country roads, winding up through Northumberland towards Edinburgh and staying north, through Dundee and Aberdeen. The roads grew narrower and windier the more northerly we rode; beautifully dangerous, with sharp bends and breath-taking scenery. I felt free. More free than I had in years. Perhaps in forever.

As the second night of riding drew in, Nat shivered against me, the grip around me growing weaker and the weight of her helmet resting between my shoulder blades grew heavier. I pulled off the road, riding down a single track, the motorbike slipping occasionally on loose road clippings. The road was desolate, flanked by a thick copse of trees before the land rose sharply to a fern covered peak.

"Hold tight," I shouted behind to Nat over the loud thrum of the exhaust, easing the bike over the uneven ground of the little forest and weaving in and out of trees until we found a small clearing way back from the road.

I set the bike onto the side, wriggling off and helping Nat down, watching as she stretched weary legs. Sheltered on the other side of the forest, just inside the treeline, I pulled off the tent, putting it up with ease as Nat sat on a boulder, gazing up at the darkening sky. We'd camp here, let Nat get some rest. The ferry to Shetland didn't leave till the morning anyway, and then we were connecting from there onwards to Norway and eventually Sweden, my mother's homeland.

Night drew in quickly, despite being this far north. I sat myself beside her on the rock, the two of us admiring the clear sky. Millions of stars twinkled down upon us, as if the sky had been dusted in them.

"You know you don't have to do this," I said, hoping I'd hidden the unease in my voice, "we can still turnaround. You could go to Ireland with Cian. He would give you more stability than I could."

"When you promised to show me the Northern Lights, I didn't expect us to be actually heading there so soon," Nat said, ignoring my question, her head tilted to the sky, sadness at the edge of her voice.

"I know, babe. I'm sorry."

"I'm not. I've done nothing other than work all my life. I've never lived. Being so close to losing everything made me realise what I didn't actually have. I want to have those things, V. I'm not talking about marriage, and babies, and big houses. I'm talking about life and freedom. About living that with someone I love, someone who loves me. I want to take memories to my grave, not regrets. And I have few good ones, so I need you to help me make more. I don't know how we'll make money, but I've spent my whole life making loads of it. And I can't take that with me either."

"What about your job?"

"I've taken a sabbatical. Told them I'd never properly grieved after my father died, and so I was taking time off to figure things out. I'm one of their best, course they said yes."

"And what if we don't come back?"

"Then I'll figure something else out. I have my whole life to think of something. I want to be with you, V. You were willing to give up your freedom for me. Now I'm willing to give up any chance at normality to be with you.

408

You're not what I thought I wanted in my life. But you are everything I needed."

She turned, her eyes fixing on me, her hand warm where she moved it across mine.

"I'd rather have a life with you on the run, than a life without you, V. I love you."

I smiled, pulling her into me, my lips finding hers, soft and full and warm.

"I love you too," I whispered against her mouth, and for the first time I felt at peace, felt that I belonged somewhere. And that, somewhere, was in the arms of a lawyer, my absolute opposite, and together we could both be whole.

℘ The End ℘

Want More?

All the books in The Northern Sins Saga can be purchased here:

https://nikterry.link/thenorthernsinssaga

Keep up to date with new releases, get access to bonus scenes and exclusive giveaways by signing up to my newsletter:

https://nikterry.link/newsletter

Follow my Facebook page to learn more about me and join my reader group.

https://nikterry.link/facebook

About the Author

I can't remember a time I haven't written stories. I wrote my first short story collection at six years old and they went a lot like this:

Once upon a time there was a goat. The goat was good. The goat met a witch. The witch was bad.....

Well you get the idea, but the imagination, creativity and story structure was there, even when I'd barely learnt to read and write.

I then took to writing thrillers and fantasy series, none of which I have ever published but are sitting, patiently waiting to be given some attention at a later date.

My very first fascination with romance came from the absolute best series of my generation – Buffy the Vampire Slayer. How I loved bad-boy Spike and how angry I used to get with Buffy over some of her rubbish romantic choices (I only approved of Angel when he lost his soul). Then there was Cole and Phoebe in Charmed and later Bella, Edward and Jacob in Twilight (I was strictly team Jacob by the way – he was much more my type – I think you're getting the picture).

One day I stumbled into the steamy romance genre (before EL James made Romance so very sexy) and bought a book that looked like a fantasy story – which it was – but with extras. I remember reading it on the commute to work and hiding it in a newspaper because I was worried about what people would think if they read it over my shoulder, because that's what I always did to others. I also remember coming across that first scene totally not expecting it and turning bright red when I realised just what I was reading. But I quickly became hooked and I've read so many in this genre since, falling in love with the passion, action, and angst and the adrenaline rush of a hot scene.

Then, just before the Great Pandemic of 2020 (this will sound much more dramatic in ten years' time), I decided to see if I was capable or writing such scenes. It seemed I was, and my hubby was happy to 'sense check' them with me. Now, between us, we have released the first book in the Northern Sins Saga, set in the North East of England where we live with our two daughters, two cats and three ponies.

I'm really excited to get you all on board the steamy romance train with me because what a ride this is going to be!

Printed in Great Britain
by Amazon

19493584R00243